T0285443

THE
SECRET
of
THE
THREE FATES

THE
SECRET
of
THE
THREE FATES

A RUBY VAUGHN MYSTERY

JESS ARMSTRONG

MINOTAUR
BOOKS
NEW YORK

First published in the United States by Minotaur Books, an imprint of St. Martin's Publishing Group

THE SECRET OF THE THREE FATES. Copyright © 2024 by Jess Armstrong. All rights reserved. Printed in the United States of America. For information, address St. Martin's Publishing Group, 120 Broadway, New York, NY 10271.

www.minotaurbooks.com

Library of Congress Cataloging-in-Publication Data

Names: Armstrong, Jess, author.
Title: The secret of the three fates : a ruby vaughn mystery / Jess Armstrong.
Description: First edition. | New York : Minotaur Books, 2024. | Series: Ruby Vaughn mysteries ; 2
Identifiers: LCCN 2024019359 | ISBN 9781250909886 (hardcover) | ISBN 9781250909893 (ebook)
Subjects: LCGFT: Detective and mystery fiction. | Paranormal fiction. | Novels.
Classification: LCC PS3601.R5753 S43 2024 | DDC 813/.6—dc23/eng/20240429
LC record available at https://lccn.loc.gov/2024019359

Our books may be purchased in bulk for promotional, educational, or business use. Please contact your local bookseller or the Macmillan Corporate and Premium Sales Department at 1-800-221-7945, extension 5442, or by email at MacmillanSpecialMarkets@macmillan.com.

First Edition: 2024

10 9 8 7 6 5 4 3 2 1

For Mom

THE
SECRET
of
THE
THREE FATES

CHAPTER ONE

Sic Semper Tyrannis

I was going to murder Mr. Owen, there was simply nothing for it. Blood thrummed through my veins as I looked up at the librarian of Manhurst Castle, struggling not to lose my temper. It certainly wasn't *this man's* fault that I'd been brought here under false pretenses. No, that blame lay squarely at the feet of my octogenarian employer who was currently enjoying his midmorning nap.

"What do you *mean* there are no illuminated manuscripts?" I asked for the second time, my voice far more strained than I intended.

Mercifully, the young man remained unaware of my rising ire as he turned back to the dark mahogany bookcase behind him, pulling the newest copy of Debrett's guide to the peerage from an overburdened shelf containing every edition published from the company's eighteenth-century inception to now. He set it on the long low study table beside me. In a desperate hope that the young man had forgotten a cache of illuminated manuscripts secreted away with the most recent month's serial novel, I scanned the spines of the next nearest shelf. Mostly modern fiction alongside some late-nineteenth-century poetry. Nothing awe-inspiring. In fact, there wasn't a single interesting book in this library—it was a rather insipid collection all told. As if someone hastily purchased everything from a rummage sale in an attempt to fill the empty shelves.

"I told you earlier, Miss Vaughn, there are no illuminated manuscripts left in the collection. The lot of them were sold off two years ago, not long after Mr. Sharpe took over the estate. I understand they paid for the renovations here."

My attention snapped back to the young librarian and I blew out a breath, my eyes lingering on the most recent copy of the who's who of the peerage on the tabletop. A more generous soul might assume that Mr. Owen had simply gotten his estates mixed up. After all, he was in his eighties and I'd known plenty of other folk his age—younger even—who had begun to forget harmless little details like that. Though Mr. Owen never forgot *anything*—an annoying habit of his.

Besides, even if he *had* gotten his estates confused, it didn't explain the telegram in my pocket offering said missing manuscripts for sale. No. I was certain that Mr. Owen was up to his old tricks again.

"Is there anything else here Mr. Sharpe is thinking of selling? Perhaps there was some mistake . . ."

The librarian shook his head, glancing to the open door leading into the main hall of the hotel. "Nothing, miss. I was as surprised as you were when you came in asking for them this morning. Mr. Sharpe sold everything of value from here not long after acquiring the estate. From what I understand, Manhurst Castle was falling apart when he bought it—and it took everything he had and more to fix this old place into a resort suitable for the sort of guests we entertain."

"You've not been here long then?" I raised a brow.

He shook his head. "I come from Edinburgh, miss. I was hired on earlier this year when the resort had its grand opening. Mr. Sharpe believed that any proper estate ought to have a librarian."

I couldn't argue with the elusive Mr. Sharpe on that score. A nagging worry lingered as I unfolded the telegram that Mr. Owen had handed me the morning we left Exeter and offered it to the librarian. He took it from me, reading it with a frown.

Have a dozen twelfth-century manuscripts for sale. Please come at once. M. Sharpe.

The young man reached up, rubbing at his smooth-shaven jaw. "That is peculiar, miss. Very peculiar. I shall ask Mr. Sharpe about it, but feel free to take your time to look around. I warn you not to get your hopes up; if there was anything of value here—I'd know it." He looked again at the door behind me, scooping up the newest copy of Debrett's and holding it under his arm. "I'd best be off. The dowager countess has requested this delivered to her rooms."

I groaned at the mention of the horrid woman. Every time I'd come across Lady Morton and her young daughter, the elder avoided me as if I carried some twelfth-century pestilence. It was a wonder the woman needed the book at all. I'd assumed a soul as pompous as she would have the whole of Debrett's memorized already. I fiddled with the telegram before folding it back up and thrusting it into my pocket. There was only one person who could *illuminate* our reason for being here, and he was currently upstairs taking a nap.

I RUSHED THROUGH the fashionably decorated hallways of Manhurst, recently redone in *le style moderne*. A stark contrast to the sparse Georgian exterior of the building. The lush green, black, and gold paper on the walls must have cost a fortune. There was no wonder this Mr. Sharpe, whoever he was, sold off everything of value to fund the renovation.

Pillaging a library for wallpapering. The very idea made my skin crawl. I blew out a breath, brushing past a cadre of well-heeled gentlemen coming in from a game of golf smelling irritatingly of sunshine and the Scottish hills.

The only positive of my morning's discovery was that now we could board the first train back to Exeter and return to our book-shop there. Perhaps Mr. Owen would feel more like himself once we returned home. As it was, he'd spent most of the forty-eight hours since our arrival shut in his room, not even taking his meals with me, leaving me to wander the castle alone. Decidedly *not* my idea of a restful vacation.

The real puzzle was *why* Mr. Owen had brought me here in the first place. It was unlike him to hare off after mysterious manu-scripts without knowing absolutely everything he could about the seller. The old man was a born meddler, and possessed investiga-tive skills that would put the Home Office to shame. He could sniff a fake from miles away—so why would he have come all the way to Scotland for manuscripts that had been sold off years before? Mr. Owen ought to have known they were not here the moment he received the telegram.

No. Something was amiss, and I was about to find out what.

My throat grew dry as I turned the knob on the door connect-ing our rooms.

Locked.

I rattled the handle as a frisson of tension inched its way from my palm up my spine and settled itself in my jaw.

"Mr. Owen . . ." I rapped on the wooden panel.

Still nothing.

I waited on the plush crimson carpet for any sign of life from the other side but was met with silence. "Mr. Owen, you're begin-ning to worry me. Please open the damned door."

Still no response.

He never locked the door in Exeter, not even when he was sick. Of all the times for him to get missish about privacy . . . My satchel sat on the dressing table and I took two steps in that direction with the intention of digging out my lockpicks, when I heard the hinges creak behind me.

Mr. Owen appeared in the threshold, wearing his bright blue silk pajamas with a garish pomegranate-and-black dressing gown tied at his waist. His fluffy white hair looked as if he'd just awoken and my stomach unknotted in response.

"Good grief, Mr. Owen, I thought you were dead. Or worse!"

He let out a bitter laugh and shook his head. "It'd take more than this old place to do me in. You should know that, lass. Now, come sit and tell me why you look like you've drunk curdled milk."

I huffed out a breath. All my worry from a few seconds before evaporated. He was fine. *Fine.* Mr. Owen was the closest thing I had to family, as my own father had died upon the *Lusitania* seven years ago now, along with my mother and younger sister, Opal. At times it seemed a lifetime ago that I received word that their bodies had not been recovered, and yet at others it was as if I'd just received the telegram.

The telegram. Suddenly I recalled my reason for seeking him out in the first place. *The missing manuscripts.* I dug into my pocket and waved the folded-up paper at him. "Do you know anything about this?"

He wrinkled his nose and took it from me, holding it at arm's length as he tried to read it without his spectacles. "Ah yes . . . that."

"Ah . . . that . . ." I repeated dryly. "I take it there are no illu-minated manuscripts here?"

He shook his head, then crumpled the telegram and stuffed it into his dressing gown pocket before turning and gesturing for me to follow into his room. As I entered, I caught a whiff of whisky—likely expensive stuff if his normal taste held true. His room was far darker than my own with the curtains pulled tight against the sun and the fireplace providing the only light.

I sank down into an old armchair with an irritated grunt. "I sense there *is* a reason we're here, and that you didn't just change your opinion on Scotland after all these years?"

He settled himself slowly into the chair across from me. His left hand trembled as he ran it over his white beard before picking up a half-full glass of whisky. Its twin sat there on the table, equally full.

"Was someone here with you?" I glanced from the pair of whisky glasses to his face. The man had scarcely left his room since we'd arrived; I couldn't imagine who he'd be entertaining in here. While I knew he'd grown up in Scotland, he had no family to speak of—at least none I knew of besides his litany of fictitious great-aunts he'd pull out of his pocket whenever he needed to make a point.

"Leave off, Ruby. It isn't important."

Of course it was important. Mr. Owen never did anything without a reason, and I knew he had no desire to be here. His temper had grown shorter with every moment we remained at Manhurst Castle. Something about this place bothered him and if he wasn't going to tell me, I'd have to figure it out myself. There was a faint scent of flowers in the air. Lavender perhaps. No, that wasn't it. But I couldn't quite place it.

I leaned forward, placing my palm on his forehead. It was cool and clammy. "Mr. Owen, you are clearly unwell. It's time we go home."

"Not yet, Ruby. Another night. We must spend another night here."

THE SECRET OF THE THREE FATES · 7

"Not yet?" I almost squeaked, my hand flying into the air. "There is no reason on earth good enough for us to stay. There are no manuscripts, the entire library is devoid of anything even remotely interesting. I cannot fathom why you want to remain here when you are clearly miserable!"

He turned back to face me, brushing away at the moisture gathered in his eyes with his palm. "I take it you haven't seen the papers yet."

The skin at my neck prickled. Newspapers were the bane of my existence. I still recalled the glee with which the New York newspapermen had picked apart my every flaw after my disgrace. I'd been scarcely sixteen at the time—manipulated and misused by a grown man I'd believed to be honorable—but it made no difference to society that I'd been the victim. *A proper girl would never . . .* that's how every backhanded comment would begin. For the truth didn't matter to society, nor did it matter to the men who profited from my pain.

My expression must have betrayed me, as Mr. Owen reached out, touching my hand tenderly. "No, lass, not those sorts of stories. This has nothing to do with you. Nothing at all. You are safe with me. I promise you that."

I let out an amused sound—*safe* was a matter of perspective considering he'd nearly gotten me killed six weeks before on an errand to Lothlel Green. My relief was short-lived, as the meaning behind his words became clear. If it didn't have to do with *me,* it had to do with *him.* "Oh no, Mr. Owen . . . what have you done this time?"

He eyed his glass of whisky, tilting it in the firelight. "I did not think you would come with me if I told you the truth straight-away."

Not again. "Told me what . . . Mr. Owen, *why* are we here?"

He grimaced, picking up a folded copy of *The Scotsman,* turned it over, and laid it flat on the table between us, allowing me to read the advertisement beneath the fold.

The Three Fates, at Manhurst Castle for one night only.
Join them to commune with the dead.
War widows. Grieving mothers. Brokenhearted sweethearts.
Take heart and find your consolation and peace for ten pounds.
TONIGHT!

I stared at it in disbelief. *Mediums?* Mr. Owen had brought me all the way to Scotland for us to commune with the dead? Anger. Annoyance. Dread. I wasn't quite certain which emotion would win out. "You have to be joking. You've brought me here for a séance?"

He rubbed at his thick white beard and tapped the paper. "This is why I did not tell you earlier. You would have gotten all into a tizzy over it."

I shot to my feet, hands on my hips. "I do not get into tizzies. It is perfectly reasonable to be annoyed when your employer *lies* to you and brings you to the middle of nowhere under false pretenses."

He shrugged, his eyes not meeting mine. "I did not lie, Ruby. I obfuscated. There *is* a difference."

"I'm not in the mood for semantics this morning. Aren't there plenty of fraudulent mediums closer to home willing to take *my* money from *you*?"

He harrumphed, not rising to the barb, as both of us knew that Mr. Owen lived off my fortune. It was part of our agreement. I had free rein over the bookshop and permission to run his household however I saw fit, and his name was on the bookshop door in large painted letters. My money bought me anonymity and freedom—two things I treasured above all else.

But arguing with the man was not going to bring Mr. Owen

around. I leaned against the arm of his chair, softening my words. "You know as well as I do that they're all frauds. I saw my share of their kind in France after my parents died. They'll say anything to get your money. I thought we were in agreement on that . . ."

His jaw grew slack as he stared at me. "After all you saw—after all that happened in Lothlel Green—you still mock the other world? You doubt its existence?"

He had me there. A great many things happened in Cornwall a mere six weeks ago, things I didn't dare think on at present. "I am not mocking it. I am simply pointing out that the dead are dead—they aren't coming back. And whether I believe in ghosts is immaterial. What *is* material is that you lied to me to bring me out here."

Mr. Owen did not believe me. His bushy white eyebrows rose in unison.

I crossed my ankles, looking away. "Nothing happened in Cornwall out of the ordinary."

"Curses and witches aren't out of the ordinary?"

Well . . . *almost* nothing. Mr. Owen didn't know half of what I'd found there when he sent me to deliver a box of books to his Pellar friend, Ruan Kivell. Nor did I even know what a Pellar *was*. I still wasn't entirely certain, only that Ruan was a type of folk healer—a witch of sorts.

Mercifully, Mr. Owen also remained unaware of the fact that Ruan could somehow hear my thoughts without me speaking, or the uncanny way I could sense his . . . well . . . whatever *it* was he did. I still was not certain how much I believed in the supernatural, but I did know that Ruan possessed . . . something. Something I feared to put to voice. He could *do things*. Things he didn't understand nor could he control. Things unbound by the laws of science, at least any science I knew. And the less anyone knew of what he was—the better.

A loud thunk came from the floor overhead, startling me out of my wayward thoughts and causing me to bite my tongue. The metallic tang of blood filled my mouth. "Damn."

He arched an eyebrow in challenge. "No such thing as ghosts, lass?"

"Very amusing. All I mean to say is that it's well known about these types of women. They go to the most absurd lengths to wheedle well-meaning people out of their money. Goodness knows, I've seen plenty of them in my life, all of them telling me . . ." *That my mother lived.* No, I couldn't bring myself to speak it—not even to Mr. Owen. Those horrible frauds had given me false hope for far too long.

"It's only . . ." He paused, twisting a simple gold band on his finger. "Ruby, I need you tonight. Please don't make me ask you twice. I do not think I'm brave enough to face the dead on my own, and I need you by my side."

My eyes widened at the rawness in his voice. "But Mr. Owen, it's not *real*. You can't possibly be planning on—"

He held up a hand, silencing me. The golden ring winked in the electric lights, catching my eye. "I must speak with my son." He pulled out a letter from his pocket and handed it to me. The paper trembled in his outstretched hand.

Owen, I know it has been years since we've spoken but I have a message from Ben. He has come to me in my dreams. He is angry and will speak to no one but you. If you have any love for your departed wife, you will come. You will come and hear what your son wants to say.

—L.C.

"Who . . . who sent you this?"

"Lucy Campbell," he said with a vague wave of his hand, as if that name meant anything to me. "In another life, I knew her well. She is a true spiritualist. The only one I've ever known to possess the gift of speaking with the dead."

"—and she's here . . . one of these *Fates*."

He nodded. "She has a message from Ben. From my darling boy. How could I do anything but come to hear what he has to say?"

Mr. Owen rarely spoke of his life before I came into it. I only knew the barest of sketches. Ben was the youngest of his children, and I got the sense his favorite. He'd been an aviator during the war and would have been about my age, had he survived. But he was shot down somewhere over the lines and wounded near the end of the war. By some minor miracle he managed to live through all that, only to die on a troop transport on his way back home.

"I understand how you feel, Mr. Owen, but how do we know that letter is any more real than the telegram we received about the manuscripts? Ten pounds for a public séance is an obscene amount of money. If this Lucy Campbell woman truly wanted to help you, wouldn't she just meet you in private to deliver Ben's message?"

Mr. Owen's eyes were glassy and bloodshot in the dim firelight. "I lost him once. I cannot bear to lose him again. I will not take that chance. I would offer up all the illuminated manuscripts in the world, burn each and every one until not a single page remained if it brought him back once more." A tear slipped down his face, running along the well-worn ridge by his nose, sealing my fate. "You of all people must understand that. If Ben has a message, I must hear him out, no matter the cost to me."

He'd won this battle before it even began, touching that fathomless wound in me that refused to heal. I reached across the table, taking his wizened hand in my own, and squeezed. "Very well. I'll go. But I won't like it."

"And no scenes, Ruby. I mean it. I need you to be by my side for this. I depend on you, lass, more than you could ever know."

"Me? Cause a scene? I'd never dream of it." I struggled to keep my tone light, to bring him away from that dark place that he'd entered. Mr. Owen needed finality—and that was the one thing I could not give, but perhaps these Three Fates could.

Chapter Two

Enter, the Three Fates

THAT evening found me in a dreadful temper, terribly over-dressed, and seated in the castle's dimly lit ballroom. I'd racked my brain—and trunk—for what might pass for suitable attire for a séance—a difficult task as I had not known upon packing that I was *attending* a séance. I was *supposed* to be appraising and ac-quiring a dozen illuminated manuscripts for Mr. Owen. Perhaps finagling a discreet love affair once matters were settled with the books, should a suitable candidate show themselves. Someone pleasant enough to eradicate those unruly feelings I harbored for one Mr. Ruan Kivell without causing any extra emotional entan-glements. That's exactly what I needed—something to help me forget the irrational pull toward the peculiar man.

Tonight, I ended up settling upon an airy green-and-gold eve-ning gown with a daring décolletage. Everyone else in the room was dressed in mournful shades of grays, lilacs, and black. Serge and wool. At least it was dark—making my inappropriate attire less obvious—but even still the gold threads caught the candle-light, sparkling in the shadows.

I shifted in the wooden dining chair, resisting the urge to tug on the seafoam silk of my skirt, and hide within the pathetically thin material. I'd never been skittish, but ever since my adventures in Cornwall, crowds made me nervous. It could be a mere gathering of ten people, and I would start feeling . . . rabbity . . . consumed by this primal need to flee before something larger came along to gobble me up, even though I knew good and well no harm would befall me in here.

A half-dozen ancient silver candelabras were set around the perimeter of the room, throwing the center into little more than shadows and shapes. All the better to disguise the sleight of hand that inevitably would follow. Two anemic electric lights battled the darkness, allowing the guests to find their way to their seats, while the candlelight danced in the breeze from the open windows. It certainly was a scene set for deception. One where strings became invisible, filament mistaken for ghostly renderings, and sticks rattling tables would remain unseen.

Mr. Owen sat beside me, a grim expression beneath his full white beard. He frowned, lifting his hand to tuck a curl back into the gold cloth that bound my unruly brown curls. "Don't think I don't know how much it is costing you to come here, my girl."

"You're a fine one to talk. Look at you. A man bound for the gallows, if I've ever seen one."

"I mean it, Ruby. I'm old and have seen and done far more than is wise. But you . . ." He reached up, thumb lingering at the slight pink scar bisecting my eyebrow. He dropped his hands limply to his lap with a gruff shake of his head. "Never mind me. This place has too many ghosts, that is all." Mr. Owen quickly changed the subject, dropping his voice to a whisper. "Do you see that man over there?" He tilted his head to the far side of the very large circular table. The man in question was probably sixty or so, with typical patrician features. A delicate nose. Fine brows and fair hair that shone like burnished bronze in candlelight. At his side was a much younger woman, not much older than I, who looked as if a stiff wind would blow her over.

A hollow and brittle thing, putting me in mind of the fictional Miss Havisham, albeit not in her wedding gown tonight. Now *that* would be overdressed for a séance. "Who are they?" I asked, swallowing down the amusing image.

"The Duke of Biddlesford. Capital fellow." He leaned closer, finally getting a bit more color again and spoke behind his hand. I'd heard whispers that a duke had arrived this morning, but I hadn't crossed paths with him yet—not that I particularly wanted to. I didn't have much use for the aristocracy, nor they me.

"Of course, the young lady next to him who looks as if she bit into an unripe persimmon is his second wife, Catherine. And before you ask—I haven't a clue why she looks miserable when she has more money than you. Perhaps marriage to old men does not suit her." He leaned closer still, whispering into my ear, with a nod toward the dowager countess. "I'm honestly surprised Lady Morton is here at all. I heard rumors that she was angling to be the second Duchess of Biddlesford before he settled on that one."

I raised my brows. "How is it that you are better versed in the history of the people in attendance tonight than I am, when *you* have scarcely left your room for five minutes in all of two days?"

He gave me a pained look, laying a hand on his chest. "You wound me, Ruby. How am I to acquire their treasures if I don't know what secrets they've hidden in the attic?"

I laughed, earning me a cross look from Lady Morton, who was reluctantly seated only a few places to my left, alongside her daughter, Lady Amelia. The girl couldn't be more than sixteen or seventeen, still with the vestiges of childhood on her face.

Mr. Owen squeezed my hand, drawing my attention back to our conversation. "I knew Biddlesford a lifetime ago, back when he was a boy." He grew wistful as he watched the duke.

"When you lived in Scot—?" I started to ask but my words died away as my attention was caught by an old man who had sat down directly across from me. His angry expression stole all the light from the room. The fellow's gray hair was scraggly, falling loose about his shoulders. Gauging from the fine cut of his coat, he had both means and access to an enviable tailor, even if he lacked a decent barber to go with it. Likely some lesser aristocrat considering the rest of the company here. Though one could never tell; after all, Mr. Owen and I were also in attendance and didn't have a drop of aristocratic blood between us. I drew in a shaky breath then a second, tapping my thigh beneath the table, desperate to will away the slow creeping panic clawing its way up my throat.

"Who is that?"

"No one to concern yourself with." Yet the tense muscle at the edge of Mr. Owen's jaw told me this was another prevarication.

A younger man came in, pulling a spare chair from the wall to settle himself beside the scraggly haired fellow, drawing the man's focus from me at long last. The addition of the newcomer caused the seats to shift, putting young Lady Amelia beside me, to Lady Morton's dismay. At least I didn't have to see her disapproving glowers any longer. A small mercy.

There was something familiar about the fellow who'd just joined the group—something in the shape of his eyes and line of his Roman nose, perhaps the geometry of the two together— but before I could ponder the question of his intriguing features anymore, the electric lights to the room were cut, thrusting us all into the dark.

"Right. Time for the ectoplasm and table shaking," I muttered.

"You promised to behave yourself." Mr. Owen whispered behind gritted teeth. His good humor from earlier had vanished.

I hadn't agreed to anything.

Lady Amelia giggled behind her hand, casting me a curious look.

A low hum reverberated from somewhere outside the room and the air filled with the unctuous scent of incense—dark and rich—putting me in mind of the old cathedrals I'd visited during the darkest days of the war, back when I still sought meaning amongst the devastation of life.

Three shrouded figures appeared in the doorway, processing into the room. The first bore a dove in a cage, fluttering noisily against its confines. The second, a pair of shears, and the third clasped a book tight against her chest. I'd give them high marks for maintaining the theme. Perhaps I'd get my ten pounds' worth yet.

I reached into my pocket for the flask I often carried with me and realized that I'd left it in my room. *Damn.*

Sensing my turn of thought, Mr. Owen cut me a sharp look and I dutifully retrained my attention upon the Three Fates. Their dark gowns were Roman in style, thin and light falling to the floor, and each wore a long black veil shielding their faces from view.

The low rhythmic hum grew louder, settling under my skin and embedding itself uncomfortably in my brain. Where was it coming from? I took in a slow breath and let it out again. Counting in my head. Fingertips drumming on my thigh. I'd been to war and back; surely, I could endure a single séance sober? But as the moments dragged on, a clawing sensation ran down my spine, followed by a cold flush to my face. I recognized it at once—fear.

Run.

Run, child. Run.

The voice in my head was clear as if the words had been spoken aloud.

The first medium immediately swung her gaze to me, holding it for several seconds, before looking to each participant in turn with an unnatural jerk of her chin.

My throat clenched. Her movements were stilted, almost inhuman. Mr. Owen clasped my hand, squeezing it against my own leg as one would to calm a fidgety child. *This was absurd.* It was theatrics, that's all, and yet I could not escape the creeping dread that threatened to devour me whole.

By the time I managed to settle my thoughts, the three mediums had taken their seats around the table at twelve, four, and eight o'clock, splitting our group into equal portions. One by one the women lifted their veils. The first medium was very old, probably of an age with Mr. Owen. Another possibly a decade older than me with fine features and auburn hair. And the third . . .

When I looked upon the third, all my earlier fears made perfect sense. The woman's distinct hawkish appearance and unusual eyes unnerved me as much now as they had the first time I saw her at the crossroads in Lothlel Green weeks earlier.

It was the White Witch of Launceton, and she was a *very* long way from home. The first time I laid eyes upon her, I thought she was a ghost. I had no idea I'd ever see her again, nor did I want to—for last time there was a murderer on the loose.

"What is it, lass?" Mr. Owen whispered in my ear. His breath rustling my hair with his words.

I was unable to speak. The memories from my time in Cornwall struck hard and fast—no more than fragments of thoughts—of how she'd mysteriously appeared portending death and destruction only to vanish again like an ill omen. I stared unblinking at her pale face, unable to form the words.

The oldest of the three women began to speak.

Mr. Owen took my hand in his own, squeezing tenderly, as did Lady Amelia, reminding me of what I must do.

Join hands.

Right.

I think that's how it went the last time I participated in one of these ridiculous charades, but it didn't matter. Nothing mattered now except the White Witch, and why she was *here*.

The youngest of the three mediums began to speak from where she sat on the far side of Lady Morton, the dowager countess.

"Arthur. Arthur McTavish. Can you reach him, see why he called for me?" Lady Morton asked.

McTavish? Now that was intriguing, my own curiosity at war with my sense of self-preservation. While I wasn't as versed in the aristocracy as Mr. Owen, I was quite certain that the late Lord Morton was not named Arthur. Nor were they McTavishes. I chewed on my lip, curious about this turn of events despite the White Witch's unwanted appearance.

She couldn't harm me.

She *couldn't*.

I simply had to make it through this farce, then I could find out what she wanted. And from the way she watched me, I was certain that I was the reason she'd come.

As soon as I latched onto my post-séance plan, the temperature dropped precipitously. The room fell into silence as a strange lilting voice rang out. "He's here . . . the one who betrayed me . . . he's here."

Mr. Owen's pulse galloped against my palm as he crushed my knuckles against his fingers.

"What's your name, spirit?" called the youngest medium. Her voice bore a faint Russian accent. "Tell us your name."

But the eerie voice continued, as if she had not heard the young medium's request at all. "Boundless ambition. Boundless desire." The lilting voice called, the words neither spoken nor sung—hovering somewhere between. "Wanting and striving. Always wanting and striving. My love was not enough. Was never enough. Never enough."

Mr. Owen tensed as the voice echoed around us.

"I tried to warn you. Tried to show you . . . but it was too late." The strange voice grew sharp, as the words died upon the lips of the eldest medium. It was *she* who spoke. Was this the Lucy Campbell that Mr. Owen spoke of? The only true spiritualist he'd ever met. I swallowed hard, unable to look away from the scene before me. The old woman's head lolled from side to side, her eyes rolled back into her head revealing only the milky whites. I'd certainly never seen anything like *this* in France. "But *you* . . . I know what you did. I know . . . what . . . you . . . did. And soon the world will know too. Too long have I lain in my stony tomb. Too long have you stolen my tongue. I will be heard. We . . . will . . . be . . . heard."

The eldest medium's expression contorted in pain as her body drew ramrod straight in the chair. Her eyes wide and sightless as her head continued to rock about on her neck like that of a newborn babe unable to control the weight—white eyes moving from face to face to face with a terrifying liquidity I'd never seen in all my days.

The spirit was seeking something.

There was no other explanation for it.

My breath was visible in the coldness of the room.

The medium grew still at last, her eyes fixed upon me with an odd gentleness before looking away, craning her neck into an improbable angle. "There is nowhere on earth you can hide from the dead. We have not forgotten . . . we shall not forgive. The dead know what you've done."

"What do they know, spirit?" Challenging a possessed spiritualist was likely a terrible decision—but she, *it*, had been looking at me before going on this tirade, and *someone* needed to take charge of this nonsense as things were quickly getting out of hand.

The unearthly voice softened as an icy breeze floated through the room, gently caressing my neck. "He knows you've come, child. He'll be coming for you now."

Who is coming?

I ought to be afraid—any rational person would—and yet I could not quite convince my body of what my mind knew to be true. Only a fool would argue with a ghost. But surely this séance couldn't be real. Could it?

"Who. Who is coming?" I asked at last.

Her mouth grew round and her word came out in a hush. "Run." And with that final word the candles all snuffed out in the room, casting us all into the darkness and cold.

"It's Mariah!" a man shouted from the far side of the room.

"She's returned."

"Back . . . she's come back . . ."

The voices began to bleed into one as the youngest medium rose to her feet, rattling the tabletop with her movement, struggling with matches that refused to light.

Someone else was looking for the lamps.

Lady Amelia squeezed my hand, causing my knuckles to ache. Her skin damp against mine. The room grew colder, as if such a thing was possible.

"I left you the key, but you abandoned me. Why did you abandon me? Why did you leave me, my love?" The old medium's voice grew shrill as she called out into the darkness. "The key will tell all and then *you—you* will pay for your sins . . ."

At long last the youngest medium managed to locate the switch, and the room was flooded with artificial light, burning my eyes which had grown accustomed to the darkness.

The room warmed instantly, and the strange specter left as quickly as it had come.

"Murderer!" the scraggly haired old man across the table roared, leaping from his chair and lunging toward the spot where Mr. Owen sat. "Murderer!" he shouted again, waggling a bony finger at Mr. Owen.

Mr. Owen shrugged away from me, scraping his chair across

the worn wooden floors, and fled the room as it descended into chaos. Everyone spoke at once, clamoring to understand what had occurred.

The oldest medium had gone utterly slack, her neck resting on the high back of the chair. A grayness settled over her features as she opened her fathomless eyes and looked at me.

This was not the face of a woman who was playing a con. No vapor or smoke tricks here—nor silken scarves masquerading as ectoplasm.

My heart thundered in my chest as I heeded that warning voice at long last.

I ran—scrambling through the sweaty bodies, struggling to make sense of what had occurred. *Where was Mr. Owen?* I strained up on the tips of my toes—a benefit of my height I supposed—where I could make out a tuft of his fluffy white hair near the west wing doors. I darted through the crowd and down the hall after him in hopes of finding out what in God's name had happened back there.

CHAPTER THREE

An Ounce of Truth, No More, No Less

"MR. OWEN!" I gasped, chasing him down the servants' stair into the bustling kitchen, past the harried staff still cleaning up after supper. The old man didn't slow his pace at the sound of my voice, if anything he quickened it, disappearing out into the rapidly cooling night.

Murmurs of what had happened at the séance had already found their way down here, if the curiosity of the staff was any indication. Muttering apologies for us both, I raced out of the kitchen, following Mr. Owen past the ruins of the previous Manhurst Castle, which loomed in the moonlight, casting dramatic shadows in the night. The overgrown lawn was tall and dew-laden, soaking the silk and lace hem of my evening gown.

A stitch formed in my side as I climbed up and over the ancient wooden stile and headed out toward the lake where an old Palladian bridge connected this estate to the neighboring one. Hawick House, I think it was called. I'd overheard the dowager countess whispering about it to her daughter, Lady Amelia, half in awe and half in warning. The place's lurid history alluded to, but never mentioned outright. Something about a murdered countess or duchess or something. I wasn't really paying attention at the time, as I was full up on murdered aristocrats after leaving Lothlel Green.

I could scarcely hear my own thoughts over my chattering teeth as I struggled on through the thick muddy ground, farther from the electric lights of Manhurst Castle.

During daylight, rolling hills and woodlands stretched out as far as the eye could see. With hidden streams that wended into dark and mysterious copses, the Scottish borders were a wild place where one could lose themselves—disappear, never to be found again. At night, such wildness took on a far more sinister tone, as if all the bloody years of history here conspired to ward off intruders.

My left foot sank into a muddy animal burrow, twisting my ankle and sending a fierce pain up to my knee. I tumbled to the ground, hands and knees in the cold mud. My gown gave a loud rip at the impact.

Lovely.

Just lovely.

Wiping the sting from my hands, I got up and limped farther into the night. I could barely make out his silhouette in the moonlight. I glanced over my shoulder, no longer able to see Manhurst at all. We must have ventured onto Hawick grounds by now. Fabulous. Mr. Owen would likely get me shot by some overzealous groundskeeper at this rate. It was dark now—with nothing but the moon and stars overhead to light our way.

A fox screamed in the distance. At least I hoped it was a fox.

Perhaps this was not the best of ideas.

Mr. Owen paused outside what looked to be an iron gate leading into a walled garden. Something large rose up from within. A grave perhaps, or a monument? From this distance it was hard to tell which. My patience had worn thin and I didn't care a jot about what it was. I was simply grateful he'd slowed down long enough I could catch my breath.

I found the old man seated on a bench at the far side of the walled garden. His shoulders slumped and his head was buried in the palms of his hands. The sight of him evaporated any remaining annoyance from chasing him halfway across Scotland. *As usual.* Weak and tenderhearted thing that I was.

The beast merely has to look at you, Ruby, and you will make a home for it in your heart. My mother's gentle chiding suddenly came to mind and I brushed her voice away.

"Mr. Owen . . ." I drew nearer. "What happened back there?"

He didn't answer. His dark eyes remained fixed on the gravel path before him, leading toward the marble obelisk. The foxes were truly carrying on now. A second screeched, sending a chill down my spine.

Drawing in another breath of bracing night air, I tried again. "Mr. Owen, please. Talk to me."

Still nothing.

"Mr. Owen, for God's sake, *say something,*" I grumbled, running a muddy hand through my tangled hair. I must have lost my headscarf when I took a tumble in the grass. A problem for morning, as I hadn't a hope of finding it in the dark.

"Uncle. There you are!"

Uncle? I turned quickly and found myself face-to-face with the same fellow from the séance. Not the straggly haired one, but the younger man who'd sat beside him. The one with the cane and familiar patrician features. Well, that certainly explained things. The man was thin and slight, and of a height with me.

"Ah, Andy, did Malachi send you to scold me for returning to Scotland as well? I didn't think you ever put much stock into those old rumors."

Mr. Owen's nephew laughed and drew nearer, his limp pronounced as he heavily favored one leg. "I am only surprised it took Father that long to dredge up the murder accusations. I fear last time you were here he'd started into them well before teatime. Perhaps time finally *is* soothing his temper?"

Mr. Owen let out a dry laugh, rubbing his hands together, staring into his palms. "Doubtful."

I looked warily at Mr. Owen's nephew. Up until this moment I had no idea he even was in possession of a nephew, nor a brother for that matter. Mr. Owen had always guarded his secrets closer than gold.

Then again, if *I* had a sibling accuse me of murder in front of a room of more than a dozen people, perhaps I wouldn't speak much of them either.

"Miss Vaughn. Meet my ill-begotten nephew, Captain Andrew Lennox. Andy, this is my . . . this is Ruby Vaughn."

Captain Lennox made a slight bow, shifting his weight onto his cane. "Miss Vaughn." His eyes grazed over my exposed shoulders, and he quickly shrugged out of his dinner jacket, offering it to me. Ordinarily I bristled at such outmoded displays of chivalry, but as I was wearing little more than a few damp scraps of silk and lace, I was too damnably cold to care.

"Ruby works at the bookshop and lives with me in Exeter, taking care of the things that I'm too old to be bothered with." Mr. Owen gave his nephew a meaningful look that I could not quite decipher.

"I'd seen something of it in the papers about a month ago. It sounded like you'd gotten into a spot of trouble in Cornwall, Miss Vaughn." He was a decent enough–looking fellow with short cropped auburn hair and features that put me in mind of the cliffs along the seaside. Craggy and sharp-hewn. It was a wonder I'd not noted the resemblance between the two men immediately. They had a similar set to their shoulders in addition to the uncanny physical resemblance. Mr. Owen might have had forty odd years on his nephew, but beyond the lines in the elder's face the only substantial difference was that Andrew had broken his nose at some point in time.

"It's been in the papers that you'd been spotted here as well, Miss Vaughn. It was how I knew my uncle couldn't be far behind. I wouldn't put it past Sharpe to have let them know you were coming in order to build excitement for tonight's spectacle. Though Uncle Owen seemed to have taken the limelight all on his own."

"Nor would I, my lad. He's a bit of an eccentric from what I hear," Mr. Owen grumbled, continuing to rub his hands together between his knees.

"Have either of you ever met this Mr. Sharpe? I've been here for two days and I'm beginning to think I'm the only person in Scotland who *hasn't* met him."

Mr. Owen grimaced. "He's an American, lass. What more do you need to know?"

My brows rose in mock surprise. "Indeed. Two of us all the way out here?"

Captain Lennox laughed, a hoarse, rusty sound. "My father and I live nearby. We've not spent much time in his company but from what little I've witnessed, Sharpe is a perfectly affable fellow—American or not. I hear he made his fortunes at the card tables. The luck of the devil and a consummate showman." Andrew turned to Mr. Owen and laid a hand on his shoulder. "I'm sure that's all it is, Uncle. He likely paid the Fates extra for that bit of drama."

Mr. Owen harrumphed again.

"Rather cynical of you. Besides, why are you certain what happened at the séance was false?" My mind went back to the way the medium's voice sounded and the liquidity of her movement— neither seemed natural. "It certainly seemed real enough to me."

"To me too, lass." Mr. Owen patted my arm through the coat sleeve. "But Andrew comes by his skepticism honestly. Men of our line are terrible cynics. Always thinking the worst of everyone. Would suspect the motives of a saint. Speaking of the saints, how is my dear half brother? Shouldn't you be off soothing his delicate nerves instead of bothering with an irredeemable old devil like me?" Mr. Owen flitted his gaze between the two of us before turning his attention back to the monument.

"He'll bide. Besides, after that outburst I don't care to speak to him myself. You know my father, all temper. I'd not even meant for him to learn you were here, thinking to avoid a spectacle like tonight—but you know how he can be." Andrew's attention drifted to the monument. Neither he nor Mr. Owen able to look away.

"As much as I'm enjoying this lovely family reunion, could one of you please tell me what happened tonight? Who is Mariah and why are we out here in the cold instead of nice and warm inside Manhurst?" My teeth chattered together, despite the meager warmth provided by my borrowed dinner jacket. The sweet scent of roses flooded my senses, then disappeared again.

Mr. Owen muttered something that sounded a lot like *insufferable besom,* the edge of his mouth curving up in a hint of a smile. Perhaps all would be well if he was hurling affectionate aspersions at me again.

I turned back to the marble monument where a woman's profile had been lovingly carved in relief. Her delicate stone features almost glittered in the night. The craftsman who'd made this had been a master, capturing every detail with an uncanny reality. A work like this must have cost a fortune to have commissioned. I glanced down at the damaged plinth, where the plate had been hastily removed.

"Forgive him, Miss Vaughn." Captain Lennox stood shoulder to shoulder beside me, studying the woman's lovely face. "My uncle, he is . . . well, suffice to say the men in my family tend to be temperamental even at the best of times. I'd best see that he makes it back to the castle in one piece."

I remained by the obelisk watching the two men disappear into the darkness before turning back to the marble bas relief, running my fingers over the woman's finely chiseled face.

"I suppose you aren't going to enlighten me either, are you?"

But the stone woman kept her silence.

CHAPTER FOUR

Medium Trouble

I lingered in the garden debating the existence of ghosts until I began to lose feeling in my toes. Six weeks before, I'd refused to countenance anything that reason and science could not explain away—but now I couldn't help but question my own perceptions. Tonight I saw a woman possessed. There was no other explanation for what had occurred at Manhurst.

Ghosts *were* the reasonable explanation. Somehow whatever spirit the old medium summoned filled her body like an empty vessel. But for what purpose? I thought back, retracing every second of the séance, my thoughts lingering upon the way the medium's body seemed to be seeking someone. *Something.* Her words rattled around in my head until they became nonsense. Meaning little more than a drumbeat of sounds and syllables.

There is nowhere on earth you can hide from the dead . . .

And why did the spirit seem to speak directly to me? I shrugged the thought away, hugging the borrowed jacket tighter around my body as I hurried back to the castle. This was a problem for another day—and preferably by then we'd be gone and the vengeful ghosts could sort out their own problems—without me.

It was well past ten when I returned to Manhurst through

the rear doors. Word of the terrifying séance must have spread quickly, as I didn't encounter another soul on my way up the stairs to where Mr. Owen's and my rooms were situated. Just as I reached the landing, I heard angry voices coming from ahead, followed by the slamming of a door. The dreadful man from the séance turned the corner and scowled at me, looking even *more* venomous than when he'd accused Mr. Owen of murder hours earlier. *Malachi.* That was what Mr. Owen had called him.

I straightened my spine, not about to be cowed by such an unpleasant person. But before I could say a word, he pointed a gnarled finger at my chest. "If you know what's good for you, lass, you'll leave this place before you end up like *her.*"

Her? What on earth was he going on about? I opened my mouth to ask but he didn't slow his pace, slamming into my shoulder with his own and continuing down the stairs, causing me to grab on to the banister to keep my balance.

Good God, what had gotten into everyone?

I gaped after Malachi's retreating form, debating whether to succumb to my temper and give him a piece of my mind, or go check on Mr. Owen. I settled upon the latter, as I was too damned tired to quarrel with strangers.

As I neared Mr. Owen's door I heard more voices coming from inside.

He wasn't alone.

I paused, pressing my ear against the wood, struggling to make out the voices within, but they remained hushed. Perhaps it was Andrew Lennox? That *would* make sense as he'd followed Mr. Owen back to the house earlier. I waited for several minutes there—cheek pressed to the wood like a child at Christmas—but there were no shouts. No angry words.

As things seemed to be settled with Mr. Owen for the night, it would be the sensible thing to go to my room, draw a bath, and get some sleep. I could deal with whatever ramifications came from the séance tomorrow with a clear head. However, there was a raw energy in my body—a dare-I-say excitement—that I hadn't felt since leaving Cornwall.

I had a puzzle here at Manhurst Castle, one that could only be solved by speaking with the Three Fates.

MY SEARCH FOR Lucy Campbell, the oldest medium, led me to the old family wing of the castle. A far cry from the garishly redesigned modern area where the guest rooms were situated. The walls here were simple stone rather than plaster, and hung with thick tapestries faded from years of use. The narrow corridor smelled vaguely damp, mildew pricking at my nose. Lucy's room was supposed to be ahead. The third door on the right—or so my well-paid informant said.

I wet my lips and paused before knocking, counting the seconds. One. Two. Three.

No answer.

I knocked again.

Lucy had last been seen heading back to her room for the night a half hour past, but evidently she was no longer here. I glanced down the empty corridor before trying the handle.

It was unlocked.

I nudged the door open with my toe. "Hello?" Not that I expected anyone to answer, but it would give me the thinnest veneer of an excuse should anyone be inside.

The medium's room was far smaller than the guest rooms on the floors below, with spartan furnishings of good quality from the last century: a sturdy bed and a rosewood dresser with a matching wardrobe. A pitcher of fresh water and a bowl sat on the dressing table awaiting her return.

The room was perfectly ordered and perfectly empty with the faintest trace of verbena in the air.

Verbena—of course!

That was the scent I'd noticed in Mr. Owen's room earlier this evening. With everything going on at the time the name escaped me—but in the quiet of Lucy's bedchamber I could place it. He must have been meeting with this medium in there. But why would he have kept *that* a secret when he'd already told me that she'd sent for him?

An oversize carpetbag sat on the dresser, stuffed to burst with all of her earthly possessions. Miss Lucy Campbell was preparing to leave. This did not bode well for Captain Lennox's supposition that the séance had been a sham—for why would one flee after pulling off such a spectacular ruse?

I blew out a weary breath and walked around the room, taking silent inventory of every surface and windowsill in the vain hope a plausible alternative would spring from the ether. Some bells. Scarves. Anything at all that could explain away what I'd seen with my own eyes. Perhaps it had been one large group hallucination?

There were intoxicants that could do that . . . weren't there? Goodness knew I'd sampled my share of the things. Perhaps there was some form of opiate in the incense? Now *that* was an idea.

I was grasping at straws and I knew it. Turning to leave, I noticed something curious carved on the back of the heavy wooden door. It was a flower of sorts—carved in a single unending line, creating six even petals. I ran my finger along the outline, then gave my head a good shake before leaving and closing the door.

"What are you doing here?"

The hair on the back of my neck rose as I turned to find the White Witch standing behind me. I didn't even have to see her to know it was her, as I'd heard her voice in my ever-increasing nightmares. Dreams I scarcely recalled, save for the notion of blood and water. Better *those* dreams, I supposed, than the ones from my girlhood—the walking dreams that my mother feared the most. The ones where she'd find me staring into water, with no recollection of where I was or how I'd gotten there. As a little girl I'd wander sometimes a mile or more from home, though somehow she'd always known where to find me.

The White Witch wore the same simple mourning garb that she had worn in Cornwall. Her raven's-wing hair lay in a thick braid over her shoulder.

"I could ask you the same thing. You're a long way from Cornwall." I didn't know what to make of her presence here, but I certainly didn't believe she was who, or what, she purported to be.

"You should heed the spirits and go home."

I gritted my teeth. First the ghost, then Malachi, now the White Witch. *Did everyone want me to leave?*

"Mariah's spirit was clear on the matter. You seek answers to dangerous questions." She leaned closer to me, her breath cool against my ear. Her voice almost . . . concerned. "Listen to the spirits, child."

"Then the séance was real . . ." I said more to myself than to her.

The White Witch nodded. "Yes, Morvoren. More real than you could know."

There was that name again. *Morvoren.* She said it like a curse, the word bitter on her tongue. The air between us grew crisp, stinging my nose with that strange electric scent that seemed to surround Ruan as well. It was the scent of power. I straightened my spine, looking up at the witch. "I do not understand why you are here, nor do I understand what *I* have to do with any of this."

"It is better you not understand—at least not yet. It is not safe here. You must go quickly. He will die if you do not leave this place."

My throat tightened at the thought. "Mr. Owen?"

"No. I care not for your mortal bookseller. I care for *him.* I warned you both before, you will destroy him. I have seen it."

The air left my lungs in a rush. Ruan. *Of course* it had to do with Ruan. She'd delivered the same warning at that crossroads weeks before. Nonsense. That's all it was. I was not going to harm Ruan any more than I'd cut off my own hand. I slammed my palm into the doorframe beside her head with an audible thump. "In case you didn't notice, he's not even *here*."

For half a second her expression softened as she looked into my eyes. "You care for him . . . that, I did not foresee."

I shook my head angrily but she continued to look through me. Into me.

"Did he tell you, Morvoren, of what he is? Did he tell you what I saw?"

My eyes burnt from the growing scent of electricity in the room. I ought to be afraid of her, but for the briefest of moments I thought that perhaps it was me the White Witch feared. "He told me the story of the first Pellar." I repeated the same tale he'd woven, how an old man stumbled across a mermaid stranded on the shore and returned her to the sea. How as reward she bestowed upon him three gifts. When Ruan told me the story weeks ago, I'd been charmed by it—and truthfully charmed by him.

The witch let out a bitter laugh. "Is that all? Did he not tell you the rest?"

The skin pricked on the back of my neck as I shook my head. I wasn't sure I trusted her, nor was I certain I wanted to hear his tale from her lips.

"He died, Morvoren. Nine years after the first Pellar fell beneath the sea-bitch's spell, the water claimed him. And thus every nine years another of his line will share that fate. It was her price for those *gifts*. One must never trust the sea-folk."

My nostrils flared as I recalled what my housekeeper, Mrs. Penrose, told me of Ruan's past. *The seventh son, born from a family of charmers.* It was on the tip of my tongue to ask the witch how long it had been since the last of his line died, but I sensed I already knew. "He is descended from the first Pellar . . ."

The White Witch nodded gently. "You understand then."

Bile rose in my throat and I swallowed it down, tapping on the wall with my palm. "It's a terrible story, but that's all it is. I don't see how I can harm him when he isn't even here . . . Now what I need is for you to tell me what those two mediums want with Mr. Owen."

She weighed her options, studying me before she responded. "I do not know why the old woman brought your bookseller here. I do not know why she brought any of you here. I do not traffic with the dead for the dead cannot be trusted—"

First sea-folk, now the dead. Did the White Witch trust anyone? I held up a hand, pausing her mid-sentence. "Do you mean to say this Lucy woman brought the others here as well?" A sickening worry clawed its way up my throat. What if this was a trap? Mr. Owen came here on the promise he could speak to his dead son. Had she done the same for the others . . . the duke . . . the dowager countess? Perhaps the Fates had promised the others things too. Mr. Owen's brother . . . Andrew intimated that he'd not meant for his father to come. What if Lucy intended for each of them to be here for a reason?

"I believe so, though I do not know why." Her expression shifted and she turned her head toward a sound I could not hear. "Someone comes. You should go now. I will find you if I learn more about the Fates and their purpose here."

"Is it Lucy? I need to speak with her."

The White Witch grew pale, shaking her head as her attention remained fixed on whatever she sensed coming down the corridor. "You must hurry. Back to your room."

I followed her gaze but could neither see nor hear what had caught her attention. She had helped us, in a fashion, back in Cornwall, but I still did not trust her. "Why are you helping me?"

"Because the sooner you do what you've come to do, the sooner you will leave this place."

I raised my brow in challenge. "Then we understand one another?"

The White Witch let out a strange sound that might have been a laugh. "Unfortunately, we do. Now go."

WHILE I DIDN'T trust the White Witch and she did not trust me, alliances had been built upon shakier foundations. I was also *fairly* confident she didn't mean me any lasting harm. My mind flickered back to when we'd met in Cornwall. Her presence in Scotland didn't make sense at all, but there was no time to worry about the White Witch's perplexing motives. She was here, and I needed to know what these mediums wanted with Mr. Owen. If the White Witch was willing to help on that score, then so be it.

I raced back to my room, opening my door with a frustrated grunt that sent it slamming into the wall behind. Through the closed door I heard a telltale snort informing me that Mr. Owen had fallen asleep in my absence. At least he was resting. I did not like seeing him troubled—and while I remained vaguely irritated at him for bringing me here under false pretenses, I could not entirely blame him for doing it.

Someone wanted him here and went to a great deal of effort to make sure he came.

I sank down onto the little dressing table stool and picked up what remained of the salve Ruan made for me in Cornwall, pulling out the cork stopper. I dipped two fingers in the very last of it and rubbed the greasy substance over the scar on my brow— much as I'd done every night—the crisp scent of lavender and mint flooding my senses.

When I opened my eyes again and looked in the mirror, I noticed a piece of paper sitting on the center of the bed behind me. *Now that hadn't been there before.* I shrugged out of Andrew Lennox's borrowed dinner jacket and moved to the bed, grabbing the envelope from the mattress and turned it over in my hand. The wax seal on the back was the color of overripe blackberries. I broke it with my thumb, unfolding the message and read the words written there.

Meet me at midnight on the bridge. Alone. There's not much time. He knows I know.

I stared at the words on the page, struggling to make sense of them. Who is *he* and what did this cryptic letter writer know? I bit my lip, staring at the slip of paper, and ran my thumb over the black ink on the page. I lifted my thumb . . . a small shape in the form of an *M* branded itself on my skin. The ink was still wet. I sniffed at the paper which bore the same trace of verbena that I'd noted in the medium's room moments before. It had to be from Lucy. Perhaps whatever danger the White Witch sensed worried Lucy as well.

I let out a hoarse laugh. This was preposterous—the product of my own overactive imagination and lack of sleep. I was putting far too much stock in the supernatural, when there had to be another explanation for the goings-on at Manhurst. There simply *had* to be.

I slipped the note beneath my jewelry box and unfastened my mother's emerald earbobs and necklace, dropping them both into their leather traveling case. Meeting mediums on bridges at midnight was a terrible idea—but I needed to speak to the woman. I opened a small drawer and pulled out the locket I always wore and affixed it to my throat before taking my own woolen overcoat from the wardrobe, slipping it over my evening gown. There was no time to change into proper traipsing-around-the-wilderness attire. Not that I'd even packed such things in the first place.

I withdrew Mr. Owen's old Webley service revolver from a drawer and unfastened it from its cumbersome leather shoulder holster before tucking it into the pocket of my jacket. One really couldn't be too careful, though after all the improbable things I'd survived to this point it was a miracle I was still in one piece: a war, an angry mob of Cornishmen, attempted poisoning. I mean really, what was the worst that could happen on the bridge?

Chapter Five

A Midnight Swim

THE damp night air grew colder by the minute as I darted into the shadows off the east lawn toward the bridge. The ruins of the old castle rose up in the moonlight, swallowing up what little light existed. The dreadful construction was the sort of thing that inspired ghost stories. No wonder I was leaping at shadows as of late.

You're in a ghost story, Ruby.

I swatted that thought away. There was no such thing as ghosts, and no matter how convincing the séance seemed, there had to be another explanation for what I saw tonight—I'd just have to figure out what exactly that explanation *was.*

The wind picked up, cutting through my woolen coat as if it were no more substantial than my pitiful gown beneath. The hem was soaked—*again*—likely ruined for good and not even my housekeeper Mrs. Penrose's estimable skills with a needle could save it now.

A shadowy, lumbering figure appeared in the distance, making his way back toward the castle. I squinted to make him out, but whoever it was disappeared as quickly as he'd appeared.

No such thing as ghosts indeed.

Thighs burning from exertion, I climbed back up and over the stile, hurrying through the muddy pasture down toward the lake. The soft light of candles appeared in the distance. There must have been a dozen of them flickering below on the bridge—a warming glow drawing me nearer. Somewhere from my left an animal splashed into the water. Whatever it was, it sounded large. My frozen fingers wound themselves around the grip of the revolver as I continued onto the bridge.

But there was no one there.

Nothing but twelve lit candles set into a circle.

Odd. But what hadn't been odd this evening?

My foot skidded as I took a step nearer to the circle of flame. Each of the candles had been set within a larger ring made of what looked to be coarse salt. I stooped down, running the substance between my fingers. I pinched a bit and held it near the flame before testing it on my tongue. Definitely salt.

I picked up a still-burning candle from where it'd been stuck to the bridge with its own wax, and began to explore my surroundings. Another of those strange flower symbols had been hastily scrawled on one of the columns in charcoal. I touched it gingerly, a bit of the carbony substance rubbing off onto my skin. Each of the bridge's columns was marked with the same symbol. I counted quickly. There were twelve in total.

I sighed, leaning back against the railing. *Where was Lucy?*

Glancing back to the circle of candles, I realized another had been knocked over and extinguished in the salt, breaking the circle. *Thirteen* candles then. Not twelve as I'd first believed. I walked over, lifting the fallen candle. The wax was still soft and malleable. I certainly hadn't knocked it over, but it had to have happened immediately before I arrived on the bridge.

At last my sleep-deprived brain placed the pieces together: a broken salt circle, an overturned candle. These were signs of a struggle. Then the splash I'd heard as I approached. With sickening certainty, I walked to the edge and peered into the water, knowing good and well what I'd find there.

A lifeless shape floated upon the surface. Bits of dark cloth billowed out from her body like a discarded doll. It was the same dark fabric that the mediums had been wearing during the séance.

Lucy.

It had to be her.

I shucked off my jacket, dropping it on the stone bridge, revolver along with it, and hastily slipped out of my shoes. Without a second of hesitation, I threw my legs over the side and dove into the water. The iciness hit me hard and fast. My heart stuttered at the sudden drop in temperature and I sucked in a pained breath. Lungs aching, I swam over to where she floated along the surface. The silk of my own gown stuck to my legs, making it hard to tread water. I only had a handful of minutes before the cold would drain my strength. I had to be quick getting her to shore or we'd both die here. I rolled her lifeless body over in the water to face the sky and kicked violently, struggling to keep the both of us afloat. My limbs grew heavy but I managed to wrangle my left arm around her chest, my hips pressed against her back.

I'd always been a strong swimmer; my mother had taught me when I was very small. Pushing hard against the lake, I moved us incrementally closer to the pebbled shore. The weight of her dress threatened to pull us both down. She couldn't have been in the water long or else she'd have sunk like a stone.

Perhaps she was still alive and the air in her lungs had kept her afloat. I didn't have time to check, I had to get her to the shore.

That's it, Ruby, just a little farther. I could almost hear my mother as I fought against the pull of the lake.

Gasping for air, I finally reached the water's edge. Droplets of churned-up water filled my lungs as I took in an accidental mouthful. I heaved her up onto the cold rocks, coughing and spitting out half the lake for my efforts.

I laid my cheek against her chest, listening for the faint thrum of her pulse. The crepe of her dress plastered wet against my skin. Nothing. My fingers went to her throat.

Still nothing.

Good God.

Lucy Campbell was dead.

I rocked back onto my bare feet, struggling to catch my breath and reorder my thoughts. Someone had killed her. They had to have. I looked around in the darkness, but it was still. There was no one around.

I slicked my short hair back from my face, and patted down her body. I wasn't quite sure what I was seeking—a clue—an answer as to why she was killed? My hand felt something inside the pocket of her dress and I fumbled with the layers of drenched fabric, before finally pulling it out. I knew, before I even opened my own palm, what it was. I'd seen thousands of them during the four years I spent on the western front. An octagonal identification disc. I held it up in the eerie moonlight, turning it over. British for certain. Then I made out the name in the darkness: *B. Lennox.*

Lennox. That was the name of Mr. Owen's nephew and before I could think twice upon the wisdom of my actions, I shoved it into the bodice of my dress and ran back to Manhurst.

I REACHED THE flags of the back terrace, panting heavily—my limbs numb from the cold and teeth chattering loud enough to drown out my own thoughts. The soles of my feet were bloodied, leaving ruddy smears across the stone.

The house was dark, most of the guests having gone to bed long before I set out to meet Lucy Campbell. I caught the edge of my toes on the frost-covered flags and toppled forward. I thrust my hands out to brace my fall, when I was caught by someone in the darkness.

"Good God, Miss Vaughn . . ." My body and mind were far too muddled to recognize the voice.

"You're soaked and nearly blue . . . We must get you inside—" I blinked, looking up at Andrew Lennox's eerily familiar face. In the darkness, he looked enough like Mr. Owen that he might have been his own son. Hell, he might have even *been* Mr. Owen in another lifetime.

Captain Lennox righted me, shifting his cane to better help me walk inside. "Come, let's get you warmed by the fire. What in God's name happened—you're soaked to the bone." His accent far broader than it had been earlier in the day.

"There's . . . there's . . . a body . . . b-b-by the lake. It's the medium . . . Lucy . . . Lucy's dead . . ."

Captain Lennox's expression darkened as he shuffled me inside the castle—and for the briefest of instants, in the electric lights of Manhurst, I saw a flicker of fear in his eyes. But more than that—I had the strangest notion that he already knew my answer long before he voiced the question.

An hour and a half later, I was curled in a deep leather chair in the library, snugly wrapped in a woolen blanket. The fire danced in the hearth before me as I struggled to make sense of the evening. Had it only been this afternoon that I'd been here inquiring after illuminated manuscripts?

I stared into the flames, testing my stiff fingers against the heat of the fire licking up in the immense hearth. The needling sensation had finally stopped. That was good, at least. About the *only* good thing to happen this evening.

It was dangerous to do what I'd done. I knew that from the moment I leapt into the lake and yet I hadn't stopped. Hadn't paused to imagine all the thousands of ways it could have gone terribly wrong. Tucking my legs against my chest and sinking deeper into the armchair, I watched as Andrew Lennox spoke with another man deep in the shadows by the far bookcase. I could only imagine the other party to be the mysterious Mr. Sharpe, the owner of Manhurst Castle. Though to watch the two of them one would think their roles reversed, as Captain Lennox had been barking out orders ever since returning with Lucy Campbell's body, while Sharpe stood meekly by, casting the occasional glance in my direction.

I'd repeated my story a thousand times already to Captain Lennox, omitting a couple key facts—details that would do no one any good to know. Firstly, not a soul knew of the note the dead medium had left for me. And secondly, I wasn't about to let anyone know about the identification discs I'd found on her body, which remained safely tucked into the damp bodice of my evening gown.

"Are you certain?" Mr. Sharpe asked in a hushed voice. I turned to see if I could make him out.

Captain Lennox took a weary step backward, leaning against the shelf and rubbing at his hip with a grimace. The subtle change in his position finally revealed Mr. Sharpe's profile to me, and I could not help but gape—half in disbelief, half in horror—as the years slipped away. Once again, I was that uncertain young debutante, head full of books and hopes and dreams. Living in New York, brought up to be her father's crowning achievement before being sold off in marriage for the most advantageous match.

It would have been considered an ideal situation to most girls of my acquaintance had my *most advantageous* match not been a grown man already in possession of a wife. My blood turned to ice as I stared at Mr. Sharpe's profile, not wanting to believe the truth. It *couldn't* truly be him. Elijah. Elijah Keene. I hadn't thought his name in over a decade. Not since my exile from New York.

And yet my eyes and heart were certain of it, even if my mind could not make the leap. Elijah had been the one person who knew the truth about my former lover. Knew the truth and hid it from all of New York society until I was well and truly ruined.

I tucked the blanket tighter around me, arguing with my own mind. The last I'd seen Elijah had been at the Vanderbilts' ball, the night of my great disgrace when I'd been caught in flagrante delicto—to put it mildly—with my supposed fiancé. But there was no reason for *Elijah* to be *here,* not when there were plenty of wealthy young socialites to swindle back in New York.

My thoughts were cut short as Captain Lennox shifted again, blocking my view of Mr. Sharpe—Elijah—whoever he might be. "I am as certain as I can be without further examination. From all accounts it looks to be suicide. The inspector will be able to say more when he arrives in a few hours. I'm sorry for it, Sharpe, I know it's the last thing you need right now."

"Fuck." Sharpe muttered beneath his breath.

My sentiments exactly.

I quietly wrapped myself in the blanket and headed to the door. No good would come of remaining any longer. Elijah Keene or not—Mr. Sharpe's identity was another problem for another day. I'd settle for a bath, and then tomorrow I'd find out what really happened to Lucy. Because I did not for one moment believe it was suicide.

CHAPTER SIX

An Unpleasant Surprise

EARLY the next morning, I was sitting in the courtyard with a large cup of black coffee, letting it wind its way down my throat before checking my pin watch. It was a little past six, and I was shockingly rested considering I had approximately three hours' sleep to my name. But even those precious few moments were marred by terrible nightmares. The sort I could not recall beyond the vague sense of searching, and the peculiar metallic tang of blood in my mouth.

I was certain that the reappearance of Elijah Keene, like a specter from my past, caused the return of my nightmares. I did not want to believe that Mr. Sharpe could actually *be* Elijah, and yet the signs were all there. What if Mr. Owen wasn't the one the medium had lured here at all? What if it was me that had been sent for? After all, Elijah and I had not parted on the most charitable of terms. What if *that* was the warning the medium was trying to give? The warning that was thwarted so violently.

But was Elijah a killer? I didn't think so—but can one ever truly know another's innermost soul? No. No, I learned that lesson long ago. One never could tell what evil lay within a man's heart.

A dense fog blanketed the grounds beyond the courtyard, sealing us away here at Manhurst. It'd likely be hours before it burnt off. I tugged at the sleeves of my woolen jumper against the damp air.

"I see you're up early."

I started at the unexpected interruption, and looked up to see Andrew Lennox coming across the slate flags with a curiously wrapped parcel beneath one arm. I stiffened, uncertain what to make of the man after the previous evening. While he'd been nothing but kind and attentive to me, he'd concealed the truth of Lucy's death.

"Did the inspector arrive last night?"

"Mmm. The man arrived not long after you went to bed. It's probably for the best. He's not the most agreeable sort. The fewer dealings you have with him, the better in my opinion."

Captain Lennox leaned heavily upon the shepherd's crook he used for a cane. Its handle gorgeously smoothed giving the creamy sheep's horn a mirrorlike finish. He laid the package down on the table, sliding it over to me. "I believe this belongs to you."

"Me?" I asked before tearing the paper and lifting the lid. My breath caught as I looked from the Webley revolver back to Captain Lennox.

His expression was grim. "It would do no good for someone else to have it found out there."

I'd forgotten completely about it in all the chaos of Lucy's death. Perhaps he had good reason for claiming it was suicide after all. I pointed to the open chair across from me with my coffee cup. "Join me? I think there may be more left in the pot. I'll have your jacket sent to your rooms later on today."

He hesitated, eyeing the silver pot. "How are you feeling this morning?"

I furrowed my brow, not understanding. I was perfectly fine— why would he even ask such a thing?

"Most women of my acquaintance would be still abed after doing what you did last night. And to have carried a grown woman back to shore with you? That is indeed quite remarkable."

I let out an irritated sound. "Well, then apparently I'm not *most* women. Though I feel it important to add that *few* women are *most* women in absurd statements such as yours. They're simply words used to divide and insult my sex. Women contain multitudes, Captain Lennox, as do men—at least in my experience."

He flushed, giving him a softer appearance as he looked down to the table between us. "Touché, Miss Vaughn. It was a poor choice of words on my part. You exceeded most men as well last night. I hadn't meant offense—only to say that the fact that you didn't suffer hypothermia is a surprise in itself. I've not known many—man or woman—who could do such a feat and be up the next morning."

My temper soothed—a bit—as I took another sip of my coffee, watching Captain Lennox carefully. "What do you know of Mr. Sharpe? You seem to know more of him than most."

Captain Lennox folded his arms across his chest and straightened slightly in his seat. "Not nearly enough. There's been a bit of gossip about him in these parts. You see, he bought the castle here after the war. The inheritance tax was too great for the Campbells to keep hold of it. Granted, I don't know why they'd wish to—not after all that happened here."

I leaned forward, interest piqued. "The Campbells? Lucy was a Campbell. Is it the same family?"

"Aye. They've had nothing but bad luck for generations."

"Bad luck?" I let out a startled laugh. "What all has happened here for you to say that?"

"What *hasn't* happened here . . ." He inclined his head toward the ruins behind me, which were little more than two turrets and three broken-down walls that looked liable to crumble at any moment. I'd been told the old castle burnt in the mid-eighteenth century, replaced by the current structure some decades later. "I firmly believe that no good ever comes from the goings-on at Manhurst. First Mariah, and now this?"

"Mariah? Do you mean the spirit from the séance?"

He nodded grimly. "She has haunted these lands for decades. Whispers of her fate have been told as bedtime stories."

"What happened to her?"

He shrugged, his tone growing icy. "A well-born woman who met a sorry end. It is not a story fit for repeating, that's for certain."

"If children are fit to hear the tale, then why not me?"

He reached out, laying a hand over mine. "Perhaps you should ask my uncle. He knows the story far more intimately than I."

A coldness lodged itself in my throat at the thought that Mr. Owen had known this Mariah. He'd also known Lucy—an inconvenient coincidence to say the least. I snatched my hand back and folded my arms beneath my chest.

"The point is, Miss Vaughn . . . women have a nasty habit of coming to bad ends here at Manhurst. First Mariah, now Lucy. It is only a matter of time before another dies."

"Why would you say that?"

He gestured to the ruins behind. "Manhurst has been the center of great misfortunes and sadness. Perhaps it's fitting for Lucy to die here as well. The last of the Campbell line extinguished. Perhaps with her death it'll be the end of it."

"She is the last of her family?"

He nodded, running a finger beneath his collar. "Aye. The last living heir. It was part of the details of the sale. Sharpe was to allow her to live here the remainder of her days."

I wet my lips, disliking the picture that Andrew was painting. "Rather convenient for him that she died only a handful of years after he took over the estate."

Andrew's expression shuttered. "Indeed."

"Do you think he might have had a hand in what happened last night?" I fiddled with the identification disc I'd taken from the dead medium's body, which I had in my pocket. I hadn't felt safe leaving it in my room. Truth be told I wasn't quite sure what to make of Lucy having it in her possession to begin with. Perhaps Captain Lennox had a brother, and it was on the tip of my tongue to ask about his own family but something in his expression gave me pause. "You lied last night to Mr. Sharpe when you said it was suicide. You know as well as I that someone killed her."

He licked his teeth, warm brown eyes not meeting mine. "It had to be done."

"Why?"

"I fear for my uncle. Owen is a complicated man, but a good one. And it would do no one any good to find *his* revolver in the field the night a woman is found dead."

"You can't possibly think Mr. Owen was involved in anything. He was asleep when I left my room."

"That does bring up a rather perplexing question, Miss Vaughn. Why *did* you leave your room last night? That part does not quite add up."

"I . . . I'd gone for a walk. To clear my head."

He looked somewhat relieved by that answer, as if he'd expected me to tell him something closer to the actual reason I was on the bridge that night.

I laid a protective hand down on the box bearing Mr. Owen's revolver. "My jacket . . . it was there too . . . Did you happen to find it?"

He shook his head. "It wasn't, Miss Vaughn. When I went to fetch the body all I found was the revolver. I pocketed it before any of the servants saw."

Behind me, a few other guests had roused from their slumber and come out to enjoy an early morning repast. In the distance I spotted Mr. Sharpe among them, making his way from table to table, presumably reassuring the rest of the guests that they were not about to be murdered in their beds. I craned my neck, trying to catch a glimpse of the man in the light of day, but he remained at a cautious distance from me.

"Why did you come to the séance?" I asked quietly.

He blinked, surprised by the question. "I told you, I heard my uncle was here and I wanted to speak with him about Ben."

"That doesn't explain why you came to the séance."

He bit his lower lip. "I'd not meant to go at all. I'd intended to slip over to Manhurst, speak with my uncle, and go home. My father, however . . . somehow he found out that Uncle was here, and he is like a dog with a bone. He wouldn't leave it be."

He had said last night that he'd not meant his father to come. The words came out on a breath. "You didn't tell him about the séance."

He let out a startled laugh. "God no. I expressly hid the papers from him. I know how badly my father hates Uncle Owen and I saw no sense furthering their quarrel. I cannot fathom who told him about the séance. As he'd left the house before I did, I had no choice but to attend, solely to keep him from skewering Uncle Owen in front of an audience. I love my father, Miss Vaughn, but I do not like him very much sometimes."

My mind went back to the letter Mr. Owen had shown me before the séance. The invitation to speak with Ben. Perhaps Andrew's father, Malachi, had received a similar one. "Do you think Lucy would have invited him? Like she did Mr. Owen?"

I had surprised him.

"Lucy sent for Uncle Owen?"

I almost regretted revealing it, but it was too late to recall the words. "She did. She told him Ben had a message for him. Do you have any idea what that message might be?"

He shook his head. "It's hard to say with Lucy. She did as she pleased for decades. Most people around here gave her wide berth because of it. She was respected, aye, but feared."

"Would anyone want her dead?"

"Not that I know of, but a woman who can speak to the dead? Who knows what secrets she might have uncovered along the way." Andrew checked his watch and shot up, expression troubled. "Forgive me. I have somewhere I need to be." And with that he disappeared, leaving me with a thousand questions hanging in the air like the very fog that refused to lift.

CHAPTER SEVEN

An Unexpected Party Guest

SPEAKING with Andrew Lennox left me with even more questions than I had answers. I entered my room, unpinning my handsome olive-colored cloche and set it gently down on the dressing table. If I could determine why Lucy brought us all here, then perhaps I could understand who wanted her dead. Not that it was any of my business who killed her—I ought to leave it to the authorities, and yet I'd pulled her body from the lake. *She wanted to tell me something.*

And because of those two simple facts I could not let it rest.

I tugged off one calfskin glove, when I heard voices from the adjoining room. I walked over and opened it, half expecting to discover Captain Lennox chatting with Mr. Owen, but instead I froze on the spot, not believing my own eyes for the second time in as many days.

Ruan Kivell.

"What are you doing here?" We both spoke the words at the same time, staring at each other.

Ruan looked different from when I left him back in Cornwall, though his eyes remained the same—that pale green with the gray mark in the left. *Partial heterochromia.* I'd looked it up after we'd met. Though having a name for it failed to make the effect any less arresting.

In truth, I'd spent far too much time digging around in ancient books looking for an explanation for both Pellars *and* Ruan Kivell, all of which turned up fruitless. The man was a mystery—as was the uncanny connection between us.

"Ah yes. Ruby came along with me. Didn't I tell you?" Mr. Owen asked as he slid something back across the table to Ruan. Quick as a flash, whatever it was disappeared into Ruan's broad palm and was secured into his green waistcoat pocket. His hand lingered there, protecting the contents from my curious inspection.

"No," Ruan grumbled. "You didn't." He did not look away from me, nor I him. The pair of us caught in some bizarre trance cataloguing the thousands of tiny changes that had occurred in the handful of weeks we'd been apart. He'd grown a beard and cut his dark curls. Instead of falling in a riot about his shoulders, or being pulled back into a knot, he now wore his hair above his collar and slicked back. It was an altogether gentlemanly look and I hated it—utterly despised the way such a simple thing as cutting his hair made him resemble all the other men of his age.

"You look well." His voice was hoarse as his keen, witch's eyes lingered on the scar above my brow—a wound he'd stitched with his own hands—before moving lower on my face, pocketing away every detail for further reflection.

"You do too . . ." My mouth grew dry with the dawning realization I'd *missed* the damnable man. Now that was unexpected.

With a sigh, I pulled my attention away from him, folding my arms beneath my chest in a failed attempt at disinterest. "What brings you here? I can't imagine you've heard about the dead medium already."

"I sent for him, lass. I needed some medicines—"

That familiar divot between Ruan's brows appeared again. He'd been fretting—not an altogether unusual circumstance—as Ruan was a great mother hen. Brooding and worrying for other people were some of his most endearing traits. Oh well, I suppose it didn't matter why he was here. Only that he was.

Ruan smirked as his eyes met mine.

Damn. I guess he'd heard that. I'd have to remember to guard my thoughts around him. With Ruan near, none of them were private. While it ought to bother me that the man could hear the inner workings of my mind, it did not feel a violation. It felt . . . like for the first time in a very long time that I was a little less alone.

The corner of his mouth tugged up in response, and I struggled not to show him how much his unexpected arrival pleased me. "Have you told him about our problems here?" I asked Mr. Owen, kicking myself from the doorframe and walking deeper into the room.

Mr. Owen frowned, pouring himself a drink from his cut crystal decanter. "A bit."

"What do you make of it?" Ruan asked me—and I spotted it at once—that familiar flicker of excitement in his eyes. I'd noticed it in Cornwall when we worked together to find Sir Edward's killer. Ruan Kivell enjoyed a puzzle nearly as much as I did. "It was all the talk at the train station this morning." He went on. "Then I overheard the inspector questioning a young girl—dressed all in pink—the one that looks like a strawberry tart."

I let out a startled laugh. "That's Lady Amelia. I swear she must have the corner on the pink fabric market. It's enough to make one ill. Her mother is Lady Morton. Awful woman."

He leaned forward, resting his elbows on the brown wool of his trousers. "They're saying the old woman killed herself. Is that so?" He looked from me to Mr. Owen.

So, *that* bit of news had not traveled yet. I checked over my shoulder to ensure I'd closed my own door before resting my hip on the arm of Mr. Owen's chair. "I'm afraid it's worse than that. I was speaking with Captain Lennox this morning . . ."

Ruan drew in a sharp breath, his eyes widening slightly at the name. How very odd.

"Andy's still here? I'd have thought he'd have gone home by now. What did he have to say? You didn't mention him last night," Mr. Owen said with surprise.

"We had coffee earlier. He agrees she was murdered before being pushed into the lake."

"What do you *mean,* murdered?" Mr. Owen growled, turning to face me full-on. "You told me yourself last night that you found her in the lake drowned. But I still cannot understand why she was out there at all. Or what possessed you to wander the grounds late at night. And on a full moon."

I hesitated, dragging my locket along the chain at my neck. "She was waiting for me."

"The devil?" Mr. Owen's expression darkened. "What do you mean she was waiting for you? I insist you tell me everything, right this instant. No more of this running about trying to figure things out on your own. I won't have you risking your neck and certainly not *here* of all places."

I held up a finger and darted back to my room, returning with the note she'd left me, and handed it to him. "Do you have any idea what to make of that?"

Mr. Owen unfolded the paper and read it to himself, before handing the page to Ruan.

"Why does she think I'm in danger?" I longed to ask him what they'd been discussing in here the day she died, or to ask who Mariah was and how the two women were connected, but there would be time enough to ask him all these questions later.

Mr. Owen's eyes grew cloudy as he stared at the paper in Ruan's fingers. "You must tell no one of this, Ruby. Do you understand me?"

"Why?"

He slammed his fist on the table, glasses rattling. "Because I said so. You shall not pursue this. You shall not meet anyone on bridges. You shall not—"

"I *shall* do as I please, Mr. Owen. I am not your child to command!" I snapped back. "And it's a fine thing for you to tell me who I shall and shall not meet when you were meeting with her yourself in this very room and lied to me. You lied to me. *Again.*" The words burnt, but they were true, and he needed to hear them.

His eyes widened. "How do you—"

"Because I'm not a fool. I smelled her perfume in here. Now will you tell me why? And for that matter why your brother was also with you the very night she was killed, storming out of here with murder on his face? I know you do not like speaking of your past, but you are going to have to tell us the truth. Even the unsavory bits."

Mr. Owen closed his eyes and shook his head. "Malachi would not harm her. He's angry, but harmless. He cared for Lucy, in his way."

I arched a brow. "He seemed rather capable of murder last night."

Mr. Owen pinched the bridge of his nose and groaned. "Ruby . . . there is only one person in all of Scotland that my brother wishes dead and that is me. Lucy had nothing to fear from him."

Something in his tone gave me pause.

Ruan cleared his throat, interrupting our little spat. "Owen said you found the body. Did you see anyone else last night, anyone at all when you were out there?" Ruan ran his wide palms over his trousers, smoothing the fabric.

Grateful for the interruption, I shook my head. "Not a soul, I am beginning to wonder if Lucy was bringing everyone here for a reason. Do you have the letter she wrote you at first? I want to look at it."

Mr. Owen stood, rummaging around in his valise and pulled out the folded letter, handing it to me. I opened it, comparing the two and laid the two pages down side by side. "They don't match."

Mr. Owen and Ruan leaned closer, both studying the script on the pages.

"Not at all." Ruan mused. "These were written by two different people, but who . . . and why?"

Bile rose in my throat as I remembered my missing coat and shoes. I folded up both letters and tucked them into my pocket. "That *is* the question."

"Well, we do have another interesting visitor at the castle to make things more muddy." The dear familiar divot formed again between Ruan's brows and my thumb itched to smooth it. But instead I clenched my hands tighter. "The White Witch is here."

"What?" Ruan growled, springing to his feet.

"She's one of the Three Fates, or at least that's what they're calling themselves. The three mediums who performed the séance last night. I still don't entirely understand why she's here, but I get a sense that she did not care much for Lucy and the other medium. She's helping me. At least I *think* she is."

"The White what? Ruby, heavens, what nonsense have you gotten into now?" Mr. Owen started before shaking his head. "Never mind it. I don't care. Would you mind entertaining Mr. Kivell in your room? I'm afraid I have a headache. It's come fast and I need to rest."

His quick turn of mood was startling, but it had been like this ever since we arrived in Scotland. One moment he'd be himself and the next he'd turn bearish and snarling. "Do you have your medicine?" I ignored Mr. Owen's grumbling and laid a hand on his brow. Cool. Damp. I didn't like that—not one bit.

"I have some powders. And Ruan brought me one of his tinctures. I'll be fit in the morning. Just . . . I think it's the strain of the last day. That's all."

It *had* been a trying twelve hours, I'd give him that. Ruan and I hastily fled to the safety of my room and I pushed the door closed before walking over to my dresser and pulling out the stopper from a decanter of Scotch. "Want some?"

"No, thank you." He settled himself in a floral armchair. I'd forgotten he didn't drink. I poured myself two fingers, taking a sip, letting the peaty liquid burn its way down my throat. I wasn't a fan of Scotch but when in Rome . . .

"You said the White Witch is here?" Ruan asked, glancing to the closed door behind me.

"Mmm. She is, and I don't know what she wants, but she's seemingly trying to help me."

"*Help* you?"

I shrugged. "That or she's afraid of me. I'm not sure which is better, but beggars cannot be choosers. If she isn't trying to frighten me away, I may as well make use of her."

Ruan didn't laugh. "It's never good when the old ones are afraid."

"Is she truly what she claims to be? A witch?"

I wasn't quite sure I wanted the answer, and Ruan did not give it. "Shall I go find her for you? See what she wants this time?"

Most certainly not, she'd be incandescent when she learned he was here. "She still thinks I'm going to kill you, by the way. Probably for the best if you keep your head down or else she might stop being cooperative."

Ruan took a step closer, reaching up and touching my cheek softly with his thumb. His strange greenish eyes fixed upon me as if he were seeing me for the first time. My breath caught in my chest as he sighed and shook his head. "It's the strangest thing . . ."

"My face? I assure you it hasn't changed *that* much since we saw each other last."

He let out a startled laugh. "No. My . . ." He lifted his hand helplessly before it fell back to his side. "I can scarcely hear you here. It's odd."

Now that was a shock. My lips parted slightly. "Do you think your . . . abilities are tied to Cornwall somehow?"

"Not at all. It's actually the opposite. Ever since arriving on this estate, everything is too loud. I hear *everything*. My head aches with all the voices clamoring for my attention. I cannot focus upon you. Upon anything." He rubbed at his temple with his left hand.

Despite the way he described it, it wasn't sound he spoke of, but his ability to hear people's thoughts. He had once said that it was akin to being at a crowded train station, catching bits of conversation and a general sense of *something* coming, with the odd word here or there. If it was worse now, I could only imagine what a burden it was.

After leaving Lothlel Green I scoured every book I could get my hands on, absorbing every word I could find about Pellars— which were not terribly many—they were born, not made. All the books seemed to agree on that part—with only the seventh born of a seventh born possessing these specific gifts. Yet in all my books and all my studies I learned no more than what Ruan had told me himself. How far we'd come, he and I, from when we first met on the shores of Tintagel and he told me the story of the poor troubled mermaid who gave her power to the very first Pellar—some distant ancestor of Ruan's. Granting that nameless soul the ability to break curses, to heal the sick, and find stolen goods. It seemed such a charming tale then, but as with all fairy stories the truth behind it is always a bit grimmer—especially after the White Witch's revelations. And as I got to know Ruan Kivell, I saw what a toll those *gifts* had taken upon the man himself. I yearned to help him, to find something to unlock the secret to what he was. And more, why he and I should be so closely linked. An American girl born an ocean away, on the very same day as he.

A part of me was glad he couldn't hear me as well here, especially as wayward as my thoughts had grown when it came to him.

"Ruby," he said softly, bringing me back to the task at hand. Right. Lucy Campbell.

"There is one thing I didn't tell Mr. Owen or his nephew." I reached into my trouser pocket and placed the identification disc between us on the table. The green one only, the red having been taken when the soldier died. "I found this on her body. Lennox is the name of Mr. Owen's nephew. Do you have any idea who this belonged to?"

Ruan touched it gently and closed his eyes. "Ben."

I sucked in a sharp breath. "Ben? As in Mr. Owen's son, Ben?"

"The same."

Mr. Owen must have given the tags to her sometime before she was killed. It was a good thing I'd taken them from her body. The ceiling creaked with the footsteps of someone the next floor above. "How is he a Lennox and not an Owen?"

"I do not know. But I knew Ben. I met him briefly after the war. I was on the hospital ship the night he died. We were all coming home together . . ."

I could see the weariness return to his expression at mention of the war, but I wasn't going to press him. Not now. "Mr. Owen said that Lucy had brought him here to relay a message from Ben. But during the séance, the spirit that spoke to us was that of a woman. A Mariah. I meant to ask Mr. Owen about her, but he hasn't been well and you know how he can be when pushed."

Ruan nodded, placing the disc in my palm, folding my fingers around it, his hand remaining there a second too long.

"You don't happen to know who Mariah is?"

His hand was warm over mine as he shook his head. "Who else knows of this tag?"

I looked down to our clasped hands. "Only you."

"Best keep it that way."

My thoughts exactly. "What about Mr. Owen's nephew? Shouldn't he know?"

The muscle leapt in Ruan's jaw as he struggled to keep his tone even. "Absolutely not."

"You know each other then?"

Ruan frowned. "We do. But back to matters at hand. You fished the dead woman from the lake. Made certain she was dead. We're at what? Approximately half past twelve?"

I was rather impressed at his ability to piece this together—even if he was prickly when it came to Captain Lennox. "Then I ran back to the castle grounds for help. I hadn't the strength to carry her back and well . . . she was dead already. I didn't see the point in it."

"What then?" His eyes sparkled, as if he were enjoying this far more than a man ought to.

"I came to the castle half-frozen, and ran into Mr. Owen's nephew. He'd been in the gardens and I bumped into him coming up the steps from the lawn."

Ruan arched a dark brow. "What was he doing in the garden at that time of night?"

"Walking, I suppose. He'd been smoking a pipe."

"But you ran into him . . ." Ruan eyed the borrowed dinner jacket still lying over my chair, piecing together bits of the night, and I wondered precisely what incorrect assumption he'd added up in his head.

"It was a long night," I snapped, before softening my tone. "But yes, I came back to the house, he found some blankets, warmed me up and went with some servants to bring the body back."

"Stay away from him, Ruby."

"From who?"

"Andrew Lennox. Stay far away. He's a dangerous man. I cannot stress to you how important this is for you to understand. He is not to be trusted."

I let out a strangled laugh. The fellow who gave me his jacket and cosseted me like a small child. Dangerous? It was laughable really. My housekeeper, Mrs. Penrose, was more likely to be a murderer than he. "Why on earth would I? He's Mr. Owen's nephew and has shown himself to be a perfect gentleman." I reached out, taking the identification disc, and stuffed it into my pocket. "And why, pray tell, do you think he's dangerous? You'll have to be a bit more forthcoming and stop sitting there glowering at me like my great-aunt Prudence."

Ruan smirked. It seemed Mr. Owen's habit of inventing distant P-named female relations was rubbing off. "I know . . . you're your own woman . . ." He ran his hand over his beard, drawing my attention to his full lower lip. "Promise me, Ruby . . . Promise me you'll be careful. Ben trusted him and look what happened."

Now that brought my thoughts back to the present. "Wait . . . is that why you're here? Does your presence have something to do with Ben?"

Ruan nodded. "I'm afraid it may. Mr. Owen sent me to bring him something of Ben's that he'd left with me for safekeeping."

I eyed his pocket.

"Don't ask questions I cannot answer. It's Owen's story to tell. Not mine."

"I dislike your discretion. You know that, don't you?"

The edge of his mouth quirked up. Arrogant man.

I toyed with the disc in my pocket. "Why do you hate Andrew?"

"Because I believe he either killed Ben or allowed him to die that night. That's why."

I stared at Ruan, struggling to make sense of his accusation. "That's . . . absurd. He's been nothing but the picture of kindness. He doesn't seem like a murderer to me."

"And *you* are the best judge of such things?" he shot back.

Ruan's words stung.

He swore beneath his breath, and stepped forward, taking me

by the arms. "Promise me, Ruby. You won't go risking your life on this. First Ben . . . now this medium . . . and Andrew Lennox is sniffing about the estate? Something isn't right about all of this. If Lucy had his tags when she died, perhaps it's because whoever killed him wants that secret to stay buried too."

I searched his face for answers. As if he were some oracle and not simply an exhausted Cornishman who'd arrived on the overnight train. "I just . . . I don't understand what's going on here."

"I don't either." He reached up, touching the scar on my brow with two fingers. "At least not yet. But I'm not risking your life trying."

My stomach jumped at his words—at his touch. This was terrible. Just terrible. I opened my mouth to say something witty. Clever even, when someone knocked at my door.

"Go on," I whispered, tilting my head to the door connecting my room to Mr. Owen's. "You can make sure he's all right before you find your room." The very last thing I needed was Ruan Kivell to be found in here with me. I had never been discreet regarding my bedfellows back in London, or in Exeter for that matter, and did not care a bit about what people thought of me for my own sake. I did, however, care a great deal for Mr. Owen's good name, and as it turned out, Ruan's too.

He nodded, recognizing the wisdom in my train of thought. I waited until he was safely behind the closed door before answering my own.

A young maid stood there, one I'd never seen before. She wasn't dressed like the other Manhurst servants who wore a lovely shade of deep blue. Instead she was in old-fashioned black with a white cap, which meant she must have worked for one of the other guests. "Miss Vaughn?"

I nodded, arms folded tight across my chest. "Yes?"

The maid kept darting her eyes back to the hall. "I've come

from my lady, miss. She asked that you come to the orangery to meet her. She says there isn't much time."

"When?" A second clandestine meeting in twenty-four hours. This did not bode well.

"Now, miss. She said her mother is being questioned, and she isn't sure how long she has."

I blew out a breath. Lady Amelia. It must be. Now this was a twist I'd not expected. I could hear the soft rhythm of voices coming from Mr. Owen's room and I wondered how much Ruan was telling him of our discussion. I'd speak with them both later, but for now I grabbed my room key and set out to find out what the girl had to say that couldn't wait.

CHAPTER EIGHT

Secret Confessions

THE orangery was situated on the opposite side of the castle from the ruin, set across from an ornamental garden, presumably positioned to better catch the afternoon sun. Though what did one call an orangery that had no oranges? The structure now sat derelict with the surviving flora sheltered by what remained of the glass roof. Vines grew up one side and shrubby plants threatened to take over the remaining soil. Broken glass roof tiles allowed rain in to feed the neglected plants. It seemed Mr. Sharpe's looted library could not fund the rehabilitation of *this* part of the estate.

I stepped inside, shoes crunching on the dead leaves that had gathered on the stone floor. "Hello?" I called into the silence, disturbing a handful of sparrows, sending them up to the glass roof before perching on the long-dead branches of a tree.

"Hello?" I called again, creeping past a broken statue of Venus. "Miss Vaughn?"

I startled, banging my knee on the old iron bench beside me as I turned. Lady Amelia stepped out from a nearby alcove. The girl was dressed all in deep rose with red piping, her golden hair waving stylishly beneath the smart hat she wore. Ruan was right. She did resemble a strawberry tart.

"I didn't mean to surprise you. I didn't want to be seen." Her cheeks flushed a pale pink, clashing with her frock. I glanced around the orangery, wondering who exactly she thought might reveal her presence here.

"I think you've accomplished it. I cannot imagine anyone would come out here. This place looks like it's about to fall in on the both of us."

She let out a tinkling laugh, which she hid behind a gloved hand. "It's for the best. My mother would never let me hear the end of it if she knew I'd actually sought you out."

I placed my hands on my hips, curious about the girl. I'd assumed her a spineless thing, based on how she clung to her mother's skirts inside the estate. But perhaps she had more backbone than I'd first assumed. "I'm not sure what you think I can do for you."

She twisted the fingers of her gloves, taking a step closer to me. The scent of her floral perfume thick in the air. "Mother said that the medium killed herself."

"I'm not sure why you think I'd know anything about it."

The girl took another step closer. Close enough her skirt brushed against my trousers. I started to take a step back, but my heel struck the wall behind me. I was trapped there, against the stone beside an intricately carved waterspout. The scent of decaying plants and mold burnt my nostrils.

What was this girl after? I didn't *think* she meant me any harm, but this was quickly becoming one of the more peculiar encounters of my life. Lady Amelia's expression shifted again and she flung her hands in exasperation and stepped back in a flurry of emotion. "I am sorry. I am going about this all wrong. Mother says I'm too much of a flibbertigibbet and need to be cautious in my speech but I do not know how to do this any other way."

I eyed her cautiously, as one would a feral cat who had hopped the garden wall. Her cheeks grew very rosy. "Let me begin again. I . . ." She puffed up her chest as if about to give a long speech. "I am worried for my mother. She has been behaving most erratically since we arrived here. Before that even."

Lady Morton? This conversation was getting stranger and stranger. "Erratically how?" I asked, sidestepping away, allowing myself room to breathe. The nervousness of Lady Amelia was contagious. I moved toward the metal bench and took a seat, pulling my knee up beneath my arm and hugging it to my chest.

"We're here—" She flung her arm wide. "I don't even know why we are here. Up until last week Mother had been planning to spend the month with my grandfather in Kent. He has an annual hunting party every year. We have never missed it in all my life."

I frowned, not quite understanding the urgency of this conversation, but I may as well hear the girl out. "Did she tell you why?"

Lady Amelia shook her head. "No. That's the more peculiar part. At first, I wondered if there wasn't some matchmaking plan of hers coming all the way to Scotland, but there isn't a single man between twenty and sixty here unless you count Captain Lennox. I suppose that wouldn't be an altogether terrible match if that was her intention . . . He does stand to inherit a title eventually, but he's *old*."

I could have laughed. The girl could do far worse than Andrew Lennox; besides, he wasn't *that* much older than I. Possibly a handful of years at most. Though I suppose at seventeen I thought anyone on the far side of twenty was positively ancient.

Suddenly a thought struck me and the humor dried on my tongue. "What happened last week to change your mother's plans?"

Lady Amelia frowned, little lines forming between her brows. "She received a letter. I remember it clear as day. We were having breakfast talking about the party and Jamison—our butler—came in with the post. She went white as a ghost."

I caught my lower lip between my teeth and prodded her on. "Do you know what was in the letter?"

"No. She stood and left the room, but not before burning it."

I swore, smacking my palm on my knee. "Did she say anything else? Do anything strange?"

Lady Amelia shook her head. "The next thing I knew we were packing for a week in Scotland."

"For the séance?"

"I don't know. I assume so. Mother doesn't ask my opinion on things, you see. She tells me what we're doing and where we're going and I go . . ." Her voice trailed off. "You don't think she's in danger, do you?"

I caught the inside of my cheek in my teeth. I didn't know. I'd know a great deal more if I had that letter she'd burnt. Or if I had a clue what the letter contained. Odds were slim of ever finding out as Lady Morton looked at me as if I were a bug beneath a glass. She'd never tell me what was in the missive, and honestly it could have been anything at all. The woman was insufferable. Perhaps she'd gotten the bill from her seamstress or the baker and decided to skip paying it and have a change of scenery instead.

"Why me?" I asked her suddenly.

The girl's expression dropped from the animated one she'd had only moments before to the shy and skittish creature who often appeared at her mother's side. "Because I've read about you in the papers. They say you're a lady detective. I think that's what we need."

I laughed. For the first time in my life the papers were not casting me in a terrible light. An unconventional one—perhaps—but at least not as a walking scandal. "I'm an antiquarian, Lady Amelia. I deal in old books, not in crimes. What happened in Cornwall was an accident—I certainly don't mean to make a habit of it."

She furrowed her brow. "But they're alike, aren't they?"

"What are?"

"People and books. They all have stories, tales they want to tell. Some give them up easier than others—but it seems to me they're the same."

She had me there. While people were alive, and books were not—there certainly were similarities between the two. Though at times I vastly preferred books to people, as they could be shut and left on a shelf if they grew tiresome. People, on the other hand, had a knack for returning of their own accord.

I plucked at the fabric of my trousers. While I didn't have firm proof of what was in that missive that she burnt, I could have bet my locket that it had been similar to the one Mr. Owen received. "Keep an eye on your mother. Send your maid around with word if she behaves strangely or if anything seems amiss."

Lady Amelia blanched. "Then you do think she's in danger?"

I shook my head, unable to lie. "I do not know, but you need to keep your head down. Don't go hunting clues, don't poke around in anything. Leave the matters to the authorities."

She gave me a bullish look. "Are you leaving matters to the authorities?"

Of course not. I cleared my throat, changing the subject. "Do you know the man your mother asked for at the séance? Arthur McTavish, I think was what she'd said."

She nodded, wrinkling her delicate nose. "That was the other odd part. Arthur McTavish was my father's valet from when I was a little girl. He's been dead ten years. Why would Mama want to speak with him now and not Papa?"

I blew out a breath. That was a very good question indeed.

CHAPTER NINE

A Tale of Two Bullies

NOT five minutes after leaving Lady Amelia in the abandoned orangery I found myself in the company of Inspector Burnett and his young constable. The pair had just finished speaking with Lady Morton as I returned to the castle and the men latched on to me at once. My timing could not have been worse.

For four hours, we remained sequestered in a cramped closet outside the dining hall, the scent of food drifting in through the closed door, causing my stomach to rumble longingly. The inspector would ask the same questions over and over and I would answer them to the best of my knowledge. I certainly doubted that they'd kept Lady Morton in here this long without food or drink, but was wise enough not to comment.

All in all, I thought I was doing quite well, functioning on three hours of sleep and a pot and a half of coffee; however, I doubted the inspector agreed. The odious man eyed me across the rickety table.

"Tell us again, Miss Vaughn, what happened that night," he growled.

I might have been more inclined to do so, had they the decency to offer me a glass of water, or a pickle and cheese sandwich. But as it was, my temper was running short. I rubbed my right eye, trying to decide if I'd changed my story at all since I'd been in here. *I* didn't think I had, but I was also near delirious with hunger and exhaustion—I might have said anything just to get something to eat.

"I have told you everything I know in every way I know how. May I please return to my room?" I asked, trying my best to appear an obedient girl, my hands demurely in my lap.

Inspector Burnett, the older of the two men, leaned across the table, his bushy eyebrows raised. He had dark hair that had gone silver at the temples and he was missing the tip of his forefinger, a fact I noticed as he rested his chin on his hand. "Funny, because I don't believe you *have* told us everything."

I let out a little harrumph of annoyance, sounding far too much like Mr. Owen, before settling back in my chair.

"It doesn't make sense to me, what you were doing out there . . . *alone,*" the young constable added, drawling out the final word.

There was that question again, and I had a sense that they would not accept the excuse I'd given to Andrew Lennox earlier this morning. "I was walking, as I told you before. I couldn't sleep after the commotion with the séance and went out to clear my head."

"Couldn't sleep, could you?" The constable waggled an eyebrow, withdrawing a large box from beneath the table. He lifted the lid and piece by piece withdrew my missing coat, my shoes, and the golden cloth hairpiece that had fallen into the tall grass when I took my tumble in the foxhole—or whatever it had been.

My breath caught in my chest. That's where the missing items had gone.

"The staff here tells us that you came back with your hair all knotted, dress ripped and stained. They also found your coat and things lying in the tall grass beside the bridge . . . From where I'm standing, it certainly looks like you were doing a *bit* more than walking last night."

"How dare you . . ."

"Then perhaps you'd care to enlighten us how your belongings got there?" The inspector flashed a wicked smile at me with his yellowing teeth.

The room was stiflingly hot. Sweat beaded up along the collar of my blouse, bleeding through and darkening the fabric. I shifted in the uncomfortable wooden chair. Good God. "I fell. *In the grass*. Then I took my shoes and coat off to jump in a damned lake to save what I *thought* was a drowning woman."

"Aye, lass, but what were you doing in the grass to begin with at that time of night? When anyone or anything may have come upon you?" Inspector Burnett probed, his stale breath hot in my face.

Clearly, *walking* was not the answer he was looking for, but it was the truth. I tugged my legs up beneath me—one of the thousand benefits to riding breeches, in my estimation—the young constable leered at my thighs and then raised his brows with a decidedly unprofessional gleam in his beady eyes.

"I'm not afraid of the dark, Inspector. After four years of driving an ambulance during the war, there's nothing in nature that frightens me, of that I can assure you." *Men, on the other hand.*

The inspector's expression softened at mention of the war, but the young constable remained unfazed, transfixed upon what I wore. Perhaps he'd suddenly discovered the novelty of a woman in trousers. "Or were you meeting someone out there?" the constable challenged. "You see, Miss Vaughn, you were overheard arguing with a woman outside Miss Campbell's room before midnight. Then for you to be the one who found her body, I'd say that's more than enough evidence to have you brought in."

My throat grew tight. "As I told you, I wanted some air."

The younger one flicked his attention over my loose-fitting lilac blouse with its sweat spots from this stagnant room. My jaw tightened in response, temper barely reined in. I was a Vaughn, after all. No one spoke to me like this.

"You see, what doesn't make sense to me is this: a lady like you—" He pointed in the general vicinity of my bosom.

I crossed my arms. My bosom was none of his concern.

"You come to meet us in broad daylight wearing trousers like one of the lads. And yet you went for an evening stroll dressed for supper and leave half your clothing in the field. Why would that be?"

"One does tend to wear evening gowns in the *evening*. And while I don't know how my coat was found in the grass, I assure you I took it off before jumping into the lake to try to save Miss Campbell. Perhaps some animal carried it off—but I promise you I did not hurt that woman. If I were you, I would spend more time worrying about who did kill Lucy Campbell and less time trying to concoct convoluted stories about me. As I have told you a dozen times—I went for a walk, saw the candles, and drew nearer. That was when I saw her floating in the water. I took off my coat—as not to drown myself in the process—jumped in and pulled her out."

"Candles?" the inspector asked, attention rapt as he leaned across the table. "You'd not mentioned that before, and there were no candles out there, Miss Vaughn. Nothing at all of the sort."

I stared at him, dumbfounded—and they saw it in my expression. "But how is that possible? There were candles. Thirteen of them. And a salt circle when I arrived. That would mean . . ."

"It'd mean that you're making up ghost stories, lass, to cover your tracks. We know you were out there. What we don't know is why," Inspector Burnett said, his voice slightly softer. "If you were out with your lover, tell us and save us the time of finding out on our own. There's no harm in having a discreet affair . . ."

I shot to my feet, not even having to feign offense. I had done a great many things in my life that I regretted, but I would never be ashamed of taking my pleasure as a man would. My personal life was none of their business, especially as it had no bearing on poor Miss Campbell's death. "We are done here, gentlemen."

The constable laid his clammy palm over the top of mine, holding me firmly to the table. "I don't think so, *Miss* Vaughn. You see, I know you're lying to me. The inspector"—he cocked his head, a lecherous smile on his face—"he knows it too. And if you were anyone else, you'd already be in irons on your way to Edinburgh."

My skin crawled as he ran a finger down the back of my hand while the inspector watched, motionless. Panic clawed its way up my chest.

"Believe what you will, I've told you exactly what happened last night." I struggled to summon my mother's chilliness, a skill I could scarcely manage in the best of times. "And if you would please remove your hand from my person." I tried to tug myself free, but he didn't release me. Instead he pressed harder against the wooden surface, causing the skin to pinch and my palm to dig into the rough grain.

Spittle flew from his lips as he leaned closer still. "You see, what I think happened is this: I think you were out with your lover, the old bitch interrupted you, then Lord Hawick did her in—"

"How dare you! That woman was murdered. *Murdered,* and you would insult her in such a way when you ought to be finding her killer?" With a firm tug, I managed to jerk my hand back, scraping it along the desktop. I spun around, snatching up my tweed jacket and made for the door, both men watching me with thinly veiled contempt. "Until you have something other than insinuations about my virtue or lack thereof, I'd appreciate you leaving me in peace. Go find the real killer, fellas, because I have better things to do than talk to either of you. Maybe you should go over to Hawick House if you're so certain he did it and leave me out of things."

I stormed out of the small drawing room into the main dining room. My pulse ricocheting through my veins. This was terrible. I'd lost my temper and in the process made things infinitely worse for all of us.

I hurried along the sunny hallway toward my room when I ran smack into a warm body. Stammering out a nonsensical apology, I suddenly realized exactly *whose* body it was.

I'd crashed into the Duke of Biddlesford. My day could not get any worse. I suppose it could—at least I hadn't knocked him down the stairs, killing him in the process. Now *that* would have been a problem.

The duke smiled down at me patiently, his golden hair neatly combed back. He was dressed for golf and had a green-handled walking stick.

"Are you all right there?" Convinced I wasn't about to topple over, he released me, patting me on the shoulder.

I nodded numbly, still reeling from my encounter with the inspector. "Fine. Just fine."

"That's good to hear. I believe you are Ruby Vaughn, are you not?"

I was surprised he knew my name at all. "I am. And you are?" I didn't need to ask, as I knew full well who he was. Mr. Owen had told me as much at the séance, but I was feeling a bit combative after my run-in with the inspector.

"James Swindon, Duke of Biddlesford," he said with an almost rueful smile as if to apologize for his title. There was something boyish about the gesture that instantly made me feel guilty for being cross. "I think I'm next."

He inclined his head toward the doors I'd just left.

"They're questioning a duke?" I couldn't disguise my surprise. In my previous encounters with the British aristocracy, any transgressions would be immediately brushed beneath the rug. To question a duke in a murder investigation was downright revolutionary.

He nodded, looking nearly as perplexed as I. "It seems so. I'm beginning to wish I'd not heeded my wife's wishes. She was insistent upon coming. I could not tell her no."

My ears pricked at his words. "Is she interested in the occult, Your Grace?" I asked politely, wondering how far I could pry before this duke would tire of speaking to me.

"Not at all. I found it peculiar at the time, but you know how women can be. And if this took her fancy, then how could I disappoint her?"

My mind was working twice as hard as before. I couldn't very well ask if she'd received a letter requesting her presence here, but perhaps I'd get a chance to speak with Her Grace later. "Have they questioned her?"

He shook his head. "No, not yet, though I fear her nerves will get the better of her. I do not relish the idea of her sitting alone with them. My wife has a delicate constitution. I worry for her even on the best of days but to be questioned by the inspector?" He grimaced before shaking his head. "I hear they ruffled Lady Morton earlier, a feat I'd like to have seen. Perhaps that alone is worth the inconvenience."

I snorted back a laugh; this duke was nothing like I expected. I'd known others of his kind. Stuffy and full of their own pomposity. But the Duke of Biddlesford was a great deal more likable than the others of his ilk. Then I remembered what Mr. Owen had said at the séance—he'd known Biddlesford as a young man. Perhaps that's why this man was remotely tolerable. He had Mr. Owen's seal of approval.

"As would I. She doesn't seem to like me much."

The duke gave me a conspiratorial grin. "Lady Morton doesn't seem to like *me* much either, if it's any consolation. I don't think she's liked anyone since she was a girl. But I had best see what the inspector has to ask."

"Good luck, Your Grace."

"I'm a duke, Miss Vaughn. I don't need luck." He flashed me a sad smile and shook his head. "Terrible business about the medium, though a woman like that, I suspect she had a great many enemies." He nodded to me and started down the hall. I leaned against the wallpaper, watching as he disappeared into the dining hall, realizing I now had a series of puzzles to solve instead of just one.

Whoever killed Lucy Campbell was inextricably linked to the reason we were all brought here. I had no proof of that, well— *little proof* besides the letter from Mr. Owen and my peculiar conversation with Lady Amelia—but signs certainly pointed to the fact that Lucy Campbell wanted us all to come to Manhurst Castle for the séance.

The *why* was the difficult part. And was it Lucy herself who wanted us here, or was there someone or something else at play that I had not yet considered? I ought to leave it to the authorities as I'd scolded Lady Amelia this morning. However, the men who questioned me this morning did not instill confidence that they'd do the job properly.

I was shaken from my wonderings by the arrival of Andrew Lennox. "Are you all right, Miss Vaughn?"

I suddenly realized he'd been standing there for several seconds before I noticed he'd been speaking to me. Andrew's gaze dropped to my injured hand, swollen and scraped with a smattering of thick dark splinters on the palm.

I'd been distracted by the duke and the mystery of Lucy Campbell's death and nearly forgotten my injury. I folded my fingers into a fist. "It is nothing. I was just questioned by the inspector. That's all."

"Did they harm you?" Andrew's voice grew grave. He reached

down, taking my hand and gently unfurled my fingers for his inspection.

"No. Nothing of the sort," I lied, wincing as he touched the large splinter in the middle of my palm. "I am fine."

He probed around, testing each finger and joint to be sure no real damage had been done. I stepped back, tugging my hand away. "I'm fine. Truly."

"Nothing seems amiss. Only a bit swollen, it might bruise. I could see to the bandaging if you'd like?"

"No. No, I'll be all right." I took a step back. Andrew nodded politely and turned, heading back to his room presumably—or wherever it was he was going—and I set off in search of the only person on this entire estate wholly unconnected to Lucy Campbell to help me unravel this mess.

Ruan Kivell.

CHAPTER TEN

Lady Detectiving

IT took only twenty minutes of wandering the halls of Manhurst before I found Ruan in the courtyard. He was sitting alone at a marble-topped table near the edge of the slate flags with a pot of tea and his head in a book. In the hours since we'd seen each other this morning he must have secured a room—or Mr. Owen secured one for him—as he'd managed to both bathe and change from his rumpled suit into a smart pair of gray trousers and an improbably green cardigan. His shorter curls were rebelling against whatever he'd used to slick them back, and I could not help but smile at the sight of them. I hesitated, drinking in the entirely un-Ruan-like sight. When I'd first met him at the seaside, with his trousers rolled up and knee-deep in the water he'd seemed free from the world around him, yet here in this place he appeared utterly confined by it. Bound by the rules of polite society. I missed it a bit—that untamed Ruan—but I supposed I could appreciate this version as well.

I cleared my throat as I approached the table.

He didn't look up at all, simply folded the corner of his page and closed the book before setting it down. "What's your plan?"

I ignored his question, staring at the desecrated medical text he'd been reading. The horror evident on my face. "I cannot believe you just did that."

He arched a brow in challenge. "It's a book, Ruby. They are meant to be used. Surely, you've seen worse than this living with Owen. Now, are you going to tell me what brought you out here or do I have to start guessing?"

The courtyard was relatively empty with the exception of the duke's wife, Catherine, I think Mr. Owen said her name was. She and Lady Morton were deep in conversation, having not taken any notice of me. Odd, as Lady Morton rarely wasted the opportunity to stare disapproving daggers at me whenever I entered a room.

I bit the inside of my cheek. "Can we go somewhere?" *Private.*

He must have heard me, because he nodded, gathering up the misused text and tucking it into the large pocket on his cardigan. He took a sip of the tea before placing the cup back on the saucer. "Shall we?"

Ruan matched me stride for stride as we walked out across the pasture with no real direction in mind. The speed at which we fell back into that easy companionship we'd had in Cornwall both surprised and comforted me. He didn't interrupt me once as I told him what I'd learned from Lady Amelia in the orangery followed by my unpleasant encounter with the inspector and how determined the authorities were that I'd had something to do with Lucy's death.

The cool autumn wind whipped at my hair as I paused, pushing it back from my face, and I looked up at him. "What do you think?"

He huffed out a breath, stuffing his hands into his pockets. His green eyes cast toward the sky as he weighed his thoughts. "What am I not thinking?"

"That's not very helpful. I wish we still had her body. The inspector indicated that they removed it from the estate early this morning."

Ruan gave me a puzzled look. "Why in the gods' names do you want her body?"

I poked him in the ribs. "I have a dead medium. Maybe a *Pellar* would be useful in this instance."

"Doubtful. My head is a disaster. I'm afraid I'm less than useful at present. I thought tea and quiet would help matters but it only grows worse by the moment. The noise in the courtyard was worse than inside the castle."

"How is that possible—you were alone—" but the word died on my lips. "Ruan, those women out there with you. Did you hear them?"

"It doesn't work that way—not usually. As I told you—most times when I can hear a person's thoughts it's a word here or there. A general sense or feeling of something. Dread. Fear. You though . . ." He hesitated, studying my face, then let out a strange laugh before shaking his head. "You are entirely different and I do not understand *that* at all."

Because you hear me.

He nodded again, his lower lip caught in his teeth. "It's better all the way out here. At the house you're scarcely louder than anyone else—imagine a whisper competing with the roar of an engine. It worries me."

"Do you have any idea why that would be?" I took a moment to orient myself. Manhurst was far in the distance. We'd nearly wandered onto Hawick lands again—probably a mile or more from the house. "Or do you think it's because we're standing in the middle of a field up to our knees in mud with only sheep to compete for your attention?" As if prompted, a particularly fluffy sheep bleated out in agreement.

He sighed, rolling his eyes to the sky. "You are maddening."

"Yes, yes. One of my numerous good qualities I'm sure. But back to the point at hand. Those women in the courtyard—did you sense anything from them? Overhear even a whisper of their conversation?"

Ruan rubbed at his dark brown whiskers and shook his head. "Not much. There was fear there—but that's to be expected as there is a killer on the grounds."

I waved off that thought. "Or if they're afraid of discovery."

Ruan arched a brow. "You cannot possibly suspect two women because they are *afraid*. That's not evidence. Half the people on the bloody estate are afraid."

No. No, it wasn't. *Evidence.* The word settled uncomfortably in my head as I recalled precisely what the inspector had unwittingly revealed to me in the interrogation closet. *There was no evidence.*

"You didn't tell me that before," Ruan murmured, evidently having overheard my thoughts. I shook my head and started off toward the bridge. I had to see for myself what remained. While the inspector didn't find evidence, maybe I could.

The night I found Lucy's body remained stubbornly in my mind. Perhaps Ruan could make sense of it. I hurried on across the pasture toward the bridge, which was just peeking out over the horizon. The trees in the distance had begun to change their colors. Greens mixed through with umbers, yellows, and oranges. Sheep dotted the landscape, grazing beneath trees. Fleece thick and white, bleating out at my approach. The splinters in my hand long forgotten and replaced by curiosity at what we might find there. *Or what we didn't find.* Either could be telling.

Ruan and I paused at the foot of the bridge. There were voices ahead. One male, the other female. It appeared to be the elusive Mr. Sharpe and the youngest medium. I held a hand out behind me to still Ruan as I drew nearer, not certain what we were interrupting.

"—You are going to get yourself in trouble if you aren't more careful—" Sharpe said coldly.

The young medium placed a finger in the center of his chest

which he snatched away, holding it in his left hand. She said something low and soft that I couldn't make out from this distance.

Whatever it was, his expression softened as he looked down at her, still clasping her wrist in his hand. I couldn't decide if I'd interrupted a lovers' quarrel or something more sinister.

Mr. Sharpe's voice dropped as he purred. "Do you now? Because I—" But the rest of his sentence died away when he saw me standing there. The impervious mask I'd once known so well in New York slipped back over his elegant features and for the briefest of moments Mr. Sharpe became Elijah Keene again. It wasn't my imagination at all. I might have even convinced myself again that it wasn't him, had he not betrayed the truth with the myriad emotions crossing his face: surprise, fear, and finally settling into anger.

As if he had any right to those sentiments after what he did back then. I was going to be sick. My stomach churned and I reached out, laying my hand on the solidness of the bridge rail, as if grounding myself would make the truth more palatable.

The medium took advantage of his distraction and jerked her hand from Sharpe before slapping him across the face. Not a lovers' quarrel then. She darted past me on the bridge, with the scent of rose water trailing in her wake.

Mr. Sharpe drew nearer to me, achingly familiar. Elijah had been a beautiful man when I'd last seen him in New York, but this man no longer possessed that boyish softness, making him even more arresting than he had been in his youth.

The wound in my chest fresh and raw as I whispered his name. "Elijah . . ."

He turned to me and the same pale blue eyes that my younger sister mooned over, looked back at me. It had to be him. It *had* to be. "I am afraid you are mistaken, Miss Vaughn. Now if you'd excuse me." He took off at a more leisurely pace, but following in the exact same path as the youngest medium.

I didn't hear Ruan approach until he settled his hip on the railing of the bridge beside me. "Who is Elijah Keene?"

"How much of that did you hear?"

He cocked his head to one side with a frown. "More than you likely intended me to. He hurt you. Badly."

"Ah. Yes. Well. I cannot be certain, Mr. Sharpe looks so like Elijah that I cannot make sense of it. The resemblance is uncanny."

Ruan shifted where he stood, shoving his hands into the pockets of his trousers. "Was he your . . . ah . . ." The tips of his ears turned an endearing shade of pink as he flushed.

"Lover?" I looked up at him through my lashes with a grin. It never ceased to amuse me how shy he could be about physical congress. For a man who has delivered more babies than I could count, he certainly couldn't speak of the act of begetting one without turning an adorable shade of pink. I cast my gaze back down to the ground and shook my head. I'd been scarcely sixteen years old when Christopher came to my father's attention. A promising young alderman with a head for politics. Daddy thought it would be an advantageous marriage—uniting our family with the man promised to be the rising star of New York politics. I'd been a girl, smitten by the idea of love and Christopher had noticed that naiveté a mile away. He and Elijah were always together—thick as thieves my mother had said—always attending the same dinner parties, the same plays, they even were in business together. It was only natural that I'd befriend Elijah if I planned to marry his best friend. Elijah had even been there the night of the Vanderbilts' ball—when Christopher had convinced me that we did not need to wait until marriage. What was a wedding when two people loved one another as we did? Granted, Christopher already had a wife that no one knew of. I still don't understand what he thought he would gain from his web of lies. Could one truly get away with bigamy in the modern age?

"Ruby." Ruan reached out and wrapped me into his arms. "It's all right. They cannot harm you now. Either of them."

I rested my forehead against his chest, breathing in the green scent of him and feeling my anxieties slowly start to melt away. His right hand stroked the back of my head, with each touch drawing out the bone-deep ache inside. "I know," I whispered. "But it doesn't make the memories hurt any less."

"No. It doesn't, but you really ought to have told me." He ran his hand soothingly down my back.

I wriggled out of his embrace, leaning back and raking my hands through my hair. "What difference does it make? I cannot even be certain it *is* him. It's been thirteen years, Ruan. And even if it was him, what does it matter? The Elijah I knew was not the sort of man that would murder a medium. Could you sense what they were arguing about?"

He shook his head. "Only emotion."

"This Pellar business of yours is not very helpful, you know."

He grinned, before turning to the water behind me. His smile faded. "This is where she died?"

"I don't suppose there are any chatty ghosts around who want to tell you what happened." My gaze dropped to his lips for a half second before I looked away. "Right. Not that kind of witch either. Pity." I slipped away from him, explaining exactly what I'd found here the night that Lucy was killed. I moved to where the salt circle had once been and bent down on my hands and knees, looking carefully along the gravelly surface. The inspector was right. Even the charcoal flowers that had been on each column had been dutifully removed in the hours following Lucy's death.

Between that and the true identity of Mr. Sharpe, it was enough to make me think I was going mad. Just as I was about to suggest we return to the house, a bit of color caught my attention. I bent down in the gravel and touched it with my thumbnail.

Blackberry-colored candle wax. The same color as the wax that sealed Lucy's note to me.

"What's that?" Ruan joined me on the ground, his sleeve brushing against my arm.

I picked up the little piece of wax and held it in my palm, showing him. "A clue."

I didn't know what to make of it, but at least I could be *reasonably* assured that I wasn't going mad.

CHAPTER ELEVEN

The Hunt Begins

I sent Ruan back to the house with instructions to get a message to Hari, my solicitor, and ask him to find out everything he could about Elijah Keene and his whereabouts. Above all, I needed them both to be discreet. A man seeing to his affairs would not be considered out of the ordinary—but with the inspector already convinced of my involvement in Lucy's death, I needed to keep my head down as best I could. If anyone could find the current whereabouts of Elijah Keene, it would be Hari. He was a brilliant solicitor and one of the few people in this world I trusted with my life. I might not always like what he had to say, but Hari had never steered me wrong. Nor had he ever *been* wrong—even when I sometimes wished him to be.

I had no solid evidence as to what was going on here, besides that Lucy—or someone—wanted us all on the estate. I wasn't even convinced that the person who wrote the letter to Mr. Owen was Lucy at all, and if that wasn't the case—then who *did* lure us here? And why cover up the séance—or whatever it was Lucy was doing out here the night she died?

Any clues she might have left behind would be long gone by now. I shoved the little blob of wax into my pocket and darted back to the house in search of Andrew, hoping that he remained on estate grounds. He'd been here immediately after Lucy died. Perhaps he'd seen something that might be useful.

ANDREW WAS IN the ruins when I returned to the castle, sitting on the top of a broken-off staircase, using his uninjured leg to steady his notepad. He was sketching something in charcoal. His eyes darting from the page, to the top of the ramparts, then back down. His fingers were smudged from the tiny bit of pencil in his hand as he captured the ruins of Manhurst on paper. This castle had burnt centuries ago and instead of rebuilding it where it stood the Campbells erected the great manor house next door. The keep and some of the outer wall were all that remained of the fifteenth-century stronghold that once proudly stood here in the Scottish borders, a first line of defense against the English. The air smelled strange. Old and acrid, with the scent of decay.

"I'm surprised you haven't left."

He looked up at me through those familiar warm brown eyes. "Haven't you heard? None of us can leave until they find the killer."

I sighed, shielding my sight from the bright midday sun. "I hadn't, but I suppose it shouldn't be a surprise. They suspect you too?"

He returned to his sketching, not looking at me as his fingers flew over the page making quick hash marks. "They must. Though they've questioned everyone—even my father. Serves the old bastard right for coming here that night. Now he's stuck with Uncle Owen." Andrew let out a cynical laugh and sighed. "What is it that brings you out here, Miss Vaughn?"

"Am I that obvious?"

He paused. "You've sought me out in the ruins, so yes. I daresay you are quite obvious."

"You are very like him, has anyone told you that?"

"Owen? All the time. Much to my father's dismay. Father used to bring me here when I was a boy. Our family had always been close to the Campbells. I wonder how long it will be before this ruin finally tumbles the rest of the way down."

My shoes crunched on the tall grass as I took a step closer to him, as if the ghosts of this old place might overhear. A part of me didn't want to disturb him from his drawing, but another part needed answers. "Do you recall the night I pulled Lucy from the lake?"

Andrew set his sketchbook down with a sigh and cocked his head to one side. "I don't very much think I'd forget—why?"

"You found the revolver."

He peered behind me toward the earthen bridge leading into the ruins. His jaw tightened. "You should not speak of it."

"Did you see anything else when you were there? Candles, a salt circle . . . anything at all? The reason I ask is that when I jumped into the lake, there had been lit candles. A salt circle. Strange drawings in . . ." My eyes drifted to the charcoal in his hands, then I brushed the thought away. "I think she was trying to *do* something on the bridge. But the inspector says that when they arrived there was no evidence of that."

Andrew leaned back, rubbing his fingers together to remove the smudges. "I don't believe so. I think I'd have noticed candles had they been lit. I did not to go to the bridge though, I was down by the water—where you left her."

"You never went to the bridge?"

He shook his head. "Why would I?"

My pulse sped as the words did not want to come. "But you found the revolver."

"Of course. It was beside her body at the water's edge. In the high grass."

I had left the revolver with my coat on the bridge, right by the salt circle and candles. For it to be down by the water by the time

Andrew arrived at the lake meant only one thing. Whoever killed Lucy Campbell was still there when I pulled her from the water. They'd killed her and stayed to watch her sink to the bottom of the lake.

The thought gave me pause. "Did you see anyone there on your way out or going back?"

He shook his head. "No. But at the same time I was more concerned with why my uncle's gun was lying beside a dead woman."

"You have a point."

He leaned forward, taking my arm and leaving a dark smudge on my lavender sleeve. "You must take this seriously, Miss Vaughn. Someone killed Lucy Campbell, and whoever it is fully intended to frame my uncle for it."

The words struck me in the stomach. "You cannot think they'd suspect him? He's eighty years old!"

"What else am I to think when I found his revolver beside her?"

"Unless whoever did it wanted you to find it. Perhaps as a warning?" I gnawed on the inside of my cheek before shaking my head. No, that didn't make sense either. The killer could not have known that Andrew Lennox would be the first to see the body—he wasn't even supposed to be on the estate at all.

It's just as well that Andrew took the gun from the scene—of course doing so meant that the inspector found only my things there. I blew out a breath and swore loudly. Considering how badly the inspector wanted me to be guilty of the crime, it was only a matter of time before he manufactured enough evidence to arrest me.

Which meant that I needed to figure out who killed Lucy Campbell. And I had to do it fast.

CHAPTER TWELVE

Setting the Scene . . . or Perhaps Unsetting It

IN the dozen years since my exile from New York, I had lived freely, without a care for polite society or the repercussions of my actions—and here at long last they had caught up with me in the manner I least expected. I suppose if one breaks the rules long enough, people begin to expect the worst of one. *It wasn't fair*—but the world has never cared a whit about fairness. And I could either allow that fact to dictate my actions, give up and allow my past to land me in prison for a murder I did not commit, or I could take the necessary steps to save myself.

I chose the latter.

And the latter led me back up to Lucy Campbell's room to see if she'd left any clues for me that I'd missed when I'd come up here the night she died. It had only been what? Not even a full day and yet the room, which had been neat as a pin earlier, now looked as if someone had thrown three alley cats in a wet sack, set them loose, and locked the door.

Jars were broken and books lay splayed open-faced on the ground. The contents of the packed carpetbag were now spilling out of the open top. Chemises and blouses pulled from the drawers of the nearby wardrobe. Dresses lying in heaps on the ground. Whoever had been here was in a hurry, and hadn't been particularly careful in their search. I gingerly stepped around the debris, holding my breath as I took in the disarray. A broken vase lay in pieces on the dressing table, water dripping from the surface onto what appeared to be glass plate negatives lying scattered on the rug. Two of the negatives had broken and I stooped down, gathering up the bits of glass, trying to piece them back together.

Once again I had been too slow. Just as I'd been the night she died. Whoever it was remained two steps ahead of me.

I picked up the negatives, hastily riffling through the plates one by one—pausing now and then to be certain no one was coming—whoever I'd interrupted must have taken off when they heard me coming down the hall. Odds were, they wouldn't return, at least not for a while—and if they did . . . well, then at least I'd know who or what I was dealing with.

Probably not the wisest course of action, but it was the one I was taking nonetheless.

I shuffled through the plates, quickly trying to make sense of what I'd found. At first blush, one might have thought I'd stumbled upon a stash of Victorian pornography, but upon closer inspection the images weren't particularly lurid—though the subject matter was decidedly carnal—there was an almost clinical or scientific feel to the images.

While the faces of the figures on these images remained obscured, the photographs left little else to the imagination. I was no novice to cabinet cards—goodness knew I'd acquired them for Mr. Owen's more adventurous customers—but these were more than simple pornography. I moved to the window, examining them in the waning light of day. A sexual ritual, perhaps? The indifference with which I studied them shocked even me. But I'd seen my fair share of this sort of ephemera since taking on my position working with Mr. Owen.

I was about halfway through the set when one particular

image gave me pause. Something wasn't quite right about it and I couldn't put my finger on it. The images were voyeuristic, and gauging from the fact that several were missing from the sequence—these were what the killer was after. They had to be. I counted them—a dozen in total—before stuffing them into my pocket for safekeeping.

A rustle of fabric froze me in my tracks, my left hand rested protectively over the pocket where the negatives were nestled against my belly. My right reached for the revolver that I realized was sitting in the drawer of my dresser on the floor below.

A creak came from outside the door.

Then nothing.

One.

Two.

I began to count my breaths, slow and steady.

Silence.

I waited several more heartbeats before I moved at last. Finally, satisfied that whoever—or whatever—had been outside the door had gone, I crept out of the room, shutting the door behind me, and hurried to my own chamber. The lamp was still burning in my room when I returned, as it had been when I left. However, the door connecting mine to Mr. Owen's room was open. He must be feeling better, that or trying to keep an eye on me. One could never tell with him.

Regardless, he was precisely the person I needed to talk to as the old man was in possession of the most extraordinary collection of early wet plate photographs and photographic equipment that I'd ever seen. Perhaps he'd have an idea as to the age of the images. Not that I'd ever seen him handle a camera in his life. It was yet another collection he kept under lock and key in the private library, housed with his most precious books and artifacts.

"You're back." Mr. Owen looked over the top of his gold-rimmed reading glasses and set down his most recent serial novel.

His color had vastly improved from this morning. Perhaps whatever tincture Ruan brought him had helped. I spied a large chunk of what appeared to be a lovely Wensleydale sitting on the table before him. I reached over, taking his silver knife and cut a piece of the wheel, plopping it onto my tongue. Yes. Most certainly Wensleydale.

"Where'd you find that?" I mumbled, licking a softened crumb from my thumb.

"A man must have his secrets."

"Yes, well. I'd appreciate it if everyone had a few less secrets at present." I pinched another bite of the grassy cheese between my thumb and forefinger.

"I bought it off a man on the train, if you must know."

I rolled my eyes, failing to disguise my amusement at the scene. "Leave it to you to clandestinely procure cheese."

He smiled again, but it died away. "You're growing thin. Mrs. Penrose will have my skin."

"Serves you right for bringing me here under false pretenses." I took another bite, letting its deliciously smooth texture melt on my tongue. "Mmm. On second thought, just feed me cheese and I'll forgive any and all sins."

A strange expression crossed Mr. Owen's face. "All of them, my love?"

"Certainly most of them. Have you any grave ones you haven't told me yet?"

"Stop torturing the cheese," he grumbled, casting a glance at an uneaten piece still between my fingers. I stuck it in my mouth dramatically. Mr. Owen continued on, eyeing me much as Mrs. Penrose had been of late. Both of them complained that I needed to eat more, but my nerves always went to my stomach. "Ruan came by looking for you earlier. Tell me you're not detecting again."

"That's not a word—"

"I mean it, Ruby. I could not bear it if something happened to you because of me. This place . . . I should not have come here. Should not have brought you here—Manhurst has been nothing but trouble." He pulled his glasses from his face and rubbed his eyes.

"That's quite the understatement." I spied an apple sitting in the bowl before him and snatched it up, taking a bite. It seemed I'd found my supper this evening. "Have you given any thought to who might have wanted Lucy dead?"

He shook his head. "No, my love. Though I fear it has to do with me coming back here. I've avoided this place far too long. The ghosts are angry. They demand their price."

I frowned, leaning forward, my apple momentarily forgotten. "Mariah, you mean? The spirit from the séance?"

He stared at his hands, flexing his fingers before sighing. "I do. Lucy was her twin sister. I would have thought she'd forgiven me after all these years but perhaps not."

I leaned forward, elbows on my knees. "Forgiven you . . . for what . . . exactly? As it stands right now the inspector thinks I killed Lucy. I really need you to tell me everything you know about this place. Anything that could help me."

His breath hitched but he did not speak at first.

"Captain Lennox told me I should ask you about Mariah. I'm asking now, Mr. Owen. Tell me about Mariah."

"Andy gossips like a fishwife." Mr. Owen took a swig of his Scotch and sighed. "But aye, I knew her. I do not know what you want me to say about her that would do any good after all these years. I once knew a woman, radiant as the sun. I loved her and now she is gone. It is the way of things I suppose."

I blinked at him, taken aback by the sudden honesty. "She was your lover?"

"She was my *wife*." He flexed his fingers, studying them in the waning light of day. "I wonder if there was truth in what she said. If I had killed her somehow. Pushed her away until she—"

"Your . . . *wife* . . ." I repeated slowly, the revelation rattling around in my brain. "Might you have told me a *bit* earlier?"

"What difference would it have made?" He grumbled, lifting his eyes to mine. "You don't tell me everything either. Like how you know this Mr. Sharpe fellow. Were you going to tell me that, hmm, lass?"

I sucked in a breath. "How did you know . . ."

"Ruan also gossips like a fishwife."

I snorted back a laugh. I had never known Ruan to gossip, but I supposed there was no harm in Mr. Owen knowing about my past—in fact there was a bit of relief in it. One fewer secret between the two of us. "What exactly did Ruan tell you about him?"

He shook his head. "Not much. Only that he did not trust him. That you were afraid of him and to watch him."

I arched a brow. "And nothing else?"

He shook his head. "No. Is there more to it?"

I wet my lips and shook my head. It was on the tip of my tongue to tell him about New York, and my suspicions about Mr. Sharpe's true identity, but I could not bring myself to add to his worries—at least not when I didn't know for certain myself. "No. Nothing. How did she die?" I asked, bringing us back to safer waters—for me at least.

He shook his head. "I don't know. She disappeared one night. Some say she drowned in the lake. Others that she ran away from me. But I loved her, Ruby. Gods, did I love that woman."

"How long has it been?"

He wet his lips. "Over forty years. I still recall the first time I saw her. Truly saw her. She lived here at Manhurst and my family . . . we had some holdings nearby."

I eyed the mostly empty bottle of Scotch on his table, the reason for his uncharacteristic honesty. I longed to ask more, but it was wise to hold my tongue when Mr. Owen was speaking candidly.

"Our families had always assumed that she would marry Malachi, as they were closer in age. Besides, I had no time for a country lass. Worldly git that I was. My head so far up my own arse . . ."

I laughed at the image and leaned across the table, setting down the half-eaten apple, and I patted his arm through the garish orange dressing gown sleeve. "I take it not much has changed?"

He gave me a soft wistful smile. "Oh, Ruby, you should have seen her that night. You'd have loved her too. I'd not so much as looked at the lass in probably five or six years. I'd been away in London leaving Malachi to handle things here. I only came back as he asked me to attend their engagement party, and as I was paying a fortune for the damned thing I thought I better show my face. He's my only brother and I loved him then."

"Do you love him now?"

"He's kin, Ruby." He covered my hand with his own and gave it a light squeeze. "Let me finish this sorry tale before I lose the courage to tell you. It's important you know. I fear . . . I fear there is a connection between the two deaths but I cannot see it. I cannot fathom how or what I could have done to have caused this."

I paused, not liking the tone in his voice. "What do you mean?"

He wet his lips. "I stole my brother's intended."

"You *what?*"

He wrinkled his nose, white mustache twitching. "It was an accident."

"Mr. Owen, one does not accidentally abscond with one's brother's fiancée. How exactly did you *accidentally* manage that?"

He leaned back in his chair, eyes taking on a wistful expression. "I was tired. My train had been delayed and then the bloody coach broke an axle and I was two hours late for the ball. I was supposed to have arrived here at Manhurst long before luncheon."

Mr. Owen took a sip from his cup, running a finger along the lip. "I dressed myself for the evening but could not bring myself to make an appearance in the ballroom. Instead I took myself off to the orangery with a book. I thought if I had a few minutes' peace I might work up the courage to face the gauntlet." He winced at the memory.

I leaned forward, intrigued by Mr. Owen's past. He'd never done more than crack open a window in the place, and this afternoon he'd opened the front door and let me come inside and I loved him all the more for it. "What happened then?"

He let out a soft laugh. "*She* happened. The foolish creature had the same thought at her very own engagement party. Book in hand, she'd found herself wandering the darkened glasshouse. She must have spied my lantern and came to see who else was hiding from the world."

"Please tell me nothing untoward happened—because I am quite enjoying this story right now."

He shook his head. "No. That was the most peculiar thing. I'd had more lovers by that time than I could count. You might not want to hear it, but I had a reputation as a bit of a rake as a young man. Until I found Mariah." I could hear the tears behind his words. "She should have run away, left me to my work and my books. If she had, and married my brother, she would still be alive. Instead the foolish woman sat down on the bench beside me. I was . . . *enchanted.* She had a book of botanical cyanotypes—I'd not given much thought to photography at the time, but the way she spoke, the passion in her voice. It was—"

"A surprise?"

"Oh, don't look at me like that, Ruby. I have always known women to be as clever as any man, but something about Mariah knocked me arse over teakettle and I haven't come up for air in nearly fifty years."

"And she chose you . . ."

He shrugged as if none of it mattered. "She threw him over that very night unbeknownst to me. If I'd known her intentions when we parted in the orangery then I might have talked her out of it. It was the worst of scandals, for after she called off the engagement it came out that we had been seen together. Oh I know I was a poor bargain for a husband, but when she told me she loved me—that she chose to be with me—I was helpless to say no."

"I am sorry."

His eyes met mine and he mustered a weak smile. "You remind me of her. Your spirit. Your clever mind. Mariah always wanted a child, but we never—we couldn't—" He cupped my hand in his own. "You are the daughter I'd always hoped we'd have, Mariah and I."

My eyes grew wet and I slipped my hand away, wiping away the irritating tears. "You should have told me about her."

"Aye, my love, I should have. But after a while sometimes the lie becomes easier than the truth. I've not been that man in a very long time. Sometimes I think he disappeared alongside her that night."

Something in his words gave me pause. *My family had holdings near here.* Dread climbed up my throat. "Mr. Owen . . . *what* man do you mean?"

"You will not like me very much when I tell you this."

My chest tightened.

He couldn't look at me as he drew in a shallow breath.

"What . . . man . . . Mr. Owen?"

"The Viscount of Hawick."

The words were sharp and I couldn't decide what was worse— that he'd lied to me, that he thought I'd be upset by his revelation, or worse—that I *was* upset by his revelation. "You're . . . Lord Hawick."

Suddenly the inspector's insinuations made a great deal more sense. That *Hawick fellow* they assumed was my lover was actually Mr. Owen. The man I had lived with for the last few years.

I fell hard into the armchair, my back against the fabric as I stared at the ceiling.

"Say something, Ruby. Please. I am sorry for keeping it from you. It's just—"

It's just you've lied to me for over three years. Tears pricked at my eyes as I swallowed down the betrayal. "It's all right." It wasn't. But I supposed it would be in time. Because for all his faults and probably against my better judgment I loved the meddling old man. Whoever he was.

"Oh, Mr. Owen. Do you have any other secrets?"

He let out a strangled sound and shook his head. "No, my love. No. I don't think I do. Will you forgive me?"

My silence wounded him. I could see it in his eyes as he watched me, hoping that I would say yes. That I'd laugh and think it a lark as I often did. But this was a great deal more important than what he'd had for supper or why he was sending me to Gloucester on an errand. Mr. Owen had *lied* about who he was. About *what* he was. That was a difficult thing to get past.

I stood, my hand bumping into the forgotten glass plate negatives in my pocket. It wasn't the time to ask him. It might never be the time to ask. I walked over, and pressed a kiss to his forehead. "We'll speak in the morning." And then I went to my room, closing the door behind me.

It wasn't the answer he was wanting, but it was the only answer I was capable of giving.

CHAPTER THIRTEEN

The Questionable Efficacy of Locks

ONCE inside my own room, I locked the door between us. A symbolic gesture at best as he had the key to open it from his own side. I simply needed time and space to adjust to what I'd learned today—neither of which I had. It would be all right. *It had to be.*

I allowed myself precisely thirty minutes of self-pity before I went downstairs to the kitchen to procure a plate for supper, and settled myself back at the dressing table with my notepad and a half bottle of wine. Hours passed while I sketched out what rudimentary information I had. Mariah and Lucy were sisters.

Both died.

Presumably at Manhurst, though that was less certain.

Mr. Owen was a *viscount.*

I underlined that bit before drinking down the dregs of my wine, licking a droplet from my lower lip. *Now that* was going to take a while to adjust to. My head ached and I finally looked up at the clock. It was half past midnight and I was out of ideas and desperate for someone to talk to—someone I could reasonably guarantee was not lying to me.

I started for the door, picks in hand, when I heard a sound outside. The rustling of feet on carpet then the sound of a latch catching. Odd. I cracked my own door, cautiously looking out into the darkened hallway in time to see Malachi Lennox walk away from Mr. Owen's room and disappear down the stairs. What on earth could they have to say to one another? After what Mr. Owen revealed to me hours before—odds were if they were in the same room they were likely to come to blows and I hadn't heard any commotion through the door.

Alas, another question to add to my notebook when I returned later this evening. *Why is Malachi Lennox skulking about?*

Shaking the thought away, I hurried down to Ruan's room, knocking softly on the door. Pressing my ear against the wood panel listening for signs of life on the other side. *Mr. Owen is a viscount!* The knowledge irked me to no end. I waited impatiently for Ruan to answer.

Nothing.

I tapped again, hoping everyone stayed in their own rooms.

Still no response.

Why wasn't he opening the door? It wasn't *that* late. Besides, he seldom slept as the man was used to doctoring cows and cats and half of Cornwall.

I let out an annoyed huff of air and reached into my roll of lockpicks, pulling out the middle-sized one and inserted it into the keyhole, gently fiddling with it until I heard the click, and let myself in.

It took a moment for my eyes to adjust to the dimness of the room. A low fire was rolling in the hearth, casting the room in a cozy glow. Ruan was *in fact* asleep. His breath slow and even in the darkness and I was suddenly struck by the intimacy of what I'd done, but I couldn't be bothered with that. I needed him.

Needed. I wasn't going to think too much on the meaning of that word.

"Ruan. Ruan, we need to talk." As I edged closer to where he was lying I realized that this might not have been the best idea.

He was lying on his back, his chest bare and his left arm thrown over his eyes. His right arm draped lazily across his stomach, partially obscuring the trail of dark hair that disappeared below the sheet. I swallowed hard, casting my eyes dutifully to the ceiling before trying again.

"I need you to wake up."

He shifted, groaning softly as he rolled over, the thin sheet slipping lower on his hips. I squeezed my eyes shut. *Get yourself together, Ruby. He isn't the first naked man you've seen.* But he hadn't agreed to be naked in front of me. Oh, why hadn't I knocked louder? I'd been so caught up with Mr. Owen's betrayal that I all but burst in on a man in his privacy. Good God. What else might I have interrupted? I squeezed my eyes tighter to preserve his remaining modesty.

"Why do I question the efficacy of locks whenever you are around . . ." There was an edge of humor in his voice.

"We need to talk." The bedclothes rustled. Good. He must be sitting up.

"And you couldn't knock?"

Eyes squeezed tight, I sighed. That was a very good question. I hadn't really expected him to be asleep. "I did. You didn't answer and this is important."

"I'm wearing trousers. You can open your eyes anytime you'd like."

The heat rose to my cheeks as I sank down in the chair beside the bed, hazarding a glance over to him. He did, indeed, wear trousers. He ran his hands roughly over his hair, doing little to calm the angry curls. My mouth grew dry, all my frustrations with Mr. Owen fading away into another entirely unrelated emotion.

Desire.

Lovely. Just what I *didn't* have time for.

"Ruby."

"Right." I swallowed down my very wayward thoughts.

The edge of his mouth curved up and my stomach unknotted. He was back. The man I'd known in Cornwall. "Are you going to tell me what can't wait until morning or must I start guessing?"

I'd nearly forgotten how much I truly *liked* Ruan. "He's a *viscount*. A viscount!"

He yawned, rubbing the sleep from his face. "Who is? Besides, we have a duke, a countess. Why not have a viscount?"

I swatted at his bare arm. "Ruan, I'm serious. Did you know about him? That Mr. Owen is the Viscount of Hawick?"

Ruan either was an incredible card player or he'd had his suspicions. Suddenly I felt ill.

"No." He reached up, touching my brow softly, a cool rush flooding my veins from the contact. "No. I didn't know. I just am not surprised."

Whether his words, or whatever it was he *did* when he touched me, it eased my mind considerably.

"I always knew he was hiding something. I just didn't know what, and frankly didn't care to ask."

I wasn't certain if that was better or worse. I drew in a deep breath and proceeded to tell him what I'd learned after leaving him by the bridge. He listened intently in the firelight as I left no detail unspoken. As I finished I looked up, waiting for him to say something. Really anything. Perhaps chime in with an *oh, I know who did it!* That would have been fabulous at this moment. We could tell the inspector and all go home.

"Owen doesn't have any living children, does he?" Ruan asked.

"No. All his sons died in the war. Ben was his youngest."

Ruan swore.

"What?"

The muscles in his jaw worked as he weighed his words.

"This isn't good, is it?"

He shook his head. "You said that Andrew Lennox was the first to check the body after you pulled her from the lake?"

I nodded.

"And he took the revolver from the scene, returning it to you?"

I nodded again, not quite liking where Ruan was headed. Coldness sank beneath my skin as I watched him in the firelight. "You cannot possibly think that Andrew Lennox killed her. Why would he?"

"I don't know, but if Owen is a viscount, then his nephew would be his heir. *Andrew* would be his heir."

"But what would he stand to gain by killing *her*? Why not just kill Mr. Owen?" The question gave me pause.

"I don't know. I've never liked him, and never trusted him. He was a beastly boy at Oxford, I cannot imagine time has made him any better."

"At Oxford? What were you doing at Oxford?"

Ruan let out a startled laugh. "What everyone else does at Oxford. Read books, sit examinations. Make questionable life decisions. Are you surprised by that fact?"

"I suppose not." I had never asked about Ruan's past. I didn't like the place—at least my own—and as a result I tried not to muck around in other people's either.

"I don't speak much of it. It wasn't a happy time in my life. A wealthy benefactor sent me up. It's not unusual for clever boys to have a patron pay their way through school. I've never been ashamed of the fact I was a charity case—it was a better option than staying in the mines—that's for certain. But it's where I met Andrew. I never finished. I ah . . . left . . . midway through my last year there."

"I'm sorry."

His features were cast in shadow. "I'm not. I never fit in with any of the lads. I saw their world, realized it wasn't for me, and when an opportunity arose, I went back home where I belonged."

There was a sadness there, and I hated it. Hated everyone in the world who put that in his eyes. I reached out, taking his hand in mine, palm to palm. "I'm glad you're not like them."

He let out a sound of amusement and laced his fingers in mine. "You came here tonight to tell me that Owen's a viscount and to remind me that Andy is a great arse?"

I let out a startled laugh and shook my head. "Yes . . . well . . . no, not entirely." I pulled my hand from his, regretting the loss of contact at once, and withdrew the glass plate negatives from my pocket, careful of the broken edges. "I found these." I handed them over to him. "Do you remember how I told you that I'd gone into Lucy's bedroom looking for her the night of the murder? I went back today and the entire room had been ransacked."

"You *what?* After all that's happened, you are still nosing around?" He sat up straighter and I noticed a silver chain hung around his neck, with a golden ring at the end. In the darkness I couldn't quite make it out. Had he a sweetheart? Jealousy coiled in my stomach. Jealousy? That's preposterous. I didn't get *jealous.* I swallowed the sensation down, clearing my throat.

"Of course, I am. The authorities are convinced I'm involved, and someone has been trying to make it look that way. Besides, I didn't come here to be chided by you. I came for your help." I pointed at the negatives in his lap for emphasis. "So, yes. I am poking around."

"And you think that sneaking around the estate stealing things will make you look *less* guilty."

I rolled my eyes.

"You must be careful. This isn't Cornwall. I can't get you out of trouble here if you wind up on the wrong side of the law." Ruan grumbled as he tilted the glass plates into the firelight, studying them intently. His expression grew comically horrified. "What are these?"

It seemed my country Pellar wasn't quite as experienced with cabinet cards as I. "I'm not sure. I found them in Lucy's room. I think it's what her killer was looking for. What do you make of them?"

Ruan's ears grew that endearing shade of pink again. "That your dead medium has very interesting hobbies."

"Have you ever seen such a thing?"

He raised an eyebrow. "Are you really asking that question? To me this looks like some sort of club or group. See how they're all wearing the same chain around their neck?"

I moved nearer to him, resting my hip on the arm of his chair, and looked down into the image in his hands. "I wish we had someone we could trust who could print the photographs. It would be a great deal easier to see what we're working with."

Ruan made a sound of agreement in his throat as he gingerly moved through the images, one by one, and indeed each of the men wore a chain around their neck which bore an odd resemblance to a livery collar.

"That seems uncomfortable."

Ruan laughed. "You are the most astonishing creature I've ever met. I ponder about the existence of sex clubs and you are concerned over what they're wearing."

I stood quickly and began to pace the darkened corners of his room. He'd been here less than a day and the place even smelled of Cornwall. Of those herbs he'd have drying from the beam in his sitting room. "What if *this* is what Lucy wanted to tell me that night and that the answer to who killed her is in those photographs somehow? Lucy was afraid of something, desperate enough to meet me at midnight on a bridge. What I don't know is what the images are supposed to tell me. Do they identify someone, or some place?"

Ruan leaned back, watching me as I tried to burn off the nervous energy taking over my body. "How does the séance fit in with your theory?"

I ran my hands roughly over my face, looking at him through my fingers. "It doesn't. I'm still not certain if it was real. But

Mr. Owen seems to think it was real enough. It *felt* real, Ruan. And you know I don't ordinarily believe in ghosts but it certainly *felt* like a ghost."

Ruan rose and walked to the wardrobe. From the shadows, I couldn't help but admire the way the muscles in his back flexed with his movement. He certainly knew how to distract me from the point at hand.

What are you doing, you peculiar man?

"Finding a shirt." He grumbled as he latched on to something in the closet. "As I presume you will not let me go back to sleep until we've looked at the medium's room again."

"No. I probably won't." My eyes lingered on the width of his back, and the deep scar that went like an arrow alongside his spine disappearing into the waistband of his trousers. *What had happened to cause such a wound?* It had to be nearly twelve inches in total, if not more.

Ruan coughed, tugging on the fresh shirt. "About that, twelve and a half I'm told. But it was nothing romantic, I assure you. A German soldier took issue with my men's and my presence in his tunnel." At times his ability to hear my thoughts was unsettling, but at others, like now, it was as if we spoke a language that only the two of us could understand.

"That wasn't very charitable of him. I'm sure you were a perfectly well-mannered tunnel-guest."

He laughed again, those creases from worry between his brows disappearing as he fastened the buttons one by one. My stomach churned at the thought of the scar—of the wound that had been dealt him. I'd seen soldiers with injuries like that that during my time in the war, back when I was driving an ambulance between the casualty clearing stations back to the main hospital in Amiens. I'd never seen a man survive a wound like that—certainly not along the rough road to Amiens.

"Evidently I'm a difficult man to kill. Now, what are you intent upon showing me?" Gauging from the tone of his voice, there'd be no more discussion about his past. Not today. Besides, we had more important things to do. Like break into a dead medium's room.

IT HAD BEEN only a handful of hours since I'd left Lucy Campbell's room looking as if it'd been raided by invading Visigoths—and yet somehow between then and now it had been fully cleaned, making me doubt my own memories. All the broken jars and pottery removed. Clothes tidily folded and returned to the wardrobe precisely as it should be. Even the carpetbag had been repacked, sitting in the middle of the dresser as if awaiting its mistress to finish the task and go on her way.

"You said it was ransacked." Ruan folded his arms from where he stood in the doorway.

"It was." I wet my lips, turning to face him as I gestured to the peculiar six-petaled flower carved in the wood. "What's that?"

He stepped farther into the room, pushing the door closed to inspect the carving.

"That's the image I saw on the bridge. She—someone—drew it in charcoal on the columns . . ." My mind flickered back to Andrew Lennox's gray fingers from his sketching. Ruan had accused him of killing Ben and I'd disregarded it—but perhaps there was more to Mr. Owen's nephew than met the eye.

Ruan let out a low chuckle.

"I don't see what's amusing."

"It's a hexafoil."

"Yes, well. What is a hexafoil? I assumed it's something related to the occult but I don't believe I've seen one before."

Ruan stared at me in disbelief. "Working for Owen all these years you haven't come across a *hexafoil*? It beggars belief . . . Half the barns and cottages in Britain have these somewhere. It's used to protect a person from evil spirits, witches, demons, and the like."

"But *you're* a witch."

"Pellar, remember? Besides, they aren't trying to protect against *my* kind. They're concerned about harmful magic. I'm not sure I could do harmful magic if I tried. Besides, I always found them nothing more than a bit of folklore and superstition. No carving—no matter how pretty—will save you if the devil's after you. You'd need something far more powerful than that." He ran this thumb over the carved line and my reckless heart responded as if it were me he touched.

I opened my mouth to point out that to most people, Ruan himself would be considered little more than folklore and superstition but wisely held my tongue on that score. "The salt too . . . do you think she was worried about the spirits she summoned?"

"It does look that way." Ruan bit his lower lip, green eyes full of pity for this soul he'd never met.

"But ghosts can't harm anyone . . ." After all that I'd witnessed in the last six weeks, I couldn't quite discount the theory as easily as I once would have. "Can they?"

Ruan exhaled, tapping his fingers on the wood.

"And you are having trouble with your abilities. You said you can't hear me as well here . . ." I gestured at him, the words melting away. "Is this killer human or is it something else?"

He closed his eyes, taking in a deep breath. The air between us growing sharp, taking on the vague scent of an electrical storm. He stayed that way for several seconds before he gave his head a grave shake. "The spirits are angry here. They're as loud as I've ever heard them, even during the war. I think *that's* why I'm having trouble hearing you. I reach out and it feels as if I'm on the edge of something, all the voices, they're clamoring for my attention, pulling at bits and parts of me—they want something—but cannot speak its name. Ruby, it's enough to drive one mad. I've never experienced anything like it. Everything here seems *more . . .*" He hesitated, taking a step closer to me, his eyes wide. "Even you."

I swallowed hard. *Even me.* What was that supposed to mean?

He ran a rough hand over his jaw. "I'm not sure what is happening, but the spirits . . . they don't trust it. Something has come to Manhurst, Ruby. That much is clear to me. I do not know what, but it's as certain as the change of seasons."

I shivered, fingers tightening on his arm. "Do they speak to you? The spirits . . ."

"Not in that way. The living, the dead. They all sound the same. A sense of foreboding. A murmur. A hush. But I can promise you that they didn't harm the old woman."

"Did they tell you that . . . just now?"

He laughed softly, tucking a stray bit of hair from my brow. "Haven't you ever sensed the dead before?"

I shook my head. The only thing I was feeling right now was him. Not precisely the same thing. I stepped away from his touch and turned back to face the wardrobe. "I'm not sure I believe in ghosts."

He started for the door. "Unfortunately, they believe in you. Now, if you don't mind, I'm going back to bed."

And with that unsettling statement, he turned and left, leaving me to an old woman's things and the horrible realization that once again I was in far over my head.

CHAPTER FOURTEEN

A Mother's Fear Returns

I was in France.

Knee-deep in water and blood, stumbling through the flooded-out trench. Fetid liquid sloshed up over my boots and wet the knees of my woolen jodhpurs.

My frozen fingers dug into the earthen wall of the trench, desperately trying to keep balance.

Each step harder than the last.

They'd told me he was just ahead. I could make out his shape at the opening. The familiar slope of his shoulders as he ran from something unseen.

Death and piss.

Metal and gunpowder.

All the familiar scents blending with the sickeningly sweet remnants of gas on the air. My teeth chattered hard enough that I could scarcely breathe. Rats, fat from feasting on both the living and the dead, followed along behind me, looking for their next meal.

I'd left my ambulance back by the regimental aid post with a handful of wounded already loaded in the back. The regimental medical officer said the soldier was just ahead. He was waiting for me and would come for no one else. Stubborn bastard, but I'd expected no less of him.

I knew him.

Had always known him.

Kitted-up soldiers pushed against me like high tide. Flooding up and over the top, met by flashes and the rumble of gunfire.

A match strike.

A hiss.

Sticky hot blood rained down my face, filling my mouth with its metallic tang.

Where was he?

A high-pitched whistle of a shell sailed overhead, followed by a blast that took the ground out from beneath me, sending bodies flying. Yet I was pulled ahead on an invisible tether.

He needed me.

I had to keep going.

Crawling over a sea of bodies, the duckboards gave way at last, opening up into an angry crimson lake.

He was there. Just ahead.

The dark water was up to my waist now.

Cold. So cold. My body grew weak but I could almost touch him.

Ruan.

A knit hat was pulled low over his ears. He had his back to me yet I knew it was him. I'd know him in any age, any time.

He was mine.

A bright poppy-colored scarf was wrapped around his neck, stuffed into his mud-streaked uniform jacket. He turned to me as the sniper fire rang out from behind me. The scarf turned into a river of blood, seeping down his uniform front.

A second shot rang out, and he stumbled backward, arms pinwheeling as the poppies bloomed across his chest.

"Ruby!"

I struggled against the hands that held me back. I could save him. I knew I could, if only the bastard would let me go. Let me go to him.

This was Ruan. I'd only just found him again, and I couldn't lose him. He couldn't die—I wouldn't let him.

And yet someone was pulling me away from his lifeless body.

Violent shivers racked me as I screamed. The sound piercing through the night.

"Ruby, wake up! Stop fighting me."

Somewhere in my deepest consciousness I heard it. Heard him calling me home.

The warm low west country cadence pulling me back across the channel. Away from the trenches and gas and blood. Through the fog of my dreams, back to Britain. Back to him.

Dazed, I stared up into the night sky—the stars above no more than mere pinpricks and streaks of distant color, universes away. Ruan crouched, his arms bracketing me against the earth. He leaned down, cupping my face in his hands.

"Ruby, can you hear me? Gods . . ." He grabbed me hard, crushing me and my soaking-wet nightgown against his warmth.

"Of course, I can hear you. What's wrong with you?" I rubbed my face, glancing around, pulling his hands from my cheeks.

Where the hell was I?

"I heard you calling me . . . I thought . . . Thought you found something. I went to your room . . ." I burrowed myself deeper into his embrace, greedily drinking in his heat. "Then I find you here, up to your waist in the water."

Suddenly I knew without question where I was. I hadn't walked in my sleep since I was a small child. I'd thought those days behind me. But if the stinging of my bare feet was any indication, they were back.

He ran his thumb across my cheek, voice thick with panic. "I thought I was going to lose you . . . I've only just found you and—" Something in his words echoed in my memory but I couldn't quite recall why.

I reached up, holding his hand against my cheek and pressed my eyes shut, willing him to be able to hear me now, though I doubted he could—his own fear drowning out every other sentiment—and I didn't have the heart to speak the words aloud.

I thought the return of my prescient nightmares had been the worst of my affliction, but this was beyond all that. Flashes of my girlhood came violently back. The fear in my mother's eyes as she held me in her arms, rocking me at the edge of the pond. Words I'd long forgotten gained a foothold in my brain. *"Not you too, my little Ruby. I won't let them take you from me."* I was too young then to ask what she was afraid of—to even realize that the words might have some meaning beyond a frightened mother soothing her firstborn.

"You walk . . . in your dreams." Ruan must have heard the memory.

My teeth chattered against his warm chest. "I haven't in years . . . I thought it h-h-had stopped."

"You ran into the bloody lake. I called your name but you didn't hear me. You wouldn't stop . . . Ruby . . . Gods . . . I called for you and you wouldn't stop." He held me tight enough my ribs might have cracked from the sheer force of him. Our hearts beating, for once, in almost perfect rhythm. Slow and steady.

"Let's get you inside . . ."

A branch broke nearby and we both froze as whatever it was crunched across the frost-covered grass.

An animal?

Ruan shook his head.

Boots, then?

A nod.

How many?

He tapped my thigh twice and I squinted into the darkness,

barely able to see the two shapes making their way to the bridge above where we sat nestled in the reeds. The pair moved quickly, keeping to the shadows as best they could.

We were safe, hidden amongst the overgrowth. Perhaps not an ideal spot during the day, but in the darkness, we might go unnoticed at least for a time.

Ruan tapped me again on my thigh, a gesture I believed meant we should sneak back to the castle. He stood quietly, pulling me to my feet, and the two of us crept out of the reeds and away from the two figures.

Hand in hand we walked through the halls until we reached my room. It was a weakness to depend on him, but there was something steady and reassuring about Ruan that called to me—reminding me of those Cornish rocks he loved so well.

He pressed the door open and ushered me inside before throwing another log onto the fire and turning on the faucet of the great claw-foot tub beneath the window. The pipes groaned and hissed as the basin filled with hot water.

Ruan hesitated before turning around to face me, jaw tight.

"We'll warm you up. Then, Ruby . . . I'm afraid we need to talk."

CHAPTER FIFTEEN

A Coerced Admission

WE *need to talk.*

Were there any four words in the English language that inspired more dread in a person's heart? Probably not. I allowed myself twenty extra minutes to soak in the tub in avoidance of said conversation, but I knew I couldn't put it off forever. Besides, the water had grown tepid. Fully thawed, dry and dressed in a fresh nightgown, I wrapped a plaid blanket around myself and entered Mr. Owen's room. Ruan had recently poured a kettle into the teapot sitting on the table, filling the room with an unusual herbal scent. Must be another of Ruan's teas. I suppose there are *some* benefits to having a witch around.

"You said she walks in her sleep?" Mr. Owen asked Ruan, eyeing me carefully across the table, as if I might turn into a newt if he looked away. "And she's no recollection at all . . ."

Ruan shook his head, his back to me, as he tended the fire. I had the distinct impression he was making himself busy to not think about what almost happened tonight.

"How very extraordinary . . ." Mr. Owen murmured.

"The sleepwalking isn't what bothers me. I've done it since I was a child." Ruan poured me a cup of tea and placed it in my hands. "I'm more concerned about who else was out there by the lake? I know why I was there—" Well, actually I didn't, but that was yet *another* problem for another day.

Ruan snorted and I shot him an irritated look. It seemed he heard me well enough tonight.

"Ruby . . ." Mr. Owen said, snapping my attention away from Ruan.

I cleared my throat and took a sip of the tea, scalding my tongue in the process. "Let's not quibble about me for a moment, I am simply saying that I am more concerned that there were two other people at the lake tonight searching for something."

"Others?" Mr. Owen's brows rose as he turned to Ruan with a frown. "Why didn't you tell me that, lad?"

"I was less interested in them than I was that she"—he pointed at me with his own teacup, sloshing the tea over the rim onto the saucer below—"nearly drowned herself."

"I'm perfectly fine." I turned back to Mr. Owen. "There were two men on the bridge tonight. I think they were looking for something. Do you have any idea what?"

"Do you think it was the inspector?" Mr. Owen's skin grew pale. "Ruby, you must stay away from him, you must give him no reason to suspect you further!"

"A fine thing for you to say, since your prevarications are the reason he suspects me in the first place." I turned to Ruan, half expecting him to agree with me, but instead he was studying the depths of his teacup in a determined attempt to avoid looking at me. I drew in a sharp breath. "You're keeping something else from me, aren't you? Something you haven't told me yet."

Ruan muttered to himself in Cornish before finally looking up at Mr. Owen, his eyes flashing with the faintest hint of silver. I'd never seen him so angry. Not even when we were in Cornwall. "I won't have secrets between us. I gave you my word to hold my tongue years ago, but things are different now. She deserves to know the truth of it all. And as you know *I* cannot break *my* word, you had better do it yourself."

"I was going to tell her. You don't have to threaten me, Pellar." Mr. Owen grumbled, hand trembling as he poured me a glass of whisky, and slid it across his table. I could only recall one other time when Mr. Owen had offered me a drink unbidden, and that was when he'd finally managed to get me released from Holloway Prison where I'd been detained after transporting illegal books for him. And frankly we both needed it after that adventure, it was his way of making amends—which did not bode well for whatever was coming next.

"Ruby, there is one other small thing I have not told you . . ."

My nostrils flared as I tugged my blanket tighter around my shoulders. "You told me there were no more secrets."

He looked up at Ruan before turning to me, his dark brown eyes glassy. "Aye, lass. I know I did and I am sorry for it."

"And Ruan knows . . ." A second betrayal.

"Do not be angry with the lad. He doesn't know what it means . . . but he knows what I sent for. I didn't want you any more involved in this matter. What with the inspector already braying for your blood and Malachi all too willing to rub my nose in it. I wish we'd never come, but it's too late for that." Mr. Owen rubbed his eyes before gesturing to Ruan with his forefinger. "Go on and show her, lad."

Ruan grumbled something in Cornish again, casting a mutinous look to Mr. Owen as he unfastened the top two buttons of his shirt and withdrew the silver chain I'd seen earlier tonight and removed it, laying the strange ring on the table before us.

I ran my finger over the warm metal. Golden and thick, with enamel banding in red and black with little iridescent bits of abalone made to look like tears. It was a very unusual piece. Lovely, yes, but unusual. I picked it up in two fingers.

"Be careful!" Mr. Owen hissed, snatching the ring away.

Ruan laid his hand over Mr. Owen's, gently unfurling the old man's fingers. "She's safe—whatever you think it to be—I won't let it harm her." He plucked it from Mr. Owen's palm and set it in my own.

Mr. Owen winced, eyes wide, but did not argue.

Another benefit to having a Pellar. I held the ring up to the light, turning it this way and that.

"After all the death it's brought. How can you know it won't take her too?" Mr. Owen snapped at Ruan, his eyes wet with tears.

"It's only a ring—" I began softly.

Ruan took it from my palm and placed it in his own. "Would it make you feel better if I held it?"

"Aye, lad . . . that it would." Mr. Owen wiped at his tears and touched my cheek with the back of his hand. "I can't lose you, Ruby. I won't let them take you. I've lost too much. I won't lose you too."

My heart tugged at his words. "You're not going to lose me. I'm cross with you for keeping your secrets—but I'm not going anywhere."

Mr. Owen winced. "You cannot promise that. You may not intend to go, but that does not mean that someone cannot take you from me."

My eyes dropped back to the ring. His secrecy suddenly made a great deal more sense. The great misguided fool thought he was protecting me. "That's why you brought Ruan. You think this ring has something sinister about it . . ."

"Aye, my lamb. Anyone who has had it in their keeping has died. Everyone except him."

I furrowed my brow, not understanding. "And it can't hurt Ruan . . ."

"He's a Pellar. Curses and the devil are powerless over him."

I doubted this tiny chunk of metal was capable of killing

anyone, but Mr. Owen was unraveling before my eyes. I could not hold his secrets against him now. Not truly.

"It was his son Ben's," Ruan said softly at my ear. His breath lifting my damp hair. "He gave it to me the very night he died on that hospital ship. Made me swear I'd tell no one I had it and to take the thing home to his father. He was delirious with fever at the time."

"Is that how you met Mr. Owen?"

Mr. Owen let out a cynical laugh. "Gods no."

Ruan let out a noncommittal grunt. Whatever *that* was supposed to mean.

My mind raced trying to catch up with this newfound information. "And Andrew Lennox was there too . . . on the ship."

Ruan nodded again. No wonder he believed Andrew had a hand in his cousin's death. Why else would Ben have trusted a family heirloom to a stranger rather than one's own flesh and blood?

I ran my forefinger over the ring, which rested innocently in Ruan's open palm. His expression remained stone except for those extraordinary eyes of his that burnt with something I didn't recognize.

"There's a hinge here."

"Aye. It's a mourning piece. Show her how it works, Kivell. See what sense you can make of it that I cannot."

Ruan placed his thumbnail beneath the enamel lip and popped open the top design of the ring to reveal a braided piece of golden hair.

"Who had it before your son?"

Mr. Owen frowned. "Mariah. It was hers. Lucy asked me to bring the ring to her. Said it would bring her closer to Ben's spirit as he'd had it in his dying days. But now . . . Now I cannot help but wonder if it holds some other answer."

First Mariah, then Ben. No wonder Mr. Owen was beginning to question the ring.

"Was she wearing it when she died?"

Mr. Owen shook his head. "No. For here is the most peculiar part of losing my Mariah. She disappeared one night and I awoke with the ring on my finger and my wife gone."

"Gone . . . which means you cannot be certain she is dead." I breathed out. "What if she's alive?"

"And how could she be? Ruby, I might have been a terrible husband but Mariah would not have left me. Not like that."

I gnawed on my lower lip in thought. "Ruan, did Ben tell you anything else when he gave you the ring? Any indication why?"

He snapped the ring shut. "He did not say. Only that it had to be me. And I had to return it to his father." Ruan fastened the strange little piece of jewelry against his neck, tucking it back into his shirt. "We were on the same ship home. He wasn't doing well." Ruan gestured to his own thigh. "A shrapnel wound that wasn't healing properly. It had started to turn gangrenous. Some of my lads thought I could help him so I went to him against orders."

"You tried to help?" My chest warmed at the thought, that even miles from home Ruan could not fight his nature. His need to heal people.

"I might have done, had I not been thrown into the brig with my men by Lennox."

Mr. Owen suddenly slammed his fist on the table, rocking his chair back. "Out, the both of you. And take that damned ring. Throw it in the lake for all I care." The suddenness of his proclamation surprised the both of us. "I do not want to hear any more of this. Not tonight."

"Are you all right?" I leaned across the table, taking him by the hand.

He rubbed the back of mine with his thumb and shook his head. "I have not been all right in forty years. But sleep. Let me sleep, lass, and we'll speak again in the morning."

I nodded, taken aback by his quick change of mood, and left

the room, Ruan following along after. He pressed the heavy three-paneled wooden door shut and turned the key. "Has he been like this long?"

"I don't know what's come over him. He's always so . . . composed . . . cynical. And now he's like this. Drinking at all times, swinging from uncharacteristically sentimental to melancholy with these flashes of anger and I—I am afraid to press him. The more he tells me of his past, the more it seems he's coming apart at the seams."

Ruan reached out, running his thumb across my brow. "This place. I've begun to fear we're all unraveling here. Tonight at the lake. When was the last time you've done that?"

"Not since I was a girl. You don't think there's something about Manhurst itself making us this way?"

"I don't know what I think. But I don't like it here. And if I could, I would take both of you back to Cornwall on the next train."

And I would go in a heartbeat. I leaned back against the door, closing my eyes. Mr. Owen had become the one curmudgeonly constant in my life since the death of my family, and Tamsyn's betrayal of me during the war. When my family died, I thought Tamsyn and I would be able to make a life together. I loved her once, beyond all reason, and yet she too left me behind. When I found Mr. Owen I was a heartbroken, scarred, and angry young woman and he took me in regardless. And now . . . now after he'd revealed the extent of all his secrets, I scarcely knew who he was. He spoke of love and wanting to protect me, and yet for more than three years he'd hidden who he was from me.

"How long have you known him anyway?" I asked softly.

"I officially met him after the war when I brought the news of Ben's death to him. And the ring."

"But why did he leave it with you? If he believes the thing cursed or dangerous, why not destroy it?"

"Because I'm the Pellar, Ruby. If the item is cursed, as he believes, then it cannot touch me." Ruan leaned against the dresser with a groan, crossing his left leg over his right.

"I've never believed in curses . . ."

"I never once thought you did. I might have met Owen after the war, but he knew of me long before. He knew of what I am from shortly after I was born."

"*Knew* of you? You mean he'd been watching you?"

"More or less, yes. Not the most pleasant thought, mmm? I told you that I'd been sent to Oxford by a wealthy benefactor. I failed to mention that it was *him.* Owen took a keen interest in my well-being. My potential. He misguidedly believed that he could mold me. Take a country boy with peculiar abilities and shape him into—honestly, Ruby, I'm not sure what he thought he could do with me."

I reached out of habit for my cigarette case, which was buried deep in my traveling trunk. "That sounds familiar. Mr. Owen always has a plan of some sort."

"How did you meet him? I realize I hadn't even thought to ask."

I ran my fingers along the edge of the blanket around my shoulders. "Nothing exciting. I was angry after the war."

"You, angry? I am shocked."

I let out a little laugh and sighed, struggling to remember the girl I'd been once. The one who came back from France with a fortune to my name, and no one to share it with. My family dead, Tamsyn having abandoned me in France so she could marry Sir Edward. It was all quite the blow to my jaded little heart. "I answered an advertisement in the newspaper."

Ruan arched an eyebrow. "I can only imagine how it was worded to intrigue you."

It felt good to laugh. "If it had told me I'd be up to my knees in witches, curses, and murder, I might have reconsidered answering.

I actually thought it would be a quiet life. A place to heal from my past."

Ruan smiled at me, warming me to my core. "Come now, we witches aren't that bad, are we?"

"No. I suppose some of you are tolerable."

Lies. He was more than tolerable. He was downright dangerous—and while the White Witch had warned that I would destroy him, I had a growing fear that it went the other way. For as wild as I was, as headstrong and independent, my heart was brittle. I'd been broken by love, and the idea of actually coming to care for someone else again—to allow myself that small indulgence, was a risk I wasn't quite ready for. And after the spectacular way both of my previous romances ended, I worried I never would be.

My stomach knotted as memories of those final days in New York returned. "Ruan, did you hear anything back from Hari?"

"Your solicitor?" He shook his head. "Nothing yet, it's only been a few hours since I wrote him."

"You don't know Hari. Promise me you'll get me as soon as you hear from him. He has saved my neck more times than I dare count since my exile from America. I need him to reassure me that Mr. Sharpe cannot be Elijah."

"You make this island sound like you were transported to Botany Bay."

"For a spoiled little debutante who'd never lived outside of New York, being sent to Cornwall with Tamsyn might as well have been."

Ruan again touched my brow, running his thumb along my temple, sending a cool rush of sensation through me, and I realized how truly tired I was.

"Get some sleep, Ruby. It's late."

The first hints of dawn began to show its face outside the window. "Early. It's early."

"You are the most argumentative woman I've ever known."

I yawned again into my fist, lids growing heavy. "Do you think the ring and the glass plate negatives are connected in some way? Mr. Owen said Lucy requested he bring the ring. I should look at the negatives again. Perhaps I'll see it there? There'll be a link or someth—"

"Bed, Ruby." Ruan took me by the shoulders and walked me backward to the mattress. "You need sleep. You're no good to anyone worn to the bone." He looked down into my eyes and I leaned a hair's breadth closer to him. His fingers traced the scar at my brow and he sighed. "I cannot bring myself to leave you tonight . . . all I can think about is what would have happened if I hadn't heard you calling for me. I scarcely did as it was—I almost ignored your voice, thinking it was just—" He cut himself off before he revealed too much of his feelings, but he'd said plenty. I wasn't the only one affected by this connection between us. The thought should have reassured me, but it only unsettled me more.

"Do you recall any of your dreams? Why you were calling for me?"

I shook my head. "I never do. I never remember the walking dreams."

The deep divot returned to his brow. "What do you suppose you saw?"

I shook my head with a tired smile. "I'll be fine, Ruan. We'll figure things out in the morning, mmm?"

He gave me a worried nod and moved to the door, lingering there with his fingers on the latch.

"And Ruan?"

He turned to look at me, the dark circles visible beneath his eyes.

"Thank you for having him tell me."

"He would have in his own time. I just nudged him to be sure he did at *this* time. He'd made me vow I would not speak of the ring. I cannot . . . I cannot go against my word as other men do."

"You cannot break a promise?"

He shook his head. "Owen—he does not mean to hide things, I don't think—but when a man spends a lifetime running from his own shadow, it is difficult sometimes to bring light into such a dark place."

"Et tu, Brute?"

Fine lines formed at the creases of his eyes. "It's the truth. Owen isn't used to being honest with anyone—least of all himself. We must be patient with him."

"You are the kindest person I've ever met, Ruan Kivell." I pulled my legs up onto the mattress, settling against the headboard.

"Do not mistake my understanding human nature for kindness. They are vastly different things." He hesitated. "We must be cautious here and trust no one but each other in this—and the sooner we solve this mystery the sooner we can leave this wretched place and go home."

We.

Ruan's words had a strange finality to them—*we* could go home—and I found I liked that idea a great deal. Not separately, but together. A small part of me wanted that more than anything else—someone to trust, to rely upon. I'd been alone long enough that I had forgotten what that must be like.

"Good night, Ruan."

And without a word he left me to another restless night.

Chapter Sixteen

A Spot of Golf

"KEEP your voice down!"

I startled awake, rubbing my eyes, trapped in that liminal space between dream and reality.

"I'll do what I bloody well please, Owen. As you've always done," the second voice said.

Not a dream then. Blinking in the dim morning light, I looked around my room half expecting to find the arguing pair standing at the foot of my bed—but there was no one there. Which meant the voices were coming from the hall or Mr. Owen's room. My money was on the latter.

The voices grew quiet again as I padded my way to the door, placing my ear to the wood.

"I will not allow it. Do you hear me?" Mr. Owen said.

The other speaker was quieter, his voice unfamiliar. A male with a deep Scottish burr—which fortunately limited the number of people it could have been. "You shouldn't have come back here . . ." There was muffled silence as I strained to hear more. ". . . her blood will be on your head."

Whose blood?

There was a rattling of something from beyond the door as I pressed myself tighter against the panel, desperate to hear more.

"And you'll kill me too? Because you don't agree with my methods."

"I'll kill you because you deserve it, you great big bastard. Now get out and leave her alone! She's mine to care for." Mr. Owen growled.

"As you cared for Mariah? We all know what happened there, brother." There was slight scuffling from the other side, followed by the slamming of a door loud enough I winced.

I pushed open the door between our rooms. "Is everything all right?"

"Ruby . . ." My name came out almost a sigh as he looked me over from head to toe. "You should be asleep."

"I heard a crash." He was holding a dinner knife in his hand, knuckles white.

"It was nothing, go back to sleep, my lamb." His voice was tender, but his jaw remained tight.

I took a step backward and nodded, not at all sure what to make of what I'd witnessed.

"I heard voices . . ."

A flicker of guilt crossed his face. "Nothing for you to worry about. I have it in hand. You will be safe here. I promise you that."

My gaze dropped to the knife in his hand. "Are you *certain* you're all right?"

"Go back to bed," he repeated. There was a steel edge in his voice that I knew better than to question, so I returned to my room.

Despite what he said, something was terribly wrong.

As I wasn't going to be getting any more sleep this morning, I had better get started finding out what that *something* was. I dressed myself in a rather fetching hunter-green drop-waist dress and started for Ruan's room to tell him what I'd overheard this morning and to see if he could make any more sense of it than I.

Just as I approached his door, I spotted the White Witch standing in the threshold between his room and the hall. Her unnerving amber eyes fixed upon me. "He is gone, Morvoren."

"Gone?" A frisson of tension crawled up my spine as I peered into Ruan's empty room. "What do you mean *gone*?"

"As in he is not here. But I was looking for you." She lifted her hand, the brightly colored bracelets jingling with the movement. I did not pause to wonder why she would look for me in Ruan's room at this hour. "The other medium. She is not what she seems."

I let out a strangled sound at the thought of adding this medium to Mr. Owen and Mr. Sharpe—or Elijah—whichever one he might truly be. This place was a den of deception masquerading as a resort.

A strange look of sympathy crossed her icy features. "None of us are who we pretend to be. Some simply do not know what they are, others are afraid of their truth, others still are afraid of what that truth might mean. We should pity them, Morvoren."

Fabulous. The White Witch was now giving me mysteriously phrased life lessons. "Do you know who she is, this other medium? Is she connected to Mr. Sharpe, the hotelier, at all?" The image of the pair of them on the bridge returned to my mind. They certainly looked acquainted, yet there was fear in her face and Ruan had sensed the same.

"I am not certain. But I do not believe she is Russian. I will keep looking. We must find the answers you seek and you must leave soon. Quickly, before what I have seen comes to pass. That vision must not happen."

Right. Before I kill Ruan. I sighed in frustration. At least she wasn't repeating that dire warning anymore and was being moderately helpful. I should be grateful for small mercies. "Thank you. I mean it."

Her head cocked unnaturally toward the corridor behind me. "Someone comes, Morvoren. Hurry. Go before they find you."

I saw no one. "What is it you sense?" But when I turned back to face her, the White Witch had disappeared and the air before me smelled vaguely of lightning. Lovely. This was precisely what happened when dealing with witches.

UNABLE TO FIND Ruan in the castle, I went outside to clear my head, pulled by some sort of unearthly call. Was it the water? I'd always loved the seaside, spending as much time in the ocean as possible—even to the point of having built a bathing pool in Mr. Owen's rose garden back in Exeter. But this was more than that—much more.

The October wind was crisp and the sky bright and clear as I set off across the pasture. The early morning birdsong was period-ically punctuated by the distant crack of a shotgun and the shatter of clay targets. I pushed through the reeds, traipsing down into the thick mud near the water's edge. I was grateful for my boots, as the soles of my feet still ached from the thorns and brambles I'd walked over the night before.

This was where Ruan had found me. Not ten feet from where I'd pulled Lucy from the lake. It had to *mean* something, didn't it? Though more likely than not, this place was simply driving us all mad. Mr. Owen's changing moods, Ruan's inability to control his powers, my returning dreams—could Manhurst itself have some-thing to do with it? Perhaps Mariah hadn't run away at all—she'd simply been driven mad.

I swallowed the thought down, unwilling to even think that a place could have such power over man. The lake was still as a painting with golden light coming through the white clouds, reflecting on the mirrorlike surface. The slight indentation of where my body had been pressed into the mud by Ruan's remained. As did the tracks we made—his and mine—on our way back to the castle.

And that was when I saw the second pair of tracks.

Once again, we were not alone.

Her blood will be on your hands, Malachi had said to Mr. Owen this morning. Had it been me that they were discussing?

Had my mysterious follower watched me go into the water as they had Lucy, waiting on me to die? Or were these the prints of whoever was on the bridge last night, seeking something they thought Lucy had left behind?

I pinched the bridge of my nose, struggling to connect the dots. Someone wanted us at the estate, someone was trying to frame me for the murder of Lucy, and presumably the photographs have something to do with all of it. I could cry—if I were the crying sort. Simply flop down on the mud and weep for all the frustration growing in my chest.

Balling my fist, I started back to the house when I noticed a figure on the bridge. It was dreadfully early for anyone to be awake, but I made my way up the muddy embankment to see who it was. As I reached the bridge, I recognized the woman at once—the youngest medium. She sat on a stone bench looking out over the water, her thoughts a thousand miles away.

She is not who she pretends to be. That's what the White Witch had said. But who was she? The witch did not believe the medium to be Russian, and considering the number of people who had fled the revolution in Russia, it would be a sensible enough disguise to assume. Or, she could simply be a woman displaced by her own country's unrest, seeking to start over.

There was only one way to find out which side of the coin was true. The medium was dressed this morning in a pale butter-colored dress with her auburn hair swept back into a delicate knot at the nape of her neck. She looked vastly more peaceful than when I'd seen her here yesterday, angry and afraid and quarreling with Mr. Sharpe. Could Mr. Sharpe be my mysterious shadow? If he truly *was* Elijah, and I was growing certain he must be, then he'd likely take umbrage with my knowing his identity. But framing me for murder seemed a bit drastic.

Admittedly, I was not the best gauge of character. Mother said it was my nature to love ferociously, claiming it to be a strength rather than a weakness, but I disagreed. My *nature* had caused me nothing but pain and was part of the reason for my current predicament. If I didn't *care* for Mr. Owen, I wouldn't be at Manhurst at all.

I'd not gotten a good look at the medium before, but up close, she was quite possibly the most beautiful woman I'd seen in my life with the sort of loveliness that only grew with age. Her hair was a medium shade of brown, shot through with strands of gold and copper that shone in the early morning sun—with not a single strand of silver in it, despite the fact she had to be at least a decade older than I. Her skin was flawless, giving me the impression of one of those delicate French dolls I played with as a girl.

"I cannot believe she is dead," the medium whispered.

If she *was* Russian, she must not have been there in quite some time as her voice carried only the faintest of accents and her diction was that of someone who had been at the finest of schools. A mark in the White Witch's column. Now *who* or *what* the youngest medium truly was—that was an entirely different question.

I took a step closer and leaned against the rail, crossing my ankles. "It's a terrible thing. Did you know her long, Miss . . . ?"

She turned the cigarette over in her fingers, studying it intently before patting the bench beside her. "Demidov. Genevieve Demidov. They say you pulled her from the water." Her voice broke as she turned around. "Thank you for that. It was a kindness."

"I thought she was alive. I am sorry she wasn't. I mean to find out who did that to her—who killed her."

Genevieve let out a surprisingly bitter laugh as she stubbed her cigarette on the bench. "Better you than those two"—she struggled for the word before saying something in Russian I didn't understand—"who are supposed to be investigating."

"Are they giving you trouble too?"

She shrugged as a pair of ducks landed on the water behind her, disturbing the smooth surface. "Nothing I am not used to. Women who make their own way often deal with such . . . men. They think to frighten me into admitting to something. It is strange though." A flicker of something flashed through her rich brown eyes, the color of a pot of hot chocolate.

"What is strange?"

She looked up at me in surprise, as if I ought to have known what she was about to say. "That they are not looking for the other medium."

What other medium? She must have seen the question in my face.

"Abigail. Abigail was the third Fate. We had been doing several shows a week, traveling the countryside—shows like the other night. Well . . ." She winced at the memory. "Not exactly like that night. It had never been like *that* before." She flexed her fingers. "The spirits do not usually come, I do not know if it was the stranger's presence or if it was—"

I straightened, turning to face her. "Which stranger?"

"Hecate."

"Hecate?" First Abigail, now this? The woman was starting to remind me of Mr. Owen with the way she talked in circles.

She inclined her head back to the house. "The dark-haired witch. She arrived a few days before you, looking for work. She fit into Abigail's costume. Lucy said that it made sense for her to step into the role. It was important to Lucy that the séance take place no matter the cost."

The White Witch had a name after all. *Hecate*. It made her seem more human. "What happened to the other medium? To this . . . Abigail woman?"

"We do not know. She disappeared. Lucy believed she was murdered—we found her valise on her dresser as if she was about to leave."

The picture she drew mirrored the one I'd stumbled across in Lucy's room.

"Packed?"

Genevieve nodded. "Everything was in her case. She'd been acting peculiar before she disappeared. She said she'd found something important, but wanted to be certain what it was."

"Do you have any idea what she'd found?"

She shook her head. "Lucy went all the way to Edinburgh to seek help after Abigail vanished, but no one would come to Manhurst. No one cared about the disappearance of a woman like us."

The thought enraged me, and yet I was familiar enough with the situation. It was a sad fact of life that many men considered women disposable. Poorer women, or those who fell outside the proper bounds of society—well, to certain sorts of men, we were a nuisance at best. "And then Hecate appeared . . ."

She nodded.

"How much do you know about her?" Several swallows on the wing soared up into the early morning sun, out of sight. I wondered briefly if Hecate herself, the White Witch, could be involved in the crime though I quickly pushed the notion away. She wanted to be rid of me; the very last thing she'd do is create a situation in which I was trapped within five miles of her precious Ruan Kivell.

"Not much. The witch keeps to herself. I'm not even certain

why she is still here. Hecate is nothing like Lucy. Lucy was a true spiritualist and was patient trying to teach me her ways. She believed the dead used her as a conduit and that she could teach me to do the same. I never put much meaning in it, but it pays the rent and I've always been good at reading people. Abigail didn't have Lucy's gifts either. No one did and I've never met another like her. Not when I lived in Petrograd, Paris, nor Rome." She stared at the cigarette in her hand as she twisted it between her fingers.

"But you said the other night was different from earlier séances . . ."

"It was beyond anything I've ever seen. I do not know if it was the presence of the stranger, or if the spirits are as angry as Lucy kept warning. She told me that they demanded vengeance. That's what she said. That the spirits would not be denied their due."

I drew in a sharp breath. "Do you think that's what happened here? That the spirits were angry at Lucy for some reason?"

She shook her head, giving me a gimlet eye. "No. I think the spirits told Lucy the truth. I think they told her something that someone here didn't want known."

"Why are you telling me all this?"

She sniffed and looked away, picking at the edge of her finely polished nail. "I cannot help myself. There is something about you that makes me . . ."

I followed her gaze and spotted a group of men coming onto the bridge. I recognized the first instantly. The lithe form of Andrew Lennox and next to him was his father, Malachi. The dreadful man had his stringy gray hair tied back in a queue and looked as miserable this morning as all the other times I'd crossed his path.

His expression turned to pure malice as he spied me. There was no doubt in my mind that he was the person quarreling with Mr. Owen this morning. I noted a nick at his jaw, with dried blood scabbing it over. My mind suddenly recalled the knife in Mr. Owen's hand when I entered his room.

Distracted by Malachi's sudden appearance on the bridge, I nearly overlooked the Duke of Biddlesford, who followed behind with easy grace alongside Mr. Sharpe. Sharpe, for his part, kept his distance from me, dropping to the back of the group. I studied every inch of his face for some tell. Some *evidence* that he truly was Elijah. Perhaps I'd get word from Hari today. That would be a boon.

All four men were dressed for golf, with a pair of young boys of fourteen or more lumbering along with the clubs slung over their shoulders.

"Miss Vaughn!" Andrew's eyes lit up and he reached out to embrace me. I kissed his cheek in greeting, feeling his father's barely tethered rage radiating beside him. "How is my uncle this morning?"

The silence that fell on the bridge was deafening. The ill blood between Mr. Owen and Malachi was clearly no surprise to the duke, nor to Mr. Sharpe who wandered on ahead of the group away from my line of sight.

Malachi grumbled to himself as he followed after the hotelier.

"You shouldn't goad your father."

"I am genuinely inquiring. Their quarrel is between the two of them. My affection for my uncle is yet another in a litany of things about my life that my father disapproves of." Andrew paused, turning to look at Genevieve, who was seated on the bench behind me. Had I not known it was her, I would scarcely believe it to be the same woman. The slump of her shoulders, her downcast eyes—she appeared every inch a beleaguered servant and not the sparkling woman who had been speaking with me moments before. It was a remarkable trick.

"Captain Lennox, have you met Miss Demidov?" I asked hesitantly.

She scrambled to her feet, reminding me of an animal that had grown used to being mistreated. Who or what had caused such a reaction in her? I turned quickly to see where Mr. Sharpe had gone, but he was no longer anywhere to be found. Neither was Malachi.

Andrew furrowed his brow and shifted his weight on his cane as he watched her. "Have we met?"

She shook her head, eyes fixed on her shoes. "I must go back . . ." Her accent had shifted again, to one far thicker than before. She made a polite bow before hurrying back in the direction of Manhurst. Andrew and I watched after her, waiting until she was out of earshot before speaking.

"Do you truly think you know her?"

Andrew frowned. "Apparently not. She looks deuced familiar, that's all. Though I'm sure it's nothing. It's only . . . Ah, Ruby, where are my manners?" He straightened, holding out his arm to me. "Have you met the duke?"

I hadn't. Not officially, at least, unless one counted colliding with him in a hallway.

"So we meet again," the duke said, a faint smile spread across his affable face. "You seem recovered from when we last met." He tapped his ornately carved walking stick gently on his palm. The carved jade pommel bore a distinct insignia with a stylized thistle, the rich green color catching my eye.

"I hope the inspector didn't keep you too long for questioning."

He smiled at me. "An hour at most. It appears my duchess had informed him where I'd been the previous evening. I had no idea she'd already spoken to him, it was simply confirming what he knew. I do not mind. Not if it helps find who harmed that poor old woman." He looked out over the water. "It was here, where the woman was killed, wasn't it?"

I nodded. "Yes, Your Grace."

He made a sound of sympathy and shook his head. "Dreadful business. Tell Hawick I hope to see him at supper, will you?"

"Hawick?" I started to ask, before I remembered that that was Mr. Owen's name. He was not Mr. Owen at all—he was known to these people as Lord Hawick. "He mentioned he knew you as a boy."

He smiled, tapping his walking stick. "He had some business dealings with my father. Whenever he'd come out to Rivenly, I'd always be underfoot. I think my father, the previous duke, hoped that Hawick's more studious habits would rub off. I confess, I did not expect to see him here, but I am glad of it. It has been too long since I've had such fine company."

He glanced over his shoulder, having noticed half the party had moved on. "Ah. It seems they have left us. Shall we, Andy?"

Andrew nodded, staring off in the direction Genevieve had disappeared.

And with that the two men disappeared back over the bridge and out of my line of sight.

I GREW MORE and more confused by the interplay between Mr. Sharpe and Genevieve on the bridge. Combined with what I'd overheard this morning between Mr. Owen and his brother, and Genevieve's suspicions about Abigail's fate, I began to wonder exactly how gnarled this knot had become. Perhaps Lucy's death was the culmination of events, not the beginning of them as I'd initially believed.

Genevieve said the other medium—this Abigail woman—had been packed as Lucy had been. If that was the case, then we now had three presumably dead women, not two. Mariah, then Abigail, now Lucy. I grew ill at the thought.

I checked my pin watch before snapping it shut. It was nearly nine in the morning, as reasonable a time as any to seek out Ruan to see if he'd come to any conclusions in the handful of hours since we'd last spoken. I rounded the corner at the bottom of the back stair and hurried past a legion of uniformed staff, starched and polished to within an inch of their lives and made my way up to the east wing of the castle. I counted the doors, my fingers absently tracing the smooth paper, a geometric treat of jet, emerald, and gold, until I found myself outside Ruan's. I could get used to relying on him—seeking him out like this.

From down the hall, I heard some of the other guests making their way back to their rooms after breakfast, the voices growing marginally closer. I knocked again, waiting patiently—as the last time I'd gone in without asking I'd embarrassed the both of us.

He didn't answer. I huffed out a breath. The irritating man was likely holed up with a grimoire. Subtle rustling came from the other side of the door.

I knocked again.

It still didn't open.

The footsteps behind me grew nearer and I dared not wait any longer, I didn't need the horrid constable or the inspector to come across me lurking outside a man's bedroom. They already thought I was Mr. Owen's mistress, I could only imagine what they'd make of this. I tried the handle and the door opened inward.

I slipped inside, closing it behind me, and prepared to launch in to Ruan on proper etiquette for answering one's door in a timely manner. However, the room was empty.

Impossible. I'd heard someone rustling around in here only seconds before. Not to mention there was still an indentation on the bed where he'd been, with an ancient Cornish grimoire lying open exactly as I'd expected. Mercifully the pages in *that* book had not been dog-eared like his medical text.

On the bedside table a cup of tea sat abandoned, steam curling up in the chilly autumn morning. *Where was he?*

I was about to question my doubt in the existence of ghosts, when a large hand clamped itself over my mouth and I was yanked into the darkness. The great wardrobe door shut behind me with a soft click. I squirmed against my assailant, fully prepared to bite the hand that held me until I caught a familiar verdant scent.

Ruan.

My body instantly slacked against him. Strange that even in the darkness I could be certain it was he, but it wasn't the first time I'd been in such close proximity to the infuriating man. His breath was hot on my neck as his fingers loosened against my lips. Before I could gather my senses, another sound came from his room. Someone else was there too. For several heartbeats I remained, nestled against Ruan's chest. His one arm clamped tight around my stomach, his left palm gently over my mouth. I willed away the inconvenient sensations this closeness brought. This was not the time, nor the place to have said sensations.

"Mr. Kivell . . . Mr. Kivell, are you here? It is important."

What was Lady Amelia doing here? I had scarcely seen her after she lured me to the orangery. Since then she'd obediently made herself scarce as instructed. If the girl had a lick of sense she'd continue to do so until the killer was caught. Then again, who at sixteen has any sense? I certainly didn't—having fallen in love with the first honey-tongued would-be bigamist who crossed my path.

At least I'd been marginally wiser the second time around.

Ruan's chest quaked again in amusement.

Stop eavesdropping.

I squirmed against Ruan's grasp, but he tightened his hold on me.

Lady Amelia said something softly to herself, before turning and leaving. The door closing behind her. The muscles in Ruan's palm flinched against my skin in warning to stay silent. He must be making certain she stayed gone. I breathed in against his palm, inadvertently flooding my senses with him. It was entirely unfair how good he smelled.

Several more seconds passed in silence before Ruan released me and I scrambled out of the closet into the glaringly bright morning light of his room. We'd been tucked away with his clothes for probably a half hour. Long enough for my legs to grow stiff. I stretched, smoothing my irreparably wrinkled skirt as he pried himself out of the tight spot.

It was an entertaining sight to behold, with his fingers wrapped around the wooden opening, one leg out and the other still inside. "The great Pellar of Lothlel Green hiding from debutantes in a cupboard."

Ruan, for his part, was unamused by the situation. He raked a hand through his dark hair, placing much-needed space between the two of us. "I was not hiding. I was . . ." He prowled to the window, angrily thrusting his thumbs into the waistband of his trousers.

"Just lurking in your wardrobe waiting on me to come by for tea?" The echo of his fingers remained warm on my skin.

"Ruby, I am not amused by any of this," he snapped, turning to face me. "A woman was killed here three days ago, you're suspected of killing her, and every time I leave my room I'm being tracked down by every woman between sixteen and sixty like some kind of bloody badger. Do you not have the sense of a hoverfly?"

I sniffed indignantly. "You could lock the door. It keeps them out."

"Why bother when *you'll* pick the lock?"

His words stung more than they should. Surely, he didn't want to keep *me* away. "It's because you're different. Intriguing. How can you blame them? The parties and scheming of well-bred men out for one's inheritance or frankly just to get under one's skirt. It's all tiresome. I wouldn't pay them any mind, they're out for a lark. You're an adventure for them. That's all."

He took a step closer, looking down at me, his eyes bright. "Is that what I am to you? A *lark*." The bitterness dripped from the final word. I had struck a nerve.

"Of course not—you're . . . I'm simply saying that I understand what they want from you—"

"Do you . . . ?"

I swallowed hard. I ought to take a step back. I really ought to, but I couldn't bring myself to do it.

"Believe me, I know what *they* want too. Gods know I've caught my share of their fanciful imaginings since I've been here. But that one . . ." He pointed toward the door, his nostrils flaring slightly. "The girl dresses like a strawberry scone but her mother ought to know the things going on her in her head."

Bravo Lady Amelia. Honestly, I couldn't blame her. She had exquisite taste if she was admiring my Pellar. "Ruan . . . women are allowed to have carnal thoughts too. It's perfectly normal. Natural even for girls of that age to want to . . . explore."

"I don't mind them having the thoughts, but I'd rather they not have them about me where I can hear them."

Well, that would be a problem. "Ah. Yes, I could see how that would be uncomfortable."

He raised his brows to underscore the point. Suddenly he recalled something, slapping his hand on his thigh before moving to his grimoire. He flipped to the cover and pulled out a telegram, handing it to me. "You were right about your solicitor."

My heart leapt in my chest. "I told you Hari could work miracles." I quickly scanned the missive. Short and to the point. Hari was never one to mince words—a trait I valued above all else in a friend.

Ruby, I regret to inform you I have no conclusive news at this point. I traced your acquaintance until 1917 when he disappeared entirely from the record. Prior to his disappearance he'd embarked upon an ill-advised business venture with one C. S. Something to do with manufacturing during the war. The business was a front. Though I have not been able to determine what for.

C. S. My blood ran cold. That meant Elijah had been working with Christopher years after I left New York. I bit hard on the inside of my mouth, willing myself to read on.

There was a messy affair in the summer of '17 where it appears that your acquaintance was utterly ruined. His reputation in tatters, some believe he took his own life, though no grave or death record has been found. He simply disappears along with approximately two hundred thousand American dollars. C. S. however escaped scandal-free and is currently rumored to be considering running for governor of the state of New York. I will continue to investigate. Would you like me to look into the business dealings of Mr. S.?

> *Your faithful friend (and occasional solicitor)*
> *Hari*

Good God. Could it be that Elijah ran off with the money and has hidden himself away here in Scotland? The timeline matches, but a great deal could have occurred between 1917 and 1922.

Ruan touched the scar on my brow with his thumb gently. "Is that the news you hoped to hear?"

"I don't know what I hoped to hear—but it helps to know it's plausible." *And that I'm not going mad.* I took a half step back toward the door, where it was safer and a girl could gather her thoughts. "I talked to Hecate this morning."

Ruan's eyes widened at my use of the White Witch's name.
So you know her true name too.

He nodded again, resting his hip on the windowsill. "She thinks that she can help me, teach me how to control it."

It. The breath left my lungs as my brain started to trip along through all the things I knew about him and the strange power he could not control. He had saved me with his abilities in Cornwall, and yet he had no idea how it was done. "Do you know why she's here?"

He shook his head. "I have suspicions. The old ones do as they will. Hecate is no different. She comes and goes as she pleases. Her kind do not follow the same laws as we do. She called on me once . . . back in Lothlel Green not long after you left the village."

My eyes widened, though I had no right to be surprised that he had dealings with the White Witch. "And you didn't think to tell me?"

He whipped around on his heels, green eyes flashing almost silver. "I didn't plan to see you again. To be close to you like this—having you invade every bloody sense I possess!" He raked his hand through his short hair before growling. "Gods, it's enough to drive a mortal mad if he isn't there already."

My jaw dropped, an unpleasant sensation settling in my throat.

His voice cracked as he took a step closer. "You terrify me. I do not know what lives between us. I have seen more things in this world than I care to admit but I cannot explain what this is." He reached for my cheek, his tone tender enough to break a girl's heart. "You are everywhere and everything to me, flooding my senses and I cannot understand it. Not one bit. I have read every book I can get my hands on. Scoured every source looking for a *reason* for this inexplicable thread between us and for this power you hold over me—" His breath hitched. "I don't know if . . ."

"Don't know what . . . ?" My voice trembled as his thumb trailed its way down my jaw to the hollow of my throat and for half a moment I thought he might kiss me, but the moment passed.

He closed his eyes. "I simply don't know. Go, Ruby. I'll come to you and we can talk about whatever it was you came for. I just need a moment . . ."

My limbs grew weak. But I nodded and cowardly ran away.

CHAPTER SEVENTEEN

A Necessary Sacrifice

I left Ruan's room and headed straight for the library, the one place in this castle where I might be able to clear my thoughts and make sense of what I knew without interruption. The halls were empty, which was just as well as I hadn't the stomach to talk to anyone, and I slipped into the darkened room.

It's never good when the old ones are afraid. That's what he'd said. Well, it's certainly not good when the Pellar is frightened either. I blew out a breath and made a circle of the library, running my fingers over the books, simply trying to regain my footing. A great deal had happened in only a handful of days. Ghosts of my own past and Mr. Owen's were threatening to strangle us both. Hari's note gave credence to my suspicions that Matthew Sharpe was indeed Elijah Keene. I'd have to write Hari and ask him to continue to investigate, however *I* couldn't do such a thing without raising suspicion. Once Ruan had gotten beyond whatever unpleasant emotions were currently plaguing him, he'd need to see to the task. This was precisely why I avoided feelings. They got in the way of more pressing matters.

I paused before the shelf bearing all five million copies of

Debrett's. Oh fine, there weren't that many, but there might as well have been.

A duke, a countess, and a viscount. Surely it was unusual to have *this* many peers at a séance, even if Mr. Owen was pretending *not* to be one when we arrived.

Perhaps that was the link I'd missed?

I pulled out the current volume of the paean of the privileged from the shelf and flipped through, not certain what I was looking for but paused as I came across the page for Mr. Owen. Or rather, the page that *ought* to have been for him. It had been torn out of the book entirely.

Dread climbed up my spine as I laid that one down on the table behind me and grabbed another. I went back through the years, grabbing an edition from the time before Mariah disappeared, and pulled it from the shelf. The exact same thing had happened. There was nothing there. The page—excised from the book. Volume after volume, I searched, fingers flying through the pages, however, each one had the entry for the Viscount of Hawick carefully removed. After going through a dozen different editions I blew out my breath and leaned against the table, the desecrated books stacked high behind me.

"What are you doing?" Lady Amelia asked.

I jumped, whacking my knee on the leg of the table, swearing beneath my breath. The girl had crept in quietly. I hadn't heard her at all.

"Looking for something," I muttered, rubbing at the sore spot on my leg.

She wrinkled her nose, looking from the books to me. "Did you . . . find it?"

I shook my head, not sure what to make of the curious girl who had just moments before been looking for Ruan. She seemed innocent enough, but he was correct in his assessment of her

THE SECRET OF THE THREE FATES · 151

wardrobe. Today she wore a pale pink frock with white piping down the front and sleeves. Definitely a strawberry scone.

"Mama was looking at this one too . . ." she said absently, picking up the most recent copy of Debrett's and turning it over in her hand. "She is not herself, Miss Vaughn. I am worried for her. It is growing worse—her moods."

"What do you mean?"

Lady Amelia sighed dramatically and flopped into a leather chair, her feet swinging freely. "Just this morning she yelled at me. She *yelled*! No . . . Mother would never yell . . ." Lady Amelia made a face before changing her voice to mimic her mother. "'Proper ladies do *not* screech, they *call*, Amelia.'"

The girl's animation made me smile. She was refreshingly full of life, a far sight from how I'd felt after the day's revelations— and it wasn't yet noon. "You said she'd been behaving strangely before you came too . . . changed your plans. Has anything else peculiar happened—besides her temper? Have you learned any more about why she insisted you come?"

She shook her head. "No. But I did learn that the duchess is the most boring woman I've ever met in my life. I'd not been introduced to her before, but she and my mother have taken tea at least three times since arriving. Mother doesn't even take tea three times in a week with *me* and I live with her. If the duchess's son wasn't only six years old I'd be convinced Mama was angling for an advantageous match." She shrugged, fiddling with one of the flimsy layers of her pink skirt. "I truly thought she'd intended to dangle me at Captain Lennox—even though he is dreadfully old."

The girl continued on, completely unaware of my raised eyebrow. "Besides, even if she did *intend* to, he's not at all interested in me. But I know who he *is* interested in." She waggled her eyebrows comically.

There was something charmingly refreshing about Lady

Amelia—even if she did think I was nearing my dotage at all of twenty-nine years of age. Besides, her innocent chatter was a welcome reprieve from the problems at hand. Between ferreting out a killer, worrying over Mr. Owen, and sorting out Ruan's newfound *feelings,* I could spare five minutes to humor a sixteen-year-old girl's fancies. "Tell me."

She looked to the door, then back to me with a conspiratorial smile. "Why, the medium."

Suddenly, all my mirth fled as I tucked a loose curl behind my ear, stepping closer to the girl. "What . . . what do you mean *the medium?*"

"The Russian one. She's ever so pretty. I suppose I couldn't blame him, besides, she's as ancient as he is!"

My stomach knotted. "Why do you think he's interested in her?" Surely this was a girlish misunderstanding. Yes. That was all it was.

"I saw him outside her room—and there's no reason for a re-spectable gentleman to be in a lady's private room. None! And I've seen him follow after her on at least two other occasions." She looked proud enough I might have wept. Not because of her assumption, but for the nagging fear that I had misjudged Andrew Lennox.

I weighed the options, none of them good. If Andrew was connected to the mediums, could *he* have been the one to bring Mr. Owen to Manhurst in the first place? Could Ruan's apprehen-sions about the man be true? My knees grew weak and I braced myself on the table.

"Miss Vaughn?" the girl snapped, drawing my attention back to her. I shook my head, focusing on her puzzled face. "You just disappeared for a moment. Did you hear what I said? I said I think they are having an affair!"

I nodded numbly, then shook my head. "You mustn't speak of this to anyone else, do you hear me?"

She wrinkled her brow. "I don't intend to tell anyone. Besides, I'm not supposed to be speaking to you at all. Mother said to keep away from you, that you and Lord Hawick were corrupting influences on young girls. She'd never even let me out of our rooms if she knew we were alone in here."

"Most mothers agree with that notion," I murmured, still struggling to wrap my mind around the prospect of Mr. Owen's nephew being a murderer. "Tell me, does your mother say much else of Lord Hawick?"

"Only that he's dangerous and she cannot wait until Captain Lennox inherits the title to bring some respectability back to the name."

My mind reeled as the girl prattled on, oblivious to my increasing discomfort. I shifted, digging my fingernails into my palms.

"Rumor says he killed his wife. Mama said that's why the spirit was angry at the séance. No one has even seen him in years—then for him to show up like that. But it's strange though . . ." She tapped her lower lip with her finger.

"What is?" I managed to ask.

"If he'd been hiding away for that long and not claiming the title, then why would someone go to the effort to remove all mention of him from Debrett's?" She wrinkled her nose at the stack of books on the table beside me. "I assume that's why you've pulled every one out. You noticed it too, didn't you?"

I nodded slowly. The girl wasn't quite as flighty as her mother seemed to believe.

"It was only after I asked Mama who he was and she behaved strangely that I decided to find out more about him."

"You're a very clever girl."

She huffed out a breath, her feet swinging, making her appear younger. "Much good it will do me. We're leaving soon and headed to my grandfather's for the hunting party. I'm certain Mother will have a match planned before Christmas. I suppose I should be happy, but I've rather enjoyed exploring this place. It's far more interesting than I expected it to be."

I furrowed my brow. "But we're forbidden to leave here until they've found the killer."

Lady Amelia's expression fell and she gave me a pitying look. "Haven't you heard, Miss Vaughn?"

"Heard what?" I leaned back against the table, awaiting whatever new horror Lady Amelia was about to reveal.

"They've arrested Lord Hawick. He's confessed to the murder of Lucy Campbell."

CHAPTER EIGHTEEN

Safe Harbor

THE earth gave way beneath my feet with the girl's words. *They've arrested Mr. Owen.* He'd confessed. Why would he do such a thing? I knew good and well he hadn't harmed a hair on Lucy Campbell's head as he'd been snoring away in his room when I left to meet her that night.

"Are you all right?" She shot to her feet, touching my elbow gently. "I'm sorry, I assumed you'd already heard the news. Everyone has been talking about it all morning. I was looking for you and couldn't find you, then I thought to go tell his gentleman friend earlier, but couldn't find him either."

I was going to be sick. The entire time Ruan and I were arguing in his room Mr. Owen was in danger.

"Is he still here or have the authorities—" My mouth grew dry and I couldn't finish the thought.

"I believe so, the inspector was waiting on someone to come down from Edinburgh. I think because he's a viscount it makes things a little more . . ." The girl hesitated.

"Complicated?"

"Yes, that." She twisted her hands nervously. Lady Amelia

went on for a few more minutes before making some excuse and leaving, but I scarcely heard a word leaving her lips.

I was utterly adrift and no closer to finding the true killer than when I arrived. All I had were a handful of glass plate negatives, a bizarre ring that Mr. Owen was terrified of, and the knowledge that no one in this damnable estate was who they pretended to be.

Hot tears flooded my eyes. *Oh, Mr. Owen.* How was I to get him out of this? I licked my lips as I heard the door creak open.

Wiping at the wetness on my face with my hands, I struggled to mask my emotions behind that well-polished veneer my mother had taught me to wear. *Hide yourself from them, Ruby darling. Don't let them know what you are.* Christ, at almost thirty years old I didn't even know who I was.

"Oh, Miss Vaughn, there you are! This is terrible. Just terrible," the duke muttered, rushing into the room, looking every bit as frantic as I felt.

"You've heard the news?"

"Andrew's driver found us and told us what happened. Have you spoken to him? Do you know where he is?" The duke had lost his composure and the words tumbled out of his mouth as if he could not control them. It felt strangely good to be with someone as horrified as I was at the revelation that Mr. Owen had confessed to a crime he didn't commit.

"I just found out myself. I'm told he's to be held at the castle until the inspector can bring in someone from Edinburgh."

The duke let out a startled sound as he rubbed his jaw, his golfing cap in his other hand. "I cannot think what compelled him to do such a reckless thing. If I had known he was at risk . . ." He shook his head. "This should not have happened. It cannot happen. I will speak to the authorities, have him released into my custody. Surely there are some privileges accorded to a duke."

I dared not hope. "Do you think the inspector would allow it?"

The duke nodded. "My family estate is on the Isle of May. I

have little doubt that I can convince the inspector to let him stay there until the trial at least. Hawick is an old man, he would not survive a week in prison. It is unthinkable."

He was right, of course. I'd briefly spent time in prison thanks to Mr. Owen's penchant for dealing in illegal books and it was no place I wished to return. It was certainly no place for an eighty-year-old man. "Mr. Owen does as he pleases. It's one of his most infuriating and endearing qualities."

The duke's expression softened. "That it is. I've always admired that about him. As a boy I used to want to be him. Thought if I read the same books and appreciated the same art, that somehow I would be able to become a fraction of the man he was."

"Is." I corrected.

The duke's brows rose in silent question.

"The man he *is*. You speak as if his conviction is a foregone conclusion. It is not." I gritted my teeth, sounding far more assured than I felt. "I simply have to find the real killer, then we can clear his name."

"I do not see how anyone can accomplish that, Miss Vaughn, but I wish you luck. I assure you I will not let harm come to him whilst in my care. Pack his things, I'll speak to the inspector and we can be on our way to Rivenly within the hour. I'll send a man back for his trunks once I have him safe. But I must get Hawick away from here before he manages to get himself into more trouble."

I nodded, but knowing Mr. Owen he'd only find himself up to his ears in more of the stuff, no matter how desperately we tried to save him.

CHAPTER NINETEEN

A Bad End

WITH newfound resolve, I spent the rest of the morning packing Mr. Owen's things. A stark reminder of my last trip back to New York. I'd returned after the war to deal with matters at our family townhome on Sutton Place. Worried about my state of mind, Hari had insisted on joining me. It would be good to have a friend, he said, when packing away the memories of my family—before selling the house for a fraction of its worth. We spent two weeks there, with the curtains closed up, hiding the fact the notorious Vaughn girl had returned. I spent two weeks drinking away the vestiges of the war, struggling to place the memories of my family into boxes and crates, to be stowed away and never thought upon again.

As I folded Mr. Owen's dressing gowns, the earlier memory was close enough I might have touched it had I not hoped—no—*known* that I would help him. I might not have been able to keep my family from dying on that ship, but I could save Mr. Owen.

What had he been thinking, confessing to a crime like that? But deep down, I knew. He'd told me as much whether I wanted to believe it or not. That must have been what he'd been arguing with his brother about this morning. He wouldn't allow me to come to harm. Mr. Owen had known . . . he'd known the inspector had intended to arrest me and instead he gave his life for mine.

I slammed the trunk lid down and screamed. The sort of scream one would expect of an animal, frightened and wounded in the woods. A scream that brought back all the pain and ache of the last decade. He loved me. He all but told me so.

Once finished, I spoke with the man at the desk to arrange to have Mr. Owen's things picked up by the duke's man, and then I set off to find Ruan. Had he heard? He surely would have by now—but if he had, why had he not come for me? Unless he intended to leave now that he was free to go.

I wouldn't blame him if he did, and I was more than capable of saving Mr. Owen on my own if I must. I just didn't want to. I made it as far as the terrace when I spotted him. He was walking slowly across the field toward the bridge in the early evening fog. He was far away but I would have recognized the slope of his shoulders anywhere. My heart squeezed at the sight of him and I raced after him.

I was out of breath by the time I reached the bridge. Ruddy-headed wigeons made their way to way to shore, noisily abandoning the water as I approached him at long last.

Ruan stood against the rail, his palms flat as he stared into the water. The sun was setting behind us. It was quiet and for once we were truly alone. Even the sound was damped from the thick air.

"I've been looking everywhere for you." His voice was hoarse, but he did not turn to face me.

"Did you hear about Mr. Owen?"

He nodded with a frown. "I spoke to him as he was leaving. He wanted me to tell you not to blame yourself."

I let out a strangled sob. *Not blame myself*—how could I not?

"None of this is your fault," Ruan murmured into my hair as he scooped me into his arms, holding me tight against him.

I let myself melt into his embrace. It was there, in the silence of the fog that I told him everything that I'd learned. Of what Lady Amelia revealed in the library, of my growing suspicion of both the youngest medium and Andrew Lennox, of how I'd failed Mr. Owen. All of the sentiment tumbled out of me and I was helpless to control it.

"Hush . . ." he murmured. "I hear you. I hear . . . all of it."

And in that moment I knew he did. All the fear, all the sadness. He knew every crack, every crevice within my very heart. Whether it was because of being a Pellar, or the odd connection between the two of us, Ruan knew me inside and out.

He pressed a kiss to my forehead, his beard scratching my skin. "We will help him, Ruby. I promise you. You are the cleverest person I've ever known. Together we can figure this out."

I paused, looking up at him, his pale eyes full of emotion that I could not name if I tried. "We?"

He nodded. "We will save Owen from himself."

I wiped at the wetness of my nose. It was terribly difficult to look dignified while weeping into a man's chest. "But you are miserable here, you said it yourself this morning. Why would you stay?"

Ruan gaped. It was as if I'd suddenly sprouted wings before him. "Why would I stay? Ruby . . . I . . ."

It made no sense. He hated leaving Cornwall. *Why would he stay in Scotland with no reason to—*

"Because of you. Do you think so little of me that you'd believe I would turn my back on you and Owen now? Walk away and go back to my cottage and my garden and never once think on that remarkable woman who wandered into my village six weeks ago determined to prove me wrong in every conceivable way?"

I sniffled again, unable to look him in the eye. "I don't remember her. Not now. I feel so . . . so . . ."

"Lost?" he supplied.

"It is truly unfair how you do that."

He let out an amused sound beneath his breath. "It's only reasonable. You love Owen, and he's an infuriating old man but you are an infuriating young woman. It's part of your appeal—the both of you."

I sniffled again. "I don't know what to do. I cannot see my way out of this."

"We'll figure it out, just as we did before. This may not be Cornwall but the mechanics are the same. A person killed someone, now we have to go dig around and ferret out the truth, mmm?"

"I do not understand how you can be calm about all this."

"Don't you?" He raised a brow. "Ruby, I . . ." He paused, shaking his head, and instead leaned down, tipping my chin up with his forefinger. The wind whipped around us and I unconsciously moved into his lee. He took me by the shoulders, gently rubbing the tight muscles there and taking away a bit of the ache inside my very soul. That familiar cold rush flooded through my veins until I no longer wept. The tears replaced by resolve I thought I'd lost. We *would* save him. Just as we'd found the killer in Lothlel Green.

An odd streak of silver flashed through his green eyes, one of the few visible aftereffects from when he'd drawn upon his abilities. I doubted he was even aware that his eyes did that, but I was altogether too aware of him. The edge of his mouth curved up as a dark curl fell into his eyes.

"Thank you . . ." I murmured, stretching up, meaning to press a kiss to his cheek but accidentally brushing the corner of his mouth. His body tensed at the contact, not certain what to make of it. But he didn't pull back and neither did I. The two of us remained there frozen in time, breathing in the other, not certain whether to give in to the growing attraction between us or to do the sensible thing and walk away.

"Of all the souls in this world for the old gods to bind me

to . . ." Ruan murmured against my lips. But before I could re-spond to the very disturbing words he uttered, he crushed his mouth against mine, washing away any memory of what came before or after. The world narrowed to only Ruan. The green scent of him, the faintest bit of honey candy on his breath. I wasn't at all prepared for this—for him.

I reached up, pulling him closer to me, and suddenly remem-bered . . . I remembered *everything*.

The sea of blood.

The mud.

The poppies blooming on his chest.

It had been Ruan I was looking for in that terrible dream and as soon as I'd found him, I'd lost him forever.

But before I could pull away to warn him that I'd seen his death, the sniper's shot rang out—just as I'd foreseen—the force of the round piercing my body from the back and pushing us both over the granite railing.

Ruan's eyes shot open, almost fully silver now with only the faintest hint of green, as a searing-hot pain burnt through my shoul-der and the two of us went tumbling into the icy water beneath.

The White Witch was right when she'd warned us in Lothlel Green.

I'd killed him.

I'd killed us both.

A COLD WHITE fire ran through my body as I sank deeper into the water. It started in my shoulder where Ruan's hand held fast to me and ricocheted through my veins with a force I'd never felt before. He held impossibly tight against the part of me that hurt the worst, tugging me down to the lake bed with him, allowing the water to claim us both.

The sea will give and the sea will take.

An ancient warning echoed in my head, whispered by a voice long forgotten. Deeper and deeper until we lay together on the rocky floor. The silver had fled Ruan's eyes at last, as he lay still beneath me. His lifeless green gaze staring right through me.

Not like this. We would not die like this.

The red blossoms spread across his chest, creating clouds in the water around us. I could scarcely see from all the blood. Mine or his, it did not matter.

I wriggled in the water to get a better position before I hooked my uninjured arm around his chest, in a mockery of our previous embrace. Struggling to find my feet, I kicked hard against the rocky bottom, sending up a cloud of water, mud, and blood. We couldn't be more than fifteen feet from the surface, if that.

My sluggish muscles rebelled.

Struggling against the water and his considerable size, I clutched his chest against my own, yet Ruan remained eerily still against me.

Please don't be dead. Don't be dead.

Come on, Ruan. You great stubborn ox.

My lungs stung as I battled the water. I needed to surface. Needed to breathe.

I kicked harder.

My own pulse slowed as my body lost more and more of its strength to the icy water. At long last, I broke the surface with a gasp. Our mingled blood and muddy water flooded into my lungs. Salty and metallic as I coughed in the chilly October air.

My tenuous grip on him slipped and his head fell down into the water. I jerked him hard, pulling him farther up my body, keeping his face above the waterline. It would do no good to pull him up only to let him drown. With a pained grunt, I shoved us both onto the rocky shore, to the very spot he'd woken me from my nightmare.

It had been a warning then, or meant to be one.

Except I hadn't remembered until it was too late.

Ruan was either dead or unconscious, but I was too exhausted to tell which. I reached up with my free hand, feeling for a pulse, but his heart had always been so eerily slow that I could not have been certain whether I felt it or not.

Surely someone heard the shot.

Someone would come.

In the shallows, I gave one final tug, dragging us another six inches toward land, when my body finally succumbed to the cold. I collapsed upon my back, water up to my ears with Ruan's head resting on my chest where the pain still seared through me. Our bodies were held together by his weight and that damned ring of Mr. Owen's pressed hard into my flesh. I could feel it digging into my belly.

Perhaps Mr. Owen had been right about the ring after all.

CHAPTER TWENTY

Not Quite the End

THE next thing I recalled I was lying in a strange bed with crisp white linens beneath me and a cool breeze kissing the exposed parts of my body. I'd flung the covers off at some point in the night and was lying there in an uncomfortably stiff nightdress, staring at the ceiling like a startled starfish.

Where was I and more importantly, how did I get here?

The air was sweet with the first blush of fall as I struggled to remember *something* from the night before. I'd been upset, I recalled that much, and had spoken to the duke. After that it grew cloudy. I'd gone to find Ruan and then . . . then my memories belonged to someone else, and I was grasping for them through frost-covered glass. Well. If I couldn't figure out *how* I got here, perhaps I could figure out where exactly I was.

The ceiling overhead was painted with a bizarre nautical battle scene. Legions of sea serpents and harpies, merfolk and men at war with one another. Armies of different species painted lovingly against torrential waves tossing the bodies upon an angry tide. It was a peculiar masterpiece that put me in mind of Burghley House's Hell staircase—except this room was an ode to Poseidon.

Blood.

Water.

A tinge of a memory rose to the surface, but remained just out of reach, pulled back on that selfsame tide.

Shades of indigo and silver adorned every surface in the room with subtle—and not so subtle—nods to the sea everywhere I turned. It was beautifully disturbing. I turned to get a better look and suddenly yelped. The pain in my chest had grown sharp enough to steal my breath. I groaned, sitting up and shifted the nightgown, noticing an unfamiliar bandage there.

My heart froze as the last few hours flooded back through my consciousness.

Mr. Owen had confessed to murder.

I'd kissed Ruan.

Then the sniper's shot.

Ruan's lifeless eyes at the bottom of the lake.

Oh God, where was he?

If I was alive, then surely he must be too. I threw my legs over the edge of the bed, but they wouldn't hold my weight, and I tumbled back to the mattress with a mocking squeak. Breathing slowly, I tried again to stand, gently pulling myself to my unsteady feet.

He couldn't be dead. He *couldn't* be. And yet I saw the blood blooming in the water. He had been limp in my arms as I pulled us both onto the shore. But with that strange connection between us, wouldn't I *feel* it if he were gone?

"Miss, you're awake!"

I turned to the sound, nearly falling back onto the overstuffed mattress for a second time. A young maid stood in the doorway with a pile of clean linens clasped to her chest. She was a round-faced thing, probably no more than eighteen, if that. Small, winsome, and terribly happy to see me up and about.

A sentiment I did not share.

"Welcome to Hawick House, miss." She smiled, revealing deep dimples in each of her cheeks.

"Hawick Hou—" That's right. I'd nearly forgotten in all the excitement—but Mr. Owen *was* the Viscount of Hawick. This was *his* house.

"Yes, miss. The young master said you were to have the best room and be treated as mistress here once you awoke. He was very worried for you."

My mind remained sluggish from my recent ordeal. "Has Mr. Owen been freed yet? Is he here too?"

She didn't understand.

I grunted, raking the hand on my uninjured side through my clean, vaguely damp curls. "Lord Hawick . . . Where is he?"

"Why, he's being kept at Rivenly with the duke, miss. At least until the trial. Captain Lennox had you brought here after the two of you were found."

The two of us. I dared not hope too much at that small word. "Where's Ruan? Is he alive? Is he safe?"

She didn't answer, instead she laid her cool palm on my brow with a quiet gasp. "You're burning up, miss. Let me find Captain Lennox, he said to fetch him when you woke. He will be cross that I've waited."

A thread of suspicion gnawed at me as I suddenly recalled my conversation with Lady Amelia before I'd been shot. How he'd been following Genevieve, the youngest medium—but there was no time to worry about Andrew Lennox's perplexing motivations. Even Mr. Owen's plight had faded slightly from the forefront of my mind. My hand shot out, grabbing hers. "Where is Ruan? Why won't you answer me? Is he dead?" I was growing frantic.

"Calm yourself, miss. You've been shot. 'Tis only a miracle you survived. You need to rest, regain your strength, or else you'll make yourself sick. Everything else can wait."

Me . . . shot? That was impossible. I'd certainly know if I'd been shot and while I felt like I'd been kicked by a mule, I'd seen what bullets did to men and I certainly didn't feel like *that*.

However, like the sun breaking through storm clouds, memories of those final moments flickered back.

The silver overtaking Ruan's eyes.

The dark shadow of his body over mine.

And the odd way his hand was fixed upon my chest, near my shoulder as we sank beneath the surface. My fingers went to the bandage covering the precise place his palm had rested.

Good God what *had* happened in the lake? I stumbled toward the open door and out into the corridor with the little maid trailing after me.

"Miss! Miss, you cannot go wandering here! You must stay in bed. The captain said you could do yourself lasting harm if you got up too quickly!"

With my right hand braced against the rich wood-paneled walls, I stumbled down the hallway desperate to find Ruan, to see with my own eyes what had happened. My head swam from loss of blood and I tried to catch myself but failed.

"Miss Vaughn . . ." Captain Lennox grunted, as he wrapped an arm around my waist, dropping his cane to the ground with a loud clatter on the herringbone floors.

I sucked in a sharp breath at the force of the impact. Andrew shifted my weight, and hefted me up to standing.

". . . it seems you are awake. How does your shoulder feel?" He took my right hand and placed it against the wood paneling to help me stand on my own power, and then bent down, picking his cane up from the floor. "Uncle Owen told me you wouldn't be the most cooperative of patients. But I had no idea you'd be quite this lively."

My fingers curled against the wood, my chest tight. "Where . . . is . . . Ruan?"

He frowned. Why would no one answer me?

My dream had been right. *Again.* My voice came out little over a whisper. "Tell me he's not dead."

Andrew steered me to his uninjured side. "Your Mr. Kivell is alive at present—though I'm not quite sure how he is or how long he'll stay that way. He has not awoken. And, Ruby, I must warn you . . . he may not."

Mine. My Mr. Kivell. His words rattled around my brain. "Need to . . . I need to . . ."

"Yes, yes. That's about enough sentiment for one morning." He placed an arm back around my waist. "Give me your weight, I'll take you to him."

Putting away my pride, I allowed him to help me down the hallway in order for me to see for myself what had happened to Ruan. While I needed to get back to Manhurst to continue my search for clues, I was in no condition at present to do so—nor did I have the stomach for it if Ruan was dying down the hall.

Perhaps that was the point of shooting us in the first place.

Had I gotten too close—stumbled upon something that the killer did not want discovered? If so that was news to me, as all I had was a basket of clues that meant nothing. At this rate the killer could knock off half of Scotland before I figured out who'd killed Lucy Campbell.

We inched our way down the corridor until we reached the door on the far side. Andrew steadied me on the doorframe and paused before opening it, his hand lingering on the catch. "I must know. Though I suppose I have no right to ask considering the bad blood between he and I—What *is* he?"

"He's a Pellar." My voice cracked at the admission. It was the truth, after all, especially considering I had the sickening sensation that his inexplicable healing abilities were the reason I was alive at all.

Andrew furrowed his brow. "Uncle said the same. But I . . . I've never seen anything like it."

"Like . . . like what?"

"There is time to explain inside. Come along."

We entered the brightest room I'd ever seen. Flooded with light and clean air. Linens hung from the rafters above, blowing in the breeze like storybook ghosts. Shelving sat along one wall loaded up with stacks of bedding and clean textiles to stock the entire manor house.

Ruan lay by an open window in a makeshift hospital bed clad in a pair of gray pajamas. Ruan Kivell was maddening and frustrating and incredibly obstinate but he was the only truly *good* person I'd known in my life. And here he was, a breath away from death, looking small and fragile.

I sank down on the mattress beside him. His skin was hot beneath my touch, warmer than my own. A hint of a bandage peeked out from the collar of his shirt.

"There's nothing more I can do for him. He has to fight this last battle himself," Andrew said softly. "You did everything you could. Ruby, by all rights, neither of you should be alive right now. You, least of all."

My eyes widened as I turned to look at Andrew in the light of day. The exhaustion was all over his face, but there was another expression there. Andrew Lennox was perplexed. "What aren't you telling me?"

"It took me half the night to get the bullet from the bone. It went straight through you, burying itself into his scapula, fracturing it."

"*Through* me? That's preposterous . . ." I'd assumed when the maid said I'd been shot that I'd been grazed, but a rifle round through that part of my chest ought to have killed me.

"It *is* preposterous. I would have thought it an old wound from the war, had I not seen you after you came out of the lake with Lucy's body. You had *no scar*. It is as if the wound cauterized itself inside and out, but I do not understand how it could have happened."

My eyes stung as I looked down at Ruan's still form. My rusty heart seized up at the thought. He'd saved me—whether he knew it or not. I wanted to scream. Drag my nails down the walls until they wept from the fury that flooded my veins.

Ruan was dying.

Mr. Owen was going to prison.

And I could hardly walk down a damned hallway without collapsing.

Andrew didn't notice my distress, or was polite enough to ignore it. He fiddled with the horn handle of his crook, running his graceful fingers over its smooth head, drawing my attention there. "You were in the war, Ruby. Uncle Owen told me as much . . . In truth, he's told me a great deal about you. You are quite the remarkable woman."

His words scarcely registered as I remained mesmerized by the slow rise and fall of Ruan's chest beneath the nightshirt.

"You saw what rifles do to human flesh, there is no way that you could have carried him to the surface after being pierced by a round. Ruby . . . this is beyond all science."

"Why isn't he waking up?" I asked numbly, though the wounded beast within my mind knew the answer.

Andrew wet his lips, removing his spectacles. "The real question is why he isn't *dead* already. I am not going to mince words with you, you deserve far more than that. We will be lucky if the infection doesn't take him before the week is out. It's only the fact that your wound somehow sealed itself that you aren't in the same sorry state."

Andrew had done everything science would allow to save him and had given the rest up to . . . to fate. All that was left to do now was wait.

"You're a clever lass, you know what filthy wounds do to even the strongest of men." He reached into his pocket, withdrawing a damaged copper-jacketed bullet, the object resting heavily in his palm. "Strange how such a small object can cause such devastation."

I reached out, wrapping my fingers around the horrid chunk of metal. "Do they know who shot us? Mr. Owen was far from Manhurst by then, shouldn't that tell the inspector that he had arrested the wrong man?"

Andrew inhaled sharply and shook his head. "Inspector Burnett assures us that it was a stray bullet. A hunter . . ."

I eyed the metal skeptically. "With one dead woman already, another missing, and the inspector believes that while standing on a bridge in the middle of Manhurst grounds, we were caught by a *hunter's* round."

Andrew raised his brows in surprise. "What other woman do you mean?"

I shifted my weight on the mattress, the heat of Ruan's fevered, damp body soaking through my nightgown. "I spoke with the youngest medium. Genevieve," I began cautiously, watching for any sign of emotion to give away why he'd been following her around Manhurst. "She said there was another woman who was working with her and Lucy. That this third medium disappeared without a trace. Supposedly Lucy went all the way to Edinburgh trying to get help finding her and the authorities brushed her off . . ."

Deep ridges formed at the edges of his mouth. "Do you think that whatever happened to this missing medium has to do with Lucy's death as well?"

I gave Andrew a curt nod, gnawing on the inside of my cheek. "But what I cannot fathom is why. People do not run about murdering mediums and shooting booksellers without a reason."

"I agree, it does seem too much of a coincidence. I shall speak to the inspector about it this afternoon, but—Ruby—I don't think he cares who shot you. I've met him several times and I don't believe him a truly bad sort, but instead the lazy kind. One who wants the easiest and simplest explanation to speed him home in time for tea. The whole mysterious death of Lucy has him angry. Agitated in a way I've never seen."

I trailed a finger over the back of Ruan's hand. "He doesn't like you, you know."

"I don't blame him for it. I don't like myself very much either most of the time." Andrew sighed, watching Ruan's still form with a peculiar expression. "I was a foolish boy back then. At Oxford, I saw Kivell as a rival for my uncle's affection. This darling boy he dragged up from the mines and elevated to polite society. I'd tried so bloody hard to be the perfect son, the perfect nephew. The perfect *everything*. Always doing what I ought, never daring to place a single toe out of line and then Uncle appears one day and tells me I must look after this boy with his rough manners and his sullen disposition. I was to ease his way . . ." Andrew sighed, watching Ruan. "The man now regrets the boy then."

My fingers curled into Ruan's hair. "Do you know why Mr. Owen took such an interest in him?"

Andrew shook his head. "Uncle has always been fascinated with the occult. The *other* world as he calls it. Always seeking out the inexplicable, gathering oddities around him like curiosities to place into a cabinet."

I bristled at the description. He did *not* collect oddities. He simply was an unusual man himself. He was bound to attract people like him. Like drawn to like, as the saying goes.

"He said this Cornish boy had no inkling what he was capable of. Uncle Owen was angry with me when he learned I had a hand in Kivell leaving Oxford. I thought he might cut me off entirely."

Ruan stirred slightly beneath my fingers, or perhaps it was just my imagination.

"I had a devil of a time getting the bullet from his shoulder. As if his very bones did not want to surrender it to me. For a moment last night, I wondered if he might decide to die on my table, just to spite me. To prove that I'm not as skilled as I think I am."

I let out a startled laugh. "That sounds a bit like him."

Ruan murmured something beside me, in old Cornish, and my reckless heart leapt in my chest. I shifted quickly to look at him, heedless of the twinge from my wound. Ruan struggled to sit up.

"Don't move, Kivell. You'll only hurt yourself more," Andrew chided, the relief thick in his voice.

A thousand emotions flickered across Ruan's face as he studied the bandage visible beneath my borrowed nightdress. "What . . . what happened?"

"It seems we were shot. Andrew said the round went through me and lodged itself in you."

His eyes widened in surprise as he looked from my wound to the sling binding his arm to his chest.

You saved me. You saved us both.

But he must not have heard me. His pale green eyes frantically darted over my exposed throat and to the bandage. "Are you well?"

"Fine. I'm fine." I placed my hand tentatively over his, and felt his tension ease.

He blew out an unsteady breath, watching me as if he'd discovered some new plant in his garden and wasn't sure what to make of it.

Andrew fidgeted with an unraveling roll of bandaging. "I had you both brought to Hawick House after the dark-haired medium found you at the lakeside. It seemed far easier to keep an eye on you both here than at Manhurst."

The muscle at the edge of Ruan's jaw tensed. "This is Hawick House . . ."

Andrew nodded. "My uncle said you'd be more comfortable

here than in one of the guest rooms. Miss Vaughn is staying up-stairs in his private suite."

Ruan's nostrils flared. "Did he? Or *did you* want to be sure I remembered my place?"

This is not the time. I laid a hand on Ruan's chest. "Andrew, could you give us a few moments—"

"Of course. Ring if you need anything. Bridget is to keep an eye on you." He pointed to the bell affixed to the wall. "For what it's worth, Kivell, I am glad you shall live to plague me another day, and I couldn't give a damn where you were in my house. We simply thought you might die more comfortably within eyeshot of the kitchen garden."

Ruan let out an indecipherable grunt, watching as Andrew slowly left the room. Once the door shut he collapsed back against the bed frame with a groan. "Gods, Ruby . . . is it true?" Ruan reached with his uninjured arm, touching the strap of my nightgown and tracing the edge of my bandage with his forefin-ger. "May I?"

"Of course . . ."

He slipped the thin fabric strap over my shoulder, seeking the start of the binding. Despite the fact he'd been unconscious mere minutes before, he'd mustered enough strength to peel away the cloth to see what he'd done to me.

As the last of the bandage came off he drew in a sharp breath. "How . . . ?"

Fear gnawed at my belly, not wanting to see how bad it truly was. For Ruan to be surprised it must be worse than I'd imagined. And while I didn't mind tending to others' wounds, seeing my own injuries made me squirm. I looked down, half expecting to see a bloody and raw hole, but instead there was a brand-new scar on my chest—deep and pink, slightly above my breast and below my clavicle. A wound that by all rights ought to have killed me straightaway.

Ruan's hand trembled as he touched the new skin with his roughened fingers. The fresh scar tissue ached at his touch, but no more than pressing a nasty bruise.

"Turn around."

It was a command, not a request, and I shifted on the bed at once, allowing him to see my back, pulling my bare feet under my bottom.

"Gods . . . what did I do?"

"Saved my life . . . evidently." I let out a breathy laugh, turning back around and took the bandages from his hands, working to reaffix them to myself. "I suppose I ought to thank you for it—it's a nasty habit you've gotten into, saving my skin—but you really should have taken a bit more care for yourself."

"You do that often, don't you?" The edge of his mouth turned up slightly.

"Do what?"

"Use humor to hide when someone gets too near to the quick."

I bristled. "I absolutely do not."

"You absolutely do. But you cannot hide from me, Ruby Vaughn." He smiled again, and my irritation fled.

I sighed, slipping the strap of my nightgown back up my shoulder. "I am fine, Ruan. Truly. But you almost died. For a moment I thought you actually *were* dead and I—" The words would not come.

He stared at me for several seconds, brows furrowed.

"What is it?"

"Nothing. I just—" His expression shifted. "I must be weaker than I thought."

I scooted back, putting a bit of distance between us before I made a fool of myself. "Sleep. Get stronger. I intend to go back to the castle later this afternoon and see what has happened while we've been gone. I also mean to get those negatives from my room before someone else finds them."

Ruan's fingers went to his throat, where the chain still held the ring. He struggled one-handed with the clasp before giving up. "Take it with you. Protect it. At least until I'm stronger."

"Of course." I clumsily removed the silver chain from his throat before affixing it to my own. The enameled ring remained warm from his overheated body and I tucked it inside my nightdress.

"Do you trust him?" I tilted my head to the door from which Andrew had withdrawn. He hadn't given me any reason to doubt him, aside from the fact Lady Amelia told me he'd been following Genevieve Demidov. Certainly, if he meant us ill, he wouldn't have gone to the extraordinary effort of keeping us both alive.

"I don't know." He rubbed his beard with the back of his hand. "Please be careful. The killer has already proved that they don't mind shooting us to keep their secrets."

Yes, well. That was a problem. I tugged the ring out again, turning it over in my palm. The intricate enamel glinted in the sun. "Do you suppose we'll ever find out what this means? Or if it means anything at all?"

Ruan's hand covered mine, ceasing my fidgeting. "It must since someone took a shot at us. But are we going to talk about what happened on the bridge?"

"We did discuss it—we were shot and you did your best Saint Ruan of Kivell impression and patched me right back up," I teased, pointing to my freshly scarred chest, but he did not smile.

"No. The other part. What happened *before* that." His eyes held mine, the intimacy too much to bear. Heat rose to my cheeks at the memory of his kiss.

We absolutely would not. I cleared my throat to erase those memories. No. That kiss was a mistake that should not be repeated. It was dangerous to get too close to Ruan Kivell. A girl could lose her head. Or worse—her heart. "What's there to talk about besides who would want to kill us?"

He took my hand, pulling it to rest over his heart, which beat steady and slow beneath my palm. "You don't have to pretend. Not with me." The tenderness in his voice broke something deep inside me. Oh, what I wouldn't give for that to be true. A better woman might have stayed there with him, carried this conversation down the path that it was destined to go. But I was not that woman, and instead I made some half-hearted excuse about why I had to go, and headed for the door.

CHAPTER TWENTY-ONE

A Curious Discovery

THERE'S always been something about sitting in a kitchen that soothed my mind—hiding deep in the belly of the home, safely away from the outside world and all the problems that came with it. As a girl, I scarcely left our family's kitchen. Always underfoot, swiping something sweet from the larder, or simply watching our cook Mrs. Carty prepare for supper. But for some reason, here at Hawick House, with all the bustling and preparation going on around me, my mind remained fixed upon the memory of my mother's simple picnic hampers. Every Saturday and Sunday for as long as I can recall, Mother would send the staff away, and the house would grow still and quiet. She would wake me up before dawn, and we'd steal away into the kitchen, filling a basket to the brim with whatever struck her fancy, and the two of us would set out—spending those precious hours together on the small catamaran Father had bought her. When we were in the city, we'd sneak out onto the Atlantic for a handful of days, but in summer Mother and I would escape for weeks on end and sail the Great Lakes. I hadn't thought about those precious days with her in years.

But kitchen notwithstanding, there would be no comfort for

me until I found out who truly killed the two mediums—for I feared that Genevieve was right and that the missing woman was just as dead as poor Lucy Campbell.

I toyed with the chain around my neck, my finger loosely hooked in the ring.

"Something the matter with your soup, miss?" Bridget asked with a cheery smile looking down at my long-forgotten bowl of vegetable stew that had grown cold before me. The young maid had been hovering ever since I left Ruan's bedside. She'd stay and fuss over me for a few minutes before going off to complete another chore, only to return and repeat the same cycle again and again. This was the fourth or fifth time we'd been through this particular routine and it was growing downright suspicious.

"When did you say Captain Lennox would be returning? I need to borrow his driver."

She paled and shook her head. "I do not know, miss. The young master is a private man. He said he would return this evening, that's all I know."

"Did he take his automobile?" I arched a brow. "I'm certain he wouldn't mind my borrowing it." I actually *wasn't* certain, but she didn't need to know that.

"No, miss. Captain Lennox said that you were not to leave without his permission. I cannot let you go." The rapid flutter of her pulse was visible beneath the thin skin at her throat.

"Bridget . . ." I began, pinning her with my stare. "Where is he?"

Her jaw worked and she shook her head, glancing behind me to the cook who offered her no aid. "I told you before, I do not know. He does not tell me such things. It's not my place to know any more than I am told."

She was lying. I could tell by the way she twisted her fingers into her white apron. The way she subconsciously placed her body between me and the servants' stair at the opposite end of the room.

What was Andrew Lennox hiding? I rose, inadvertently knocking the spoon from my bowl and splattering the cold stew all over the tabletop. I grabbed a nearby cloth and hastily mopped it up.

"Miss, where are you going? You must stay calm and rest. The young master said that you must rest yourself."

"Am I your guest here or am I not?"

"No, miss. No. I mean yes you *are* a guest, but you were shot, that is, but . . . it's only—"

"It's only what?" I folded my arms beneath my breasts. I knew I was intimidating her and I didn't mean to—at least not wholly—but the young maid's caginess about Andrew's whereabouts was making me increasingly concerned that she was hiding something. The only question was what that *thing* was?

"He said I was to keep an eye on you," the girl said at last in exasperation. Her cheeks flushed.

"Am I in need of a keeper?" *Well, considering the fixes I found myself in, probably so . . .*

She shook her head again, face beet red. An iota of guilt rankled. The poor girl was simply following orders, but I couldn't see why would it matter where I went as long as I had someone accompanying me. At last, I decided to spare the maid any more discomfort and took a different tack, one taken from the pages of Mr. Owen's very own book: I would lie.

"I believe I shall take a walk in the garden. Assuming *walking* is acceptable to Captain Lennox?"

She worried her pink lower lip before nodding. "In the garden . . ." she repeated. "I suppose there's no harm in that. I'll fetch you a shawl, miss. You wait right here and I'll accompany you."

I waited until Bridget disappeared down another corridor. Once her footsteps grew quiet, I darted up the servants' stair in search of Andrew, determined to find out for myself what the girl was hiding.

IT ONLY TOOK a handful of minutes to locate his room. The door, of course, had been unlocked, which was his error—not mine. If the man didn't want interruptions he should employ locks. Not that locks deterred me either, but as my picks were back at Manhurst they would have given me pause in *this* instance. However, immediately upon entering the shadowy room, I recognized my grievous mistake.

I had misread the clues *entirely.*

Andrew Lennox was asleep, his expression peaceful in the muted light breaking through the parted curtains. The exhausted lines on his face smoothed in his dreams, making him look far younger than his years. I looked over to his partner, whose stubbled cheek rested against Andrew's bare chest.

It was an intensely domestic scene: two lovers partaking of a midafternoon nap and my own treacherous heart ached with jealousy. Not over Andrew—goodness, no—but of his ability to find a moment of peace when the world had gone utterly mad around us. Oh, what I would give for one second without the voices in my head, the increasing nightmares or my worsening headaches. One damned second without remembering that everyone I ever cared for had either left of their own accord or been taken from me.

I started for the door, furious at myself.

Andrew opened his eyes and his entire body tensed.

That brief moment of peace melted away into anger. A righteous rage as I'd intruded on his privacy and witnessed something we both knew was illegal.

He mouthed the words, "Get out."

I obeyed without argument, silently shutting the door behind me. I waited for several seconds in the hall, watching as Bridget came barreling up the stairs, a gray woolen shawl clutched in her hands. She made a sound of horror in the back of her throat. "Miss! Miss! You must come away!"

The girl had been protecting Andrew all along and I felt wretched for the way I'd treated her downstairs.

I opened my mouth to say the same when the door opened again and Andrew stepped out, tying a saffron-colored dressing gown tight around his waist. "It's all right, Bridget, you may leave us."

She murmured something beneath her breath before bobbing and scurrying off.

As she disappeared his expression hardened. "You, on the other hand—"

"—I see Mr. Owen's extravagant taste in dressing gowns runs in the family."

"Amongst other things," he grumbled. "Did no one teach you to knock in your American finishing schools?"

"I never went to finishing school."

Andrew muttered beneath his breath, then let out a weary sigh. "May I ask what was important enough for you to intrude upon my privacy when I specifically gave instructions to be left alone for the afternoon?"

His tone sounded precisely like Mr. Owen's when he'd noticed I'd misshelved his Romantic poets.

Andrew rubbed his jaw. "I presume you know enough to hold your tongue about what you saw in there."

"Of course, I do. I'm not a fool." My chest ached and I reached up absently, rubbing at the tender scar. "I don't even know why the government *cares* what happens willingly behind closed doors between adults. One would think with everything going on in the world that they would have better things to do with *their* time than worrying about what we do with *ours*."

Andrew arched a brow. "Pretty words without action, Miss Vaughn."

I bristled, but deserved his ire. "Be that as it may—in my experience, one cannot control whom one loves. Trying to do so would be like changing the tide or making the sun rise in the west—a pointless endeavor at best."

The edge of his mouth twitched slightly as he leaned back against the dark wood paneling. "My father does not hold such modern opinions. I think he'd prefer to be well shut of me if I weren't the heir. Unfortunately for him, he's quite thoroughly stuck with me." Andrew's face took on a wistful expression as he stared into the empty hall behind me. "Uncle Owen understood though. I think sometimes that's another reason Father despises him so. He thinks that Uncle had some hand in the fact I prefer the company of men to women. An absurd notion as I scarcely even knew Owen until I was at Oxford, and by then I'd already had my first lover and was plenty old enough to know my own mind."

"Your father knows about him?" I tilted my head to the shut door.

"I'd not meant for him to learn of it, but yes. Father begrudgingly accepts the fact I will not give him up. Though I think he does eventually hope I'll do what Uncle Owen did." Andrew's accent broadened dramatically as he did a terribly good impression of his father's speech. "'Why don't you go on and marry a bonny lass, boy? Surely you can get at least *one* bairn on her before you go back to your way of sin.'" He gave me a sad small smile and shrugged. "But alas, poor Andrew. See that's the difference between my uncle and me. I cannot bring myself to live a lie. I won't do it."

A shiver ran up my spine. "What exactly do you mean, *do what Uncle did*?"

"Come now, Miss Vaughn. Surely you know some of his past. How can you not? What has he told you?"

"Little," I admitted with a frown. "I know he's Hawick and

that Mariah had been engaged to your father before Mr. Owen married her and that's why the two of them don't get along."

Andrew cocked his head in acknowledgement. "That was certainly *part* of their bad blood, but not all of it. From what I understand Uncle Owen and my father were nothing alike. My father's always been a religious man. Strict and hard like his mother. Uncle Owen . . ." Andrew sighed. "He loved books and art and the unknown. He had a healthy disregard for rules of polite society, even when he ought to have been a bit more careful in his dealings."

"I don't understand what you're trying to tell me . . ."

"Only that my uncle was one of the greatest rakes in British history. His list of lovers as a young man was legendary, and put even Lord Byron to shame. It's a wonder he settled down at all to marry Mariah. But after she disappeared—the way they tell it—he nearly drowned himself in liquor, leaving a trail of devastation a mile wide before he finally disappeared, only to reappear a few years later with a proper second wife. Father was angry with him before, but after that . . . he forbade Owen from setting foot in Hawick House ever again. I don't think he's ever forgiven Uncle for moving on with his own life after Mariah died. Father saw it as an insult to her memory. It's mad, I know—but my father has never been a reasonable man."

"I need to speak to him."

"My father? Why on earth would you want to talk to him? The man is an utter nightmare."

I let out a laugh. "Well. Yes, I probably ought to speak with him too—but I meant Mr. Owen. I need to get to Rivenly. I have some questions for him that I'd meant to ask before he confessed to killing Lucy."

"Are you still seeking out the killer?"

"I cannot let Mr. Owen suffer for something we both know he didn't do."

Andrew hesitated, but thought better of whatever he was about to say. "Hugh, my driver, can take you as far as the ferry to the Isle of May then bring you back here straightaway. I'll try to keep Kivell from killing me before you return."

A smile tugged at my lips. "That would be splendid, but Andrew, I have one more question. And I need you to be completely honest with me."

"Of course, Miss Vaughn." He mirrored my position, folding his arms across his chest.

"Why were you following Genevieve? I don't believe you wish Mr. Owen harm. I don't believe you wish *me* harm. But there is one—possibly two—dead mediums now and you were seen in the third's room. I need you to tell me why."

Andrew shifted where he stood. "For the same reason as you. I love my uncle—and I am determined to find out who means him harm."

"And what would you do if you found them?" I asked.

He cleared his throat and straightened. "Let me have Hugh bring the car around. You should make haste to Rivenly, it'll take most of a day to get there and back."

And as I watched Andrew walk away, I began to wonder what I might do if I found the person who meant Mr. Owen harm. He wasn't my blood, but he was family all the same. Mr. Owen, Ruan, Mrs. Penrose, even the dreadful cat. They were mine, and I had learned one fundamental truth about myself in the last few years—I would allow no one to harm what was mine.

CHAPTER TWENTY-TWO

Rivenly

HOURS later, in fresh clothes and once again in possession of the stolen negatives, I finally reached the Isle of May. It was just before dawn, having taken several hours to traverse the country roads from Edinburgh to Anstruther where I was able to catch a ferry across the Firth of Forth. A maelstrom of seabirds cried out overhead, swooping down around the little flat-bottomed boat as we approached the great stone cliffs of the Isle of May rising from the swirling waters.

The sun crept over the horizon, illuminating the lighthouse with morning sun. The damp sea air whipped around me from the west, pulling my hair from my scarf as I paid the ferryman at the dock and tipped him extra to await my return. It wouldn't take long. No matter how desperately I needed to speak with Mr. Owen, I also needed to get back to Manhurst before anything else went wrong.

THE YOUNG BUTLER led me through the elegant center hall into the library where Mr. Owen was waiting. It was dreadfully early, but he often had trouble sleeping even at home in Exeter. I'd not expected how much it would hurt to see him taking his morning tea, now that the weight of what he had done finally settled into my mind.

"You should not be here." He frowned, setting the delicate china cup into the saucer on the table beside him.

"I shouldn't do a lot of things," I grumbled, closing the library door and walking over to him. The air in here was crisp with a hint of citrus. "Mr. Owen, what were you thinking?"

He inhaled slowly and let it out again. "I could not allow it to happen again. It was the only thing I could do to keep you safe."

I leaned forward, touching his brow with the back of my hand. He felt fine. "But you didn't kill her, now it's twice as bad. Not only do I have to figure out who did kill her, but also prove *you* didn't."

With his forefinger, he gestured for me to take the seat across from him. I did, wincing as the movement jostled my injury.

His eyes widened. "Andrew said you were not injured. He said it was only Kivell that was shot."

"No, I'm fine, just grazed," I lied, grateful that Andrew had spared Mr. Owen the details of the extent of my injury.

"And how are you being treated at Hawick House? I trust that my staff there is allowing you all the freedoms you'd have at home?"

Strange. This was the first we'd spoken of it since he told me who he was. Who he *truly* was. We'd left things unsatisfactorily that evening, with me walking away from him after he'd given me his truth. I owed him something—and while I wasn't sorry for being upset, I regretted hurting him in the process.

"What . . . what should I call you?" It wasn't elegant, but it was a start to a conversation that we should have had a long time ago.

"Owen is fine. It is my name after all."

"Is it?" The words might have been bitter if said with any force, but there was none there.

"Owen Alexander Lennox. That was my name, but I put it away—put all of it away after Mariah disappeared."

I reached out, covering his hand with my own. "What happened to her? You told me a little of it but I still don't understand entirely—I am convinced there is a connection between her death and Lucy's. There almost has to be."

Mr. Owen slumped back into the chair and looked at the ceiling. "The truth of it is that I do not know. Sometimes I've wondered if I killed her myself, like they all say."

"That's absurd, you wouldn't kill anyone!"

Mr. Owen arched a white brow at me. "But I don't remember. I don't know I *didn't*. Who is to say what truly happened the night she disappeared?" He let out a strangled laugh. "I love her still. Isn't it strange how that is? More than forty years have passed since last I saw her face and I still recall the exact shade of her hair, the scent of her warm skin, the sound of her laughter in the parlor on a rainy day. And it kills me that I still do not know what happened to her. For nearly half my life that same question has dogged my every step. I have my suspicions, but in order to know what happened that night you must know something about Mariah first—she was *extraordinary*. Cleverer than anyone I'd ever met."

"You told me about that night at the ball and how she showed you her photography book."

He smiled faintly, growing lost in his own memories. "There was strange symmetry to our love affair, I suppose. I'd only just returned from London the night she disappeared. Mariah was not herself that evening. I likely told you this already, but we'd been unable to have a child and she'd wanted one desperately. It didn't matter to me—and I told her as much—she was all I ever wanted and goodness knew I didn't need an heir when I had my brother Malachi to carry on the Lennox name. He was a far better steward of the estates than I. But Mariah had fallen down this rabbit hole, fascinated by the spirit world. Convinced that perhaps the answer to our worldly problems could be found in the *other* world. That somehow she would find something to help her to conceive our child."

"Is that how you became interested in the occult?"

Mr. Owen nodded.

"I take it things are about to take a tragic turn?"

He squeezed my hand. "I'd been in London for weeks. Mariah hadn't been feeling well and asked to stay behind in Scotland until she'd recovered. I'd hoped that perhaps the reason for her illness was that she was with child, not for my own hopes but hers. She felt things keenly. The judgment from peers, the expectant looks every time she appeared in society without a thickening waist. I didn't give a damn what the world thought of me—but I cared about Mariah. She wanted that child and I wanted it for her sake. I'd have done anything, Ruby. Anything for that woman."

It ached to see how similar we were.

He sighed, finishing off his tea, and rubbed his hands over his bristly white beard. "I'd only returned home because she'd written this curious note that said we had important matters to discuss. Mariah would have told me at once had she been with child—but a small part of me hoped that she simply could not find the words after hoping for so many years. I'd been home at Hawick House twenty minutes at most when Mariah asked me to join her at her sister's séance that very evening. She said there was something at the castle she needed to show me, something important and she knew I would be angry when I saw it—"

"Angry? What would you be angry about?"

He lifted a shoulder.

"You didn't go . . ." I whispered.

His voice cracked. "I told her I was tired, that she should go and I'd come fetch her in the morning and we could discuss whatever it was she wanted to then." His brows raised at the memory.

"I daresay she didn't like that. She flew into a rage like I'd never seen her."

"And then what?"

His expression flickered and he shook his head. "The next morning she was gone." He snapped his fingers. "As if she'd never existed at all. There was blood on the bridge. At first—" His voice broke as he swallowed down a sob. "At first we thought she'd been set upon by—"

I laid my hand over his own, stomach knotted. "And they never found her body, did they?"

"Never. Malachi dredged the lake, but there was nothing there. For a while I held on to hope that she had left me—it would have served me right for failing her as I did. She asked one single thing, and I did not listen. I searched for years before finally giving up. People . . . people began to whisper that I'd killed her. My reputation being as it was—" He gave me a queer look. "I assume Andrew informed you about all that."

I gave him a slight nod. "He might have mentioned it."

"They concocted all sorts of fantastical tales of the wicked things I'd done. One more lurid than the last. The morning she left I tore the house apart looking for her. Went to her rooms and they were perfectly ordered. All the things precisely where she'd left them, and that was when I noticed that sometime in the night she must have slipped her ring on my finger. It was there, on my left hand."

My mouth snapped shut. "The ring you had Ruan bring back?"

"She never took it off. She had to have wanted me to have it. I thought at the time it was a token of her love, a promise she would return, but what if it was not? What if there was a message in it, one I failed to heed?"

I rested my hand atop his on the table and he covered mine with his other.

"Now enough of that. Tell me how the lad is. I hear he was

shot too," Mr. Owen said, shutting the door on that conversation and locking it tight.

Ruan.

My face must have betrayed me, as he gave my hand yet another squeeze. "He'll mend. Don't worry on that. It's keeping *you* safe that matters to me. I'm an old man who has lived and loved more than one could ever dream." He cleared his throat with a crooked smile. "Besides, they haven't hung a peer since the fourth Earl Ferrers. You need not concern yourself for *my* neck. And now yours is perfectly safe too."

I rolled my eyes. Only Mr. Owen would shun his title, then rely upon it when it suited him. Perhaps it was the fact that I'd been shot two days before, or the fact that I was not a proper detective, but suddenly Mr. Owen's words took on a new meaning. What if Mariah *had* left him the ring as a message? What if she was trying to tell him something then, and again at the séance? My blood chilled in my veins.

"Mr. Owen . . . the spirit said she left you the key . . . could the ring be the key her spirit mentioned?" I whispered half to myself.

He stared at me, open-mouthed. "What sort of medicine is Andy giving you? A ring is not a key, lass. It is a ring."

I held up a finger, reaching into the pocket of my borrowed coat and withdrew the negatives I'd stolen. "I found these in Lucy's room after she was killed. I'm fairly certain that the killer was also looking for them. I can't help but think that these images . . . they somehow hold the answer to why Lucy was murdered."

Mr. Owen leaned forward, looking at the negatives I'd spread on the table before him.

"Do they mean anything to you?"

Mr. Owen's mouth curved into a slight O as he studied the photographs. A thousand memories flickered across his face as he went from one to the next.

"You know what they are, don't you?"

He tilted his head toward the closed door behind me that led back to the public areas of the house. "Lock it, lass, if you would. It wouldn't do for the servants to overhear what I'm about to say."

I quickly turned the key in the lock and returned to my seat.

"I don't know what to think." He did not look up from the negatives in his fingers. "No wonder they shot you, lass. I suspect they'll try again when they realize they didn't manage the thing the first time."

An unpleasant thought. "What is it, what is going on in them? Is this some sort of . . . ritual? Ruan and I couldn't quite agree."

"Of a sort, yes. I'd been to their gatherings a time or two with Mariah, but I didn't approve of how they carried on."

I blinked, not understanding, but his focus went unerringly back to the images between us.

"It's Eurydice's Fall."

"Eurydice's what?"

He waved his hand airily over the negatives. "Eurydice's Fall. It was a gentlemen's club."

When Mr. Owen got this tone, things were starting to get very interesting. I leaned forward in my chair. "Were you a member?"

He looked affronted at the thought. "Heavens, no. While I was more open in sexual matters than other gentleman of my age, I wasn't content with the tenets upon which the club operated."

I let out a startled laugh. "Too avant-garde for you? Truly Mr. Owen, what exactly went on at Eurydice's something-or-other, if it was too wild for you?"

"Fall . . ." he murmured, studying the negatives. "And it wasn't wild, in many ways it was terribly restrained. You see, the club was founded upon a philosophy that sexuality was something one should be able to explore, regardless of marriage—regardless of status. Intellectually, I understood the underpinnings—agreed with them, even. After all, the sexual act itself is natural and when everyone understands and agrees to the rules I see no issue with the whos or wheres or whats of things. However, some of the most influential and staid men in Parliament were members of the club. They toiled tirelessly, passing laws to prohibit the very same behaviors they committed in private. Punishing those who did not have the means or will to live such a duplicitous life. I could not stomach hypocrisy. I didn't need their permission to live as I pleased, and they well knew it."

I could see why Captain Lennox admired him so. Mr. Owen lived bravely and honestly, in a time and world when that was not allowed. But not even he, with his title and privilege, could manage it unscathed. The rumors surrounding Mariah's disappearance were a testament to that. But there was something else—something in Mr. Owen's voice that gave me pause.

He tapped one of the masked figures. "I've been many things in my years, Ruby—a liar, a rake, and a roué—but I have never been a hypocrite." He paused, his expression shifting as he held a negative up, catching the morning light. He slid his glasses higher up his nose and tilted his head back, inspecting it in detail. "This though . . . I know who took these photographs." Mr. Owen squinted, his thoughts tens of years in the past, lost in a sea of his own memories. "Mariah always had a way with her art. She was captivated by doorways." A sad little laugh escaped his lips as he pointed to the staging of the image in his hand. This was the same one I'd been stunned by in Lucy's room—the participants posed with their backs to the camera. The image drew the viewer's eye past the figures in motion, to the darkened doorway beyond, pulling one's attention to the unseen and ephemeral. This was . . . art. Categorically so.

His expression grew wistful as he laid it down on the tabletop and wiped at his eyes with the back of his hand. "Would you mind if I kept this one?"

"May as well, it's likely safer here than at Manhurst."

"This is Mariah's work. I'd stake my life on it."

"Was she a member of the club?" I asked hesitantly, not wanting to reopen old wounds.

"Goodness, no. She found social organizations as tedious as I did—but she was curious about the club. It was the secretive nature of it that intrigued her. She always liked a puzzle. You are like her, Ruby." He touched my cheek softly with the back of his hand.

"What else do you know about this Eurydice enthusiast club?" I asked, desperate to change the subject back to firmer ground.

"Nothing useful. I haven't been openly in polite society since Mariah died. All the members I'd once known are likely long dead." He sighed heavily. "I'm afraid I'm next to useless, my love." He paused before turning quickly to me. "Wait . . . Lady Morton . . . she was at Manhurst, was she not?"

I gathered up the negatives, scooping them into a pile, and wrapped them back into a cloth. "Yes. She and her daughter, Lady Amelia. Why?"

"Her husband. He was one of them. An Eurydicean. Dead some ten years now, but he was a member of the club. Horrible man. Particularly fond of younger women. There were many a housemaid forced to leave their house quietly. He knew my opinions about his private dealings. Bloody git. I was glad when I heard he choked to death at supper."

I wrinkled my nose. "I can't say I disagree, but that must have been a terrible sight for poor Lady Amelia."

Mr. Owen made a sound of displeasure. "What is his wife doing at Manhurst? That is peculiar, indeed."

I nodded, thinking back to my conversation with Lady Amelia. "I think she was brought to Manhurst as we were. The daughter, Lady Amelia, was intent on talking to me earlier."

Mr. Owen leaned forward in his chair. I hadn't seen him this animated in weeks. "How very curious."

"It really is. She said her mother had been all set to go to a hunting party, but she received a letter and did a complete about-face. They arrived at Manhurst practically the next day. Sound familiar?"

His warm brown eyes lit up. "That it does. I take it you inquired about the whereabouts of the letter already?"

"Burnt. But I can see what else I can find out. Do you think Lady Morton might have something to do with what happened to Lucy?"

Mr. Owen furrowed his brow and exhaled loudly. "It does seem that way if the Eurydiceans are involved."

I bit the corner of my lip in thought. "If we assume Mariah left the ring for you when she disappeared." I held up one finger. "And that the photographs are hers." Another finger. "*And* we assume that the spirit truly was Mariah."

He raised his brows as I raised the third. "You believe in ghosts now, child?"

"Ghosts are irrelevant. We are *hypothesizing*."

His mouth curved up into an indulgent smile. "That's my lass. Hypothesize away."

"*If* we assume all that to be true. And we allow for the fact that Mariah was at Manhurst the night she died . . . that tells me that whatever Mariah wanted you to know—and whatever the mediums were after—must still be at Manhurst. Does it not?"

Mr. Owen paused, his fingers drumming on the table. "If that's the case, then you'd best return and find what secrets that ring holds before anyone else gets hurt."

My sentiments exactly.

CHAPTER TWENTY-THREE

An Unrepayable Debt

"I wanted to thank you before I left." My fingers rested lightly on the doorframe to the duke's private study as the light from the open window cast cheerful diamonds on the rug. "For what you did for him."

The duke looked up from his ledger with a start. His shirt-sleeves were rolled up, giving him the rumpled appearance of a schoolboy. Deep lines on his forehead were etched from concentrating on his work. "It's nothing, Miss Vaughn. Truly. For all Hawick has done for me over the years. I simply could not bear the thought—" He pinched the bridge of his nose, his golden brows lifted. "I owe him an unrepayable debt, and protecting him in this way is the very least I could do to even the sum."

I smiled at that. "It is appreciated, Your Grace. While Mr. Owen is convinced they won't hang him, I am . . . less sanguine about matters. I'm grateful for you giving him refuge here. The idea of him in a jail cell is unthinkable."

He twisted his pen in his fingers. The enamel casing caught the light. "I cannot fathom why he would confess to a murder he did not commit. I've not known a man *less* likely to commit murder than he." The duke's puzzled expression would have been comical were the situation not dire.

"You truly cannot understand why he would confess?" I arched a brow, stepping into the well-lit room.

A sad smile tugged at the corner of his wide mouth. "Ah . . . *love*. Yes, well. Hawick has always been driven by his heart. Far fuller of the stuff than he ought to be. It is his greatest strength and now looks to be his greatest weakness."

It was the truth, no matter how much I wanted to deny it. Mr. Owen loved me and this was his misguided way of showing it. I cleared my throat, drawing closer to the duke's desk. "He spoke of something called Eurydice's Fall. Have you heard of it?"

The duke removed his wire-rimmed glasses, setting them neatly on the ledger before him. "What was Hawick *thinking*, even bringing up such a club to you? Its doings are not fit for your ears, that's for certain. A wicked club, full of wicked and dangerous men."

I disguised my amusement at the thought. For the life of me, I couldn't recall the last time someone showed an ounce of concern for my delicate feminine sensibilities. "I think he knows I'm a grown woman, Your Grace." I wet my lips. "You said it was full of wicked men, do you know of any those men?"

"I doubt the members themselves know who else belongs to the group. The wise give them wide berth and do not ask questions, for good reason. But I *can* tell you that at one time, some of the most powerful men in Britain were members." His expression clouded and his mouth grew into a thin line. "He doesn't think the Eurydiceans have something to do with Lucy's death, does he? That would be very worrisome if so. Those men, Ruby. Those men are not to be trifled with."

I worried my lip. "I'm not certain. But I aim to find out."

The duke stood, laying his palms on the table. "Miss Vaughn, please be careful in this venture. These men—if it *is* the Eurydiceans behind this—they do not take kindly to interference in their dealings."

"They do not frighten me, Your Grace."

He inhaled sharply, his eyes not leaving mine. "Perhaps they should."

I took a step deeper into his sanctuary. "Do they frighten you?"

He scoffed and returned his gaze to his books. "I'm a duke, Miss Vaughn."

"Dukes are men too, last I checked."

He inclined his brow in acknowledgement. "Yes, we are. But you will keep my secret, won't you?" There was a rawness there, a phrase meant to be flippant—but instead tipped his hand. He *was* afraid of what these Eurydiceans were capable of doing—even to a duke. Well, if they were involved, then it would certainly answer who took the potshot at Ruan and me the other day. Mariah's images, though old, must be a threat.

"Will you take care of him? At least until I can get to the bottom of what is going on at Manhurst."

The duke's expression softened. "Of course. But I must urge caution in this, Miss Vaughn. If Hawick was willing to offer up his neck for yours, you would be wise to accept that gift and not risk yourself again."

My nails dug into my palm. "I cannot let him suffer. Not when I know he's innocent. Mr. Owen is dear to me, and if he was willing to offer up his security to protect me—it is only fair if I try to do the same."

The duke nodded gravely. "And I shall protect Hawick with my life if it comes to that. After all, I owe him far more than I can ever repay."

I harbored the same feeling toward Mr. Owen. He'd saved me in those bleak months after the war—when I showed up in Exeter reeling from the loss of my family, brokenhearted by Tamsyn's betrayal, plagued by what I'd seen and done during the war. All of it together had created a soul-deep wound that had only now begun to mend. I owed Mr. Owen a great deal—more than I could ever repay—but I would try.

CHAPTER TWENTY-FOUR

Forti Nihil Difficile

FOR as bright as it had been on the Isle of May this morning, by the time I returned to Hawick House a thick fog had settled upon the mainland, shrouding the house from view. Hugh, the Lennoxes' driver, had grown slower and slower with each mile back to the estate. It was a wonder he could even see the road before us. I shifted in the seat, unable to calm my body, nerves increasing to near crescendo. Thoughts of a shadowy group of powerful men plagued me. Could it be as simple as Mariah threatening to expose the Eurydiceans' hypocrisy? No. There had to be more to it—powerful men were exposed for bad behavior all the time and always walked away unscathed. Unless she'd *seen* something . . . witnessed something truly terrible and had proof of it. Now *that* would be reason for them to harm her.

I blew out a breath, reaching for my locket, and found the chain horribly tangled with the one that bore Mariah's ring. I'd nearly forgotten that I'd placed it around my own throat before leaving Hawick House. I unfastened them both, making quick work of the knotted chains and replaced the locket around my neck.

Could the ring be the key? I examined the enamel band in the dull afternoon light and flicked open the hinge, revealing the intricately braided hair. Tilting it into the dim light, my pulse began to speed up. There was something inscribed there beneath the small braid. I could only make out the ghost of a shape, but I could have sworn there was something obscured by the hair.

"Hugh . . ." I squinted at it. "Do you have a light—a torch or something?"

"Aye, miss." He rummaged around in a haversack of tools in the front floorboards beside him, stashed for the occasional roadside repair that inevitably occurred, before handing a flashlight over his shoulder to me.

I flicked it on, shining the light on the small plait. Yes. I could make it out clearly, an edge of a letter just beneath the hair. Now that was intriguing, indeed. I snapped the ring shut. "Thank you, Hugh."

"Did you find what you were looking for back there?" he asked, not taking his eyes from the misty road before him.

"I rather think I have."

I RAN THROUGH Hawick House, past the disapproving butler and the curious underbutler. Past young Bridget, with her basket of soiled linens and straight into Ruan's sickroom where I found him sitting upright in bed. He was reading with a book propped against his knee—right arm bound to his chest. His color was vastly better than it had been when last I saw him and my heart squeezed at the sight.

Now's not the time for sentiment, Ruby.

I hurried over to the bed and climbed in beside him, fully intending to tell him all about what I'd discovered. The mattress gave a perturbed squeak at the addition of my weight. He shifted over to make more room for me and winced. Suddenly my reckless heart remembered just how close I'd come to losing him.

"You know this is rather novel. . . ." I said, mustering a carelessness that I did not feel.

He closed his book, thumb marking his page.

I could not bring myself to look at him—too afraid he'd see how deep my growing sentiment for him ran. "Last time we were chasing a murderer, it was me who kept trying to die. This time, it's you!"

"I'm pleased that I can amuse you from my sickbed." He tilted his chin toward my pocket. "What do you have there?"

I glanced down to where my hand was unconsciously covering the ring. Usually Ruan and I didn't need to speak so plainly. His peculiar ability to hear my thoughts made our working together easy. Whatever was giving him trouble at Manhurst must still be causing him difficulties.

I reached in my pocket, pulling out the ring and sidled closer to his left side, mindful of his bandages. "See here?" I pointed to the edge of the etching.

Ruan made a sound in the back of his throat, taking the ring and holding it up to the light. "There *is* something beneath the hair."

"Do you happen to have a penknife?"

"I'm a witch, not a barrister, in case you've forgotten."

I hadn't. But he must be feeling better if he's grousing again. I folded his fingers around the ring and patted his fist. "Wait here. I'll be back."

I climbed out of bed and scurried off to the library, which was blissfully empty. A desk sat at the far side and I began rummaging through drawers in search of something sharp and thin enough to pry the hair out from the channel of the ring. The first drawer was empty. I started to open the second when I heard voices coming from the hall. Every muscle in my body went rigid.

"Do you think they know?" The first was clearly Malachi Lennox. I'd gotten rather accustomed to hearing him grumbling through closed doors.

204 · JESS ARMSTRONG

"No. I don't think they do. I've only now discovered it," Andrew replied. He was trying to keep his voice down but I heard him clear as day. "I am duty bound to tell them. After all, Uncle's life is on the line. This is more important than any petty squabbles between you."

Tell us what?

"He deserves his fate after what befell Mariah."

"But you know he didn't kill Lucy," Andrew argued. "Why let him suffer for a crime he did not commit?"

Malachi made an unpleasant sound in his throat. "He may as well have done. Look at what trouble my brother has already brought with him. That strange man in the laundry and that harridan of an American. Andrew, this is an untenable situation. You must send them away at once before anyone else learns what you've discovered. My brother made his bed long ago, and now he must live with the repercussions of his intemperate actions."

My hand toyed with the brass knob of the drawer. I quickly took stock of the room for potential escapes—only one way in and we were on the second floor. The footsteps grew closer. Oh, blast it, I was trapped. Without a second thought, I dropped down below the large desk and tucked myself deep into the shadows as the door to the library creaked open.

I closed my eyes, slowing my breath, and awaited discovery. Hiding beneath the desk was an ill-conceived notion. I could have perused the shelves and pretended I'd been looking for a book, but no. No. I had to choose the most suspicious option.

However, if I *hadn't* hidden, they would have certainly known I'd overheard them, and that would have been doubly bad. Who knew what Malachi was capable of? The man's irrational hatred for Mr. Owen made my skin crawl. I could not fathom willingly partaking in a decades-long estrangement from my little sister. Good God, I'd have given anything to have one more argument over ribbons or frocks, and no matter how I tried, I simply could not conceive of a world in which a stolen bride was worth forty-odd years of bitterness between brothers. Family was *everything*. But then again, perhaps I only felt that way because I no longer had one. I bit my lower lip trying not to think overmuch on that notion.

The heavy footsteps made their way farther from the desk, followed by the telltale clink of crystal and a slosh of liquid. A chair groaned.

Damnation.

There was nothing to do but wait. So, I sat there, curled beneath the desk until my unwitting companion tired of drinking.

It was approximately half an hour before the door snicked shut again. With a sigh of relief, I crawled out from my hiding spot and continued my search for a penknife. As I opened the third drawer, I found a travel writing box tucked inside. Within it was a lovely silver folding knife. I tucked it in my pocket and fled.

"WHAT TOOK YOU so long?" Ruan had grown downright irritable in my absence, but who wouldn't be after having a bullet taken from one's shoulder. He'd be even more cross if he knew what I'd overheard upstairs. I hoped he couldn't hear my thoughts at the moment. He already mistrusted Andrew Lennox, and there was no need to fuel that particular fire, at least not until I'd parsed out what exactly that conversation meant.

"Shall I?"

Ruan gestured at the penknife. "I'm useless at the moment." The deep divot between his brows returned as he looked at me.

I reached up, smoothing it with my thumb out of habit. "Something's wrong, isn't it?"

He hesitated, struggling for the words.

"Ruan, what's happened? You're starting to frighten me . . ."

"I can't . . . I can't hear you at all. I thought it was just—the distance. You went off to see Owen, but now . . ."

"You can't . . ."

"I can't hear *you*. I can't hear *anything*. It's silence." He tapped his temple.

My guilty hand went on its own to the fresh scar on my chest.

"It's not your fault . . ." He must have guessed my turn of thoughts.

But it *was*. If he hadn't been with me on the bridge, then none of this would have happened.

"It will be fine. We'll be fine." He touched my arm gently before opening the hinge on the ring. Even days ago, when he'd touch me that way, I'd feel the cool rush of his power washing away the tension in my mind—but now the only sensation was that of his skin against mine. I could have wept.

And there was that damned word again. *We.* I brushed it away like a hoverfly, wetting my lips and tugged the knife from my pocket. "Hold the ring still, will you?"

I flicked open the knife and gently pried the hair from the channel.

There *was* something beneath it. Neither of us breathed as I carefully extracted the small braid and placed it alongside the ring in Ruan's scarred palm.

My throat constricted as I struggled to focus on the task at hand and not on the fact that the White Witch had been right in her warning. I might not have killed him but I most certainly destroyed Ruan Kivell.

I struggled to shove those thoughts from my mind, and focus on the ring. On what it *meant*. I had to find what the mediums were hunting, and this ring and those glass negatives were the only clues we had. I studied the now-empty inner channel filled with decades' worth of debris and dirt. And there, beneath it all, was a very faint engraving.

"You clever, clever girl," Ruan murmured, his voice humming with approval.

Warm with praise, I shot up from the bed and went to the worktable on the other side. The white sheets drying from the rafters billowed in the fragrant evening breeze. I picked up an old pewter ewer and poured some water into a basin before submerging the ring, taking a small bit of clean bandage in my nail and running it along the channel. The water grew cloudy as decades of dirt dissolved.

I withdrew it from the water and rubbed a dry corner of the bandage through the channel, repeating the process until I could read the words.

Forti Nihil Difficile

"'For the brave nothing is difficult,'" Ruan murmured over my shoulder.

I jumped at the sound of his voice, not noticing that he'd left the bed and come to my side. "I didn't realize you read Latin."

The edge of his mouth curved up into a small smile. "Oxford had its uses."

I looked at him curiously, tucking a dark brown strand of hair behind my ear. "What other languages do you speak?"

"Speak? None but English and Cornish. But I can read Latin and ancient Greek. I knew a chap at school who was fascinated by languages, but I never had the knack for them as he did."

This Pellar of mine was full of surprises.

He's not yours, Ruby, that wicked voice reminded me. And he never would be if I knew what was good for him.

"What do you suppose it means?" he asked.

I didn't know. Perhaps the ring was not a clue at all and Mariah had left it with Mr. Owen for some entirely unrelated reason. A token to say she loved him and wanted him to be brave. My throat constricted. It was all utterly hopeless. Mr. Owen would be convicted and Lucy's killer would be free and I—

"Miss Vaughn?"

Andrew Lennox was standing in the doorway looking grimmer

than I'd ever seen him. I had no idea how long he'd been there, or how much he'd overheard of our conversation.

"May I speak with you in the hall?"

I nodded, tucking the ring into my pocket and followed him out. He pulled the door closed behind me.

"I must apologize in advance for what I am about to do, and I want to make abundantly clear that if this were *my* home, and at all within in my power, I would not do this thing, but my father is most adamant on the matter."

His expression was pained and earnest and yet I did not quite believe his words. I'd known Mr. Owen too long to judge a book on the basis of its cover, no matter how fine the lettering.

"My father . . . he's set in his ways and he has . . . a certain way of doing things . . ." Andrew hemmed, leaning against the wall, waiting until a pair of maids passed by and were out of earshot.

"Spit it out, Andrew."

"My father wishes you and Mr. Kivell to return to Manhurst at once. He believes that . . . that you are a danger to us."

"He's not the first to think that," I grumbled.

Andrew furrowed his brow.

"It's quite all right. We'll go. But first, I want to speak with your father. There are quite a few questions I have for him."

Some questions more pointed than others—but I had a sense he wouldn't answer them. At least not to my satisfaction.

Chapter Twenty-five

Persephone Visited the Devil

MALACHI Lennox sat in the family dining room as if he were holding court, though there were no courtiers around. That is, unless one counted Irish wolfhounds as part of a royal retinue. The man wasn't even the viscount, and yet because of Mr. Owen's misfortunes, Malachi had carried out the role for most of his life. He didn't bother looking up from his supper to acknowledge my presence. Three dogs—brutish and hairy—lay lazily on the marble floor of the dining room, following me about with their dark eyes.

Malachi studied his supper plate with an expression torn between surprise and disgust at my sudden appearance in the dining room. He must have assumed I'd skulk away after receiving Andrew's message. Clearly, he did not know me. Malachi gestured for me to enter, and for his servants to leave. Both of which happened immediately. He was a man used to being obeyed, and had grown far too comfortable filling Mr. Owen's shoes as the head of the Lennox family.

My mind darted back to the state of our town house in Exeter when I first moved in. How it had been slowly decaying for years, while by all appearances Hawick House was in good order. More than that, it thrived. Had this man withheld funds from his own brother? Anger boiled beneath my skin.

"Say what you intend and be gone with you," Malachi said, ripping apart a roasted game hen and biting a chunk of meat off the leg. Juices coated his lower lip and dripped down his jaw. My stomach turned at the sight of it. "I don't have all day, girl. I presume my son delivered my message and that's what brings you here." He looked up then, pinning me with his cold stare. Eyes like Mr. Owen's yet vastly different.

I held my ground, back straight. "We are leaving, Mr. Kivell and I, as you requested."

"Weak boy. I told him not to give you excuses, to send you back to where you've come from."

"It seems your son is in possession of the manners you lack," I snapped back, unable to guard my own temper.

The old man's stringy gray hair fell in his face. "Well, get on with it and be off with you."

I stepped closer to the mahogany table, my hands curving around the back of a Victorian dining chair. "Why do you hate him so? I know about what happened with Mariah, but he is your *brother*. Why let him be punished when you know as well as I that he didn't kill Lucy?"

Malachi blinked at me. "Innocent? Lass, I don't know what fairy stories he's beguiled you with, but my brother hasn't an innocent bone in his body. He's a wicked and cruel man, and it's best you learn it now before any more harm befalls you."

Cruel? I'd known him long enough to be fairly certain he was anything but.

"He neglected Mariah." He mumbled between wet chews of the meat. "Ignored her. Stole her from the virtuous and righteous path and took her down to hell with him. She was my Persephone—light and beautiful and he stole her away. And once he had his prize, he used her and cast her aside like a broken plaything. Leaving her alone in Scotland while he did God only knows what down in London."

My knuckles grew white on the chair back. The way Mr. Owen spoke of Mariah wasn't that of a man who had cast aside his wife.

"Year after year she faded away, wilting under his pitiless care. There is no question that my brother killed her—if not by his hand then by his deeds."

"Perhaps you were blinded by your jealousy. Saw only what you wanted to see," I spat out.

"*Saw,* lass? I'll tell you what I saw. I saw Mariah on the bridge the night she disappeared. The same night my brother returned from London drunk enough he could hardly stand on his own two feet. Did he tell you that when you took *my driver* to see him today?" But Malachi didn't want an answer; he carried on, his voice growing louder with each word. "Who knows what unnatural deeds she'd interrupted in London when she sent for him?"

Mr. Owen hadn't mentioned being drunk. "He said she wanted to speak with him. Do you know why?" My palms grew damp as I flexed my fingers on the wood.

One of the dogs began scratching itself, paw thumping on the floor. "I don't. She would not speak of it to me, but I know she was afraid. I found her weeping in the garden that very morning. She told me he would come. That he'd know how to fix things. How to make things right."

Cold dread crawled up my neck. "And then what happened?"

He waved a meaty drumstick at me and my stomach roiled. "The servants heard them arguing that night in his room not long after he returned. A mighty stramash. I dinna ken what happened *inside,* but I was there *outside* when she left his room. Tears streaming down her face. She wouldn't speak of it. Wouldn't tell me what he did to her behind that door. But I could see plain as day that she was afraid. If I'd realized . . ." His own eyes grew misty as he took another bite of the bird, grunting in annoyance.

"What about your brother? Did you see him again after they argued?"

"Aye . . . we had words, he and I. I told him if he wouldn't be a proper husband to her he ought to leave her be. That I'd take care of her. Owen was as drunk as I'd ever seen him, slurring his words."

That didn't sound like him at all. "What did he say to that?" I didn't like the picture he was painting of his brother.

Malachi let out a dark laugh. "Told me to mind my own wife and stop bothering his."

"Why are you convinced he killed her? Many men get roaring drunk and simply wake up with an aching head. They don't kill their wives."

His expression shuttered. "I followed her that night. Saw her go to him on the bridge. They argued. Then he took her into his arms. At the time I believed they were reconciling. I waited in the shadows then once I believed she was safe, I returned home."

"You saw Mr. Owen on the bridge with Mariah the night she disappeared?" This was terrible, and pulled into question everything I'd learned. My heart sank. "You're certain it was him?"

"It was dark but there's no one else it could have been. Who else would Mariah have gone to? She loved my brother against all her better judgment. She'd not go willingly with another man. But my brother? He simply wanted her as another of his curiosities."

"Did Mariah have any . . . *gifts* as Lucy did?"

"Aye, she thought she had the sight. A seer. It's heathen nonsense, but she believed it. And my brother was intrigued by the idea. A medium and a seer in one family. He was giddy with what sort of child they might have. It sickened me."

Mr. Owen told me that they'd tried for a child, but that it was Mariah who was desperate to have one, not he. Could he have been lying to me yet again? Or was he simply shifting the truth as he was fond of doing? No. I couldn't countenance that. I *knew* Mr. Owen. He was a good man, even if misguided at times. His brother must have misconstrued what he saw, looked at the facts, and miscalculated the sum.

"As I said, I returned to the house. The next morning, she was gone."

I thought I might be sick.

"There was blood. A great deal of it on the bridge to Manhurst. Smeared across the stone rail and one of the columns. Along with bits of her fair hair." He squeezed his eyes shut. "That bastard must have crushed her skull and killed her. I know it. And if I'd stayed—if I hadn't been such a great heartsick fool . . ." His voice broke at last as his eyes grew glassy with tears.

There was no artifice here. Malachi too had loved Mariah. Where was the truth? Was it Mr. Owen's or his brother's or something in between? My throat constricted. "Mr. Owen said the body wasn't found . . ."

He gripped the silver-handled table knife hard. "No. I had the lake drained. My brother refused to do it himself, told everyone that she couldn't be dead, that he would find her and bring her back to Hawick House. It was all to cover his tracks, is what I say . . ."

My pulse thundered in my veins as I struggled to keep up.

Malachi waggled his gnarled forefinger in my direction. "Why else would he leave as he did after she died, never to show his face here again? Guilt. That's why." He grimaced at his plate, shoving it away, dishes clattering and scattering his supper across the tabletop. The dogs perked up at the sound, eager to snag a bit of discarded meat. "Damn you, you've put me off my food. This is why I wanted you gone. Gone!" His shout rattled around in my head.

Truth be told, I *wanted* to be gone. Pack my bags and head back to Exeter—but I was in too deep now.

CHAPTER TWENTY-SIX

A Second-Chance Séance

MY conversation with Malachi rehashed all the small insecurities and fears I'd had about Mr. Owen since arriving in Scotland. Each lie and prevarication over the last handful of years, things I'd once deemed benign, suddenly took on a more malevolent tone. He'd hidden his entire identity from me, and yet here I was, willingly ready to believe yet another lie. I might not have shared the details of my past with him, but I never once pretended to be someone I was not. I'd always been Ruby Vaughn.

But could he be a killer?

I swallowed hard, not ready to answer that question.

The three-mile journey along the main road back to Manhurst exhausted Ruan enough that he went straight to bed and fell fast asleep before I managed to close the door behind me. A greedy part of me wanted to stay with him, to reassure myself he was safe here and that I hadn't done him any lasting harm. But my mind was too cloudy for all that. Instead, I locked him in and made for the library to sort my thoughts.

The tale that Malachi Lennox wove was one of passion, betrayal, and murder. I twisted the ring in my pocket. His story also echoed what the spirit had announced at the very first séance. She too spoke of betrayal. Of greed. Of love.

I had known Mr. Owen for several years, and yet that entire relationship had been built upon a foundation of lies. What did one do when confronted with an unpleasant truth? How did one even know what *was* the truth? I desperately needed a drink, but couldn't risk further clouding my thoughts. Besides, even if I allowed the most improbable of options—that Mr. Owen killed Mariah and Lucy—he most certainly did not shoot me and the odds of there being *two* killers on one rural Scottish estate beggared belief.

No. Mr. Owen was innocent. He had to be.

The fire crackled low in the hearth and I toyed with the idea of tossing a new log onto the dying flames, or letting it fade to embers and seeking my own bed for the night. Everyone else, with the exception of myself and the angry ghosts of Manhurst, had long done the same.

There is nowhere on earth you can hide from the dead. The dead know . . . they know . . . they always know what you've done.

What precisely do the dead know—and why wouldn't they just say the thing plainly?

I pulled the ring from my pocket and turned it over in the firelight, leaning closer to get a better look.

The door creaked open and I turned to the sound, slipping the ring on my little finger.

Mr. Sharpe—Elijah—whoever he was, walked in, closing and locking the door behind him. A frisson of fear climbed up my spine at the sound.

He *locked* the door.

"Oh, Ruby . . . what am I to do with you?" He tapped an envelope against his palm.

I stood at once, heart hammering in my chest, and backed up

from the chair until I was pressed against the bookshelf. "Elijah?" I tried cautiously.

He sniffed and nodded, again tapping the envelope in his hand. "You've grown up."

Was that all he had to say? No apologies, no indication for why he'd locked me into this room with no way to escape. "What do you want?"

He raked a hand through his hair and shook his head, his expression bleak—broken—I might have pitied him were he not keeping me from leaving. "The same as you, I suspect. To hide. To start over. A little of both. I never anticipated running into anyone from New York all the way up here. I never did hear what happened to you after . . ."

"After your best friend destroyed my reputation?" I arched a brow, feeling suddenly emboldened despite the fact the only thing I had to protect myself were books.

He wet his lips and nodded again. "I regret that. I know it was not my doing, but I wish to apologize for my role in what happened to you . . . I should have seen him for what he was. Should have stopped him."

Now this was unexpected. I opened my mouth to speak but snapped it shut again. I did not trust this sudden honesty. I glanced back from the locked door to the envelope in his hand. I knew this man once. He'd worn that same weary trepidation on his face in New York—back when Christopher would suggest some mad scheme and Elijah would play the voice of caution. I was too young then to realize that I was being manipulated. The idealistic young pawn in a rich man's game.

I could only imagine the mutinous expression on my face, because he raised his hands in silent surrender. "Christopher mistreated both of us. It was a surprise to see you . . . to have you recognize me after all these years. I ought to have confronted you at once—told you the truth and not risked you learning on your own. If I could do it again I would—but I was startled to learn you were alive and here. I thought if I stayed away from you, then perhaps you would never need to know who I truly was."

My eyebrows raised at his audacity. "Mistreated us both? I was sixteen, Elijah. A *child*. You were a grown man—you both were!"

Elijah sank down into the chair before me with a sigh. "I did not know the truth about him either. He fooled us all. If I had known that he was married . . . I would have spoken to your father—told him of my suspicions before any harm befell you."

"And yet you continued on in business with him long after I was sent away. Why was that?"

He cast his eyes to the carpet and shook his head. "Because I was afraid. I saw how easily he walked away from what he did to you. How he manipulated the papers, turned the public eye to see him as the victim and transform a mere girl into a temptress for all the world. I was horrified how quickly he could change the story to suit him."

"Evidently not horrified enough to cut ties."

He winced. "I am ashamed of how I behaved, and my shame is no excuse but it is at least an answer. I do not expect forgiveness, nor do I deserve it. I only want you to know that I did not see the monster within the man was until it was too late."

Nor I. "How can I believe you?"

"It does not matter—it is the truth. Christopher ruined me as well as you. Even had I tried to disavow him earlier, our financial futures were entwined. I could not have escaped him without ruining myself in the process. There is a reason, Ruby, that I am here in Scotland and not still in New York. My debts—the men that he'd defrauded. He used the same methods on me that he used on you, for I was the one who took all the blame for his fraudulent schemes. I too left America under a cloud of shame. I have not even spoken to my own mother since that day in 1917. My entire life, my businesses that I'd built—all sand beneath his schemes. And yet he walked away without a scratch. Yes, I do regret not knowing the depths of his villainy *far* sooner. It would have saved both of us a great deal of heartache."

"I am sorry for it."

"It is done. I cannot change what happened, and I do not want your pity."

"I don't intend to give it."

He let out a strangled laugh and ran a shaking hand over his jaw.

I didn't believe his pretty words, but I no longer wished to dwell on what happened in New York. It was a long time ago, and I was no longer that shy girl who'd been maneuvered and played. Now I was a *grown woman* who was being maneuvered and played. I eyed the decanter across the room.

Elijah must have sensed my turn of mood and he quickly went to it, pouring himself a snifter of brandy. "Care for some?"

"Please."

He poured a second and brought it to me, the round glasses cupped gently in his nimble fingers. "I was relieved to hear you were not more grievously wounded at the lake." He took a long drink of the amber liquid, leaning against a tall bookshelf. He was still a strikingly handsome man—long and lean, with an expression that gave away little. "I have always been afraid of just that thing happening. It's why I do not allow hunting on Manhurst grounds."

"You don't allow hunting?" I could not disguise the surprise in my voice. "Why would the inspector be certain it was a hunting accident then?"

The amber liquid in his glass winked in the firelight. "I asked the very same thing, because if it *were* a hunting accident, I would wish to have whoever did it arrested for trespass. While the bridge leads to Hawick lands, there is no way a bullet could travel onto my estate at that direction. It is simply impossible and in that weather . . . ?"

I let out a bitter laugh. "The inspector is probably disappointed that Mr. Owen confessed and he couldn't watch me hang. Is that why you suddenly told me the truth about who you are? Guilt from my being shot on your property?"

He flushed slightly, giving me a sheepish look before handing the envelope in his fingers to me. "No. I'm afraid my hand was forced in the matter. I thought it best to confess before you saw the news yourself."

I looked at what he'd handed me. A response from my solicitor, Hari, addressed to Ruan. The seal had been broken. "Ah."

"Ah, indeed." He cleared his throat, changing the subject. "Manhurst is getting quite the bloody reputation. First poor Lucy Campbell . . . now this."

I lifted my glass to that and took a sip, letting the brandy do its work. "While on the subject, Miss Demidov mentioned there being another medium here before. A woman who disappeared shortly before the séance. Do you know anything of her?"

"You mean Abigail? No. Not much at all. Though I did take Miss Lucy to Edinburgh to seek assistance in finding the poor woman, but she disappeared without a trace." He snapped his fingers to underscore the point. "You don't think the two cases are connected?"

I weighed how much to share, but decided it did no harm to tell him what I knew. At least about the mediums. "I do. I think they were looking for something here."

He made a low sound of understanding in his chest. "That's an interesting ring." He tilted his head toward Mariah's ring, which I'd been rubbing absently.

"It is, isn't it? It was my mother's." I was beginning to lie as smoothly as Mr. Owen, which was a damning thought considering all.

"I had forgotten about that. Christ, I am an utter ass, aren't I?"

I smiled faintly at him, there was the Elijah I remembered. "Only a partial ass."

Elijah's eyes lingered on my finger. "Do you miss her—your mother? It was international news when it happened."

"I do." More and more with each passing day.

"Forgive me. I was only thinking, that if you missed her, perhaps you could put Miss Demidov to use. Help you find a bit of peace. I know I have no right to speak to you as a friend after all that's come before."

No. He didn't, but I'd once counted him as one. "I suppose I will allow it."

He stared at me, stunned. "You have changed—I remember you as such a shy girl, always with your freckled nose in a book, hiding in corners until Christopher dragged you into the light. And now—now you are utterly fearless. I think he would tremble at what he made."

"It's amazing what disgrace will do to a girl. You either die of the shame, or you learn to rise above it." My words held far more venom than I intended—but it was the truth. I had been given a choice when my father sent me away from New York. I could mourn the loss of the future I'd imagined and blame myself for what Christopher stole—or I could create my own life. One that suited *me*. I chose the latter and thus far it has not disappointed.

"Again, I apologize—"

"Enough with the apologies, Elijah. What are you dancing around?"

He studied his decanter intently, long enough that I thought that he might not answer at all. "It is real. That's what I mean to say."

"Pardon?"

"The séances. They're *real*. It seems strange to admit now, but as you recall my sister died in childbirth the summer we met. When I purchased Manhurst, I spoke with Lucy about her death—about how I missed her, how desperately I wanted to say goodbye but that she passed too quickly. Lucy asked me for a piece of her clothing, or a token to call her spirit close—all I had was a handkerchief my sister had embroidered for me. But Lucy was able to reach her from the grave. It gave me peace to speak to her one last time, to know she had found peace herself—I know I cannot change what happened in New York—but perhaps one of the mediums here could bring you that solace too."

I stared at him in disbelief. Of all the conversations to be having . . . But a curious thought struck me. What if I could use a séance to draw out Lucy's killer? If Mr. Owen was right, and that the killer was after the ring, then what if I used it as bait? An object to bring forth the dead—or in this instance—the living.

Elijah's eyes lingered on the ring. "It couldn't hurt."

I seriously doubted it would bring me peace, but if it could bring me Lucy's killer, that would be the next best thing.

"OVER MY DEAD body!" Ruan growled as he shrugged away from my hands and began prowling about his bedchamber, incensed by my idea of creating a trap with the ring. He was remarkably hale considering he'd been barely able to keep his eyes open when I left him in this room a few hours before.

"That *can* be arranged if you don't hold still," I growled, holding the clean dressings in my hands. "Now get back here."

He grumbled, sinking down on the mattress. I grabbed a little jar of salve that he'd made earlier and unscrewed the lid. The herbal scent was overpowering. I dabbed my fingers in it, and gently began rubbing it over his stitches as he'd instructed.

Ruan winced, his beautiful eyes closed. "Ruby . . ." His voice was gentler this time. "The idea is reckless. We've already been shot once."

I caught my lower lip beneath my teeth as I wiped the remnants of the sticky medicine from my fingers onto his unmarred other shoulder. "We don't know for certain that it was the same person."

He held a clean dressing to his chest as I unraveled the long bandage, preparing to wrap him up again. "And you think someone else here would decide to use you for target practice?"

"How do you know they weren't aiming for you?" *I certainly would be right now.*

He sighed, rolling his eyes up to the ceiling.

I finished wrapping the long cloth around his shoulder, securing the bandage, careful not to let my hands linger too much on his bare skin. The man was temptation, even in this sorry state. "Ruan—we are out of ideas. And there's something else . . ." I sank down onto the dresser, pulling my left leg up under my rump, my right dangling loosely.

He watched me, clutching his clean shirt to his chest. "I can't hear you, Ruby, you're going to have to tell me."

I nodded with a frown and proceeded to tell him what I'd overheard at Hawick House between Andrew and his father, what Mr. Owen had told me earlier that morning about the last time he saw his wife, his oddly convenient lapse in memory—his brother's recollection of the same events and my own growing suspicions about Mr. Owen. "Oh . . . and we were right. Mr. Sharpe is Elijah Keene."

He stared at me, his eyes dark with emotion. "Have I missed anything else while I've been napping?"

I let out a startled laugh and shook my head. "What do you make of it?"

"It sounds to me like Owen killed his wife."

"I know—but I refuse to believe it. Besides, I know he didn't kill Lucy, and he certainly wouldn't have harmed us."

He raised his brows.

My stomach knotted. "Even if it *was* Mr. Owen, it doesn't explain the photographs. The mediums were afraid of something—afraid enough they sent for him. They had to believe he could help them. Besides, I learned one other thing at Rivenly. Lady Morton? Her husband was one of the Eurydiceans. A particularly nasty one, if what Mr. Owen said holds any weight."

"It comes back to the ring again," Ruan murmured.

I swung my leg aimlessly, bare heel gently thumping against the wood of his dresser. "I can't help but think he's right. Mariah knew something. She had some proof—some evidence—and the ring is the key to all of it."

Ruan exhaled loudly, drumming the fingers of his good hand on his blanket. "Is she still here?"

I blinked. "Who?"

"Lady Morton?"

I shook my head. "I don't believe so. I was told she was leaving before we got shot. I cannot fathom she'd remain."

"Are you sure you want to do this second séance?"

"I'm out of other ideas."

Ruan remained silent for several seconds before he stood and started struggling to pull his shirt over his wounded shoulder. "Very well. We'll do this your way. I don't like the idea of another séance. But remember, I cannot hear you anymore, Ruby—and *that* frightens me a good deal. I could not bear it if something happened to you."

Nor I you. I straightened my spine and turned to the door. "Tomorrow then?"

"Tomorrow."

CHAPTER TWENTY-SEVEN

A Twist of Fate

ANY hope I'd entertained of having a *good* night was dashed upon entering my room and finding the White Witch sitting there waiting on me. She was dressed in her usual black mourning gown and seated at the table with a cup of tea in her hand, as if she'd dropped by for a visit—albeit at one o'clock in the morning.

Her amber gaze settled upon me in the same fashion my cat, Fiachna, would eye a field mouse before giving chase. She lifted the teacup to her lips in silent greeting.

At the best of times, I struggled to look her in the eye—but the effect was even worse after what happened with Ruan at the lake. "I am sorry. I should have sent him away."

I braced myself for the anger that did not come.

"It was vanity to think I could intercede in what the gods have decided." Hecate sighed, placing her teacup down in the saucer before turning her attention to the fogged-up window behind the bathing tub. "My visions have never erred before, not until you crossed his path. But I suppose not an unexpected turn of events considering what you are."

"I do not get your meaning." I shifted, hugging myself against the cool night air.

"You are not ready to understand. Not yet. But in time it will become clear."

I blew out a breath and grabbed a log, tossing it onto the fire. This was the most preposterous conversation to be having at this hour. But at least if we were going to have it, I'd be warm. I poked angrily at the hot embers until finally the new log fed the dying flames. "Your vision wasn't wrong."

"What do you mean, child? He lives. I felt it when I found you upon the shore."

I stood—joints aching, and squeezed the handle of the poker— twisting it in my hand. "He does, but it seems that he lost his . . ."

"He lost his *what,* Morvoren?"

I turned back around, fixated on the fireplace as if there were answers there within the flames. It was easier to stare at fire than at the curious look of the woman behind me.

"I repeat. What has he lost?"

"His power. He's lost his power." *There. I'd admitted it at last. Put voice to the things I could not bear to think upon.*

Hecate remained silent for several seconds before she let out a chilling laugh. "Foolish child . . . Pellars are born what they are. They cannot be unmade. The boy simply exhausted himself. What he did . . ." She stared as if she could see through the clothing to the scar on my chest. "What he did in that lake was beyond anything I've seen in centuries. It is ancient and dangerous, the power he drew upon. And I wonder—"

Centuries? My hand rose in a futile attempt to hide the scar, leaving a sooty mark on my blouse.

"Do not fear for him. His body needs to heal, as does his mind." She ran her hand through the flame of the candle on the table, drawing my eye. "Ruan Kivell is stronger than any mortal witch I've seen, but he does not know how to use his power. It is for the best that it is resting. Especially in this place. This is an unstable site. It has been a seat of power for my kind for thousands of years. It is *also* why the spirits have sway. But I sense you did not want to speak of your Pellar to me this night."

My nostrils flared. No. I didn't. Truthfully I did not want to *speak* to her at all. She laid her unnaturally cold hand on my shoulder and gave me what could only pass as a smile—an unnerving sight. "Tell me what troubles you, Morvoren."

I let out a strangled laugh, my free hand going to my hair. "Hecate, there is a murderer here. One, possibly *two* dead mediums. Someone *shot* me. Ruan almost died. And my employer's fate depends on whether or not I can figure out who actually killed Lucy Campbell. And you ask me *what troubles me*?"

Hecate looked past me into the flames. "Be mindful of the remaining medium. I do not believe she works alone."

My eyes widened in disbelief. "Truly. *That* is what you tell me? To be careful of quite possibly the most suspicious person on this entire estate." I gestured, forgetting for a moment I still held the poker. "You call yourself a witch and tell me no more than what I've already surmised. Can't you ask your old gods? Summon a vision. Something useful?"

She gave me a bemused look, not at all disturbed that I was waving a fire poker at her. "Do you not think, child, if we had such vast power at our disposal that we would have altered just one single moment of human history, halted one of their foolish wars, or prevented the slaughter of so many of *our* kind by theirs over the years?"

Exhausted from the day, I laid the poker on the table and slumped full-bodied onto the bed, staring up at the beams on the ceiling above. "I don't suppose you deal in miracles then, do you? Because I most certainly am in need of one."

"Those are the province of *your* kind, not mine."

This was more frustrating than conversing with a drunken Mr. Owen, but I no longer cared. If I was going to succeed in my plan for a second séance, then I needed her help. "Do you believe in ghosts?"

She tugged her long dark braid over her shoulder and glided across the room. "I do."

Hecate drew in a haggard breath and continued. "It is a dangerous game to call for the dead, as one can never be certain who will answer. Especially in a hallowed place like this."

The scholar in me might have questioned her more, had we more time. But there simply never was enough of the stuff. Not when I remained stubbornly two steps behind the killer. "Ruan says the spirits are angry here."

"They are. Dark and terrible things have happened to those who dwell in this house. They do not forget it." She frowned. "I do not like this turn of conversation. I beg of you, do not even think of doing what you are about to ask."

I slammed my hand helplessly on the mattress. "I do not know what else to do. Everyone in this godforsaken castle has secrets and there are so many lies that I cannot see my way out of it. The only thing I can think is to have a second séance."

She sucked in a sharp breath, quite possibly the most human emotion I've seen from Hecate in our brief acquaintance. "I will not summon the dead. Not even for you, Morvoren. And you cannot force me."

"It isn't the dead I want to find, it's the living." I tugged the ring from my pocket and thrust it at her. "I believe this is the key that Mariah's spirit spoke of. I am certain of it. But what I cannot understand is what it means."

"You believe that is why Lucy was killed."

"Perhaps even Mariah too. She left it with Mr. Owen the night she disappeared. '*I left you the key,*' the spirit said at that very first séance. *This* must be that key."

The only sign Hecate was listening was the slight widening of her golden eyes at my words.

"I don't give a damn about the dead—they can answer or not—but I believe the ring will bring the killer to us. It's our only chance."

For a half second, I worried that Hecate might continue to argue with me as Ruan had earlier. The White Witch plucked the ring from my palm and held it up to the candlelight, wordlessly studying it before dropping it back into my palm.

"I accept, Morvoren."

Only I wasn't quite certain what the terms were for her aid. But if it saved Mr. Owen, I would have agreed to them all without question.

CHAPTER TWENTY-EIGHT

A Spirited Guest

WHILE I was correct in assuming Hecate would have unspoken terms that went along with her help, I wasn't prepared for *quite* how many she would have. I thought I had been more than clear I wasn't interested in speaking with the dead, but Hecate would not hear it. As a result, I spent most of the morning fetching and carrying, gathering supplies intended to keep the spirits at bay should they choose to answer. Hecate had even managed to compel Ruan into making charms intended to repel evil spirits. A feat that filled me with concern rather than reassurance, as Ruan ordinarily refused to do any charm work.

I felt no safer for any of it—not for the salt, or the burning herbs, nor the great twisted hazel rod that took me halfway to Edinburgh to acquire which Hecate had lying across the table before her. She might fear the dead, but my concerns remained amongst the living. Someone had been willing to kill to keep their secret, and here I was trying to draw them out like a splinter from a festering wound.

The large round table was set up much as it had been the night of the first séance, however this time it was dusk—not full dark— and Hecate assured me that there was great power to be found in transitions. Between dusk and dawn, the solstices and the like. Perhaps that was why she was taking such precautions. Ruan's unease was palpable. The two of them had been arguing in Cornish for most of the day. Some of their disagreement, clearly having to do with me, as I distinctly heard the word *Morvoren* more than once.

By the time Hecate proclaimed us ready, and I entered the room for the séance, Genevieve Demidov had already taken her seat at the twelve o'clock position—directly facing the window overlooking the ruins. There was to be no grand entrance this time. No chanting. No costumes. And without all that artifice, the second séance felt all the more real. Genevieve wore mourning dove–gray tonight, with her lovely hair knotted into a chignon at the back of her head. Hecate sat directly across from her, her back to the window. The two women in balance.

I spotted Elijah, no longer could I think of him as Mr. Sharpe, standing in the corner—cast in shadows by the candelabra. He fumbled nervously with his pocket watch, his attention trained on Genevieve as if his very next breath depended on whatever word she uttered. It was a strange intensity and I wasn't sure what to make of it.

Despite our shared past, and his strange confession to me the night before, I did not fully trust him. Elijah's presence at the séance was to be expected. It was his suggestion after all, and he did own the estate. It would be odd if he wasn't in attendance.

But I could not disguise my surprise when I spotted Andrew Lennox entering the dining room, followed by Lady Morton and her daughter, Lady Amelia. The girl looked nervously about the room before spotting me, and the tension immediately left her shoulders. She held my gaze for several seconds, as if she wanted to impart something important but was tugged away by her mother at once.

I looked to Ruan. Had he known they were here? But he gave his head a slight shake. It seems their presence was a surprise to him as well.

Andrew took the seat beside Hecate across from me, much as he had the night of the first séance. I twisted Mariah's ring on my little finger in the darkness as Hecate began the ceremonies. Hecate's voice carried a rich earthy timbre as she began the proceedings, and even though I knew this was not a real séance, the hairs on my neck rose with each word she spoke. I hazarded a glance from her to Andrew, whose curious attention was fixed—not on the witch—but on Genevieve, just as Elijah's was.

We scarcely had enough attendees to fill the chairs now, causing us to spread ourselves out to balance the table. What had I been thinking? Did I truly think the killer would walk in and reveal themselves to all of us?

Foolish, foolish girl.

Ruan stared unblinking at the window behind Genevieve. I nearly asked what transfixed him when Hecate called to me. "Have you anything belonging to the spirit, Miss Vaughn?"

I quickly slipped the ring from my finger, handing it across the table to her. She had been adamant no one else touch it—a rule I was happy to comply with as it was my most important clue.

The little ring glinted in the dying light of day.

Making deals with witches, Ruby Vaughn? Did you learn nothing in Lothlel Green?

"Speak the spirit's name, Miss Vaughn. Who do you seek from beyond the veil?"

Up to this point, the séance was purportedly to summon my late mother. Ruan gave my hand a reassuring squeeze and I opened my mouth to speak. "Mariah. I seek Mariah Lennox."

A hush overtook the room as I uttered her name. I repeated

myself a bit louder, sounding far more courageous than I felt. "I've come for the viscountess—if she'll speak to me."

As soon as the last word left my lips the temperature in the room dropped precipitously. From behind Hecate, the window to the garden slammed open, the wind howling and rattling the glass in the panes as it struck the wall behind. The candles flickered before sputtering out and thrusting the room deeper into shadow.

Young Lady Amelia yelped, clutching onto Andrew's arm.

Hecate's hawklike gaze shot to me then Ruan as if we had any part in this. *This,* whatever it was, was certainly not part of the plan.

My chest tightened.

The autumn winds moaned over the hills, reverberating in the silence of the room and I began to understand why Hecate feared the dead.

"Sh . . . sh . . . should we close the window?" Lady Morton asked, her hand clutching her daughter's. Evidently real spirits were more than either had bargained for tonight. It was a wonder they even came after the scene that first night. It seemed we were to have a repeat performance.

Ruan was intent, fixated on something in the distance out the window—something only he could see. His hand covered mine and with his forefinger he started tracing something.

L-O-O-K.

I struggled to see what he saw, but there was nothing there. Nothing but an open window clattering in the frame. He tapped again to underscore. S-E-E?

Do I see it?

Of course not. There is absolutely *nothing* out that window but the ruin of a castle.

Growing increasingly frustrated, I shot to my feet and started for the window to close it—but Elijah beat me to it, fastening it back tight.

She broke the circle. The words came, hushed and low, from somewhere behind me. I turned for the source, but couldn't find the speaker.

She broke the circle.

The voice whispered again, its breath at my ear, ruffling my hair.

Cold fingers wrapped themselves around my throat as I saw what the voices meant. I'd disturbed the salt circle, just as it had been the night Lucy died.

She broke the circle.

She broke the circle.

Again and again the voices chanted in my ears. Did no one else hear it? Had I gone fully mad here in this castle? I looked from face to face, but they all were staring at me, open-mouthed. Perhaps it was their own thoughts I heard? But that made no sense. I couldn't hear the living any more than I could hear the dead.

Genevieve stood at the far side of the table facing me, my back to the now-closed window. Her rich brown eyes grew darker—nearly black in the dimness of the room—and she began to rock on her feet. "The dead have a message . . . a message . . . the dead have a message."

That unearthly voice returned again, with the same lilting not-quite-song that had taken over Lucy in the hours before her death. Genevieve's lovely eyes closed.

Hecate shot to her feet, grasping the rod in her hand. "This must stop. It must stop now!" She began to speak in a language I did not understand. It wasn't Cornish. It was something else. Something older.

But there was no stopping what we'd unintentionally begun.

The spirits ignored the White Witch as the cold air wrapped tighter around me. I could not have moved if I wished to.

"She will not speak to you, Ruby Vaughn."

I stared at Genevieve, not believing. This could not be real. It could not be. Genevieve herself told me she couldn't speak to the dead.

With bravery I didn't feel, I confronted Genevieve again. "Didn't she rattle the window? Do the dead have a taste for theatrics? Storming in and then refusing to speak to the one who called them? Sounds like my great-aunt Pulchritude."

"Morvoren, we do not taunt the dead!" Hecate snapped, her eyes possessing strange brightness. "You will sit and restore the circle before you unleash something we cannot trap back."

It wasn't real.

It *couldn't be.*

Genevieve glared at me, her lovely face contorted. "The dead will have their say."

"I want to help them. That's why I've come."

The temperature continued to drop—cold enough I could see my breath coming out in clouds before my face.

Lady Amelia whimpered.

Agreed, Lady Amelia.

"Tears of the mother bring the daughter's rage, and you think *you* can help them, Ruby Vaughn?" The strange voice let out a shrill laugh. "*You* think *you* can help, when you do not even know what you are?"

I hazarded a glance to Hecate, whose knuckles had grown white wrapped around the hazel rod. Hecate silently pleaded for me to move back to restore the circle.

This was bad.

Very bad.

Genevieve's left arm rose as she pointed at the center of my chest. My breath would not leave my lungs. We were trapped there, she and I in some sort of spiritual détente.

Until she screamed.

In that very instant the window shattered, spraying me with shards of broken glass, which fell to the ground like piercing rain and along with them tumbled the lifeless body of Genevieve Demidov.

CHAPTER TWENTY-NINE

A Feint . . . of Sorts

IT was hard to say who reached the medium's side first, Ruan or Andrew Lennox. Andrew hastily waved Ruan away with the clipped air of the medical officer he'd once been. He first checked for her pulse, then listened to her breath. Which now flowed easily. A good sign, based on my dim recollections of battlefield triage.

My mind reeled. Had I been attacked by a ghost? It was impossible. Improbable. And yet a slight trickle of warm moisture dripped down my neck. I reached up, pulling my fingers away. Blood.

Ruan's eyes widened as he looked from my fingers to my throat. He lifted my hair from my neck, quickly inspecting the damage before letting out a soft sigh. "It's only a scratch."

His voice was hoarse and uncertain. Likely as discomfited about what he saw as I—a frightening proposition considering he was a Pellar. Demons and spirits were his purview, not mine. Ruan reached out with his left hand, gently dusting the tiny shards of glass from my hair and shoulders.

What had happened?

He shook his head. "I do not know."

I must have voiced the question, though I didn't recall the words escaping my lips. "What were you trying to tell me earlier . . . out the window?"

Ruan leaned closer, his warmth enveloping me at once. "A woman. I saw a woman near the ruins."

My eyes widened. "Then the séance wasn't real . . ."

Ruan's jaw tightened. "I don't know."

"She's simply fainted," Andrew said loudly, jerking my attention from the uncertainty clouding Ruan's expression.

He'd roused Genevieve at last, her eyes were clear, and she rubbed at her temple.

She was alive.

Elijah hurried from wherever he'd been lurking, pushing his way through the curious bodies surrounding Andrew and Genevieve—likely drawn from the commotion. It looked as if a munition had gone off in here. Bits of glass strewn everywhere. Candelabras on the ground, candles fully snuffed.

Elijah stooped down, pulling Genevieve into his arms. The glass crunched beneath his shoes. "Give the poor woman some space."

Her head lolled against his shoulder as he murmured something into her ear. A far cozier sight than the last time I'd see the two together—back when they were quarreling on the bridge.

Hecate touched me on the shoulder. "I will see to them. Are you well?"

"Yes. Perfectly." My words came out a whisper as I stared at the broken window that lay motionless against the wall. It certainly seemed real—and yet, it could not have been. Hecate had taken precautions to keep the dead at bay, hadn't she?

I inched closer to the broken window, carefully avoiding the shards of glass, and stooped down, checking along the edges and behind for a string, a catch—anything to refute the evidence I'd seen with my own eyes. My frantic mind grasping for any bit of logic to explain what had occurred. Though my back had been to the window when it slammed shut—I could not have *seen* anything.

Ruan, however, had seen a woman by the ruins during the séance. What if the missing medium wasn't missing at all, and she and Genevieve were still working together somehow—but for what purpose? I latched onto that vain hope like a sailor lost at sea, for I vastly preferred human explanations to supernatural ones.

Ruan grabbed me by the arm, pulling me into a nearby alcove. "I *know* her." His voice rumbled in my ear.

"Who?"

"Genevieve. I have seen her before—during the war."

"*During* the war?" I could scarcely believe the words coming from his lips.

He shook his head. "I don't understand it. But Lennox saw it too. I saw it on his face when he was tending to her. He recognized her and didn't want me to see her. The two of them had been together on the ship when Ben died. I'd stake my life on it."

Bile rose in my throat at the thought. "You think Andrew and the medium have something to do with the murders . . ."

"Why else would she be here?"

Why else indeed. I stared at the empty spot where Genevieve had been lying moments before. "Andrew said the same too. He thought he recognized her and she denied it. I don't think he was lying then—but I do think he knows more than he's telling us."

The room had grown empty by now except for the table, with fragrant smoke rising from the long-forgotten burning herbs.

The table.

Good God. I'd forgotten the ring in all the commotion. I darted out of the alcove as raw fear took hold. It had been a ruse—the broken window. The fainting. Whoever it was that meant to steal the ring must have planned this descent into chaos in order to snatch it up. What a fool I was. A damned fool, and I'd played right into their hands.

I could scarcely draw breath as I rushed to the table, certain that I'd lost the ring. But there it was, sitting in the center of the table—gold winking mockingly at me in the dim candlelight. I scooped it up, sliding it upon my finger for safekeeping.

"What do you think?" Ruan asked softly.

"Fancy you asking me that."

He let out a dark, somber laugh from behind me.

"Do you miss it? Hearing people's thoughts?" I hazarded a glance up at him. How could this man steal my very breath without trying? It was unnatural. That's what it was, and yet I could not look away.

"Not theirs. I couldn't give a damn what anyone else in this world thinks. But yours?" He hesitated, his green eyes searching mine. "I miss hearing your thoughts terribly."

"You once complained that I think too loud."

"You do. So bloody loud that I didn't get a moment's peace." He smiled, wiping away the bit of blood that had pooled again on my neck. He rested his thumb there and inhaled deeply. "It's strange, but for the first time in my life, having you in there with me, I didn't feel quite as alone. I had someone to share my truth with. I do miss *that.*"

The intimacy of his admission was too much to bear, so I did what I always did when one got too close. I feinted. "Alone? You have an entire village to take care of, you're the least alone person I know."

His finger rested on my pulse. "And there is not a single person there besides old Arthur Quick who I can truly talk to. And if I dared tell him I can hear other people's thoughts? That I can . . . could . . ." His eyes drifted down to the spot on my chest that he'd somehow healed. "Ruby, they'd lock me in a madhouse, and I can't say that I would blame them. But you *know* what I am. You've seen it and you do not look at me any differently for it."

"Because you're only a man. No more, no less." I reached up, touching his cheek with a sad smile. "I'm sorry for what happened. If I'd known—"

"I am not sorry." He rubbed his rough beard on the palm of my hand like a greedy house cat. "Ruby . . . surely by now you know how I fe—"

I laid my hand on his lips, silencing him. "No." And like a coward, I walked away and out into the night, leaving whatever he was about to say hanging there in the cold evening air.

CHAPTER THIRTY

A Fetid Discovery

UNWELCOME things—*feelings*. I'd known I was infatuated with the irritating man since leaving Lothlel Green, and that sentiment had only grown worse since he appeared in Scotland. Once we were shot—and I was faced with the very real prospect of losing him—I realized that my feelings ran far deeper than mere infatuation. But feelings were not to be trusted—mine least of all.

Sentiment sorted—for the time being, I darted up to my room and grabbed a woolen cardigan and thrust my trusty flashlight into the pocket. The evening was growing dark, and I was determined to prove to myself that what happened downstairs had been a farce and to find that woman Ruan had spotted. She must be the answer to what happened tonight.

How do you explain the cold?

Oh, do be quiet. My never-ending cavalcade of thoughts were not aiding in finding the killer. I was unraveling—minute by minute—and I needed to find a rational explanation. What did it matter if Ruan had seen a woman that I had not? A woman that I ought to have been able to see from where I sat.

My breath was visible in the night air as I hurried along the beaten path toward the dining room's window, desperate to find a pulley or cord. Anything to reassure myself that it had all been a show. I slowed my step, flicking my anemic light over the ground, looking for clues of human involvement. The ground here was damp and muddy—granted, everything at Manhurst was vaguely damp and muddy, reminding me of the inside of a cave. The benefit to said state was that it ought to show if someone had been here. But no matter how I looked, there were no obvious footprints, nor any sign of a tie or contraption to cause it to slam with such force.

This did not bode well for my hoax hypothesis. I turned back to the inky night sky where the ruins of the old castle loomed in the shadows. This was where Ruan had been staring, where he'd seen a woman.

Well. He'd seen *something*.

I rubbed absently at the aching scar on my chest. What if Genevieve had not been pointing at me at all during the séance? What if she had been looking past me and pointing toward the ruins instead? I'd scarcely explored them, having been inside only the once—when I'd spoken with Andrew Lennox. I'd not looked around at all. What if *that* was where the secrets lay? The ruins certainly would have been here during Mariah's time.

I darted off through the damp grass toward the earthen footbridge leading into what was once the main keep. Overhead a cloud of rooks soared up into the night sky, disturbed by my approach. The sound of their flapping echoed off the broken stone walls.

The air here was all wrong.

I sniffed again.

Not wrong—it smelled of death. That strange sweet undercurrent of decay that sent my stomach into free fall. I'd thought it my imagination when I'd been in here several days before, but perhaps it had only begun to smell then.

I was going to be sick.

From the ramparts above the lone remaining pair of birds began to heckle me, calling down as I walked deeper into the keep, searching for the origin of the scent. It was stronger near the back, where a narrow passageway went between the old stone walls leading to the left turret. The opening was barely wide enough for me to walk through with my shoulders brushing each side. Ruan would have to turn sideways at places to make it through here. Slits intended for arrows pierced through the thick walls, allowing in only the faintest moonlight to illuminate my path.

The scent was far more intense now.

My eyes watered.

I ran my light over the floor and walls, but there was nothing out of order—at least out of order for a *ruin*. The ground was littered with stones from where the ceiling had given way over time, making it difficult to traverse, but such things were to be expected when a place was slowly returning to the earth.

The cloying scent filled my lungs and I pulled my cardigan up over my nose, but my body remembered the smell. A soldier never forgets. And while I did not fight alongside those men in the trenches, I spent far too much time there with them to not be keenly aware of death.

Cold sweat pricked my brow as I struggled against my instinct to run.

Moving deeper and deeper into the broken corridor, I had to use my left hand to keep my balance as I approached the curving tower stair. Some newer wooden planks lay across the floor ahead, spanning a gap where the stones had given way to a dugout chamber below.

I was close now. Very close.

I flicked my flashlight down to where the planks spanned the gap and knew without a doubt that that I would find the body there. I nestled the light between my cheek and shoulder and hefted one of the planks up to confirm my suspicions.

Acid rose in my throat as I stared down at the decaying form lying some three feet below where I stood. A woman—by the state of her clothes—wearing a burnt-gold cotton dress, the color of winter wheat. Similar to the one Genevieve had been wearing when I saw her on the bridge a few days before. While the woman's face was unrecognizable, I knew without fail it must be the missing medium. My light began to flicker, and for half a moment I thought my flashlight was failing—before realizing it was my own hand that shook.

Get yourself together, Ruby. It's only a dead body.

I drew in a breath, then a second before lifting the other plank to make room for myself in the grave beside her. This was no worse than anything I'd done during the war—vastly easier in many ways as this poor woman was already dead. There would be no screaming. No groaning. Nothing but silence. I could not harm her now. My feet hit the stony debris beside her. I stooped down to get a better look and noticed a large rectangular fieldstone lay alongside her hand, much like the ones that formed the walls of the corridor above.

I lifted the rock, turning it over to reveal dried blood staining the surface. Whoever it was that killed her must have dropped it in after her to hide the evidence. I flicked the light over it, revealing hastily scratched graffiti on the smooth side, partially obscured by the dead woman's blood.

Forti Nihil Difficile

The same words from the ring.

My skin pricked. She'd found it. This poor woman had found whatever Mariah had hidden—long before the ring ever made it to Manhurst. I caught my lip between my teeth as I struggled to add the pieces together. This *had* to be Abigail, the missing medium. Mariah. Abigail. Lucy. All three women disappeared in a similar fashion. All had been afraid, and all in a hurry to leave—

which meant that Abigail must have discovered Mariah's secret. Lucy must have known as well.

I blew out a breath, rocking back onto my heels, suddenly dizzy.

But what had they found? My muddy fingers trembled of their own volition. I flexed them, willing myself to be strong—but it didn't work. With uncharacteristic gentleness, I patted over her body in case her killer had left something behind. Gently, I lifted one of her hands to inspect it. Despite the discoloration and decay, they were not damaged. Her nails not broken—and very little dirt or blood beneath them.

Whoever had done this had surprised her, caved in her head with the rock, then buried her here.

The poor woman.

The stars overhead offered no answers nor were there any to be found down here. Whoever had killed this medium had taken whatever she'd discovered with them. With a frustrated groan I stood, climbed out of the hole, and promptly vomited up the contents of my stomach.

Chapter Thirty-one

Ghosts

I do not know why I did not immediately run for help. Nor do I know why I paused, sitting at a table in the empty courtyard waiting . . . I do not even recall what I waited for, only that I couldn't bear to be amongst the living until I'd rid myself of the dead.

Once I managed to compose myself enough to return to my room, I headed inside, determined to find Ruan and then contact the inspector. My hands still trembled, but I could do that much for the poor dead woman. The inspector would likely try to accuse me of killing Abigail as well, but I had no choice in the matter.

Ruan found me before I found him, catching me by the arm as I started up the stairs. "Where have you been?"

He was dressed in only shirtsleeves and a herringbone waistcoat, his right arm and shoulder bound tight to his chest with a white cloth sling.

I opened my mouth but snapped it back shut, the words not coming.

He touched my temple with his forefinger. "Please talk to me, Ruby."

Again, I opened my mouth, wanting to tell him about the poor dead woman in the ruins and yet the words would not come. My eyes burnt and silence surrounded us. The clock on the hall struck twelve.

How long had I been outside?

Ruan laid a hand on my cheek. "Gods, you are frozen. I have been looking all over the castle for you—where have you been?" He looked down at my hands. "You're shaking . . ."

I looked down to my filthy hands and clenched my fist to stop the trembling, finally finding my voice. "There's a body . . . in the ruins. The missing medium."

Ruan shifted his weight, taking me in fully. What a sight I must be with my knotted hair, my stained dress, and mud-caked shoes. As the meaning behind my words sank in, he pulled me against his warm chest—heedless of his own injury or the state of my clothes.

"You need a bath," he murmured, his lips pressed against my hair as he inhaled deeply.

I let out a startled sound. Yes. I did. But there was no time for it. Tears pricked my eyes. Stupid. Stupid tears. "I must go to her, I must help . . ."

"Help who?"

"The dead medium."

Ruan muttered something beneath his breath in Cornish before stepping back and tilting my chin up to look him in the eye. "She's dead. There is nothing you can do for her that can't wait until morning."

His words soaked through the frozen expanse of my thoughts. He was right. The poor woman had lain there in that shallow grave for a week. Surely another few hours wouldn't hurt. But leaving her alone seemed cruel. Someone had killed her and left her like carrion. Forgotten.

He frowned and met me with that irritating stare of his. The one that reminded me why he held such respect in Cornwall. "You will do no one any good like this. Let me help you—you can hardly stand on your own feet."

I wriggled away from his kindness. "No. No, I'm fine. I promise. I'll be all right." A lie. I hadn't been fine in a very long time, but I was a Vaughn, and Vaughns always managed to get by.

He stood there, perhaps six inches away from me, his eyes bright. He swore again beneath his breath, muttering in Cornish before pressing a gentle kiss to my brow.

A girl could grow accustomed to this sort of thing. "What did you say?"

The edge of his mouth curved up and he shook his head. "You don't want to know. Good night, Ruby."

Good night, indeed.

I started up the stairs, leaving him behind. Just as I turned the corner, I heard a pair of voices coming from behind a cracked door at the near end of the corridor. I ought not have stopped—not paid it any mind at all—had I not recognized Elijah's voice. The other speaker, I could not identify. My fingers rested lightly on the gilt wallpaper as I leaned closer to the opening.

"—it will be fine. Believe me. I won't let them harm you—"

"—it's too late, Elijah . . . the plan will never work now," the other person replied. An Englishwoman, though she had a strange accent I could not quite pinpoint. Perhaps it was the woman Ruan saw outside the window earlier tonight? Whoever she was, she also knew his true name—an unsettling revelation.

"I was frightened for you. When you fainted I—"

Fainted? My stomach knotted as I strained to listen harder at the door. Suddenly I recalled the ease with which Genevieve had mutated herself on the bridge. Her change in posture, her thickening accent upon the appearance of Andrew, Malachi, and the duke. At the time I thought she was afraid of Elijah, but what if her reason for being here was something else entirely?

I've always been good at reading people. That was what she said to me on the bridge.

Perhaps Ruan and Andrew Lennox *had* seen her before. I swallowed down the bile in my throat as images of the dead woman in the ruins came back to mind. Genevieve herself had told me that Abigail—the other medium—had been afraid before she disappeared, that she was running away. I struggled to remember fragments of the conversation but they were ephemeral.

"I will protect you, Gen. Please. Forget this place. I can keep you safe from them. You must listen to reason. People like that . . . They will not give up. They will not forgive this offense."

Them? A soft sob. She was crying. Could she be afraid of the Eurydiceans? Or did she mean me? I pressed closer to the wall, trying to make sense of this new thread. Genevieve and Elijah were in league, that was for certain—but was she in danger as the other two mediums had been or was *she* the killer and simply afraid of facing the consequences of her own actions?

Footsteps came up the hall behind me. There went my eavesdropping. Besides, I'd learned far more tonight than I'd bargained for. I was getting close now—I felt it in my bones—if only I knew *what* I was close to. I started down the hall in hopes of making it to my room before whoever it was found me.

"Ruby? What are you doing awake?"

I groaned, coming face-to-face with Andrew Lennox.

"I could ask you the same," I shot back, far sharper than I'd intended. I wrapped my fist tight, out of fear my trembling would return before I reached the safety of my room.

"Couldn't sleep. I confess I find it harder and harder these days."

An unwelcome thought struck me—Andrew had been in the ruins with me too that day. Surely a physician would have noticed the scent of death, far quicker than I. "Why are you still here . . ."

The shiny white horn of his crook glinted in the electric

lights as he shifted his weight. "My father and I do not see eye to eye these days. I find myself needing to apologize for the way he treated you. It was abominable—for that reason I came to the séance. I didn't expect—" He waved his hand in defeat and sighed. "I do not know what happened earlier this evening, but I certainly did not anticipate *that*. You have blood—" He gestured to my neck with his forefinger.

I shrugged him away. "It is nothing."

His nose twitched in that same way Mr. Owen's did when he was biting his tongue. "I fear if I stay at Manhurst much longer, I might be returning to medicine as a full-time occupation." He cleared his throat. "I'll see you to your room. You should not wander the halls alone. It is ahead, is it not?"

I arched a brow. "Do you think I'm in danger here?"

He let out a strangled laugh as we paused outside the door to my room. "Miss Vaughn, you have been shot and nearly killed, and the person who broke poor Lucy's neck still walks free. Not to count that other missing medium. If I were you, I'd keep your head down and go home. My uncle has made his bed with his lies and no matter how much I love him, you are far too young to get tied up in his trouble."

I bristled at his words, but it wasn't as if I hadn't thought the same thing. A wiser woman would have gone home and let Mr. Owen handle the chaos he'd created—and yet I remained loyal to a fault.

"Good night, Captain Lennox." I reached into my pocket and withdrew the key to my room and placed it into the lock, hand trembling.

He looked at my hand, brows drawn up in concern. "Are you certain you are well?"

I twisted the key and pushed the door open. "Perfectly." I locked the door behind me, hoping it would keep the ghosts of Manhurst at bay for at least one night.

Chapter Thirty-two

An Unwelcome Intrusion

THE pipes groaned as hot water poured from the brassy lion-shaped faucet and filled the bathing tub. I might have relished the luxury of it all, if I didn't reek of death. I drove my thumbnail beneath the nails on the other hand, trying in vain to remove as much of the dirt as I could before stepping into the tub. A habit I'd picked up during the war—worrying them until they bled. I could not rid myself of the filth quickly enough. I shimmied out of my dress, unsteady fingers struggling with the buttons, and left it in a heap on the floor. I would burn it in the morning and hope Mrs. Penrose forgave the transgression against my wardrobe. I sensed she might in this instance.

The dead medium's scent permeated my clothes and clung to my skin and hair. I quickly divested myself of my sweat-stained undergarments, pausing briefly before the dressing table mirror to look at my nude body in the reflection. A body not unlike that of the woman in the grave. With lines and curves. Softness and bone. Scars and imperfections from a life well lived. A dozen or more angry scrapes were visible on my neck from the broken glass.

Were the dead woman and I so very different?

252 · JESS ARMSTRONG

Someone had crushed her skull and left her there like rubbish. I squeezed my eyes shut, willing myself to forget the image—to not see my own face staring back sightlessly from that rocky grave. Turning away from the mirror, I unfastened my locket from around my neck and laid it on the dresser, before slipping off the ring and placing them there together.

The tub was nearly full to the white enameled rim. Steam rose up in the cold room as I stepped in. Thousands of needles pricked my skin where the heat chased away the Scottish cold, and the water slowly went from clear to cloudy to yellow. I sank deeper beneath the surface with only my chin above, scrubbing hard enough that my skin stung from the effort.

And yet her scent would not go away.

I let out a muffled scream, throwing the fragrant bar of soap across the room, where it landed with a wet smack on the floor before I finally descended fully beneath the water.

At last in the silence and warmth, I found peace in the one place the dead could not follow. I remained submerged until my lungs burnt and my body threatened to surrender to the water's call. Just as I came up for air, I heard the door latch click.

I wasn't alone.

My heart hammered in my chest.

"Ruan?"

Perhaps he'd come to make sure I was safe. But I'd locked my door and Ruan didn't know one end of a lockpick from the other.

The cold air pricked my skin as I rose from the tub, my voice cracking. "You know this isn't amusing."

Silence.

Had whoever shot me come to finish the job? If so, I wasn't about to die naked. I grabbed a thin towel, wrapping it around myself, and stepped out from behind the screen. The key remained in the lock as it had been when I came in. The door to Mr. Owen's room, however, was now wide open.

I slipped open the drawer on my dressing table for Mr. Owen's revolver, when I realized one terrible thing.

The ring was missing.

I'd set it on the dressing table, not ten steps from where I'd been submerged in the tub. My breath came in short bursts. Someone had been in here with me—waiting . . . watching for the moment to take it.

I threw a clean chemise over my damp skin, wrapping myself in Mr. Owen's dressing gown—one I'd kept for myself—and thrust the gun into the pocket, before entering the next room.

Empty.

Heart thundering in my chest, I darted out into the hallway looking down the corridor, left then right.

Empty.

Fool! Fool! Fool! What was I thinking? I should have allowed Ruan to come with me, for no other reason than to keep the ring secure. But no—my fear of appearing weak had caused me to lose the best clue we had.

Barefoot, I ran down the hall to Ruan's room, pounding on his door with a flat palm. I didn't care if I woke the whole damn castle. There was a thief here. A murderer *and* a thief. I shivered as the damp chemise clung to my skin.

The door flew open and Ruan quickly took me in, from my dripping hair to my bare feet, and grabbed me with his left arm, tugging me into the room and slamming the door behind us.

He held me against his chest as if he could will away whatever bothered me if he only held me tight enough. "What's wrong? What's happened?"

My breath evened as I listened to the slowness of his heart.

After several moments he stepped back wordlessly, taking my face in his one hand. A flurry of emotions crossed his face. Frustration. Fear. Anger.

But not at me.

He knew.

Somehow, he knew without me uttering a single word that something had gone terribly wrong. "You have to tell me, Ruby. You must talk to me."

I opened my mouth and a sob came out. Good God, why was I being such a ninny tonight? It was only a stolen ring. I'd already found the body, and whatever Mariah had been hiding was long gone. The ring didn't even *matter* anymore and yet the tears would not stop. I sank down into a chair by the fire and buried my face in my hands.

I was broken and couldn't even articulate *why* I was upset.

The floor creaked as he stooped down before me, brushing my wet hair back from my face with a rough hand. "Are you harmed? Has someone hurt you? Touched you?" His voice was achingly tender. It made me want to scream.

I squeezed my eyes shut, shaking my head, and the words came out in a rush. "The ring is gone."

His shoulders sagged in relief and he whispered something in Cornish, rocking back on his heels. It was in that moment I realized he was wearing only his trousers. I must have interrupted him while he was changing his bandage as the red wound in his shoulder was completely exposed—Andrew's stitches on fine display. The air around us was thick with the scent of yarrow and calendula.

Ruan brushed the tears from my cheek, his roughened fingers still vaguely sticky from the medicine he'd been applying and my beleaguered heart cracked fully open.

"I can't stop crying."

"There's no shame in it." He was close to me now. Close enough his green scent invaded every pore of my body, pushing away the memories of the dead woman and replacing them with him.

"I was in the bath. They . . . they waited until I was submerged and—" I shook my head. I didn't want to speak of it. Didn't want to think on it.

No. I needed to be useful. To *do* something. I reached for the jar sitting on the table beside him, my hand knocking into it clumsily. "Let me help you."

He pushed my hands away, taking the jar from me. "You can help me by sleeping. By not haring off and trying to get yourself killed every time I turn my back."

I smiled despite the ache in my chest. "You're a mother hen."

"Someone needs to have a care for you . . ." He grumbled beneath his breath, uncorking the lid and placing two fingers into the substance, slowly pulling them out before carefully working the salve into the muscles around his wound.

I swallowed hard, unable to look away. *Good God, Ruby, how can you think such things not five seconds from tears?* He turned toward the fire, revealing that deep scar that went along his spine. I wiped at the wetness of my face, trying not to laugh at the inappropriateness of this bone-deep need I had for him. Just being near him was enough to make me . . . content. Easy.

The room was unbearably hot from the roaring fire and I slipped out of Mr. Owen's dressing gown and adjusted my chemise. Soaked as it was it left little to the imagination. But this wasn't the first time he'd seen me in my underthings. I'd been wearing little more than this when we first met on the shores of Tintagel.

"What do we do now that they have the ring?" I asked, watching as he set about dressing his wound.

He mumbled over the bit of bandage he held in his teeth. "We worry about it in the morning. At dawn, I'll go see to the body." He finished fastening it, and looked at me squarely. "But you need to sleep."

My pulse sped up at the thought. "I . . . I don't think I can go back there tonight. Not after . . ."

He turned back to me with the strangest expression. "Why the devil would you go back there? You're staying with me. Here. Where I can be reasonably certain you won't get yourself killed before I wake up."

The narrow bed was scarcely wide enough for him. "And you think you can give me orders . . . Honestly, Ruan Kivell, you should know me better than that by now." But I was grateful for his offer, such that it was. I would make myself a pallet by the fire and be perfectly happy being near him. It would be enough.

It'll never be enough, you little fool.

I brushed the thought away as I went to his wardrobe, grabbing a spare blanket. Ruan took me by the hand, turning me to face him. "You're shaking."

I glanced down at my hands.

So I was.

I tugged my hand away, laying a thick woolen blanket on the wooden floor.

He swore again. "Get in the bed. Now." He jerked his chin toward the narrow bed in the corner.

"I'll be fine right here."

Ruan sighed heavily and took a step closer to me. Then a second. I swallowed hard, looking up into his green eyes—bright in the firelight. He placed his hand on my arm, his thumb rubbing the bare skin there. "Ruby . . ."

Oh God, this would never do.

He walked me backward in this strange hypnotic dance until my knees hit the mattress and I sank down onto the soft bed. Ruan's eyes never left mine, nor did I want them to. I swallowed hard as he stooped down, lifting my legs with his warm hand and tucked them neatly under the heavy bedding and sat down on the mattress beside me, gathering me to his side.

"I should have never left you tonight," he whispered half to himself, reaching up and rubbing my temple with his thumb.

I closed my eyes against his uninjured side. "You did exactly as I asked. What happened tonight is no more your fault than my own. I do not want to talk about what happened. We will deal with it in the morning. I want—"

Ruan pulled me closer against him, cautious of his wound, and I allowed myself this small indulgence. "What do you want?"

You. "Peace."

"I know that feeling." His mouth moved against the skin at my brow as he spoke, sending a shiver down my spine. "When I was at Oxford . . ." he began, his one hand lazily running a finger up and down my arm, lulling me into complacency. "I hated myself then. Lost. Confused. Taken away from everything I knew and wildly different from all the other lads in ways they had no way of comprehending. Hearing their judgments, their prejudices. Gods, Ruby, I knew I didn't belong there but they certainly agreed with the notion."

I closed my eyes and allowed myself to listen to the rumble of his chest. "They were asses."

He chuckled low. "I appreciate your support in this, Miss Vaughn."

My mouth dried. I shouldn't like it so much when he called me *Miss Vaughn.* "Go on then. I'm fond of stories."

"At that time in my life there wasn't anything I wouldn't have given to be like them. To sound like them, to look like them. To *think* like them. To play the games and wear the clothes. I would have gladly excised that part of me that made me different and thrown it into the fires of hell. Gods know I tried back then to make it stop. To be ordinary. And yet my difference is what put you in my path. I wonder sometimes . . . if I would have met you at all if I were an ordinary man?"

I opened my eyes, resting my chin on my fist, and looked up at him at last. "I'm glad you're not. I don't like ordinary people with ordinary lives. They're boring."

A flicker of something crossed his expression, that deep divot forming between his brows. Worry.

I reached up, smoothing his brow with my thumb. "I'm not afraid of what you are . . . what you might yet be. I never have been. Besides, you could never be boring, Ruan Kivell. Even if you were an ordinary man." The words relaxed him somehow. As if he feared that I might no longer care for him if he was no longer the Pellar.

Ruan leaned closer, his nose touching mine, and I might have let out an undignified whimper. I certainly inhaled, breathing in his scent. How could this man ever be ordinary? Even now, unable to hear my thoughts, he controlled every one of them without even trying.

He moved slightly closer, silencing me with a kiss and stealing the last of my good sense. It was madness. Utter madness the way I craved him and yet I could not stop. Could not walk away.

Witch indeed.

The edge of his mouth curved up as he broke the kiss, then pressed a far more chaste one to my forehead before pulling the blanket over the both of us. "Now. Sleep."

I let up a startled laugh. "I cannot believe you."

He chuckled beneath his breath, holding me closer against his left side. And for the briefest of moments I saw it—a glimpse of peace, locked away as we were from the rest of the world.

"You tricked me into your bed. I thought . . ." *Well, I had perhaps an idea of where this might have gone.* But neither of us was in any condition for that sort of exertion.

"I wasn't about to let either of us sleep on the floor. Besides, it's not the first time you've spent the night in my bed."

"It's the first time *you've* been in it with me."

"Good night, Miss Vaughn," he mumbled with his eyes closed and his fingers tangled loosely in my hair, holding me against his heart like some precious thing he could not bear to lose. My lids grew heavy and I fell asleep memorizing the scent and feel of his body against mine. Angelica and rosemary. Sage and feverfew. Primrose and calendula.

Oh God.

I loved this man.

And that would never do.

Chapter Thirty-three

A Tiny Problem

RUAN was gone the next morning—a realization which might have stung, if I hadn't been debating how to extricate myself from the situation. It wasn't as if anything *happened* last night. But whether we intended it or not, something had shifted between us and I feared that we would never go back to how we had been before. We were beyond friendship now. We were . . . well, I didn't know *what* we were, which meant that he would want to *discuss* matters. Especially as he could no longer hear my thoughts. Dreadful man.

A ghost of a smile crossed my face as I recalled the scent of his skin as I fell asleep. Oh, good God, I was in deep water. I'd have to deal with this when I had more time. *Much* more time.

I threw my legs over the side of the bed, before noticing that he'd left a stack of fresh clothing and my locket on the chair by the recently stoked fire. A hastily scratched-out note sat on top.

Gone to deal with the body. R.

Not the most romantic of notes, and I was grateful for that. At least he wasn't spouting off sentimental nonsense when we had a job to do. I quickly donned the emerald-green suit that he'd fetched from my room, and had started for the door when a loud knock came from the other side.

"Morvoren, let me in."

Hecate.

Pinching the bridge of my nose, I tried not to think on precisely how bad it looked that I was alone in here, especially as my chemise and dressing gown were now in an incriminating heap by the fire.

Heat rose to my face. Ah, well . . . in for a penny . . . Bracing myself for her scorn, I opened the door.

But instead of sharp words Hecate stormed past me into the room. She wore a pale gray dress this morning, the shade of smoke from a dying fire. It was the closest thing to a color I'd ever seen her wear. "Where is he?" The bracelets on her wrist jingled as she shut the door behind her.

I rubbed my face hard, struggling to gather my wits. I'd not even washed my teeth or run a comb through my hair and was in no condition to carry on intelligent conversations with anyone— let alone her. I gestured to the closed curtains. "He's gone to search the ruins."

The witch's expression shifted to one of alarm. "What do you mean by *search them,* child?"

Images of the dead woman's body flashed in my mind and I squeezed my hands to keep the damned tremor from returning. "I found the missing medium . . . the woman you replaced . . . she was murdered."

Hecate exhaled with a rush of cool air. "Then she is on the other side. I suspected as much."

"Someone hid her body in the ruins. I found it after the séance and . . ."

Hecate held up a hand. "I do not need to know your reasons

for being here, Morvoren. If what you say is true, then there is not much time at all."

"I do not understand. There is a murdered woman in the ruins!"

Hecate stopped me. "Miss Demidov is missing, as is Lady Morton. No one has seen either of them since the séance last night. I have reason to believe the young medium is in danger."

"That's preposterous, I . . ." I suddenly recalled the conversation I'd overheard last night, and the words withered on my tongue. Distracted as I was by the thief and then by Ruan, I'd almost forgotten the very real fear in Genevieve's voice. Mr. Owen had told me that the late Lord Morton had been a Eurydicean. Could Lady Morton be involved somehow? Oh God, I'd ignored her all along. I caught my lower lip between my teeth. "We must check Genevieve's room, see if there's any clue to where she went. The girl . . . Where is Lady Amelia?"

"Her mother sent her south to her grandfather's estate after the séance. Something is wrong, Morvoren. Very wrong."

I moved to my pile of discarded clothes, pulling the Webley revolver from the pocket of Mr. Owen's dressing gown, and headed for my room to pick up the shoulder holster from my things.

If Hecate noticed the bathtub full of filthy water, she did not speak of it—and I was grateful for her discretion. I slipped the stained leather holster over my shoulder, tightening it to my chest and placed the gun inside. It was an uncomfortable apparatus at the best of times—pinching and restricting movement—but with the fresh wound in my shoulder, my every subtle motion screamed in pain.

"There is no time. We must hurry," Hecate hissed at me.

We were certainly in accord on that one. Genevieve's disappearance took on a more sinister tone after finding the body in the ruins and overhearing her conversation with Elijah. Perhaps he'd simply taken her to safety, but a nagging voice within me said that was not the case.

The two of us raced up the back stair to the family wing of the house. I'd snooped around enough that I was able to find Genevieve's room in minutes, two doors down from Lucy's.

As I nudged the door open with the toe of my shoe, my earlier fears coalesced. Genevieve was going to die—if she wasn't dead already. Her hard-sided traveling case sat atop the dresser fastened and belted shut. The wardrobe doors were flung wide, contents missing precisely as Lucy's room had been on the night she was killed.

I hastily unfastened her bag, desperate for some idea where she had been going. All of her belongings were stacked and neatly folded within the case. I gingerly pulled them out—one by one—setting each to the side as I had with Lucy's things a handful of days earlier.

Hecate stood at the window, her gaze fixed on the ruins. Beside her was a cheap glass vase, holding a handful of dried dahlias, their paper-like petals illuminated in the early morning sun. Hastily drawn hexafoils adorned the windowsill.

I folded my arms uncomfortably across my chest, thanks to the revolver. "Do you have any idea what she was running from?"

The White Witch left the window, allowing the white lace curtains to fall behind her. "I do not. Keep looking." She tilted her chin to the suitcase.

Right. Genevieve's belongings and the glass plate negatives were all we had to go on, and I'd already exhausted the negatives. I ran my fingers over the fine leather. It was an exceptionally fine case. Too fine for an impoverished medium. "Who is she?"

"Now *you* speak in riddles, Morvoren."

"She's an Englishwoman, not Russian," I murmured to myself as I continued rummaging through her things. "I heard her speaking with Elijah—"

Hecate furrowed her brow.

"Mr. Sharpe. He is not who he pretends, his true name is Elijah Keene. He's from New York. I knew him . . . once . . . I overheard the two speaking last night, and I'd bet my soul she's an Englishwoman."

"Is anyone who they pretend to be?" Hecate asked me kindly. "Hiding one's true self does not make them a killer."

I had to give her that. Returning to Genevieve's suitcase, I withdrew a little bottle of rose water and set it with her unmentionables. "Someone here *is* a murderer though." I hefted out more underthings. Silken ones.

My hand hit something hard and wrapped in fabric. "What are you? . . ." I pulled out what might have been a book wrapped in a nightdress.

I gently unwrapped the parcel from its linen packaging. Hecate drew nearer, craning her neck to see what I'd found. The scent of death on the linen was unmistakable. I peeled back the fabric to find a tattered plaid cloth beneath, covered in dirt and decay.

More negatives.

My eyes met Hecate's.

This had been with Abigail's body. The same grave scent that flooded my senses in the ruins permeated the inner fabric. Only one question remained: did Genevieve put the medium in that grave herself, or had she simply found what had been hidden? I set aside the wooden-cased photograph on top, and focused upon the glass plate negatives wrapped in the soiled fabric. There were two dozen at least. Likely the remainder of the set that I'd found in Lucy's room earlier. I lifted them one by one, inspecting each in the brilliant morning light.

Mariah's photographs.

These had to be what we'd been looking for—what Mariah wanted us to find. But as I continued going through the images, I realized that they'd been irreparably damaged. Naked bodies with faces hastily scratched out and identities removed. I wasn't quite certain how it was done but the effect was jarring all the same.

"What is wrong with them?" Hecate asked.

"Either someone found these before Genevieve did . . . or . . ."

Hecate interrupted me, pointing at the background of one of the plates. There was a man there, fully dressed and cutting a fine figure in his suit, wholly unaware of the photographer's presence. He was the only person in the image whose face was fully visible. His body radiated anger, the image was blurred where his hand would have been—the likeness captured mid-motion.

"Isn't that the one they call Captain?"

The man bore a striking resemblance to Andrew, though whoever he was—his nose had not been broken. This wasn't Andrew Lennox at all. Not to mention the clothing was far too old-fashioned. I sucked in a sharp breath as the gravity of what I held in my hands sank in. Mariah had most certainly taken these photographs, and this man . . . whoever he was, could only be one of two people—Mr. Owen, or his brother Malachi—both of whom would have looked a great deal like Andrew as young men. This was bad.

Very bad.

Had Mr. Owen also lied about his involvement with Eurydice's Fall? I tucked the glass negatives under my arm and reached for the wooden-cased photograph. "Dare I see what you are?"

Hecate clucked at me. It seemed that ancient witches did not talk to themselves.

Ignoring her disapproval, I released the latch and opened the case, revealing an image of two figures—a young girl of about ten, and an older woman who looked an awful lot like Genevieve except her hair was fair. Based on their clothing alone, I would have put the image around 1890, which made sense as Genevieve was easily a dozen years older than me. The woman held what looked to be an 1890s Kodak Number 3 camera, a fact I only knew as I'd managed to find one for Mr. Owen's collection not long ago.

"What did you find, Morvoren?"

A mother's tears . . . a daughter's rage . . .

My stomach knotted. I knew well the depths of a daughter's rage—of the lengths one would go to fix past slights.

Mariah's body had never been found.

My head began to swim. What if Mariah hadn't died all those years ago at all? What if she was still alive? Alive and angry. "We need Ruan . . . we need Ruan now."

"What do you see?"

I could scarcely form the words, scarcely *think* them. I latched the wooden photograph case, slipping it into my pocket. "You said that Genevieve and Lucy were close . . ."

"Lucy was very protective of the girl, why?"

I thought back to the image in my pocket—of mother and daughter—afraid of what it would mean if my suppositions were true. Of course, Lucy would be protective of Mariah's daughter, of her own niece.

Hecate's expression fell as she sniffed the air in alarm. "Fire!"

Hecate and I bolted from the bedchamber, out into the corridor, down the back stair and toward the source of the flames. The smoke grew thicker, filling my lungs, and I fell to my knees, crawling toward the door that opened into the garden and the ruins beyond. The muscles of my chest hurt from the exertion, but I clutched the glass plates tight against me with Hecate trailing at my heels.

Shouts of *Fire* rang out from elsewhere in the castle.

My pulse pounded in my ears as I struggled to remember where the door was. I'd only seen it twice, but I was not about to die like this, not when I was this close to saving Mr. Owen.

With each labored breath, I grew increasingly unable to think of anything but clean air. Water. Life.

Ahead I spied the edges of the door, visible through the smoke. My eyes burnt. I blinked back the wetness there.

Just a little farther.

All I had to do was make it a few more feet. My lungs rebelled against the rapidly warming air around us. The flames must be close now.

A little farther, Ruby. Go a little farther. My mother's voice echoed in my head. I was dying. I must be to hear her voice again. Coughing, and body weakening, I finally found the door, reaching up for the catch. Warm but not hot. A good sign. It meant the fire was behind us, not ahead. Cool air rushed in when I pushed it open and the pair of us scrambled out onto the cool grass.

Sooty and coughing we collapsed on our backs, watching as the black smoke billowed from the upper floors of Manhurst, orange flames licking up into the smoky clouds—a beautifully terrible sight.

"Morvoren . . ." Hecate rolled over onto her knees, panting for air, as she stared at the ruins behind me.

Gasping, I struggled to sit and spied two figures high up in the ruin and recognized them both at once. One was Ruan—making his way cautiously along the uneven rampart with his right arm in the white cloth sling. The other figure appeared to be Elijah. His fair hair shining like gold in the morning sun. His hands were up as he spoke to someone else—someone deeper in the shadows.

Elijah did not notice Ruan's quiet approach.

I crept closer, hugging the glass plates to my chest. Elijah and the unknown man were arguing, I could hear the tone in Elijah's voice, but couldn't make out the words. The wind whipped around me, catching on my sooty skirt and plastering it to my legs.

Ruan edged closer to the two men. *What was he thinking?*

He paused and turned straight to me, holding my stare with such intensity I could have sworn I felt him graze my hand. The wind rose up, stronger than before—the air sharp and full of energy. Elijah's coat flapped angrily around him as he stepped to one side, revealing the man in the shadows.

Inspector Burnett.

Ruan must have already sent word about the missing medium.

A short-lived relief rushed through my veins only to be quashed when Elijah lunged for the inspector. They were grappling over something twenty feet in the air.

This was decidedly *not* normal.

Ruan edged closer to the fray.

Get down, you foolish man.

The inspector slammed Elijah's head into the stone wall, making a sickening thunk. Elijah stumbled, teetering near the edge. He reached out to steady himself, latching onto the inspector's coat sleeve.

The two men tumbled forward, and I saw a flash of steel.

Good grief, Elijah had a gun!

The two men struggled, grunting and swearing—and there was absolutely nothing I could do but watch. The inspector knocked the pistol from Elijah and it tumbled from the ramparts, striking the ground near me as a shot rang out, ricocheting back up. All three men paused and Ruan dropped to his knees behind a broken piece of crenellation.

Elijah took this moment of surprise to draw a knife, slashing wildly at the inspector. Inspector Burnett dodged backward, a miscalculation, as the ragged stone beneath his foot gave way. I scrambled back from the edge to avoid the falling debris.

Elijah did not hesitate. Instead of waiting to be sure the inspector fell, he turned and ran across to the far side as the inspector pinwheeled, struggling to regain his footing. My breath caught in my chest, watching helplessly as the man finally lost his balance and fell to the ground in front of me with a sickening thump and the distinct sound of breaking glass.

I started after Elijah, when I noticed Ruan stumble and changed course.

I would have to catch Elijah later, and I had a sickening feeling I knew exactly where he was headed. If Genevieve was Mariah's daughter as I now believed, then there was only one place in the world she'd go—and her accomplice would follow along behind.

A daughter's rage.

The one person I knew who had caused Mariah's tears. The same one who had been lured to Scotland under false pretenses. I hoped I was wrong, but if the daughter wanted vengeance . . . there was only one place she'd go.

To Rivenly and Mr. Owen.

Hecate hurried to the inspector's lifeless body as I raced through the narrow wall to the turret stair after Ruan.

Foolish stubborn bull-headed reckless man.

With my right hand on the center column to keep my balance, I made it halfway up when Ruan met me on his way down.

Infuriating.

Insufferable.

Impulsive.

My internal litany of complaints against him continued, despite the bone-deep relief of seeing him alive.

"What were you thinking, you foolish man?" I started in, poking him hard in his chest. "You could have died. You could have—"

But the words died in my mouth as I took him in, his expression as stricken as my own. He reached down, running his thumb down my cheek, his finger coming away black with soot. He sighed, muttering to himself before pressing me hard against the wall and kissing me as if his very next breath relied upon it.

It took a remarkable amount of willpower to pull myself away from his embrace. I laid a shaky hand on his chest to steady my own galloping pulse. I missed the strange way he could ease my mind. The peculiar way he'd touch my brow, and that rush of cold that would ricochet through my body, easing each bit of tension and fear. I could have used a dose of that now for what we were up against.

My throat burnt from the smoke. "Ruan, we have a problem."

He straightened, rubbing his hand over his face, leaving a smudge of my own soot on his skin. "Only one?"

"Several," I admitted. "But at the moment the one most concerning me is that I have reason to believe that Mr. Owen's wife might yet be alive and that she and Genevieve mean to kill him."

His breath hitched and he paused, hanging on to the center column, the width of his shoulders taking up most of the narrow castle stair. "You what?"

"Well, it's that or he's been killing women one by one over the last oh . . . forty years . . . And I must admit I really don't care for that option." Either I'd placed my trust in a murderer, or I was about to lose the man I'd come to love as a father just as we'd truly begun to know one another.

In the few minutes that I'd been inside the ruins, chaos descended upon Manhurst. Most of the new castle was embroiled in flames, licking at the hazy sky overhead, all the old wood and varnishes and lacquers having fed the blaze into an uncontrollable inferno. The scent of burning timbers and fabrics coated my lungs. I couldn't pause to think of what—who—might be left inside. Ruan placed his palm low at the center of my back—a quiet bolster to my flagging courage—as we approached the White Witch where she remained crouched over the inspector's body.

"Did you find anything?" I stooped down on the stony ground beside her.

She rocked back onto her heels and wiped her sweaty brow, leaving a streak of pale flesh amidst the ash. "More glass."

I pulled out my filthy handkerchief and gently lifted the inspector's coat. Inside his jacket was a leather folio strapped across his body. It'd come open at some point, leaving fragments of broken negatives scattered on the ground around him. Gingerly I unhooked the case from the strap and withdrew it from his body. "Do you suppose he's our thief?"

Ruan caught the inside of his cheek in his teeth and shook his head. "He must be. But why, what does he stand to gain?"

I pulled some of the large pieces from the folio, attempting to reassemble the old glass plates, but they were broken beyond repair.

"He must have found them here," Ruan murmured. "He or the other one."

"Elijah?"

He nodded. "I heard the pair of them arguing when I came out this morning to find the body. I wasn't close enough to make out what the quarrel was."

I sniffed the air tentatively. After the fire, I'd nearly forgotten that Ruan had come to the ruins to find the dead woman. "It doesn't smell . . ."

Ruan winced as he shifted his weight. His shoulder aching from where he'd caught himself against the stones earlier. "I doubt you could tell over all the smoke, but you're right. There is no body. I found the spot you described. The hole reeked of death, but it was empty."

"The killer must know I found her."

Ruan nodded. I tucked the Webley revolver back into the holster and stood, dusting my hands on my ruined skirt.

"Go. I will take care of things here. But you should leave before too many questions are asked about how this came to be."

The White Witch turned back to the dead man between us, yes, a wise idea.

I gave her a curt nod and squeezed my eyes shut, trying to make sense of what had happened over the shouts and the ferocious crackle of the fire. If Elijah and Genevieve were working together, that meant he would be headed to Rivenly as well, and I was not certain if I hoped or feared I was right.

CHAPTER THIRTY-FOUR

The Bitter End

WITH Hecate left at Manhurst to sort out the dead inspector, Ruan and I set off on foot. The fewer people who knew we had left the castle grounds the better. It was an eight-mile walk into the nearest town, but mercifully after two of them, Ruan flagged down a farmer who agreed to let us ride in the back of his truck alongside his produce—a mean trick considering I was covered in soot with a revolver strapped to my chest and Ruan didn't fare much better.

"We need to think this through, carefully . . ." Ruan began, tracing circles on his thigh with his thumb.

I leaned my back against a sack full of turnips, drawing in greedy lungfuls of clean country air. My throat was raw. "None of it makes sense. Why would she come back after all this time? It's been over forty years." After what I discovered in Genevieve's room, I had a growing suspicion that Mariah had not died that night on the bridge at all. That she'd simply run away. But why come back and kill her own sister? No. Lucy's death did not fit neatly into any scenario I could concoct and I'd grown tired of guessing. Tired of the what-ifs and wrong turns and dead ends.

Grumbling, I picked up a lopsided turnip that had rolled free of its sack and tilted it to the sun. "I detest turnips."

Ruan arched his eyebrow, far more amused at our current predicament than I.

"If I never saw another I'd be content. They taste like dirt."

"And you've eaten much dirt to compare?"

Cursing him beneath my breath, I shook my head.

Ruan chuckled and brushed a filthy strand of hair from my brow, his warm fingertips lingering on my skin a half second too long. "You know, Ruby Vaughn. I wonder sometimes how you get yourself in the troubles you do. In the month since we met—"

"Seven weeks . . ." The truck hit another rut, throwing us against one another.

He took in a sharp breath at the impact. "In the last *seven* weeks . . . I've had to quell angry mobs, am now solving my *second* murder, and have gotten myself shot. I think I've seen more action with you than I did during all four years of the war."

"Blame Mr. Owen. I'd have never set foot in Cornwall if left to my own devices. Besides, your old life sounded boring."

"It was." He gave me a half smile before turning away and watching the miles tick away. I was glad he didn't try to discuss what happened last night. No matter how muddied my feelings were for him, there could be no future for Ruan and me. Not in the stark light of day. He belonged in his old life—that boring one delivering babies, making teas, and tending the sick. Not here with me risking his life day after day. I was a magnet for danger—it just saunters up and falls in my lap like an overcurious kitten, begging me to stroke its ears.

Ruan laid his hand over mine, interrupting my thoughts and grounding me squarely in the present. *Damn him.* I grunted, snatching my hand back and folding my arms across my chest. The farmer would only take us as far as Glenrothes. From there we'd have to hire a car to get to the ferry out in Anstruther.

This was taking too long.

Mr. Owen could be dead before we got there.

The truck groaned to a stop as we neared the edge of town and I struggled to shove *that* cheerful thought from my head. I hopped out, stumbling as I landed—and patted my pockets, taking inventory of what I had on me. We needed money to hire a car from here and I had only the clothes on my back.

My hand went to my throat and I started to unfasten my locket. There was no choice but to pawn it and come back later to retrieve the thing once we'd sorted matters on the Isle of May. *If* we managed to sort them.

I'd unfastened the clasp when Ruan covered my hands with his own. "No. I won't allow you to do that."

My nostrils flared. "*Allow me?* While I might have let you into my bed last night, you are not my keeper."

"My bed," he corrected, his hand lingering over my locket. "I allowed you into *my* bed."

I had to give him that. "Just look at us! We look like we've escaped from Hell's operating theater. No one is going to help us out of the kindness of their hearts. We need money to get to the Isle of May. While I'm perfectly good at picking locks, I am not a thief, and my locket is the only thing we have of value between us."

Ruan groused in Cornish, and shoved his hand into his own pocket, pulling out a fine silver-cased half hunter that he thrust into my hand. "Use this instead."

"Where did you get a thing like that?" I gave him a bemused look. That was the watch of a dandy, not at all the sort of thing for my country Pellar. *Mine.* The thought flittered there at the edge of my mind and I swatted it back away.

"Perhaps I didn't eschew *all* the things Owen gave me when I left Oxford."

I choked back a laugh.

"I'll let you buy it back, mmm? You cannot lose that locket.

You are your mother's only living daughter." He pressed the warm watch into my palm, closing my fingers over it.

"My . . . my mother?" Now that was a peculiar thing to say. I hastily fastened my necklace, hurrying to keep up with him. "Ruan . . . what do you know of my mother?"

He quickened his step.

"You know something, don't you?" I called after him, hurrying along the road. He shook his head, eyes downcast. The fiend. I hardly knew anything of her. Only that she'd been in an orphanage, taken in by a childless farmer and his wife when she was three. We'd been told she was born to a poor Irish couple on their way to America, the sole survivor when their ship was broken apart by rough seas off the New York coast. My mother had been scooped from the wreckage and placed in a New York orphanage as a darling little thing. My grandparents had been charmed at once by a three-year-old girl with messy black curls and fathomless brown eyes. Always dreamy and distant—as if nothing in the whole world could touch her.

"Ruan . . ." I started again. "What do you know of my mother?"

"It's nothing." He kept his eyes trained on the shopkeeper's sign in the distance, not daring to look back at me. The wind whistled through the narrow street.

"What do you know?" I struggled to keep up with him, gasping for breath. My lungs not fully recovered from all the smoke.

"Nothing. It's only something Hecate said."

"And *what* did she say?"

He paused, turning to me with a weary look. "You are your mother's daughter, Ruby. You are *Morvoren* born." He said the word as if he was telling me everything I could possibly need to know. Except it was meaningless to me.

"Yes, but what does it *mean*? I've searched for it in every book I can find—?"

"Perhaps *you* are not meant to know yet." He pointed at a green painted sign across the street. "The pawnbroker is ahead."

Fine. As we were in the middle of catching a killer, I supposed it could wait. But once this was sorted out, Ruan and I had yet *another* thing to discuss.

THE FIRTH OF Forth was angry by the time we reached the ferry landing. Wind sang eerily through the rigging of the docked ships like the trapped souls of lost seabirds. Sharp droplets of rain pelted my skin, making it hard to keep my eyes open. I walked to the ferryman's hut and knocked on the door. He answered, recognizing me at once from my trip earlier this week. His weathered face grew more and more incredulous as I explained the situation and asked if he could take us across in his skiff.

His eyebrows rose as he looked from me to the angry waters swirling in every possible direction. "To the Isle of May . . . in this storm? Are ye mad, lass? One wrong swell and we'd all be drowned."

I could see he wasn't about to be swayed. *Five miles.* It was five miles across the mouth of the Firth of Forth to the Isle of May. Nearly to the North Sea, if I recalled my Scottish geography.

"It's imperative we get across . . ." I wiped at the rain, which pelted the side of my face.

"I don't know what trouble you're in, lass . . ." The warmth coming from his little hut was tempting. "But you can rest here until it passes, then I'll take you both across."

"It's trouble we're trying to stop—" Ruan interrupted.

The ferryman did not understand.

"A murder. There's been a murder at Manhurst Castle and I have every reason to believe that there is about to be another if you don't help us get to the Isle of May," I spluttered out.

He straightened, looking far more imposing than he had moments before. "Are you threatening me?"

I held up my hands in a gesture of peace. "We're trying to prevent one. I believe that the killer from Manhurst is headed to Rivenly." Something in my voice must have reached him as his expression softened.

"No one is getting to the isle in this weather. No one. The last ferry went across perhaps two hours ago with an American lad, but that was before the winds picked up. I wish that I could help you, lass. I do. But until the storm passes, it's not safe for anyone to go out."

Two hours? Gracious! Elijah must have driven himself straight from Manhurst at breakneck speed to beat us here. I reached for my locket yet again, clumsily unfastening it with numb, half-frozen fingers. They moved too slow, but I found the clasp and pulled it from my neck and gave it a good final look—something I had not done in quite some time. I ran my thumb over the seed pearls which surrounded the stylized compass rose inset. The whole piece was crafted from both platinum and gold. In the very center of the compass was a deep green cat's-eye emerald. The stone alone was worth a small fortune. I squeezed my eyes shut as I remembered my father's parting words to me as he gave me the locket.

"You've always been an unbiddable thing, my darling girl. As is your mother. You are like her." He'd tucked a lock of my hair behind my ear. The ruby on his signet ring winked in the sunlight as I waited on the dock to board the ship to England. I'd known he would send me away—I only hadn't known quite how far. My parents had moved quickly to remove me from the newspapermen and their cameras, far away from the scandal where my naïve heart could heal in private. Confused tears stung my eyes as he leaned close and whispered softly in my ear. "Do you know what we do with the most unbiddable of things, my love?"

I shook my head, wiping at the wetness on my cheeks.

"We let them go." He brushed a kiss to the top of my head, his face soaked from his own silent tears. "You cannot tame wild creatures unless they wish to be tamed, remember that." Then he pressed the small package into my palm.

I wasn't ready to leave them. I didn't want to go. It didn't matter to me if I had an illegitimate child, I simply wanted to stay with my family—with my mother and little sister. But he didn't care what I wanted—intent on sending me away for my own sake. I didn't bother to look at what he'd handed me until I arrived in London weeks later. I hadn't understood his parting words, not until I realized what he'd gifted me. He'd given me a compass—a means to find my way home.

I placed the locket in the ferryman's hand, closing his fingers over it. "If I don't return, sell it. You will have more than enough to replace the boat."

"Ruby—this is madness," Ruan said in hushed tones.

Undoubtedly, he was right, but I had already lost too many people I cared for in this world—if there was the remotest possibility that Mr. Owen was alive, I could not take any chances.

The ferryman quietly calculated the cost of replacing his skiff against the treasure he held. He couldn't possibly know that it was worth more to me than my own life.

"It's your heads," he said in defeat and gestured to the skiff, docked nearby. This was by far the most dangerous thing I'd ever considered doing, but there was no other way to get there in time. I should have known Elijah was duplicitous. He'd shown me who he was back in New York, but once again I'd been too trusting. Too naïve.

Ruan gave me an apprehensive glance. "Are you certain this is what you want to do? We could wait on the storm . . ."

I looked up into his pale green eyes. Oddly brighter than before as he looked out onto the surging water.

"Do you trust me?"

The edge of his mouth twisted upward in answer, and he followed me into the howling winds and out onto the angry sea.

THIS WAS A mistake.

Even without the rapidly healing wound in my chest, this would have been a fool's errand. My entire body ached from steering the small craft, and we were barely halfway to the isle. I could just make out the lighthouse perched high up in the distance through the sea spray. This far out, the waves were higher than I'd anticipated, and it took every bit of my strength to keep us to the flats.

The boat lurched, lifting high in the air on a particularly rough swell before crashing back down. The wooden hull made a sickening crack that reverberated beneath my feet. Icy seawater slammed over the sides, filling the boat and soaking me from the waist down.

We were going to die.

I dared a glance back to the severely reefed mainsail. It was holding at least. A small mercy granted by the storm. This little skiff would not survive a second wave like the last without cracking in two. Though I wasn't sure which would be worse—to be swallowed up by a wave, or to have the tiny vessel be torn apart, timber by timber, beneath us.

I lost my footing a time or two but by the grace of Ruan's old gods, we kept speed, steady and straight toward the island.

Somewhere from the darkest recesses of my memory my mother's voice came to me, bringing back the lessons she'd taught me during those summer months we'd spend sailing together through the Great Lakes. We'd been surprised a time or two by a dangerous squall, but never before did I get the distinct sense that the seas wanted me dead.

Stay to the flats, my darling. Stay to the flats and you'll see this through.

That's my girl.

You're almost there.

Over and over her voice echoed in my mind as my body moved of its own accord. Weathering a storm that we had no hope to survive.

They will not take either of you today.

I kept my eye on the rocky inlet where the ferryman had docked earlier this week. The distance between us and it quickly disappearing. We were close enough to the pier, I could make out the waves crashing against the rocks on either side. I spat out the salty water and remained focused on the shore, on the last steady thing in the world.

"Ruan, can you tie a line?" I shouted into the wind.

He growled something in response that did not sound reassuring, but I took it as agreement all the same. I pointed out the rope lying wet by my feet. "You take the bitter end in your good hand, when we get near, loop it over the piling and then—" But before I could finish my rudimentary sailing lesson, a large wave tossed the skiff onto the shore.

It seemed the sea did the job for us.

The force of the impact threw the both of us into the shallows. A sharp pain shot through my knee, where it struck the rocks below. I stood, reaching back for Ruan, jerking him to his feet as another wave struck us.

Only sheer stubbornness kept us upright. I grabbed the bowline from the little skiff, tugging it toward the dock before climbing up and securing the craft as best I could.

I turned back to dry land to see Ruan there, left palm on the ground, retching up the contents of his stomach. He crouched on the ground, before looking up at me, his coloring as gray as the stormy seas.

"I swear to the gods, never again, Ruby Vaughn." He spat out more bile as he drew himself to standing, and shook his head, water droplets flying from his hair.

I grabbed ahold of a spare bit of line someone had carelessly left wrapped around a nearby piling, and tossed it to Ruan, who caught it in his free hand and slung it over his uninjured shoulder.

As I turned to walk away, down the path to the house, he started to mutter to himself in Cornish, and I distinctly heard the word *Morvoren* followed by what I'd come to understand as a term of frustration. Perhaps I didn't want to learn Cornish after all.

CHAPTER THIRTY-FIVE

And into the Fire

WHEN I last left the Isle of May, I'd not expected to return this soon. Nor had the jagged stones jutting out of the sea seemed as ominous. I'd foolishly believed the killer would be at Manhurst and that Mr. Owen would be safe here with the duke and the thousands of seabirds. But the more I unraveled the secret held by the Three Fates, the clearer it became that Mr. Owen was somehow at the center of it all. Mr. Owen and these Eurydiceans. He'd disavowed the secretive club before, but I had seen the negative. A negative bearing the likeness of someone who looked an awful lot like him disturbing the goings-on.

I blew out a breath. It couldn't be him. It just *couldn't*. Why scratch out the faces of everyone but himself? Mr. Owen was meticulous and calculating. If he *were* going to be involved in nefarious dealings he'd certainly not leave incriminating evidence behind.

Ruan touched my elbow, and I spun to face him. "What?"

"Are you well?"

"You were the one vomiting up your breakfast and you ask if *I* am well?" I choked back a laugh, gesturing widely at the stormy seas behind us. "Ruan, in the last week we've both been shot, I've nearly drowned us, and now we're trying to keep Mr. Owen from getting killed—so no, Ruan, I'm not well. But I am doing my best." I turned back around and continued storming up the muddy path toward the house. The trail forked, one way rutted and leading to the cliffs, the other to the house and the old lighthouse that still served as a beacon after all these years. Ruan stopped me again.

"This is not the time for your overprotective tenden—"

"Look." He pointed with two fingers at the mud. It had been recently churned up, with clear evidence of struggle. There were at least three different sets of footprints there.

I stooped down to get a better look and spied a thin gold chain nearly swallowed by the muck. I lifted it from the filth with my fingers and looked over my shoulder to where Ruan towered behind me. "What do you make of it?"

He sniffed, wiping the rain from his face with his uninjured arm. "Shall we see where the tracks lead?"

I nodded, pocketing the chain, and continued, following the single heavier pair of tracks up onto the cliffs. The storm showed no signs of abating as we moved higher up the slope against the icy rain. Teeth chattering, I withdrew Mr. Owen's revolver from the holster.

Ruan made a sharp sound, and I stopped, noticing a familiar shepherd's crook laying in the mud beside us, half covered by wet leaves—likely kicked off the path and into the windswept underbrush before the storm set in. There was a distinct reddish streak down one side. Blood, and recent too.

"Andrew was here."

"*Is* here . . ." Ruan tilted his head farther up the rocky incline to the outside of a tumbledown croft near the top. I squinted, struggling to keep my eyes open against the frigid rain. Half the croft's roof was missing—ravaged by the intemperate weather along this part of the world. The other half nearly consumed by low-growing brush and vegetation.

Andrew Lennox lay partially propped against the side of the building, barely sheltered from the rain by the decaying eaves. I tore off up the hill after him, Ruan at my heels.

"Andrew . . ." I sank down beside him in the tall grass. His breath was ragged as he laid his hand on his blood-splattered satchel. *His blood.* A pair of surgical scissors lay on his thigh atop the gory makeshift bandage. "What happened?"

Andrew didn't answer immediately, weak from loss of blood.

"Ruan, can you help him?"

I saw the hesitation there—brief though it was—before he grunted what I took to be a yes.

Andrew reached out, grasping Ruan's left hand. His dark brown eyes were frenzied. "My cousin. I tried to stop her . . . followed her here."

I continued scanning over his body, looking for other wounds for Ruan to tend to. It seemed Andrew had only been shot the once. A strange mercy.

He grabbed on to my hand. "You need to see to my cousin . . . she . . ."

"Who else is here? You're the first soul we've seen on this island," Ruan grumbled, reaching for Andrew's bloodied medical kit.

Andrew jerked his head angrily toward the other side of the stone wall behind him. "Can't . . . can't get to her. Was trying . . . trying to stop her. Too . . . too . . . dangerous. He knows . . . he knows she knows . . ."

Hair rose on the back of my neck. "Andrew, who knows . . . who did this to you?"

He clenched his jaw and groaned as Ruan shifted Andrew's

weight in order to slip the medical kit off of him. "I wouldn't b-blame you if y-you let me d-die . . ."

"The old man would never let me hear the end of it. Now hush and let me take care of things." Ruan continued rummaging through Andrew's medical supplies. While his words were gruff, there was an edge of tenderness in his voice. I pulled the Webley revolver from the holster and handed it to Ruan.

His eyes widened and he shook his head. "No, you keep it."

"You have a fractured shoulder and a wounded man. Get him stable and take him to the skiff. Find shelter in the rocks by the shore. I'll come back to you. I promise."

Ruan stiffened. I could see he wanted to argue, but thought better of it. He grabbed me by the hand and tugged me down, pressing a hard kiss to my lips before letting me go. "Don't die."

I nodded before ducking around the corner into the croft, peering into the darkness. A part of me wished I had taken Andrew's surgical scissors with me, at least then I'd have something to protect myself with beyond my wits and sheer luck—but Ruan had far greater need of them, gauging from the amount of blood seeping through Andrew's trousers. We'd be lucky if he didn't bleed out before Ruan could stop the flow of it.

The overgrowth provided little shelter from the storm raging outside. Wiping the water from my face, I looked around. The room was mostly empty with broken shelves long since abandoned by whoever once lived here. In the corner, beneath what remained of the roof, was a filthy boy, and a lumpy blanket covering a pile of debris beside him.

I stepped closer, and my mouth grew dry as I realized it wasn't a boy at all—it was Genevieve. She'd cut her hair short and was dressed as a young man. Her cap was slung low on her head as she looked up at me, her cheeks streaked with blood and mud.

Her wrists were bound with iron shackles, affixed to the wall by a thick chain.

Her eyes grew wide. "You should not be here . . ."

The lump beside her moved.

Elijah.

His face was swollen beyond recognition but I knew to the very marrow of my bones it was him. Whoever had captured her had taken their venom out on him. "He's alive?"

She wet her cracked lips and nodded. "For now. But you should go before he comes back. He'll do to you as he did to him. He will not harm me. But you . . . you he will kill . . ."

I hurried to the windowsill, looking for a key or something to free her from the barbaric chains binding her. "Who are you?" I spat the wet hair from my mouth and continued searching through the broken and rusty tools scattered around. "If I'm risking my neck to save yours, the least you could tell me is who it is I'm saving?"

Genevieve looked again to the opening behind me. "There isn't time. I've told you. You need to go—the inspector betrayed us. You must save yourself."

"Inspector Burnett?" I asked, resting my hand on the nearby table.

"He must be in his pocket. He stole the only proof we had."

"In whose pocket? Who is *he*? *What proof*?" My voice grew increasingly panicked with each question. I needed names and needed them now.

Her chains rattled as she tugged against them, the rough fabric of her coat stretching with the movement. "My father will kill you."

Her father.

If Mariah was her mother then who was her father? My stomach knotted. No. Mr. Owen would not harm anyone. My treacherous gaze drifted down to Elijah's beaten body. *No.* He certainly wouldn't do that. Couldn't. The man I knew was incapable of such brutality. He was kind and gentle and . . .

The earth shifted under my feet as my knees threatened to give out. "Who is your father?"

Genevieve's face grew pale as she looked past me, over my shoulder to that same damned opening she'd kept searching the entire time I'd been there. Straightening my spine, I turned to see what she'd been awaiting.

The duke.

He stood in the doorway to the croft, his feet shoulder-width apart, and he held a hunting rifle in his hands. His tweed cap sat low on his brow as the rain spluttered down.

"I'm surprised you hadn't pieced it together yet, Miss Vaughn. Hawick told me you were a clever little thing. But it seems he was wrong about you too."

A short-lived wave of relief surged over me at the realization that Mr. Owen was not a killer, followed by growing panic as the duke was aiming his rifle directly at my chest.

"*You* killed them." The last piece of the puzzle finally snapped into place. The duke had also been at that initial séance. Mariah had told us as much. *He's here.*

"Tell her, Duke." Genevieve snarled, tugging against her binds. "Tell her what you did to my mother."

"I don't know what you are talking about. I have told you all this before but you did not listen. Going on with your baseless accusations against me. Mariah would come to Rivenly to photograph seabirds. That is all."

"Seabirds didn't leave her with a baby in her belly," Genevieve snapped, showing far more backbone than I was feeling in our present circumstance. I searched for something—anything—to protect myself with before spying a rusty pair of shears on a table a few feet to my left.

"What happened to Mariah . . ." I asked quickly, drawing his attention back to me and away from his two captives.

The duke shrugged, facing me with that casual grace I'd noted several days before. "Hawick was too busy. Spending all his time in London. She would grow wan and listless when he was away. Women are feeling beings, not thinking ones—surely you recognize that truth about your own sex. I saw no harm, at the time, in letting her come to the island to take her photographs."

Bile rose in my throat. *Not thinking,* indeed. My fingers tightened into a fist. Useless against a rifle. I needed to get to the shears without catching his attention, but even those gave me little advantage over him.

"If she later chose to join me in my bed, it was no one's business but ours. Things simply got a little out of hand."

Out of hand? My pulse rioted in my veins.

"She did not choose your bed," Genevieve shouted. I winced, willing her to lower her voice—it would not help either of us to draw attention. The last thing I needed was to have one of the duke's men join us here. "My mother never chose you. She told me what you did to her!"

The duke's eyes flashed as the monster behind the man revealed himself and he turned to her. I sent up a silent thanks to Genevieve for catching his attention, and quickly grabbed the shears, burying them in the filthy folds of my skirt.

He prowled closer, the gun no longer aimed at me. "Mariah never said no. I don't know what twisted lies she told you but she came to Rively of her own accord. Why else would she have come if she was not willing?"

Poor Mariah. I could take no more. I'd known far too many men like him. Manipulating and cajoling for their own aims, then denying the truth when it was right there before them. My fingers tightened on the cold metal of the shears. "Not saying no does not mean yes." Rage surged through me like a hot tide.

"It's lies. All lies . . ." the duke protested with a wave of his hand. But the truth was written all over his face. This was a man intoxicated upon his own privilege. His own power. "I cared for her . . . I did. Mariah was a lonely woman, as I told you. Hawick was always too busy in London. Besides, what woman wouldn't prefer a duke?"

I am going to kill him. That is, if he doesn't kill me first.

Genevieve tugged against the chains again. "You insinuated yourself into her confidence, preying upon her insecurities . . . you are a monster. And a monster's blood runs through my veins—but I will fix it. I will expose you and I vow to you—"

The duke smacked Genevieve hard across the face with the back of his hand. "Silence, you little bitch. It's only for your mother's sake you still live."

Genevieve did not make a sound, not giving him the pleasure of her pain. My palm grew damp around the shears as I edged closer to the wall, glancing out the open window to make certain Ruan had taken Andrew to the skiff before the duke arrived.

My chest loosened as I saw only grass where they had once been. While I might not survive this, they'd at least have a chance.

The clouds overhead broke, the rain letting up at last. I had to keep his attention focused on me.

Think, Ruby, think.

"You were the one arguing with her on the bridge the night she disappeared, weren't you?"

The duke turned with a serpentine smile. "Ah, Malachi did see us that night. I wondered. He always was sniffing around her skirts to the point he even came to one of the Eurydicean meetings looking for her. Now *that* was entertaining, Malachi Lennox full to burst with fire and brimstone, thinking himself so morally superior to the rest of us . . . Owen was the better of the two brothers. More interesting, more intelligent. Malachi had been a jealous zealot his whole life, just like his mother before him. The man was sick with lust for his brother's wife. A far greater sin, I'd wager, than any of mine."

My stomach roiled at the dismissive way he spoke of Mariah. I could hear the clanking of Genevieve's restraints behind me. His words affecting her as well.

"How could you betray them like that? Mr. Owen took you under his wing, he was kind to you. You said yourself you could never repay the debt you owed him and yet you harmed his wife!"

The duke shrugged with the ease of a man who had never faced a single consequence for his actions in all his days. There was rustling of an animal from the bushes behind the croft, drawing my attention for a half second before the duke spoke again. "What is a woman, to a man? He should be grateful that I rid him of her."

"You killed her . . ."

He turned the rifle toward me and took a step closer, the ground wet beneath his feet. "I did what had to be done. I'd not meant to do it at all—but she wouldn't stop talking. Idiotic woman nattering on about how she would expose me for what happened that night if I did not confess. It wasn't my fault she slipped from the cliff." He rubbed his temple, his signet ring catching the light breaking through the clouds. "It was a relief after all that time to be done with it. At least she ceased endlessly going on about what happened with that girl."

Girl? My mind reeled as the duke kept unfurling more and more of this twisted tale.

"She would have brought down all of the Eurydiceans with the scandal. Of course none of it would have mattered had I not allowed her to bring her camera to the island. It would have been her words against ours."

And who would believe a woman against the might of a duke . . .

Genevieve's attention moved to Elijah. He was waking up. Good God, this was bad. I had to keep the duke looking at me. Especially as I doubted Elijah was restrained.

"And what *did* Mariah know?" I took a step closer to the duke in challenge. "What did she see that she wasn't supposed to?"

Now what, Ruby? What are you going to do when the man has a rifle aimed at you?

He started to deny it, I could see it on his face before he flashed me another of those sickening smiles. "I suppose it doesn't matter as you won't be leaving the island. Pity the inspector was such a poor shot. I gave explicit instructions to deal with you, but he couldn't even accomplish that task. It would have been a great deal easier to clear Hawick's name after his foolish confession without you nosing about."

He told me nothing I had not already guessed. I was not leaving this island alive, but I could buy Ruan and Andrew a little more time. I wet my lips. "I ask again. What did Mariah know?"

The duke took a step closer, cutting the distance between the end of his rifle and me, a ghost of a memory crossing his expression. "There was a particular girl there at that final meeting of the Eurydiceans. Lord Morton brought her as a gift for me. I got carried away . . . as one will . . ." That oily self-satisfied smile spread across his face and I longed to rip the expression from him. To drive the shears into his face and ruin it forever, damn the consequences. "Needless to say, she did not wake up the next morning. All the world was told she caught a fever while visiting the island. No one wanted the truth of it brought out in the open. Scandal would be the least of our problems. For a wellborn girl to have died during one of the rites? Unthinkable. We would all be ruined. Morton. Myself. I could not allow it to happen."

"Does Lady Morton know what a monster her husband was?" I asked softly.

The duke shrugged. "Why should I care? The foolish woman only cares for her laces and ribbons. Do you think she would mind what her husband was up to?"

"How many girls have you killed?"

"That was an accident. I'd have never intentionally killed one of our kind."

"How many girls . . ." I gritted out, not giving a damn about his misguided moral relativity.

The duke drew nearer, jamming the muzzle into my chest.

My pulse thundered in my veins. The bastard would kill me, kill me and get away with all of it. My grip slipped on the shears from sweat and rain, but I pressed myself harder into the stone wall behind me.

Suddenly I recalled the photographs from Lucy's room. The one of the girl in the middle of what I'd thought to be some sort of ritual. I could only see her back in that image but I was certain that was the poor murdered girl he spoke of. "And Mariah had photographs of her on the island. She had photographs of all of you," I breathed out. I was either foolish or brave, but had to keep him talking, because if he was talking, he wasn't shooting.

He nodded and took a step back, the muzzle now gently resting on my breast. "At first, I did not know that Mariah had witnessed what happened—let alone had captured images of the ritual—but when she fled the island that very night, I knew that she had to be kept quiet one way or the other."

"Mariah was running away from the Eurydiceans . . ."

The duke yawned. "This is growing tedious. I have never understood the appeal of stubborn women. Owen seems downright captivated by your kind, but you're all too much trouble if you ask me." He gave me a considering look.

"No . . . you never did understand anything, did you, James?" I turned to the sound of Mr. Owen's rich voice, echoing in the roofless walls of the croft. I'd never seen him this angry and for the first time since the duke arrived, a brief bubble of hope for myself rose in my chest. A hope that drowned the instant I spotted Ruan, coming up the hill behind him.

Stubborn, foolish man. Why can't he let me get killed on my own?

"Hawick, go back to the house with my wife—you don't need to bother yourself with this bit of baggage."

"I daresay this *bit of baggage* is entirely my business." Mr. Owen's violent gaze shifted to Genevieve, drinking in her features, and his expression softened. "Gods, she is Mariah's girl. How did I not see it before . . ." He started to take a step toward Genevieve before recalling that the duke still had a rifle aimed at me. Torn between his wife's daughter and me, he turned again to the duke. "James, put the bloody gun down before you kill someone else."

A sound came from beside Genevieve, and we all turned to it. Elijah shifted and groaned in the pile of old hay. And I *saw* . . . I *saw* in that fraction of a second exactly how it would all unfurl, moment by moment. The duke would realize Elijah was alive and shoot him, his dark life's blood pooling out over the hay and Genevieve. Ruan would respond a heartbeat too slow, and would be struck down by the second round.

Without a thought, I lunged for the rifle, putting my good shoulder into the duke's belly, in hopes of disarming him. He anticipated my move, spinning back around, knocking me hard in the temple with the butt of the gun. My vision went black, and I stumbled, reaching out to steady myself with my left hand—forgetting entirely that I had the shears, and drove them hard into the duke's groin, pulling as I fell to the ground. The duke let out an agonized scream, tumbling down atop of me.

The foul man would not stop screaming in my ear, as his impossibly hot blood soaked through the front of my skirt, coating my own legs.

The bastard was dying.

Good.

Death was the only thought in my head as I stared up at the sky, struggling to breathe, but my lungs could not draw in air with the duke's weight pressing me into the wet ground.

He was crushing me.

Ruan rushed to my side, shoving the duke off me. I clutched the shears tightly as they came out of the duke's thigh, blood gushing out in rhythm to his pulse.

It would not be long now.

I could not regret it. Not after hearing what he'd done to Mariah. To that poor nameless girl. To Lucy. To countless women over the years. I may hang for killing a duke but I would not regret a single one of my actions this day.

I hugged my legs to my chest. Ruan was close now, I caught the familiar green scent of his skin, of his sweat—but could not bring myself to look at him. Could not bear to be reminded of what might have been that can never be. I'd killed a duke, and would face the consequences of my actions.

Chapter Thirty-Six

The Prodigal Daughter

I stared at the duke long after he quit breathing, unable to look away from him. I scarcely noticed that Ruan had moved Elijah from the hay, deeper into the croft and away from the elements. He was awake now, talking with Ruan, who was busy stitching his wounds and assessing the damage. The sling binding Ruan's injured shoulder annoyed him, and he strained against it as he pulled a small brown bottle from Andrew's bloodied medical kit.

Andrew.

Mr. Owen eased down in the mud beside me, his dressing gown brushing against my ruined clothes. He swept my filthy hair back from my brow with a shaking hand. "Andy is fine. Kivell got him to the house—a sight the pair of them making their way—Andy with a wounded leg and Ruan with a broken shoulder . . . The duchess and Lady Morton are taking care of him. The duchess sent her man to the mainland for the authorities."

Cold dread clawed its way up my jaw. "Mr. Owen . . . that's not a good idea. Lady Morton . . . Her husband was a Eurydicean." I looked at the dead peer lying in the mud before me. "The duke was in league with Inspector Burnett; who knows who else is involved?"

"You have nothing to fear from Lady Morton. Nor is there any love lost between the duchess and that one—" He grumbled beneath his breath, reaching around and tucking me against his side. "She learned her husband was a monster not long after the wedding, but there was little she could do about it by then. She warned Kivell that he was armed as we left the house."

I wrinkled my nose, looking at him. "And you still came out here, knowing he was a madman with a hunting rifle, and you in your nightclothes . . ." I looked down at the persimmon dressing gown.

He smiled at me, resting his temple against mine and drawing in a deep breath. "I could not leave you to the wolves, my lamb. It will be well. Trust in that. It will be well. I will not let you come to harm."

Oh, how I wished that were so. A ball of emotion lodged itself in my throat. "Did you know what he'd done to Mariah?"

He pressed his lips tight, running his fingers over his white mustache before shaking his head. "No. I had no inkling the depths of his depravity. I—" Mr. Owen's deep voice sounded small for once. Helpless. "I only wish Mariah had spoken to me, come to me . . ."

I pulled my knees up, hugging them to my chest as Mr. Owen glanced past me to Genevieve.

"I do not know how in the gods' names that lass thinks she's James's git. Has she not a mirror to her name?" Mr. Owen studied her with that mercenary gaze he usually reserved for particularly valuable tomes. Assessing every flaw, every crease. It was evident that he was coming to a similar conclusion as I when it came to Genevieve Demidov, and I suspected that Andrew had the right of things. She was his cousin. Whether she knew it or not.

"I wonder if her mother told her . . ."

He let out a dark laugh. "Just look at her. That lass is no more James's bastard than she is yours."

I let out a strangled laugh—but even that hurt.

He pressed a kiss to the top of my head and cleared his throat, clearly done with emotion for the moment. "Go talk her around, lass. You've a way with you. Besides, it'll do you good to get away from this stench." He toed the body of the duke with his slipper.

Here I was—having escaped a fire, an angry sea, and a murderous duke, and the old man wanted me to break the news to his long-lost daughter that she is not the illegitimate daughter of a dreadful duke but the prodigal one of an exceptionally eccentric viscount. "Mr. Owen, look at me! I'm in no condition to talk anyone anywhere."

"I see you, lass. I've always *seen* you. Now go break the sorry news to my daughter that there are two of you instead of only the one."

I blinked, not comprehending his words, but there was no time to question what he meant, as he'd already turned on his heels and started out of the croft, presumably back to the duchess and Lady Morton.

Ruan looked up from Elijah. His eyes bright—brighter than I'd seen them since we were shot.

I grabbed a nearby bucket and carried it over to Genevieve's side and sat down. I'd had enough mud and blood for one day. "How are you?"

She looked up at me through her wet lashes. "Do you think Elijah will be—" Her voice trembled. "I did not mean for him to come to harm."

I laid my palm on her shoulder. "Ruan will take care of him. I promise you that."

She eased beneath my touch and looked up at me. "Thank you. For everything you have done." Her gaze drifted to the duke's lifeless body. "You did not have to help me and I would not blame you had you not, considering the secrets I kept from you. I put you in danger. I'd thought . . . I'd thought the fewer who knew the truth of him, the safer we'd all be."

I looked into her dark eyes. Full of self-hatred, fear, and righteous anger. Emotions likely echoed in my own. There was no doubt in my mind that she was Mr. Owen's daughter. It was written in the proud set of her jaw, in the very way she carried herself. She might have never known the man in life, but she carried his blood in her veins. I would have bet everything I owned upon it. "You have his eyes."

"I do not understand you."

I stretched my neck from side to side, letting the sweet pull of my muscles ease the tension. "Why are you convinced the duke is your father? You have the look of Mr. Owen. You and Andrew— you have the same eyes."

She lowered her lashes and fiddled with a piece of dry straw. "Brown eyes are common."

"What color were your mother's?"

"Blue." The word more curse than anything else.

"As were the duke's." The edge of my mouth curved up into a lopsided smile. "That monster was not your father."

"My mother could not be certain. She dared not hope. I did not even know she had been married until I met Aunt Lucy."

"Did Lucy believe you were Mr. . . ." I corrected myself. "Hawick's child?"

She shook her head. "She said it didn't matter who my father was. That Hawick was a madman, chasing after his ghosts and fairy stories and that I was safer in the shadows with her."

"Funny for a medium to be judgmental of the occult."

Genevieve let out an amused sound. "I told her the same. We did not intend to summon Mariah's spirit . . . Well, we did, but not at the séance. Lucy had hoped that if Hawick brought the ring, that Mariah would reveal where the photographs were hidden in private. We had been looking for weeks to no avail."

"What about the others? Lady Morton . . . the duke . . . why bring them all together?"

"I did not invite the duke. Lady Morton, yes. I thought I

could bend her to our will. Her husband had been a Eurydicean and rumor has it she loathed the man once she realized what a monster he was. I thought perhaps we could have used her anger to our advantage. If I had known that the duke would come to the séance . . . I . . . I truthfully don't know what I would have done."

"I found Abigail—the other medium. It was the night of the second séance. Someone had killed her and left her body in the ruins."

Genevieve winced. "Elijah discovered her that same morning, along with the missing negatives. We'd hoped having them would be enough to prove the duke's guilt. It was a vain hope."

I leaned forward, resting my elbows on my knees. "But your mother . . ."

Genevieve frowned, running her thumb along the inside of her manacle to relieve the raw flesh there. "She must be buried here somewhere. I know she came to confront the duke one last time. She had hidden all of the glass plates at Manhurst the night she fled—terrified if she traveled with them they would break. It was her insurance to protect her against him. Against all of them."

"A clever woman. How many negatives were there in all?"

Genevieve smiled faintly. "I'm not certain. I believe there were over thirty hidden away at Manhurst. More than enough to implicate the duke. Aunt Lucy managed to find roughly half of them, before you arrived. The rest . . . Elijah found the rest, on Abigail's body."

The missing medium.

"Those were the most incriminating ones. I took the best ones and gave them to Elijah to turn over to the inspector, claiming he'd found them in the duke's room after he left. A flimsy tale, but I was beside myself. The remaining negatives were left with my things."

My head was beginning to ache.

She must have misunderstood my expression as she reached out and took my hand. "My mother was extraordinary, Miss Vaughn. You must know that. And he cut her life short. The last time I saw her I was ten years old. She'd left me in Paris with friends of hers. She was always frightened the duke would find us. And every time before when she'd leave me, she'd come back. But not that time."

"This must have been after that photograph was taken of the two of you."

She gasped. "You went through my things."

"It was how we knew where to find you."

Genevieve shifted, uncertain about my invasion of her privacy. "She told me in Cairo what he'd done to her, she said I was young but I needed to understand why we lived in the shadows. She said if she failed to return then I should go to Hawick. That she'd left him a ring that would be able to keep me safe, I only needed to tell him to look inside the ring. She never once said she was his wife, only that he was the best man she'd ever known, and that he would do what was right."

Tears welled up in my eyes. I wiped them away with the back of my hand. "Why did she not come back to Hawick House if she had such faith in him?"

Genevieve licked her teeth and shook her head in anger. "Mother blamed herself for what happened with the duke. Said if she'd not allowed herself to be alone with him, if she'd been more of a lady or not trusted in her friendship with the duke, that perhaps he would not have taken liberties with her. She could not forgive herself for forgetting that he was not the young boy she'd once known, that he'd grown into a man . . ."

"It is not her fault what happened. It's *his*." I pointed at the duke's now lifeless body.

"I am glad you killed him. My mother was a strong woman,

but strength can only go so far in a world that values a man over her. She had been taught from the cradle that her sole worth lay in her ability to make a man's heirs, to remain virtuous to the world, and a good wife her husband." The acid words dripped from Genevieve's tongue. "It is the same world that made her that destroyed her, allowing a monster to prey upon her fears and get away with his crimes."

Genevieve was not wrong, nor had the world changed much over the last forty years. I'd long fought against the same expectations of how a woman *should* be, but even still those claws remained snagged in my own flesh, refusing to let go.

"Aunt Lucy did what she could to make sure I was fed and clothed and cared for, but she was afraid if the duke learned of me that he would take me for his own."

"A valid fear."

"I am sorry I did not tell you more—I was not certain I could trust you and I thought—I hoped—that once we'd collected all of my mother's missing negatives we'd be able to expose him once and for all." She looked again to Elijah and Ruan.

"You care for him."

Her expression softened. "We are alike, Elijah and I—becoming someone new because our old lives had failed us. I met him not long after he purchased Manhurst, I'd come to visit Aunt Lucy. He has kind eyes. I always liked that about him. I did not expect to fall in love with him."

I couldn't help but smile. It was a lovely thought. Starting over anew. But there would be no starting over, or starting at all until I found the keys to unlock her manacles and get us out of here.

CHAPTER THIRTY-SEVEN

Ablutions and Absolution

I sat in the bathing tub in the kitchen at Rivenly, washing the duke's blood from my skin. We'd already filled and refilled one big copper tub, and I was on my second round of rapidly cooling water. I'd killed a man. I drew in a breath and let it out again, allowing that realization sink into my bones. It wasn't the first time—I'd done it once during the war too—but each time took its toll. And in truth, I worried it took a bit of my soul along with it.

I heard the door to the kitchen and turned, half expecting it to be the young serving girl who had been helping me bathe—or, more likely, making sure I didn't faint in the tub. Mr. Owen and Ruan had both been giving me wide berth after what happened in the croft, and I couldn't blame them. My breath caught when I saw Lady Morton enter with the Duchess of Biddlesford at her side. Lady Morton had a towel in her hands and her eyes . . . God. Her eyes were full of pity.

I was going to vomit.

"Hush, child," she said as she drew nearer. "You have done what needed to be done. There's no need to punish yourself for it. Heaven knows someone had to do it."

The duchess sucked in a breath. "Caroline, you mustn't—"

Lady Morton turned to the duchess with a raised brow. "She finished what we'd begun and we owe her our thanks." She opened the towel and gestured for me to stand. I struggled to balance the disapproving Lady Morton from Manhurst with this new woman before me. I stood, water trailing over my body, and stepped out of the copper tub, my feet on the cold flags of the floor. Lady Morton wrapped the towel around my body and guided me to a wooden chair near the fire.

"What do you mean by *what you'd begun,* Lady Morton?" I asked, toweling off my hair as the duchess laid what appeared to be a plain cotton dress and underthings on the chair beside me.

Lady Morton didn't answer, but the duchess did. She lifted a small enamel box from the table beside her and placed it in my hands. "Open it. I think you will understand."

What madhouse had I entered? Too tired to care, I lifted the lid and looked down, my breath leaving my lungs in a whoosh. I couldn't make sense of it. "More negatives?"

Lady Morton nodded. "Yes. I found them in Lucy Campbell's things the night of the first séance. Unfortunately none of them were enough to implicate His Grace, but I believe now . . . considering all . . . that it will be enough."

The duchess let out a shaky breath as she looked to her friend in disbelief. "Is it truly over, Caroline? Truly?"

Lady Morton wrapped her arms around the duchess and pressed a kiss to her temple. "Yes, darling. You're free of him as I promised you would be." She made an odd expression. "Though perhaps not precisely how I intended."

I could not believe it. I looked from Lady Morton to the duchess. "You've been . . ."

"Conspiring?" Lady Morton asked with a raised brow. "I have a daughter, Miss Vaughn. I must do what I can to protect her and others like her in this world from men like that."

"But . . . how . . . ?" I furrowed my brow, struggling to make sense of what they were telling me.

Lady Morton took the duchess's hand in her own. "The world sees what it wishes, Miss Vaughn, though it never has the whole of us. An overbearing mother foisting her daughter upon society. A nervous wife who spends more and more time in Bath." She paused and raised her brows knowingly. "Even perhaps a scandalous heiress?"

I let out a startled sound, looking at the two women in disbelief. I too had seen only what they wanted me to—the superficial masks they wore. Not so very different from my own. Lady Morton and the duchess quickly filled me in on the rest of the sordid tale. Of the girls who disappeared after coming to Rivenly. Usually serving girls who came seeking summer work or to make a delivery and were never seen again. Suspicious, yes, but never enough evidence against the might of the Duke of Biddlesford. The duchess had begun to suspect not long after her husband brought her to Rivenly, and at long last she wrote to her oldest friend—Lady Morton—to seek assistance.

Between the negatives that Lady Morton had stolen and the fact that the duke had shot Andrew Lennox, it was more than enough to clear my name.

Self-defense.

SEVERAL HOURS LATER, I sat on the dock in Anstruther staring across the Firth of Forth in the direction of the Isle of May. I could not see the island, but it was just as well. I hoped to never lay eyes upon it again. My legs swung aimlessly off the edge as I threw a bit of bread to the greedy seabirds. Ruan had brought Andrew and Elijah back to the mainland earlier and settled them into a nearby inn to rest.

Genevieve, Mr. Owen, and I came several hours later aboard the constabulary's vessel. Mr. Owen and Genevieve had gone off for a walk as soon as we docked, but I was not fit company for anyone but the birds. In the distance, I could barely make out the shape of Mr. Owen and Genevieve ambling along the shore, slowly getting to know one another. She was so like Andrew it was surprising that no one realized it sooner. It must have been why both Ruan and Andrew thought they recognized her.

I heard the door of the ferryman's hut close behind me as Ruan lowered himself down to the dock alongside me. His long thigh pressed against my own.

"He commended you on your mastery of his boat. Though I think he was a bit disappointed we returned it in one piece." He held out his hand, dropping my locket into my palm by the chain. The warmth of his skin transferred to mine as he cupped the necklace there between our palms.

This was the second time he'd returned it to me, though this time was more portentous than the last. Ruan withdrew his hand and raked it through his tangled dark hair. The silver strands caught in the sun that stubbornly broke through the clouds. A greedy gull hopped closer, nudging at my skirt and I handed him the piece of bread which he gobbled up with gusto.

"You shouldn't feed them, they'll get spoiled."

I shrugged, staring down at the metal locket in my palm before affixing it to my neck and resting my hand over the compass.

Ruan cleared his throat. "I hear you."

I looked up at him, not understanding his words—those pale green eyes of his full of emotion.

"Ever since that night of the second séance . . . I thought I heard you when I was on the ramparts. Then on the skiff as we were crossing the firth it grew louder. Ruby, it was the strangest thing. I heard a second voice. I heard a woman who was speaking to you."

My skin pricked. "You heard *what?*"

He furrowed his brow then turned back out toward the water, taking a bit of my bread and throwing a chunk to the birds. "I don't know what it was. It wasn't you—but she sounded the same. Who *was* she?"

My mouth grew dry as his words sank in. "It was my mother."

His breath hitched. "That's not possible. You said she was *dead.* I barely hear the living that loud—I can assure you the dead have never been that clear."

I squeezed my eyes shut. "I do not know what it means. But I need to go. I cannot breathe here. I cannot think." I scrambled to my feet, not wanting to think of her—of him—of what had happened across the firth, but Ruan wouldn't let me go.

He stood and took me by the hand, his fingers twining with mine and for a moment I almost gave in and closed my hand around his, allowing him to lead me anywhere. God knew I'd go with him.

But coward that I was, I snatched my hand away and started to walk back to the inn.

"Ruby, wait. We don't have to speak on it. We don't have to *ever* speak on what happened on that boat. It's only—" He hesitated and I unconsciously took a step closer to him.

"It's only what . . ." I gritted out.

He raked his hand again through his hair, tugging on the ends. The man was as unmoored as I. "Come with me, Ruby. Come with me to Cornwall—it's quiet there. Peaceful and I don't know how we'll manage, but I am worried for you. I—"

I put my fingers to his lips, cutting him off, and shook my head. "Please don't ask it of me."

A wounded look crossed his face. "I'm not asking you to give up your life in Exeter or the bookshop. I'm not even asking you to care for me—I'm asking you to let me take care of you. For a few days, for a week . . . for as long as you like . . . It does not have to be more than that. Sleep and read and bring your bloody cat and the old man. I do not care as long as you are happy and safe. You're not well—"

I winced at his words. He was right. I wasn't well, and there was nothing more that I longed for than the peaceful salt air of the Cornish coast, but I was afraid. Afraid of him. Of my feelings. Of whatever it was that lived between us.

The man had heard my *mother*.

He swore in Cornish and raked his hand through his hair. "I'm making a mess of this. What I'm trying to say is that I love—"

"—you're confusing lust with love. Besides, *love* is the problem"—I waved a hand in the direction of the island behind us—"Mariah and Mr. Owen loved one another and see where that got them."

"You are afraid . . . of this," he whispered. The damn man saw right through me.

"I am not—I am simply saying that I cannot see a future for us that ends in anything but heartache." *And I do not have the strength to suffer that again.* "Go back to Cornwall. Find some pleasant, well-mannered girl to marry—have seven sons—lead your boring life." The very notion made me ill.

"Fuck boring and fuck my old life." He growled. "I don't want a pleasant, well-mannered girl. And the gods know we don't need any more Pellars in this world. If you must know, I want *you*."

"*What* did you say?"

"I want *you*. Every impetuous and clever and maddening inch of you. Gods know I wouldn't be laying myself bare if I didn't. But I will not beg and I will not ask again."

I shook my head—unable to summon the words to send him away, nor could I bring myself to ask him to stay. Feelings were not to be trusted—least of all mine.

At first, I thought he'd continue to quarrel. Or worse—perhaps he'd come closer and take my hand as he had earlier. I knew if he did such a thing I would never be able to let him go. But he did neither of those things.

He simply gave up and walked away. I heard his footsteps on the wooden planks, each one a nail into my own heart. This was the right decision—for both of us. I was greedy and selfish and headstrong and irreparably broken. Ruan deserved more than that. More than me.

Ruan paused perhaps twenty feet from me and called back across the distance. "My offer stands, whenever you stop being so bloody afraid of what we are." He rubbed his hand roughly over his jaw, watching me with the strangest expression. "I love you, Ruby Vaughn, and whenever you decide what you want, you know where to find me." Then he turned and left me there—standing alone in the cool mist blowing off the Firth of Forth, regretting every single word that had escaped my lips.

"Where's Ruan gone off to now?" Mr. Owen asked with a groan as he climbed the steps back up the dock alone.

"Home, I suppose."

"Ah. I see." Mr. Owen sighed.

Unlikely. But I wasn't about to argue. "Where is Genevieve? Did she agree to come back with us to Exeter? At least until she decides what to do with herself?"

"No. She said she needs to think. I gave her what money I had on me. Told her to write if she needs more. But I doubt she will—the lass is a Lennox through and through." He shrugged off his heavy woolen overcoat and slid it around my shoulders. "You're half-frozen. What good will you be to me in the bookshop if your fingers fall off, mmm?"

I'd not even noticed, but he was correct on that score. My

hands were ice. I blew into them, rubbing them together for warmth. "Do you think she'll come back?"

Mr. Owen gave me a peculiar look. "She doesn't have much choice with the title to inherit—and how pleased will Andy be when he finally recovers enough to realize that fact? He can set up a house with that lover of his and finally get my brother to leave off with all that marriage nonsense."

I paused, whipping around to face him. "What do you mean, a title to inherit? She's a woman."

"It's Scotland, my love—the laws around my title are not the same. My daughter can be viscountess in her own right once I am dead and then the inheritance issue is her problem—not mine."

Well that certainly put a different end to things.

"Does it bother you?"

I blinked, looking up into his warm brown eyes. "What do you mean?"

He gestured at his broad chest. "Do I need to make a list of all my shortcomings? I do not apologize lightly, lass, but I am afraid I owe you a long one."

I let out a soft laugh and shook my head. "I cannot change any of those things."

He took me by the hand, turning me back to face him. "It does not matter if you can change them, I ought to have trusted you with the truth of who I was. You do not often speak of your past, but you have never before lied to me. If I enter the world again as Hawick, then things will be different for you and me. We can go along as we have been—I do not mind the wagging tongues of gossips—but you cannot hide from society like you have."

"The *gossips* are what you worry about? *You?*" I arched a brow, almost amused at his sudden prudishness.

He exhaled. "Ruby, I don't give a damn about them. It's the

fact that now that people realize that I am Hawick, you will be subjected to . . ." He hesitated, unable to meet my gaze. "Scrutiny. I would not blame you if you left my house and did not come back. I would deserve it after all that I've done."

"Do you truly want me to go?" The thought stung more than I'd anticipated.

"Gods, no, child. I want you to stay as long as you please, but I have caused you no end of misery. I was simply wondering if you might not be better off without me."

I arched a brow in surprise. "This sudden sentimentality is very unlike you."

He snorted, his mustache twitching. "*That* man did not have the week that *this* man had. I nearly lost you, Ruby—and all because I did not tell you the truth sooner. Had I done that, perhaps none of this would have happened."

"And if you had, then the duke would have found some other girl to hurt. No. I do not regret that you brought me here. I only regret I wasn't able to stop him sooner."

Mr. Owen harrumphed. "Well. As long as you know what you're in for. Let's go home before the cold and damp finishes what the duke began."

Now *that* sounded more like Mr. Owen. "Come now, it's not even *that* cold out. It's well above freezing." I linked my arm into his and rested my head on his shoulder.

"Says the lass wearing my overcoat."

"Shall we go home, then? For your delicate sensibilities?"

He nodded sadly as we began to walk down the pier. "Mrs. Penrose will never forgive me for allowing you to get shot."

"You know, we don't have to tell her that part."

He scoffed as we followed the path into town and back to our old life. "As if you can hide the scar. Besides, you know as good as I, that woman is clairvoyant. Why don't we skip Exeter?

Go to the continent . . . or beyond? You know I've never been to America . . ."

"Mr. Owen, it would take nothing short of the second coming of Christ to get me on a boat again."

The old man laughed, knowledge deep in his dark eyes, and I dreaded what that laugh meant.

EPILOGUE

IT was late November. Nearly a month had passed since the tragedies at Manhurst, and I still had not written to Ruan. Nor had he written me, for that matter. He was right, of course—I was afraid. I had known that from the moment I sent him away. And no matter how much I tried to push those *feelings* away, the man remained stubbornly in my waking thoughts.

Of course, now the only trouble was I had to overcome my considerable pride to tell him as much. But there would be time for me to sort that out in the spring as Mr. Owen had plans for us to spend the entire month of December in Oxford while he attended some cabal of aging antiquarians.

Investigators still did not know what caused the blaze at Manhurst. They had checked all the wiring, the fireplaces, even the outside, tirelessly seeking a plausible explanation. But for all that, they came up short. Perhaps that was Mariah's final act, destroying the castle that had caused her such pain in life. It would be a fitting end, but I had my suspicions that the inspector had a hand in the burning of the castle—even if such a thing could never be proven.

After all, there were no such things as coincidences.

I received a letter two weeks ago from the detectives investigating the duke's affairs. They told me they'd found at least three bodies hidden on the Isle of May, high up in the cliffs overlooking the sea. All three tucked away into the stone, sheltered from the elements for all these years. At first, they believed they'd discovered an old ossuary tied to the abbey that had once been on the isle, but again it was Mariah that gave away the truth, as she'd tried desperately to do in life.

For on the day she died, Mariah had been wearing her wedding band. An innocuous gold ring that might have belonged to anyone, except inside bore the simple inscription:

NUNC SCIO QUID SIT AMOR—2ND OF MAY 1872

The very day that the Viscount of Hawick, one Owen Alexander Lennox married Miss Mariah Campbell.

Upon learning of the discovery, I immediately set about having her body moved back home to Hawick House, where she could rest in peace overlooking Manhurst in the grave that Mr. Owen had built for her decades before. It was a sad occasion to be sure, but Mr. Owen appeared oddly at peace with the fact.

We'd found Mariah at last.

Early snow drifted lazily from the clouds around us as we stood by the monument at Hawick House. Mr. Owen cleared his throat, a handful of hothouse blooms clutched in his hands, uncertain as a new suitor.

"We are not that different, you and I," he said at last, his voice breaking.

"What do you mean?"

"For years I held on to the forlorn hope that she would return to me. Just as you did with your family. Clinging to that notion far past the time I ought to have given up. And hope. Oh, hope is a treacherous thing."

"I don't . . ."

He held up a hand, silencing me. "When someone is gone, and you know they will never return, there is no choice but to let them go. Oh, I certainly would have raged and blamed myself for her death. Drowned myself in drink and opium until inch by inch her memory hurt just a little bit less. Carrying on much as you did in that first year you spent with me in Exeter."

I might have been offended were he not entirely correct.

He reached out, taking me by the hand, and kissed my knuckles, holding it against his heart which beat rapidly in his chest. "A cleanly cut wound will eventually scab over, and in time—even the most grievous ones will heal. It may scar and be tender, but in time the pain will pass . . . Hope, however, is a festering sore." His eyes grew wet as he dropped the bouquet of crimson and purple blossoms onto the snow at the foot of the monument. "How can a wound heal when it is rent back open each time there is a knock at the door? Or the post arrives? Or you catch a familiar scent on a crowded street? Each time—" His voice caught in his throat.

I threw my arms around him and hugged him tight. "Oh, Mr. Owen. I'm sorry! I shouldn't have brought you here. I shouldn't have—"

"Hush, Ruby," he said, stepping back and putting his finger under my chin, tilting my face up to look him in the eye.

"For the first time in forty years I know the truth. I know there is no hope that my Mariah will return. I can *heal*. Because of you. You cannot underestimate the importance of that to me."

"You truly loved her all these years?" I could not fathom that sort of love. Or at least, I could not fathom someone loving me in such a way despite the disturbing confession Ruan had hurled at me on the dock.

He nodded. "Isn't it strange? She was gone more years than she was here and yet I scarcely drew breath without wondering where she was, and if I might find her again."

"And yet you married again."

He nodded. "I tried to move on. That's what they always say, isn't it? That wounds get better with time and distance. Ben's mother was a wonderful woman. She knew of Mariah . . . not the particulars . . . but she understood that I was not the man that I had been before. She had lost her first husband too." Mr. Owen sighed and stepped closer to the marble obelisk, running his finger over the etching of Mariah's profile.

"*Nunc scio quid sit amor,*" he whispered before pressing a kiss to the monument.

Now I know what love is.

I wiped away a tear with the back of my glove, unable to keep them from falling. What must it be like to have a love like that?

He turned to me, tilting my chin up with a finger. "You are brooding. It is making me bilious."

I let out a startled laugh as I brushed the snow from my lashes. "Mr. Owen, this *is* a funeral, of sorts."

"Yes, yes, but Mariah would detest all these tears for her sake. Yours and mine both. Besides, your brooding is giving me a headache. When are you going to write to Kivell and end my suffering?"

"That eager to get rid of me, are you? I thought you wanted me to stay with you in Exeter."

"I do, my dear. I cannot imagine a day without you there re-arranging my bookshelves and destroying my gardens and filling my parlors with the most frivolous of pompous peacocks trying to gain your affections. I would not have you any other way. I am simply growing weary of you being morose. It's terrible for a girl's constitution. Just ask my great-aunt Penitence." He tried to make light of it—but it was the truth—I'd become a dreadful bore as of late.

"You've had some bad luck when it comes to love, I'll give you that. But there's no one to say that this affair with Kivell will end poorly as well." He tucked my hair behind my ear. "I thought I taught you that. If not, I've been the worst of fools."

I rolled my eyes, slipping away from his embrace. "You've told me a great many things, but I don't think I've once heard you pontificate on the merits of love and second chances. In fact, I believe you *just* called hope a festering sore not five minutes ago. One could argue that these two things are contradictions."

He harrumphed, his breath visible in the cold air. "Clearly, I have been remiss in my paternal duties. I should have taught you more in that vein, and less about binding glue and beetle larvae."

"I did rather enjoy the demonstration on the difference between furniture beetles and deathwatch beetles."

"I mean it, lass. You spend too much time with books and not enough with flesh-and-blood people."

"Says the pot. The way I hear it, before I moved in with you, you didn't see anyone besides your housekeeper and your library for months on end."

"I find books better companions than most people," he grumbled, before taking my hands in his own and giving them a squeeze to underscore the import of what he was about to say. "You have a chance, Ruby. A chance to be happy right here. Right *now* and you should seize it. Grab on with both hands and don't bugger it up like I did."

I settled down on the bench, gazing up at the gray sky. "Yes, well . . . It's complicated."

"All the best things in life are. Would be dreadfully boring otherwise. Oh, I know you aren't the marrying sort—but I don't believe Kivell minds. The lad has been alone for years. It'd probably be good for him. He's far too set in his ways, it's made him old before he's earned the right to it. You're a pair of lovesick pups—the both of you—go put the lad out of his misery. As my great-aunt Patagonia once said—"

"You don't have a great-aunt Patagonia."

He waved me off.

"Mr. Owen, you don't understand—"

"—that he's a Pellar? Believe me, girl, there are far more things in this world that we cannot explain than those we can. So what if the lad's a witch? You aren't exactly adhering to your copy of Emily Post now."

I groaned at his reference to the daintily wrapped etiquette book that had been deposited anonymously on our doorstep not long before we set out for Scotland. The book had scarcely been published in the States when a copy arrived one morning addressed to me. "It wasn't as if I sent for it. I couldn't care less what some American socialite has to say about decorum."

"You *are* an American socialite. And it was addressed to *you*."

Touché. "I still think it was that meddlesome lady down the street trying to make a subtle hint."

"Or not subtle, as it may be."

I rolled my eyes and opened my mouth for some sort of witty retort when I spotted Andrew Lennox's driver running down the path and darting over the bridge—the scene of so much misery as of late.

"Lord Hawick."

Oh, no. What now?

He panted, hands on his knees, a folded-up telegram in his hand. "Lord Hawick. There's a"—another huff—"an important message."

"I can see that." Mr. Owen appeared rather amused, his dark brown eyes watching the driver. He gestured with his forefinger. "Do get it from the poor lad, Ruby. See what it is that's important. Has there been a demonic possession in Devonshire? A haunting in Little Humby?"

I took the telegram from Hugh's gloved hand while he caught his breath. "Not amusing, Mr. Owen. Thank you, Hugh. Please ignore him."

The driver let out a breathless laugh and shook his head.

"I know!" The old man laughed at his own joke. Cheeks turning a jolly shade of red. "There's been a selkie spotted in Skye."

I furrowed my brow. "Are there selkies in Skye? And you shouldn't make light. You're the one who went and found yourself a Pellar of all things."

I glanced down to the telegram to see who it was from.

Lord Carnarvon, the peer who had been financing Howard Carter's numerous expeditions in the Valley of the Kings. There was only one reason that Lord Carnarvon would be writing to Mr. Owen, as the two had been corresponding furiously back and forth for at least a decade over antiquities and Egypt.

My hands began to shake.

Three words.

Three simple words.

Carter's done it.

The edge of my mouth curved up slowly. I ought to have been jealous. Dreadfully so. Howard Carter must have found a new tomb in the Valley of the Kings while I'd been dabbling in the occult for the last three months.

"You owe me ten pounds." I stuck out my hand.

Mr. Owen blinked. "What the devil is in that telegram to earn you ten pounds, lass?" He tilted his chin, straining to get a look at it. I handed it over and watched as the color drained from his face.

"Ten pounds, Mr. Owen. Or should I say Lord Hawick? As I recall, *you* were the one who said Howard Carter would find nothing new in the Valley of the Kings."

"Wee besom," he grumbled, reaching into his pocket for his money clip.

Viscount or not, he was still my Mr. Owen. And nothing in the world could change that. I snatched his entire money clip, dropping it into my own pocket.

He swore loudly, crumpling up the telegram and dropping it to the snowy ground. It seemed things were going to get very interesting when we returned to Exeter. Very interesting indeed. But first things first. I had a letter to write.

Now how precisely did one apologize to a Pellar? Now perhaps *that* was something Miss Post might know.

ACKNOWLEDGMENTS

There are so many people who played a part in getting this book from my brain and onto the page, and I am grateful for each and every one of you. They say it takes a village to raise a child—well, I swear it *also* takes a village to bring a book to life. From my team, to my family, to my community. Thank you. Each and every one of you.

The Secret of the Three Fates would not exist at all without the hard work and support of my fabulous team at Minotaur who have worked tirelessly to bring Ruby's adventures to life and into readers' hands. Thank you for all you do. I also want to thank my incredible editor, Madeline Houpt, who has a keen ability to see to the heart of my stories. Her insight and feedback have made the Ruby Vaughn books so much stronger. Also, I want to give a giant thank-you to my amazing agent—Jill Marr—I could not imagine a better partner on this literary journey, and it's an utter joy to have you in my corner!

To all my family and friends who have been supportive throughout this process—your excitement and love mean so much to me. You know who you are. From showing up to my book events to the book club invites and talking up Ruby to your own circles of friends—you are my village and I am unbelievably grateful for each and every one of you.

Also, I want to thank Paulette Kennedy, Celeste Connally, Rose Sutherland, and Lindsay Barrett—y'all have been there with me on this ride over the last couple of years. I don't know what I would have done without you to hold my hand (if virtually) through it all.

Reine—thank you for always being there for me, enduring not only messy early drafts but also my endless brainstorming and plotting over cheese. . . . I owe you so much for your patience and friendship.

My boys—your curiosity inspires me every single day. You always make me ask the hard questions, and find the harder answers.

And last—but not least—to J, who has always believed in my writing, even when I didn't have the heart to put pen to paper. You told me to stop being afraid and just write it down. So, I did, and here we are.

ABOUT THE AUTHOR

CHRISTY LORIO

Jess Armstrong is the *USA Today* bestselling author of the Ruby Vaughn Mysteries. Her debut novel, *The Curse of Penryth Hall,* won the Minotaur Books/Mystery Writers of America First Crime Novel Award. She has a master's degree in American history but prefers writing about imaginary people to the real thing. Jess lives in New Orleans with her historian husband, two sons, yellow cat, speckled dog, and the world's most pampered school-fair goldfish. And when she's not working on her next project, she's probably thinking about cheese, baking, on social media, or some combination of the above.